The Man Who Walked
Out of the Jungle

The Man Who Walked
Out of the Jungle

Jeff Wallace

To Nan
for her friendship

2017, Jeff Wallace

Historical suspense fiction / detective fiction / thrillers / Vietnam War / Saigon

The Man Who Walked Out of the Jungle / Jeff Wallace
(a version of this novel was published previously as 'The Known Outcome')

ISBN
978-0-9983291-3-0

Day 1

In Tuyet's apartment, the sunrise flared against the rust streaks in the window screen. Outside revved scooters; leaves rustled; a clothesline pulley creaked. A moth fluttered onto my arm. Listlessly I flicked it away. The numbness of sleep clung, and I didn't wish to dislodge it.

Tuy was awake. Her hair made a silky starburst on the pillow. With her fingers she gathered the strands, and I noticed around her nails half moons of white from Ivory soap, a present from me. Our bed was a straw mat on which we threw sheets and pillows. To rise seemed a long way. She did so now, a rice stalk springing up after a windstorm.

I twisted to sit cross-legged. Zippoed a cigarette. She called this my Buddha statue, and maybe I resembled one. She'd taught me about Buddhism. It stood for the rectification of suffering. Noble truths. Paths toward a virtuous life.

Toward me, she wasn't above mockery.

I pondered the problem that had awakened with me for so many weeks it had become like the sounds of Saigon. Today, Friday, 24 April 1970, marked my thirty-second month in South Vietnam. Finishing my first one-year tour, I'd opted for a second, at whose conclusion I'd added six months. Now I clung week to week. Before I left, I had to talk her into going back with me to America—the so-called World. The topic always netted her stubborn silence. I knew why. She couldn't imagine herself in the United States, or anywhere other than in this city where she'd grown up, where her mother resided. I couldn't convince her to go, and I couldn't stay. My thinking resembled the intractable American conundrum in Vietnam: I wanted to shape the outcome, but my partner wouldn't conform to my notions.

This morning she didn't concern herself with my preoccupations. Her mood was airy. Often, despite my usual inability to answer, she asked me whether I was coming home tonight. Now she asked, "What did you dream about?"

"How do you know I dreamed?"

No reply. I was to take it she simply knew such things. An educated, sophisticated woman, she tended dreams like a soothsayer.

And the dream? Already it had faded, but I knew it had been about death. Yesterday I'd read an incident report of an unidentified man killed by a claymore fragmentation mine in the rain forests of Tay Ninh Province, 100 kilometers north of Saigon. The man had walked up on an American infantry outpost at night, an act so dangerous as to be unsurvivable. I'd perused the report with my usual callous eye, death being the commonest event, though sometimes it tracked me into my sleep.

"A war dream," I told her.

"You should dream of better things."

Through the window wafted the cacophony of horns, bicycle bells, and river-barge gongs; the musty incense of the river and its canals where the gray house boats pronged like a betel-nut chewer's teeth. In the street below, a scooter snarled, and its smoke blended with the other smells.

I looked at Tuy and knew she'd accompany my every thought or memory of Vietnam for the rest of my life. Which was why she had to go with me.

After coffee, in front of her hanging mirror, I straightened my uniform. The humidity had blemished the brass insignia on my cap, and I buffed it with the rag I kept on the high sill. Tuy had retrieved the delivered morning newspapers and was opening them to read. Leaning down, I kissed her. "I'll try to be home early tonight."

* * *

I saw her for the first time in the spring of 1968, late in my first tour. She'd leaned from the open window of her second-floor landing, calmly regarding a jeep overturned in the street below. Capping the window, a decorative Roman frieze, an architectural nuance not surprising in a city that imitated Paris that in turn mimicked ancient Rome. I'd noticed the frieze before; it was what had caused me to glance up.

The inverted vehicle belonged to the Vietnamese military police company I advised then. No act of war here, just common carelessness, and I stopped to make sure nobody was hurt. Scraped but otherwise unharmed, the driver and two occupants were righting the chassis, and as I had nothing to do but watch, I said, "I hope we didn't wake you."

"You did. I was in the middle of a dream." Her English was pristine.

"A pleasant one, I hope."

"Yes. Of peace and beauty. And you turned over a jeep on it."

I tried to think of a reply, but she'd receded inside.

On the map, Saigon looked like a ravenous, steep-finned fish eating an egg. The city was built on a marsh, and the streets would have flooded but for the drainage canals. The canals and the river ushered the water toward the South China Sea, while everything else rushed in: a glut of dollars; imports that had turned the city into a vast shopping mart; and foreigners, the Americans currently preeminent.

Only six kilometers separated Tuy's door from the gate at Tan Son Nhut airbase, yet to move this distance I traversed four cultures. She lived in the district called Cholon, among the ethnic Chinese merchants who spoke a dialect of Cantonese and kept themselves politically aloof from the Vietnamese. Few Americans ventured into Cholon's narrow side streets; you could get lost under the hanging bird cages and flax awnings. When I told Americans how to reach me in an emergency, I used the address of a grocery store on the main shopping street Dong Khanh. The proprietor was an old friend of Tuy's family and knew where she lived.

On the Lambretta scooter cab's back pad, gripping the chrome rail, the sole purchase save for the driver himself, I saw the neighborhood go by in blurs. The tires cut bubbly wash streams, knocked aside chunks of ice littered from the ice-truck deliveries. In bins ruckused chickens, monkeys, iguanas—the bigger lizards suspended upside down by their tails, their claws tied as if they were prisoners about to be executed. The motorbike's sputter joined the medley of voices, the clank of chains, the percussions of crates crowbarred open. Headed fish sizzled on grills. Thick-calved drivers pedaled their bicycle cabs called cyclos. Each block disgorged its peculiar wares: washtubs of porcelain and stainless steel; televisions under the headachy geometry of TV aerials; pyramids of cooking oil and dry beans—American aid products—meant to be distributed free, but of course the people sold them. The practice vexed visiting U.S. congressmen, who asked why something was not done, as if anyone could regulate this labyrinth.

On Nguyen Trai we coasted into central Saigon. Colonnaded buildings and balustraded houses recalled the city's history as a dominion of the French empire. Gliding under the trees of a lush park, we skirted *Le Cercle Sportif*, or sports club, a social locus then and now. Nearby were the Presidential Palace, churches, embassies, monuments. In their long stay, the French had styled Saigon to remind them of Paris, a city I didn't know, and I wondered if someday Paris might summon Saigon for me.

Even if thousands of French remained, they were no longer the masters. The famous battle of Dien Bien Phu in May of 1954 had felled their empire. The columns might be thought of as its blanched skeleton. Journalists wrote that the Vietnamese saw the Americans as its conjurors. We propped up the bones, peeked out through the skull's eyes, breathed through the lipless teeth. Was it true? After thirty-two months in country, I should have known the answer.

The driver zigzagged through the downtown streets to hook left at Cong Ly. Dodging cyclos, buses, and the petite blue and yellow Renault taxis, we reached a camp of cardboard and cloth houses fringing the Thi Nghe canal. Sometimes the land flooded, and the cardboard walls floated up sideways, bumping into their former inhabitants who posed like high-water markers. The camp was in Saigon but not of it. The dwellers were refugees from evacuated or obliterated villages, and the slum was no more Saigon than it was Da Nang or Nha Trang or another city where the displaced crowded. The statistics said there were millions of them.

The French would say *beaucoup*.

A flight roared overhead, and the gray exhaust trail widened until it blended with the low overcast. At the traffic signal by the Seventh Day Adventist Hospital, I licked my lips and tasted the chemical blow of Saigon's air.

I should be gone from here. Gone like the receding airplane, its smoke a ribbon of doubt about what might have happened with Tuy. How long could I stay, hoping she'd change her mind and leave with me? So far my arguments had failed; to argue with Tuy was like remonstrating with the Mekong River. I could only wait, as time slipped. Repeatedly postponed, the day was coming when they'd put me on a flight home. With luck, I might get twenty-four hours notice.

*   *   *

The driver dropped me off at the triangular plaza by the gate, and I entered the joint American-Vietnamese military airbase known as Tan Son Nhut. In the cantonment, the buildings squared on parallel streets; traffic moved in orderly files. The edifices spread from the bunker-fronted, bone-white headquarters of the U.S. Military Assistance Command—MACV.

Wheeling a jeep out of the motor pool, I peered over the hood through steam wisping from the overnight condensation. At the corner the airfield panned into view. In the hazy distance squatted a DC-8 Freedom Bird, the smog obscuring the troops who filed on board. President Nixon's Vietnamization and troop-withdrawal plan had begun to rake out our soldiers in large numbers. My unit of investigators had been among the first to go, leaving me behind, a unit unto myself, because I'd volunteered to stay. Last year, when U.S. troop strength had topped 530,000, I couldn't have ordered, bribed, or coerced a spare jeep from the motor pool. Now jeeps were served from a long row like candies from a Pez dispenser—one with a dragon's head, I mused. In its daily press briefings, MACV's spokesmen uttered withdrawal figures with the prideful tone once heard in their body counts. MACV was a stat machine, and to listen was to get an earful.

B. C.

I swerved toward a compound of three stucco buildings, more reminders of the French empire, the dead one we'd resuscitated. The old wall was long gone, the name survived—the French Fort. Over the red tile roofs, tamarind branches brushed, parrots fluoresced, iguanas turreted their eyes. If Tan Son Nhut stood for military orderliness, the French Fort softened its edges. The closest reminder of U.S. military regimentation was a facility for replacements two hundred meters away. They were still coming in, paradoxically, and in the right wind you might smell their fresh canvas duffel bags and hear their cadence calls. This morning the calls didn't carry, and the French Fort barely stirred when I arrived at the civilized hour of zero seven fifteen.

My assistant was Staff Sergeant Javier Lopez. The veteran of two combat tours, he'd seen more gunfights than Emiliano Zapata, his historical idol. Now he carried no weapon, and his simple fatigues featured none of his decorations. His placid eyes gave the impression he was staring into an Arizonan dusk. Stepping with a slight limp, his old wounds having left him unfit for line duty, he typed, filed investigative reports, and answered the phone in his Mexican accent that seemed to insinuate irony into his phrases. I didn't understand why Lopez had come back for a third tour, and being himself, he didn't explain except in sardonic one-liners: "Hell, why not?" We got along because both of us reveled in our contradictions. He was almost prissy in his personal hygiene habits, yet he loved scatological metaphors. Relating one of these, he'd edged on why he'd returned: "When I got home, I couldn't stop thinking about 'Nam, and it was like taking a shit knowing that a big bug was running around in the crapper. I kept telling myself that the bug wasn't gonna bite me on the ass, but all the time, I just couldn't get comfortable."

"Must have been a scary bug," I'd said.

"I think so. Never got a good look at it."

Sagacious non-commissioned officers always had been hard to come by. Now, try to find one, and you might as well be looking for snow in Saigon. It surprised me every week when his name escaped the departure-transfer list.

He said, "Colonel Crowley phoned. He's headed over to talk about the report he sent yesterday."

"The claymore KIA?"

"Yeah. Fucker walks up on a rifle company at night and gets blown away. What did you *think* was gonna happen?"

"Did Crowley say why he wanted to talk about it?"

"Only that it was urgent."

"To him, everything is urgent." I thought for a minute. "When was the last time he was here?"

"Never, far as I know."

I unlocked the drawer of my desk, removed the report, and leaned back in my chair. Before the drawdown, there had been three desks in this room. Now, a single desk, three metal-framed chairs, and a pedestal fan whose fluttering manila tag was stamped March 1965, the month when the first major U.S. combat units deployed to South Vietnam. The walls tapered to a vaulted peak and an inert ceiling fan. Louvered glass strips, randomly clear or opaque, looked out on the tamarinds, a few stubby palm trees, and a garden that bled the odor of dung. Which wasn't in short supply.

I reread the case that had tracked me into my dreams last night and grabbed the attention of my commanding officer. Attached were copies of statements from two infantrymen, Captain David Ulrich and Sergeant Henry Joshua. Almost a week ago, their company had occupied a hilltop in eastern Tay Ninh Province, and late at night, soldiers manning an outpost had detonated a claymore on a figure walking out of the rain forest. The dead man turned out to have been a Caucasian outfitted in U.S. military gear. No insignia or unit patches. Nobody had a clue to his identity.

The scrape of tires. Lopez shouted the area to attention, and the sun glared off Colonel Crowley's close-cropped head. He wore polished jump boots—the footwear of a garrison officer—and crisp khakis not yet drooping in the humidity. Less display-worthy was the man himself. His face was sunburned, and his arms stuck out of the starched sleeve hoops like pencils from tin cans. His chin stuck out too—the chin of self importance. I saw his lips moving and realized that he was talking: "See that Freedom Bird on the airfield this morning? I put five investigators on it. The troop withdrawal is bleeding me dry. Nobody cares that I have cases to assign. At least you're still around. I can run one competent investigation."

No doubt, given a chance, Crowley would have booked himself on the next Freedom Bird. His one-year stint in Vietnam was nearly finished. He wouldn't extend. In the war's hopeful early years, multiple combat tours had spit-shined an ambitious officer's career. Now, one was enough. He wanted to punch his ticket and get out. No surprise.

You didn't need a calendar to know that the sixties were over.

He stepped to the window and gazed at the garden and the parking space where his driver lounged. "How fast can you chase up those friends of yours downtown?"

"Friends?"

"Your gook cop buddies."

"I don't know. How fast is necessary?"

"Today."

Of course today. Why had I asked?

"You've read the Tay Ninh report?" He lit a cigarette, and the smoke snaked through the louvers. The wind had awakened outside; branches swished, herringbone-patterned leaves fluttered to the tilled soil. My dream came back to me, of the claymore shattering the night's stillness.

"Yes sir."

On my desk he slapped down three items: A newspaper, a manila folder, and a map. The newspaper was the New York Times folded to an article under the headline, 'TAY NINH KIA MAY BE UNKNOWN SOLDIER.'

"The press is claiming that the casualty is a GI we can't identify." He traced the print with his nicotine-stained fingertip and read: "'Unlike prior wars, Vietnam has produced no so-called unknown soldier. Speedy evacuation and sophisticated forensics all but preclude an American serviceman who dies in this war from becoming one, according to experts. Yet, despite these advances, the identity of the Caucasian killed early Sunday morning at the base of Hill 71 in Tay Ninh Province remains a mystery.'"

"He died Sunday," I remarked. "That was only five days ago. Why didn't the reporter just wait for an official statement?"

"Hell, the press will print anything negative it digs up about the military—the more sensational the better. It's how they sell newspapers. When the reporter learned we had a casualty we couldn't identify, he asked MACV for our statement, and when we couldn't give it to him quick enough to meet his deadline, he ran the story. But we're going to have the last word, because the identification procedures are reliable, and the chances are fucking *zero* that the KIA was a U.S. serviceman or anybody else working for the U.S. government."

I wondered where Crowley came by his certitude. You needed an inch-thick directory to list the U.S. military and civilian organizations in South Vietnam. Even the Library of Congress had people here. How anybody kept track of them was beyond me.

"What about allies? The Australians and the New Zealanders?"

"We asked. They denied he's one of theirs."

"And CORDS?" Responsible for pacification programs, Civil Operations and Revolutionary Development Support had representatives in every province in South Vietnam. CORDS staffed a liaison office at MACV Headquarters.

"Not theirs either. We contacted all U.S. civilian agencies. Ran fingerprints checks with DoD and FBI. Compared the records of registered MIAs. No hits."

"So there's your answer—he's not an American."

"Correct. But the newspapers don't give a shit. To them, all that counts is that we don't know *who* he is."

Flagging a priority case, three red candy stripes treaded the folder. I opened it and picked up the personal effects inventory. The first item listed was a rifle, M16A1, serial number 537629.

Crowley said, "Records match that serial number to an M16 delivered in 1966 and issued to the 1st Cav Division. The rifle was crossed off the unit's books in May '67 as lost in action."

A man comes out of the jungle with a rifle lost three years ago. Weird.

"The casualty was carrying this map sheet." He opened the map, scale 1/50,000, under whose acetate-sealed surface ran grid squares a kilometer on each side. The calligraphy of the contour lines was so complex as to appear psychedelic. There were green beards of jungle; blue rivers and tributaries spread like a doctor's chart of blood vessels; red or black roads zigzagging; the mauve scabs of built-up areas. Puncture holes recurred in the same pattern in multiple sections, from claymore pellets ripping through.

He poked a swirl of brown lines. "He came out of the rain forest at the base of Hill 71. The area's unpopulated, a free-fire zone. The best explanation for how he got there is an air crash. The Second Infantry Brigade commander, Colonel Larsen, has mounted aerial searches for wreckage. So far, they haven't found any. The AO is triple-canopy jungle. If an aircraft went down there, it got swallowed in the trees."

"Missing aircraft?"

"All of ours are accounted for. As for Vietnamese civil and military flights, no reports of crashes, but who the fuck knows?"

On the map, moss green matted the ovals of Hill 71. Resistive to encroachment, so dense that the Viet Cong and Americans might pass simultaneously under the same tree and not see each other, the rain forest was not the place where a man hiked alone at night. Not even a Viet Cong guerrilla. Rumors had long circulated of Caucasian VCs, though I'd never encountered one or met anybody who had. Most people thought the 'white cong' stories were bullshit.

"Larsen flew down to talk to me. He's been around long enough to recognize the kind of incident that gets you in trouble. When he found out that his soldiers had blown away a white man, he requested a formal investigation. I've authorized one, despite objections from MACV Headquarters. General Cobris is MACV's program officer for Vietnamization—which puts him in the middle of everything. He insists that the fingerprint checks and the absence of a dental-chart match are sufficient to confirm that the casualty was not an American. He says an investigation merely whets the appetite of the press and incites bullshit speculation like this article."

"Sounds about right to me."

"We're got to look like we're doing something. Until Cobris stops us, which he will soon enough."

"So this is all for show?"

"What do you expect? Cobris hates the case, but Larsen's a combat commander with admirers in high places, and Cobris can't shove him around." His tobacco-stained teeth bared, and he plucked out the cigarette whose smoke fled over the reddened skin of his forehead. What he meant, but didn't say, was that Cobris could shove *him* around.

Too bad. Crowley was MACV's acting Provost Marshal, and his office, along with the Inspector General's and the Staff Judge Advocate's, stood for the integrity of the regulations. The Army's watchdogs theoretically enjoyed an independent line of dissent that ran all the way to the Chief of Staff. In practice they exercised restraint. Crowley knew it was career suicide to enter the catfight between Cobris and Larsen.

So many generals roamed the labyrinthine corridors of MACV Headquarters—nicknamed 'Pentagon East'—that I thought of them like the residents of an insane asylum, not particularly relevant unless you visited the place, to be treated warily if encountered, otherwise to avoid. Brigadier General Kyle Cobris was among the few I'd met personally. Four months ago, he'd presided over an inquiry panel where I'd testified as a witness. He'd just begun his third tour in Vietnam, his first as a general officer, at which level the conventional wisdom about multiple tours no longer applied. His contemporaries had bestowed on him the most esteemed of sobriquets—*water walker*—implying divine qualities and reserved for those so anointed in success that they seemed inoculated against anything less. After earning an advanced degree from Cal Tech in systems analysis, he'd excelled as a combat commander, then shifted his extraordinary energies to senior staff assignments in Washington. He'd certified his political astuteness by completing a stint as a military liaison officer to the White House. In the sweltering afternoon, as the chugging pedestal fans failed to keep his sweat from slapping onto the précis, his ice-blue eyes had stayed sharp. Afterward I'd heard Cobris described as the most ruthless self-promoter in country. Intolerant of those who lacked the requisite sense of urgency—he referred to them as *non-expeditious*—he'd reportedly fired a slew of officers from their jobs.

I asked, "What do you want me to do?"

"Try to learn the dead man's identity. Put aside everything else."

"Yes sir."

"The remains are at the Wister Forensic Facility. See what you can make of his effects. Then, fly up to Second Brigade and interview the soldiers involved. Send me frequent MFRs on your progress. I'll keep MACV informed."

I walked him to the door, where he glanced up at the sky full of the roiling clouds typical of the pre-monsoon season. The jeep spun across the macadam, and he sank into it and sped off as the drops began to whack the roof tiles.

We were both career officers. The similarities went no further. Crowley would not have lived with a Vietnamese woman in Cholon. He did not befriend Asians, or 'gooks' as he called them. He thought it best to deal with the locals from a distance, the way an artilleryman could shell a target he never saw.

The rain began to avalanche, the drops to ping on the louvers. Lopez, working wonders with the old coffee percolator, had a steaming cup in hand. Staring at the map and the pattern of holes, he said, "The mystery man came from nowhere and was going nowhere, and he managed to get hosed in the process. Sound like someplace familiar?"

* * *

My earliest memory was of a day when, three years old, I witnessed the Tanner clan gather on a Massachusetts lawn under the sun-speckled shade of trees. The Tanners' roots stretched to the American Revolution. A relative reportedly had seen action at Lexington, and a rifle of his had existed until early in this century, when a fire or theft or other misfortune had claimed it. The sorrow of losing the relic rang in the tone of every family member who'd mentioned it to me. Our forefather from the revolution had bequeathed a more lasting memento, a flat-topped hill called Tanner's Woods on the western shore of the Connecticut River. Almost two centuries later, it retained the name, and I grew up tracing its crest with my finger, following its plunge to the river's edge. Within sight of its green skirt, I learned that a man's duty was to pass something to the next generation. Land, community, family—all ran parallel to the

Vietnamese custom of ancestor worship, and when I got to Saigon they helped me understand the unraveling this ancient society had suffered.

The Tanners lived far enough from Boston so that we spoke with no trace of its accent. As with most Mass folks, we had family connections there, the most renowned an uncle who'd studied and later taught at Harvard. In poor health, as thin as his repp-tie, Vaughn Tanner was rarely seen, save for on Christmas Days when he joined the clan for dinner. The Tanner women, the family's tradition keepers, collaborated to put on a spectacular feast in the modest spaces of my uncle Frank's white-plank house. Too numerous to sit together at a table, we balanced our heaped plates on trays, the males invariably clustering in the living room while the TV played a program nobody could hear. Vaughn sat in a stuffed chair, tray on his lap, napkin tucked over his tie, smiling with mock charm at the children who occasionally dashed in.

I was a teenager before I understood that he wasn't popular with the rest of the family. Alone among them, he questioned the authenticity of our links to the Battle of Lexington. The historical records did not list anyone of our name, he said with a shrug, as if it wasn't significant either way. Imagine the effect of his comment on the Tanners, their family legend having become grist for a Harvardite's skepticism.

The last time we spoke was Christmas 1966, soon after I'd received the notification for my deployment to South Vietnam the following June. True to his dissonance, Vaughn had asked me why I was going. Why? An irrelevant question to ask a soldier, yet he'd stared at me, apparently expecting an answer.

"To fight communism." It was a stupid sentiment, but I'd had to say something.

Vaughn had smiled. "Communism is an economic theory."

"It will force a dictatorship on those people."

"On the South Vietnamese, you mean. Have you studied the government of South Vietnam?"

It wasn't possible to hold a private conversation at a Tanner Christmas dinner—the relatives circled around each other like tree rings, and before I could answer, my uncle Frank joined us. A sportsman, veteran of the Merchant Marine in World War II, he made the legend of our relative at Lexington believable.

"Now Vaughn, you're not saying we shouldn't be fighting communism?" So bulky next to the diminutive Bostonian, Frank might have crumpled him like one of the beer cans he'd put away. And Frank's words tripped a bit over his tongue, maybe on purpose, to make it obvious that an intellectual debate wasn't what he had in mind.

"Not my point," Vaughn said.

"Good. 'Cause it wouldn't be right. Nobody second-guessed us when we went off to war."

Vaughn, in his seventies, his charcoal herringbone jacket mottled with white hairs, his skin pallid from the indoors, nodded once, not an apology, merely an acknowledgment, for he knew, as we all did, that Frank didn't care one way or the other about politics; ours wasn't a political family and nobody railed against communism. It was etiquette at stake. None of them wished for me to be going off to war, but they'd honor me for it. Vaughn left the gathering then, or soon after.

At the time it meant nothing to me.

A man is taught lessons that don't stick; he might not even remember the subject matter. Other things he learns incompletely, bearing the knowledge around like fruit still in its skin. My first tour gave me a practitioner's understanding of Vietnam. Though limited, it counted for more than anyone else in my family possessed or ever would possess, Vaughn included. Yet his question echoed: *"Have you studied the government of South Vietnam?"*

* * *

After phoning ahead, I drove to the forensic mortuary at Bien Hoa. My jeep was a sputtering shit dog, the slowest vehicle on the road; even the trucks with bald tires and welded body patches made of flattened tin cans passed me. Squatting on the landfills above the rice paddies, American-supported industries spread smoke as if from smoldering joss sticks to merge with the hazy air. Sandbagged checkpoints beaded the highway, and between them roved joint South Vietnamese-American military-police patrols in machine-gun jeeps. On the outskirts of Bien Hoa, I spotted a South Vietnamese MP waving his riot baton to halt traffic. On the shoulder hulked a pistachio-green Citroën *Deux Chevaux* with its front windshield blown out, the shards littering the roadway. Smoke frothed from the driver's compartment. A second Vietnamese MP approached the car, pulled open the door, and tugged at the driver's shirt until the limp body flopped onto the pavement.

Along the roads, you passed cars crumpled, scorched, or partially melted, shoved off to the sides. This was how they accumulated. Welcome to South Vietnam.

The cops began to direct traffic around the wreck. An American MP about eighteen years old, the soles of his combat boots crunching the broken glass, waved cars forward. When my jeep rolled alongside, I asked him what had happened.

"The guy was an ARVN deserter, sir. His paperwork looked suspicious. The Viet MPs told him to pull out of traffic, and he popped a grenade on himself."

"Christ."

"Happens all the time, some gook gets shot, blown up, or run over on this highway. I just don't want to get hit by flying body parts. One hundred and six days and counting."

The Vietnamese MPs dragged the body off the road. Traffic was picking up. "You'd better get a move on, sir."

Most American soldiers calculated their chances of survival as the reciprocal of time left in their tours. For the kid MP, the odds were reasonably good. The war's tempo had slowed since the era sandwiching the Tet Offensive, '67 to '69, when American combat deaths sometimes had topped a thousand each month. Nowadays, attacks were uncommon around the capital. If you wanted to find the war, you had to head farther out, to places like Tay Ninh Province, where the unknown had died.

I turned off the highway to enter the Bien Hoa airbase, drove for ten more minutes past warehouses, crates, parked trucks, tanks, and helicopters. There were bowling alleys, swimming pools, and theaters. A movie marquee read, 'Yellow Submarine—The Beatles.' On this post in 1959, before American logistics turned the place into what it was today, the Viet Cong had attacked a group of U.S. advisors at a makeshift movie show. Two Americans became the first of our servicemen to die in the war. Somewhere a plaque memorialized their sacrifice. At military installations across South Vietnam, you saw plaques for the Americans who'd lost their lives in Vietnam.

How many plaques were there?

Beaucoup.

I reached a sign that read 'Wister Forensics Facility, MACV Logistical Command.' Rolling up to the drop gate, I presented my credentials to the guard. Wister handled special autopsies, its scale diminutive alongside Tan Son Nhut's Central Mortuary that processed the dead like a factory, and in whose hangar-size spaces forklifts carried the caskets.

At the reception desk, a black soldier in black-framed glasses lifted his attention from a magazine. "Sir?"

"Major Tanner. I have an appointment."

"Sir, don't you know you got to be *dead* to have an appointment here?"

"Does half-dead count?"

"Okay, we letcha in this time, only half dead. Go on in, see Spec-four Marvak."

I pressed through a set of swinging metal doors marked STAFF ONLY, into a chamber where formaldehyde and disinfectants blunted the odor of decomposition. In the autopsy room, a soldier I presumed to be Marvak leaned over a stainless steel table on which stretched a body, the brain exposed at the crown. Marvak probed the tissue with the angled beak of his forceps, and blood and cerebrospinal fluid dribbled into a gutter that washed to the drains.

"Hey there, sir." Marvak was a kid too, no older than nineteen. His job description labeled him a forensic specialist, and he seemed comfortable at his work. If the Army could train teenagers to be machine gunners, it could make them detectives of human remains. "You're here to see our notorious backwoodsman?"

"Uh-huh." You'd have thought, after thirty-two months in Vietnam, the night of a dead man wouldn't have bothered me.

Stripping off his rubber gloves, he led me to the next room, past a Vietnamese man who drowsily slicked a blood-stained mop back and forth on the white tiles, painting a mural of crimson arcs. At the far wall, Marvak tugged open an insulated door. Cold air whooshed in, fog billowed across the floor. Striding to a palisade of drawers, he nosed up to the inlaid cards. "Here he is. Killed in action. Unidentified. We haven't had an unidentified KIA here, at least in my time. Oh sure, we've seen some grisly cases, took a while to verify them from the dental charts, but this guy's in one piece, and nobody knows who he is. Explains why he's so popular, right?"

"Popular?"

"Yesterday Colonel Crowley and Major Vangleman stopped by. Today, you show up. That's like Hollywood around this place. We don't get many visitors."

"Who is Major Vangleman?"

"From the MACV staff." Marvak slid open the drawer, removed the plastic covering, and revealed the death face, eyes slightly open. I noticed thick, wavy hair that the body-tenders had washed so clean it might have starred in a shampoo commercial. Not the face, though. His skin had turned as gray as the monsoon sky. It had taken a long time to get him off Hill 71. Unlike the wounded, who were given the highest priority for evacuation, the dead were a routine logistical errand, and he'd lain body-bagged in the heat for hours before a helicopter came to lift him out. Stepping closer, I saw that a claymore pellet had punched a hole in the lower right cheek.

"How far does the drawer come out?"

"All the way."

"Open it."

He tugged the platform to its full length, and it seemed to levitate above the floor. The autopsy incision ran from the thorax to below the navel. Astride the stitched line, more identical holes peppered the flesh. A larger cavity sank in his lower abdomen, a prominent second navel. The arms changed color at the elbows, a farmer's tan that ended at fingertips stained black from the post-mortem fingerprinting.

"A mask helps, sir. You can rub in some Vicks, hides the smell."

"Not necessary," I said. "Can you roll him over?"

Marvak pulled on a fresh set of plastic gloves and tipped the remains sideways. A massive exit wound marred the lower back just above the buttocks. In the tissue, fragments of pink claymore wadding, signature of a point-blank blast. "He came out of the body bag pretty messy, sir. Loose intestines trailing out this hole. The claymore did a job on him."

After he'd eased the body to its original flatness, Marvak tapped his palm to an unsounded beat.

I asked, "Did you attend the autopsy?"

"Yeah. Hold on, I'll get the report."

On the soles of the dead man's feet, crevices cut toe to heel. Broken blisters cratered the skin. He must have been limping at the end, I thought. The jungle played hell on unhardened feet.

Marvak returned holding a form with onion-skin sheets attached. "They opened him on Monday afternoon. Cause of death: trauma associated with overpressure typical of a blast, and multiple high-velocity wounds from claymore pellets. Hit him all over, as you can see. His heart stayed intact. So did his stomach. Minimal contents—he ate five or six hours before he died."

"Did you determine what he ate?"

"Sorry, the stuff was too far digested. I remember a few yellow remnants. Fruit, I'd guess."

"What about drugs or alcohol?"

"The blood tests were negative for chemical substances."

So confident was the teenager of his death facts, he made me feel younger than him. "I need a photo," I said, wishing I'd gone for the Vicks.

He rolled over a rack-mounted Polaroid and snapped three overhead frames. The photos showed the chin fallen back, exposing the upper teeth. The reflected flashbulb sparked the illusion of awareness into the half-open eyes. The gray skin took on a purple hue, slightly sinister; you might expect to find cobwebs hanging off.

"You can close it. I'd like to have a look at his effects now."

Marvak slid the drawer closed, thumped the freezer door shut behind us. Longing to splash water on my face, wondering why it mattered to show no weakness in front of the kid, I followed him to a room where boxy gym lockers pressed around a bare wood table. He opened one, removed a carton, and dumped out the dead man's gear. The jungle fatigues—cotton interwoven with rip-stop nylon—were in tatters. No insignia or patches. The fabric bore stains but no human debris; somebody, probably the Vietnamese mop guy, had rinsed it thoroughly. "Did you go through the pockets?"

"As soon as we cut them off the body. Empty."

Methodically I squeezed the shredded garments, from whose spaghetti-tangle scudded the yeasty scents of soil and mildew. There was a small canvas butt pack, also washed. I picked up a plastic canteen half full of water, unscrewed the cap, and sniffed the faint odor of iodine. "Did you find a bottle of iodine tablets?"

"No sir."

Clipped to the web belt were an ammo pouch and two nylon canteen holders. Only one canteen. "What happened to the other one?"

"This is everything that came in, sir. Except for the map—Colonel Crowley took it with him. Oh, and the weapon—we keep that in our arms room."

The ammo pouch contained two twenty-round M16 magazines. I combed through the gear until I came up with a third magazine, badly dented. All empty.

He said, "The ammunition is with the rifle."

"How many rounds?"

"Twenty-eight 5.56 and one nine millimeter."

"One?"

"Yes sir. A pistol bullet. No pistol to go with it, though."

"What about other ordnance, like grenades, flares, or claymores?"

"Weren't any."

An infantryman would consume twenty-eight rounds in the first minute of a firefight. This man had trudged through the jungle with soft feet and a paltry supply of ammunition. He wasn't a field soldier.

From the litter I picked up a standard-issue bevel-ring compass. They'd found it a meter from the unknown's body. He must have had it in his hand when the claymore went off. Gently I pried up the lid. Underneath clinked the lingering chips of the glass bevel the explosion had shattered. The breakage was unfortunate; if the glass had stayed intact, it might have shown an azimuth via the luminous line used for land navigation at night, and I could have back-plotted his direction of march.

The rolled-up poncho felt heavy. Something inside. I found the seams and unrolled it, uncovering five D-cell batteries. "Was there a flashlight among the gear?"

"Like I told you, sir..."

I lifted a hand to stop him from repeating himself. "Did anyone else uncover these?"

"No. Colonel Crowley didn't look at the stuff too closely. Major Vangleman just poked at it, like he didn't want to pick anything up."

"I'd like to examine the rifle and the cartridges."

He was back in three minutes. I checked the ammunition first. The headstamps on the rifle cartridges were identical and showed they were of U.S. manufacture, year 1966. The 9mm Parabellum round looked older. Its base bore a letter-number stamp that began with GE, which I knew signified West German manufacture. So much ammunition had glutted into Vietnam over the years from so many sources that tracing a single round was impossible. Nonetheless I made a note of the headstamp data.

Undamaged but for a cracked hand guard, probably from a claymore pellet, the rifle hadn't rusted in the jungle for the three years since the 1st Cav had lost it. Before I field-stripped it, I made sure the chamber was empty—I'd lost count of the accidental shootings I'd investigated, caused by men handling weapons they'd not bothered to check. With my fingers I rubbed the bolt carrier and inner wall of the lower receiver, yielding clean oil, no carbon residue. Nobody had fired this rifle recently. I was about to reassemble the components when I noticed the stock screw.

"Did somebody take off the stock? There are scratch marks on the screw face."

"No sir. You're the only one who's broken it down."

With a screwdriver Marvak supplied, I loosened the stock screw. It turned easily, which was surprising, usually they put up a fight to unfreeze. Separating the stock and the buffer housing wasn't a standard step in individual rifle maintenance, and Marvak gaped with curiosity at this procedure he'd not witnessed before. Inside the receiver was another, smaller screw. With these out, I tugged off the stock. Sprouting from the well's interior, a triangle of cellophane. Gently I disgorged a clear plastic bag that curled in my hand like a giant frito.

"How did you know to look in there, sir?"

"Dope heads sometimes take their stashes to the field this way. There's just enough space to hide a gram or two."

Carefully I opened the plastic wrap, revealing not a dope stash but a black-and-white photo of a Vietnamese woman. On a stage, she posed in a sequined dress, high-heeled shoes, and stockinged legs, one kicked outward in a dance step. A jeweled tiara crowned her head. The photo was an odd print, not a size that the PX developed for GIs, rather a professional photographer's marquee pic that Saigon clubs posted outside their doors to showcase the dancers the way restaurants displayed menus.

"Wow, sir. That is fucking weird."

No comment. With all things fucking weird, I had the edge on him. I tucked the photo in an envelope to take with me. Ever efficient, he found a hand-receipt form, slid it onto a clipboard, filled out the top, and passed it to me to sign.

"How long do you preserve the effects?" I asked.

"Until the remains move on. Then we burn the stuff in our incinerator. If it's serviceable, we turn it in to supply."

"Keep everything until I tell you otherwise." I handed him my card, whose validity might not stretch beyond the week. "If I don't get back to you within ten days or so, call MP investigations. They should be able to give you the case status."

"Getting short, sir?"

"I'm afraid so."

He laughed. He couldn't imagine the reality, that I was afraid to leave Vietnam.

Outside, sprinklers scattered water over grass still brown from the just-ended dry season. I breathed to clear my nostrils of the morgue's sweet-rotten scent, the kind that persists long after it should have dissipated. In the jeep, under the creepers of a tree overhanging the parking strip, I wrote down what I'd noticed. Three observations begged to be explained.

First, the body. It told the tale of a man not inured to his situation. Scantily equipped, pained from his blistered feet, he'd persevered at night over arduous terrain. What had pushed him to keep walking when the smarter choice would have been to hole up until morning? In the light of day, he might have survived his chance encounter with the U.S. Army.

Second, the paraphernalia: A rifle lost in 1967, a pittance of rifle ammunition, and a single 9mm bullet. The U.S. military did not issue 9mm weapons. He'd had a compass. Five D-cells fitting nothing he'd been carrying. No food. In the one canteen, water purified with iodine. No bottle of iodine tablets. A second canteen was missing. A man so meagerly equipped should not have been deep in the jungle. The collection implied that his sojourn there had been inadvertent.

Third, the most ethereal of all and the single item that allowed me to glimpse anything personal: a photograph of a pretty showgirl on a stage. He might have carried the photo in his shirt; instead he'd sealed it in the expedient locket of his rifle stock. Whoever she was, she'd been important to him.

Experience teaches a cop to beware of quick solutions. Yet I couldn't help thinking of the photo as a gift. Through my friends on the Saigon police, a chance existed to locate this woman. Find what a man loves, and you will find him, right?

Experience might also have warned me that what I had was an aberration. To act on it was to set in motion an unbalanced thing, a whirling helicopter blade broken off and careening into a crowd.

* * *

After I'd signed up for my second tour, the Army granted me a 30-day leave, and I spent it in western Massachusetts among the Tanners. My connections to Vietnam were not only mental but exuded in the odors seeping from my pores. I gazed at the woods sloping to the river, and I could smell the rice paddies. In the cloud-draped nights, I scanned for the flares over the Nha Be marshes below Saigon, only to discern the far-off lights of Hadley town.

That was June 1968. Because I was home, it was requisite that I attend the funeral of Vaughn Tanner. His wish to be buried in the family plot annoyed no one; on the contrary, the Tanners welcomed him, their Harvard man who no longer could dispute their family legend. In his coffin, Vaughn was as light as a Vietnamese, and bearing him from the church service to the hearse, I thought the incense smelled like the joss sticks that had burned in the Buddhist temples after Tet, and the saints in the gallery above, their alabaster heads bowed, resembled the Buddha statues. In the drizzle-wet graveyard after the ceremony, my father stood silently for a time, until he muttered, "So you decided to go back."

"They need people with experience." The bullshit you told your dad.

"Experience," he echoed. Like uncle Frank, he'd served in World War II, and he distrusted the military with his son's life. "You really think you can make a difference?"

"A modest one."

"You know, folks here have turned against the war. Seems like the country is full of draft dodgers and flower children. They smoke pot and shout and protest."

"Let them."

"Haven't you done your part already?"

He meant that I'd done what my country had asked, instead of finding ways to hide behind a college deferment or to run away to Canada. I measured the situation differently, for I saw things beyond his imagination: the haze on the rice paddies, the fires over Cholon during the Tet Offensive, people squatting on their flattened houses. The images in my head made me as alone in my point of view as Vaughn had been. I'd not changed so much that I couldn't understand why my family wanted me to stay home. They were the ones whose name I carried, and I did them no favor to get myself killed in an incomprehensible war.

Staring at Vaughn's grave, I thought I should do what the Harvard man had suggested the last time we spoke.

It was a good thing I started my readings *after* I'd finished my first tour. Captains were not asked to judge the legitimacy of South Vietnam's government, and it might have disconcerted me to have fought Tet with my head full of dark cognizance. My timing was important in another way too. Earlier in the conflict, American popular reporting had cast South Vietnam as a beacon of hope, its then-President Ngo Dinh Diem as a savior of freedom, the embodiment of the can-do spirit. Now the judgments had flipped, and criticism of the war abounded.

I read Bernard Fall's *Street Without Joy*, the books of Gerald Hickey and David Halberstam, Time and Life magazines. I paged through Larry Burrows's evocative color photographs that spanned from 1962 to the present, his frames catching the terror and tedium of the conflict. The Tet Offensive had opened a floodgate of controversy, and the information rushed too voluminous for me to drink. My father boosted my education. Every day, he brought home a book or clipped an article for me to read. He wanted me to change my mind about going back. His reasons were obvious; the news out of Vietnam was so bad as to make serving a second tour seem insane.

Journalists often referred to the Vietnam War as a quagmire—something you stumbled into and couldn't extract yourself from—evident once you were stuck. In the years following World War II, clutching to an empire slipping through their fingers, the French portrayed their reclamation of colonial Indochina in the self-serving light of an anticommunist crusade. The United States logistically sustained the French counterinsurgency. In 1954, after suffering a defeat at their mountain outpost of Dien Bien Phu, the French agreed at negotiations in Geneva to relinquish Indochina and to partition Vietnam. According to the agreement, countrywide elections were to have followed in two years to decide whether the partitions—the communist north and the newly post-colonial south—would unite or remain separate. Nobody doubted that Ho Chi Minh's communists would have won. But neither Washington nor South Vietnam's President Ngo Dinh Diem had signed the Geneva Accords, and the elections never happened. We'd lost China to communism only five years before, and we couldn't give up another Asian domino, according to the theory of the time. So we propped up Diem, a staunch anti-communist and a Catholic in a country overwhelmingly Buddhist. Aloof from the people, he ruled South

Vietnam through cronyism and oppression and his influence with us—his nickname became *My* Diem: the American Diem. In 1963, we gave up on him and abetted a junta of generals that seized power. They proved incompetent, and South Vietnam was on the brink of losing to the communist guerrillas when, in March 1965, the United States stepped in with major combat units. Now here was a new sheriff in town, the world's best army against a bunch of fucking rag tags.

Had we really been so naïve? Sure, but that was way back in the middle of the '60s. Long time ago.

My R&R was growing short. I read my books, discussed them with my father, struggled to come to terms with the disquiet we both felt. I tried to explain to him about the flattened houses of Cholon, how they had presented me with unfinished business. "All wars cause suffering," he said. "How can you change anything?"

"I'll do better next time."

Occasionally I thought of the woman in the window above the overturned jeep. In my reveries I pictured her, a goddess looking down, benevolent though not without judgment.

A few days later, I left for four weeks of training and out-processing. In August 1968, I returned to Saigon.

I hadn't gone home since.

* * *

The reporter who'd written the article on the Tay Ninh incident was preparing a follow-up piece. Clamoring for an interview, he'd beseeched Crowley's office, and the colonel had arranged for him to meet with me. Talking to a reporter was the last thing I wanted to do, but I hadn't been consulted, merely directed in the late afternoon to wait at the French Fort until he and his Army Public Affairs escort arrived. In the interval, I typed out a standard Memorandum for the Record with two carbon copies. I described my morgue visit and added my comments on items of possible significance. Then I signed the MFR and sent the original to Crowley in a courier envelope. Lopez took the morgue photos and the marquee shot to the investigations support section. Before the Vietnamization reaper scythed them away, the warrant officers in the fully staffed unit had been wizards at crime-scene photography. Today Lopez had to show the kid who remained how to tape the morgue Polaroids to the wall and snap 35mm frames through various filters. Lopez sifted through the negatives, had the clearest ones printed, and brought me a stack.

I was sliding them into my leather pouch when knuckles rapped the door. In starched khakis stood an officer holding a garrison cap and a vinyl folder with a gilded MACV crest, the kind the PX sold alongside American Soldier stationery. "Good morning, sir. I'm looking for Major George Tanner."

"That's me."

"I'm Lieutenant Hazelton from Public Affairs." He shook my hand robustly and smiled like a salesman. "This is Alton Gribley from the Randolph Press Syndicate."

For their Vietnam bureaus, the American news organizations tapped two brands of journalists: seasoned war correspondents and temporary stringers. The former counted among the war's most informed observers, men and women with years of experience in strife-ridden countries. I judged Gribley to be the latter, an opportunist who knew little about Vietnam or the military and was here purely to notch his reputation. In his late twenties, his blond hair finger combed, he wore black-framed glasses like the ones issued to soldiers. His forehead shone with perspiration and skin oil. Tan slacks and a pleated white shirt gave him the look of a Saigon pigeon, so called because he pecked crumbs from MACV's daily press briefings at the JUSPAO building downtown. Had he spent time in the field with soldiers, he'd have sweated off the thirty excess pounds rounding his middle.

Gribley slumped into one of the metal chairs; Lieutenant Hazelton sat down without allowing his shirt to touch the back—it would have wrinkled the starch. Aligning his folder in his lap, Hazelton said, "As I've explained to Mr. Gribley, it's unusual for the military police to comment at this stage of an ongoing investigation. He still insisted on talking to you."

Gribley's smile showed no pique; he was probably used to depreciating tones. The Tet offensive had changed the relationship between the military and the press. Overnight, Walter Cronkite had gone from the war's patriotic proponent to its most influential critic. Voices like his and the graphic evening news footage had done much to sour American public opinion about the conflict. No surprise that the military distrusted journalists. Officers saw them as the embodied contradictions to MACV's claims we were winning, insidious bystanders who tattled in modulated phrases always prefaced with gainsay, backstabbers who oozed sympathy for the other side and portrayed the U.S. military as so incompetent that it had become evil, the institutional gun hand behind the March 1968 My Lai massacre in which a unit of clown-led miscreants had murdered hundreds of unarmed Vietnamese villagers.

Gribley flipped open his notebook. "Do you mind if I ask you something off the record?"

Hazelton cut in. "The press generally honors its promises to keep comments off the record. But there's no guarantee."

I said, "Go ahead."

"How do you feel about General Cobris running your investigation?"

"The Provost Marshal controls investigations."

"Maybe *overseeing* is how to put it."

"It's not."

Gribley's eyebrows went up. "So you haven't heard?" He turned to Hazelton. "Can Major Tanner and I have a few private words?"

"Up to the major. Standard procedure is for a PA officer to sit in, sir, for your protection."

"It's okay. Sergeant Lopez can get you some coffee."

Ruffled, Hazelton pushed up from his chair, leaving the folder on it to mark his territory. When the door fell shut, Gribley slouched lower, as if in the presence of an old friend. He said, "Sorry, I must have sounded like a smart aleck."

"Don't feel bad. It's your thing."

He shifted in his seat, mouth ajar, unable to determine if I was joking. "I just took a statement from Major Vangleman. He said Cobris is overseeing the investigation—his words verbatim."

Here was the MACV staffer Vangleman again, and I had no idea who he was or what he was doing.

Gribley went on. "He said you're close to proving the Tay Ninh KIA wasn't an American. I understand you can't comment officially, but can you flesh it out a little? What are we dealing with? Fingerprints, documents, forensics? Have you found somebody who knew him?"

"You're right. I can't comment."

"The incident happened ten kilometers from the Gavet Rubber Plantation. Outfits like Gavet and Michelin are staffed by Europeans. Any significance?"

"None that I know of."

His mouth canted like a shovel digging in the sand. "French bigshots run those places. They don't like publicity. When I hear that an unidentified vagabond got blown up right outside a rubber plantation, and that General Cobris is putting both his feet in the investigation, it makes me think the Gavet Company has a line to MACV Headquarters."

"Been out in the jungle, Alton?"

"To firebases once or twice, sure."

"Firebases. You probably sat on the sandbags and ate C-rations and smoked and joked with the GIs. Maybe you witnessed a firepower demonstration, a noisy *mad minute*. You got a briefing from some Army major in clean fatigues in front of a map board. And when you plotted the point on the map where the man you called an unknown soldier died, you spread out your fingers, like you saw the major do, and the distance from thumb to pinky is about 10 klicks. Sound right?"

Gribley squirmed. "Yeah."

"But I asked, have you been in the *jungle*. It's a different world entirely. In places the vegetation is so dense, men carve toeholds in the hillsides so they can stand steady enough to whack their machetes against the walls of bamboo. To go a few meters, they chop until their forearms balloon up and they can't hold the machetes anymore. They don't use trails. Trails are death traps. On foot, ten kilometers isn't *right outside* the plantation. You would take two days to cross it."

He straightened in his chair. So we were not to be friends after all. "Okay, so it's bullshit, the connection to Gavet. I won't mention it in my next article."

"Glad to hear."

"Believe it or not, I appreciate your comments. Obviously there's a lot I don't know." He stood, leaving a film of sweat on the seat. Set his card on the desk's edge. "If you think of anything, you can leave a message for me at the Caravelle Hotel."

Hazelton scurried in to collect his folder and followed the reporter out.

My turn to slump. My speech about hacking through the jungle clanged in my ears. A show-off lecture worthy of a rookie. In delivering it, I'd opened a window on myself, declaring I'd been in the jungle and it mattered to me enough to pontificate about.

I was grateful the door had been closed and Lopez hadn't heard.

Worse, my speech was inaccurate. The jungle wasn't a uniform state of dense undergrowth and obstructions. In places, yes, there were impenetrable walls of bamboo. In others, you could move easily under the canopy, traverse the terrain quickly...

I unfolded the map. With a grease pencil I drew a line from Hill 71 to the closest edge of the Gavet Plantation. The line equated to 10.5 kilometers.

Having seen Hazelton and the reporter out, Lopez reappeared, coffee cup in hand. He leaned in the doorway. "What's next, sir?"

"Call G-5 and ask them to get in touch with the Gavet Rubber Company. Have them set up an appointment for me with somebody in the company's management."

"For when?"

"As soon as possible."

* * *

I returned the jeep to the motor pool, walked to Tan Son Nhut's main gate, and caught a scooter cab into Saigon. In my lap nestled my leather pouch with the photos, the map, and my Colt .45. Not many U.S. servicemen had unrestricted access to Saigon, fewer still were authorized to carry a firearm downtown. I always brought my pistol. Going unarmed might be safe on protected avenues like Tu Do and Nguyen Hue, but I roamed deep into the alleys of Cholon, where Americans were like the albino pheasant, rarely seen except in a fancy cage.

Scooter drivers took varying routes depending on traffic and checkpoints. Tonight's ride sped me along the Cach Mang commercial strip. Lancing past the bars and stalls that crouched shoulder to shoulder, I watched the merchants ratchet down the grates on their storefronts. It was dinner time. They'd reopen later, to cater to the whimsical tastes of GIs who bought the rococo fans and ceramic elephants—favorite trinkets to send home. Less tangible mementos availed in the whorehouse bars where greed and naïveté enacted their age-old exchange. On the sidewalk, a peddler shouted as I buzzed past.

Saigon was an armed camp, a city of nightclubs, a center of commerce, the locus of an existential storm. Really there were two Saigons: the precinct of facades protected by martial law and barbed wire and gun-jeeps; and the realm of catacombs—the backstreets and alleyways, their balconies rigged with clotheslines that gamboled as if they were all tied together and plucked by a hidden hand. Detouring into the city, my scooter driver stopped at an intersection where a joint Vietnamese-American military-police roving patrol checked papers. The streets lay nearly empty; rain impended in swarthy clouds. The patrol stopped us and examined my ID card. A duck merchant pedaled past, the caged fowl on his head like a distended hat in the gloom, the animal honking out a warning.

At this intersection seven years ago, a Buddhist monk named Thich Quang Duc had burned himself as a protest against oppression. Tuy had told me about the incident. A crowd had gathered, summoned by loudspeakers. The monk posed cross-legged on the pavement while a helper doused him with gasoline, pouring liquid over his slight figure, upending the jerry can as if well practiced at human immolation. Thich Quang Duc didn't falter when the match ignited him. Fiercely aflame, he didn't topple, not right away; he balanced on bent legs fused together, his skin turning black and his body's effluent boiling and crackling. The smoke swirled into a vortex that convulsed like a snake whose head is caught in a trap. His death set off a crisis in South Vietnam. More monks burned themselves. Fire alarms went off in the Kennedy White House—

the realization that President Ngo Dinh Diem might be a bad bet, antithetical to our values. The American shuddering stoked a Vietnamese military plot. In early November of that year, the participants murdered Diem.

Murder in the pursuit of American values. Was it justified?

I didn't know.

Three weeks later, Kennedy was assassinated.

What had changed? Saigon remained a city at war. But if the South Vietnamese government still survived upon the elites that suckled to a foreign power, they were smarter now. More attuned to the Vietnamese people. Succeeding in ways that had eluded them in the past and overcoming the legacy of French colonialism and the ugliness that had surrounded Diem's era. So said MACV's briefers.

Were they right?

Not a clue.

The scooter entered Cholon. Years ago, it had been a separate municipality from Saigon. The sprawl that knit them together had left no obvious seam. Even so, I felt the vibe change from crass city to small town. A block from Tuy's apartment, I paid the driver. I always dallied in the shadows to test the surroundings before I took the final leg. An attempt at security. Yet there was no way to be an anonymous American on this side street. So often had I ambled along these cobblestones that the neighbors recognized me, the lanky paleface who came and went from address number 18. They smiled politely when we crossed paths. As to what they thought, I had no idea.

At the alley's far exit stood the policeman my friend Trong had posted to watch the neighborhood. The policeman regarded me with the aloofness of a high mandarin, and I wondered whether his indifference was pretended or real. He was helpful to discourage street thugs and urchins who might otherwise bother me; he wouldn't deter a resolute enemy. If I learned that the Viet Cong had targeted me for assassination, my plan was to flee to a military base and take Tuy with me.

From the doorstep, I collected the evening newspapers. Tuy read as many of the dailies as she could get her hands on; her average was four. Typically she sat cross-legged on the straw mat, the papers spread in front of her in a fan between the floor lamp and the portable radio—another present from me—its handle flipped upward for easy toting. Absorbing the printed news, sometimes she laughed her quintessential three-syllable laugh, each syllable a pure tone. I couldn't imitate her laugh any more than I could reproduce the phonemes of the Vietnamese language. It was the sound of her spirit, and the newspapers brought it out in her. She described her late father, a publisher, as having been similarly obsessed with the dailies, and I wondered if he'd been as reluctant as Tuy to discard the old editions. When I left for work in the morning, I adiosed them to the trash bin outside. In the corner behind the tub she kept a pile of them I wasn't allowed to throw away. A meter tall, its topmost paper formed a handy shelf where she kept her shampoo, soap dish, and ashtray for smoking while soaking.

I sat on the floor and unlaced my boots. She said nothing. The radio bleated last summer's incessantly played Fifth Dimension hit *Aquarius*, a song of the peace generation that had nothing to do with me. Even so, sliding my leather pouch and .45 into the corner, I became, momentarily, a non-combatant.

For tonight's dinner, she served slivers of crab, chopped asparagus, spicy Nuoc Mam sauce, and Rang Chon—an elegant, long-grained rice whose name in the villages meant 'fox fang.' We ate on the floor above a straw mat that served as tablecloth and table alike. Few American servicemen would touch authentic Vietnamese cuisine. In newcomer briefings, the sergeants warned the soldiers that local food would give them the infamous green runs. Men who went to the jungle with the runs slashed open the seats of their pants—they barely had time to step out of column and squat, let alone to undo their belts and web gear. Toting loudspeakers, strutting around in their starched fatigues, the indoctrinators heaped misinformation. Most of them had neither sampled the food nor been in the jungle.

I said, "Do you know the Cercle Sportif?"

Tuy tilted her chin high, a haughty gesture, perhaps a gift from her French grandfather. "Yes. Why do you ask?"

"I have to go there tomorrow to meet a French bigshot from the Gavet Rubber Company."

"So, you need to know the way?"

"I want you to come along. For help with the translation."

Eyeing me, she chewed a clot of rice and crab as if it were the permutations my request represented. Though she was a quarter French, it was the part she'd consciously abandoned, as her father had done. He'd died when she was eleven years old, and she'd spent her adolescence in the household of her uncle, a colonial-administration functionary who, like others of his social caste, had wanted to be the thing he served. Her uncle's identification with the French had been so complete that it survived their defeat. His ambition for her had been that she too would imitate the supercilious colonialists, some of whom had remained in Vietnam. In this he'd been successful for a time, particularly in summoning her to their perusal, where she became a curio, worthy to be held up to the light, though not to be invited into their society.

"People will recognize me at the Cercle Sportif." She sounded irritated, and I wondered on what level she'd have to deal with these people, whoever they were. By Vietnamese standards, she was not poor. She owned this building and another below Tran Quoc Toan Boulevard that she rented to a European airline for its offices; from time to time she gave Vietnamese language lessons to the airline's employees. In a city where hopelessness sloshed at your feet, she was a successful person, with no cause to humble herself. Yet what was a gathering of former colonialists, if not to humble those they'd once subjugated?

I asked, "Do you have a dress to wear?" When we went out, she normally wore the ao dai, the traditional Vietnamese woman's garment that hugged the torso and hips and draped loosely around flowing pantaloons. Not the Americanized image I wanted her to show at *Le Cercle Sportif*.

"I have a dress. It's not new."

"Perhaps a new one would be better."

"And make them think I'm a whore for the Americans."

I retreated into silence, hoping that whatever vexation I'd caused would subside.

It didn't work. Her eyes were bayonets. "Are you going out tonight?"

"I have business with Lieutenant Trong."

"Business?"

"Tomorrow I will be asked if I have seen my contacts. I want to say yes."

She shifted her gaze to her rice and crab scraps. "You're very proud of your contacts, aren't you?"

"Yes."

"And I am one of them, I suppose."

"Not the same."

"No?"

She looked at the food scraps she'd arranged in a little crescent, the kind of plate doodling you pause before eating, because you've spent time constructing it. Perhaps she was thinking of my contacts. She said, "You'd better go. It's starting to rain."

* * *

At a vender's stall, the rain slapped the canvas awning and gamboled into a gossamer screen that helped obscure my presence in Cholon's red light district. In French Saigon, Dong Khanh had been Rue Des Marins—Sailor's Street—the site of the infamous Grand Monde Casino, run by a criminal gang that had flourished until President Ngo Dinh Diem crushed it in the mid-1950s. Tonight the mood was more subdued than grand. The downpour smocked the modest opium dens and hash dives. The taxi drivers had parked to wait it out, and I was lucky to spot one of the yellow and blue Renaults nudged against the curb. Ducking in, I directed the driver northeast toward Trong's neighborhood.

To Tuy, the police were parasites who treated themselves to every sop and kickback their sticky fingers could grasp. Her view might have softened had she known Trong, a modest family man and lieutenant of detectives. Yet I'd resisted an introduction. I worried that she wouldn't read him as I did, and that she'd brand him according to her preconceptions. And what would Trong think of her? She was my woman, to be honored. Yet an introduction inevitably would include his wife, who spoke almost no English, and whose views I didn't remotely apprehend. Tuy and I were not married. Would Trong's wife classify her as a whore?

His standing invitation to me was to call on him at his house between eight and nine at night. He worked long days, and he gave few people carte blanche to puncture the hours he reserved for himself and his family. I did what I could not to abuse the privilege.

Dealing with the Vietnamese apparatus, most Americans paid formal office calls and dispatched memoranda through channels. The few who cut their own way did so by handing out booze and other goodies, befriending corrupt bureaucrats or corrupting those who were straight. I'd come across Lieutenant Nguyen Quan Trong in a different way. Soon after the Tet offensive, he'd visited me at the Long Binh military hospital, where I was recovering from wounds from a Viet Cong ambush at Phu Lam, on the southwestern edge of Cholon. The same ambush had trapped Trong's son, an enlisted man in the ARVN MP company I advised then. His son had related how I'd saved his life by shooting my way through the kill zone to reach him and a few others. I explained to his father that the rescue had been serendipitous—I'd been shooting my way out of a situation just as bad a few feet away. Maybe he thought I was being modest. Or, to him, the distinction was irrelevant. His son was alive, and Trong wanted to say thanks. He was still doing so.

He lived on a street where colonial Saigon blended into Cholon, in a neighborhood where French bureaucrats fifty years ago had built houses more fashionable than they might have afforded in Paris. Wrought-iron gates under street lamps lent the illusion of stateliness. Over the sidewalks arched tree limbs that softened the traffic murmurs from Tran Hung Dao a block away. I sniffed jasmine and Nuoc Mam. Decades of wood smoke had steeped the bricks ash gray.

I knocked and waited a polite step from the entrance, until the throw-bolts clicked and I faced Trong's wife, a short, doughy woman who peered like a turtle from its shell. Inside, I deposited my boots and followed her across the tiles to a walled garden, where, cross-legged on a straw cushion on the stones, reading a newspaper, reposed Trong. His hair was dark and rich. He slicked it with oil, parted it with a razor line. Strands sometimes flopped over his forehead, and he restored them with a characteristic two-fingered flick. Alongside crouched a little propane stove like the one Tuy used. I'd given it to him a year ago.

Languidly he turned the news pages. The garden was full of bugs, and the pages might have been the wings of a giant butterfly. He asked, "Where have you been, my friend?"

"Working at Tan Son Nhut."

"A waste of your talents. What other American knows Saigon like you do?"

"I don't know it well enough. That's why I'm here to see you tonight."

He acknowledged my remarks with the slightest smile. The banal exchange had become our customary greeting, and we both played along. "To drink?"

"The same tea as you're having."

Trong was among the few of my Vietnamese contacts whose command of English did not require the presence of an interpreter. He was a northerner, a Catholic who'd grown up on the outskirts of Hanoi. As a youth, having impressed the French nuns with his intelligence and diligence, he found himself cast as a priest. His enrollment at the pre-seminary coincided with the end of the collaborationist French regime that the Japanese had allowed to administer Vietnam through most of the Second World War, and which in early 1945 they ruthlessly snuffed out. After the Japanese surrender, communist resistance leader Ho Chi Minh set up an independent government that the returning French soon forced into the mountains. By then, Trong had advanced to the high seminary, a fortunate status that kept him out of the conflict—he wasn't sure which side would have recruited him first. After the 1954 debacle at Dien Bien Phu and the ensuing Geneva Accords, he joined his parents along with hundreds of thousands of other Catholics who fled south, fearing repression at the hands of the victorious communists.

Had he mastered the priesthood the way he had English and French, he'd have ascended to bishop by now. Instead he'd become a detective, and he brought his northern qualities of persistence and hard work to the job, though, like everything else in Saigon, these had to be weighed against the consequences. Saigon's officialdom tarnished men as thoroughly as the tropical air corroded metal into brittle chips. Competence alone wouldn't advance a policeman with his superiors. Installed in their posts through family connections, running side businesses they bolstered with their police leverage, they valued loyalty, and they sneered at American-brand naïveté. Trong couldn't afford to be labeled as a fool. He'd spoken to me of this candidly in the weeks after the Phu Lam ambush: "All comforts are stolen ones. If we lose, this will be the reason."

An experienced cop, he was brave, which perhaps explained his admiration for how I'd saved his son. Across his forehead below the unruly strands ran a scar whose outlines blushed red. By coincidence I'd been with him when he got it. He'd been hosting me around the police headquarters when a crazed Cholonese tried to knife his way through the police. Trong had waded into the rumpus and wrestled the cutter to the ground. Rising from the melee, blinking the blood out of his eyes, he'd registered no anger, merely grit. He was the most valuable contact I might have had in Saigon, a friend who transcended police business, notwithstanding that it was invariably the reason I visited him.

Handing me a steaming teacup, he regarded my leather pouch conspicuously awaiting its turn. I fished out the photograph of the girl. "I need to find her."

"A club dancer? Are you certain she works in Saigon?"

I explained how I'd found the photo in the rifle stock of an unidentified man killed in the jungle. "He died in Tay Ninh Province, closer to Saigon than to other cities with fancy clubs."

"Club dancers are not loyal like your girlfriend Tuy. This one might not remember him from a hundred others."

"I think she would. He hid her picture away for a reason."

Examining it, he evinced a frown, unusual for him. "To find her, we have to approach the clubs. They are protected by powerful interests. They don't like the police."

"You're just asking about a girl."

"They do not see it that way. Cops are an intrusion. If the owners thought I was investigating their clubs, they would complain to their patrons, who would chastise my superiors. They would have no choice but to rebuke me. I have seen it happen many times."

Never before had he thrust out an objection to one of my requests. Maybe he wished for me to withdraw it. He had to live with his decisions; a bad one could ruin his reputation and conjure enemies. How easy, for someone to lob a grenade over the wall into his garden, the playground for his two youngest children, and where in the evenings his teenage daughter and her friends gathered to peruse the latest fashion magazines—more gifts from me.

We sat for a while, Trong studying his tea leaves while I studied mine. I didn't let him off the hook; without his help I couldn't find the dancer. Out of the corner of my eye, I glimpsed a large brown spider crabbing up my shirt sleeve. Casually, trying not to flinch, I swatted it away. Trong paid no attention.

Eventually he said, "Perhaps there is another way. Have you met Phan Quang Giang?"

"No."

"He is one of my sergeants. A strange man, but loyal to me. He knows Saigon's underworld quite well."

Day 2

Tuy had donned her midnight-blue dress. The garment had been her mother's, imported years ago from Paris and re-tailored to the current style. The hat was silk and mesh and meant to be canted rakishly. While we waited for a ride on Dong Khanh, the brim's shadows crisscrossed her face.

A seagull might wing the distance between Cholon and *Le Cercle Sportif* in five minutes across the neighborhoods and streets and police checkpoints. The cyclo took considerably longer, and I worried that I'd miss my appointment. The guards disallowed cyclos beyond the street, so we had to proceed on foot along the lengthy promenade. From a second-floor balcony, armed sentinels perused us. The sidewalk echoed the clicks of Tuy's heels and the dress's swish against her legs. At the main door, the French security men held us for awhile. They rooted warily through her purse in search of bombs, guns, knives—the implements of well-dressed Viet Cong women who accompanied American officers to sports clubs. Me they regarded with apathy. Lots of Americans attended the club. In Saigon we were like solar radiation, irritating but unavoidable.

The Saturday luncheon crowd mingled on the verandah. We heard the splashes and shouts of children in the club's swimming pool. Tennis balls sailed to and fro beyond the enameled rails where we balanced our drinks. From a court unseen, metal pétanque balls clinked their hollow clinks. Most of those present were Caucasians. Quite a few were French, vestiges of the colonialists who'd taken Indochina by force nearly a hundred years ago, only to lose it in 1954. Since then, to retain their business interests, they'd cut deals and siphoned influence from their American successors. I noticed on some of the white sport shirts the Gavet Company's colorful rubber-tree logo.

We were ignored until a man in a poplin suit, his physique like a pear, bulging abdomen trimming upward to diminutive shoulders, sidled up next to Tuy. His goatee masked a face of deep pocks, probably from a childhood illness, that served to obscure his age. I guessed him to be in his late forties, more than twenty years older than her. He flashed huge incisors. "What a long time since I've seen you!" Kissing her on both cheeks, he glanced briefly at me, and the teeth submerged. To Tuy he spoke now in rapid French. She came back with two or three words, then ignored him until he left.

I asked, "Who's he?"

"His name is Christian. He is a wealthy businessman and a busybody. I met him through my uncle years ago. Since I was with an American, he queried if there were financial hardships. Why else would I be seen with an American officer, unless you'd paid for me?"

"He said that?"

"He intimated."

The man was a pig. Yet he was exactly what Tuy had expected to encounter, and I was grateful she'd been willing to put up with it just to accommodate me.

"Why is he so eager to do favors for you?"

"Since I was sixteen and men began to notice me, men like him have introduced themselves. He used to give me money in an envelope. To help me with the expenses of my studies, he claimed. Really it was his way of saying he wanted to fuck me."

"And you took it?"

"The money yes. The fuck, no."

"I think I owe him a broken jaw."

"Sometimes it is better to accept the favors and ignore the innuendo than to refuse the favors altogether. He thinks he is making incremental progress, you see."

"For ten years?"

"People are long suffering in this town."

A busboy ushered us to the second-floor sitting room where electrified oil lamps glowed tepidly over an oriental carpet that the treads of privileged insiders had worn thin. Mssr. Leon Gavet, Managing Director and predominant owner of the rubber company bearing his name, extended his hand with difficulty across the width of a lacquered coffee table. His stout lips forged a modest crescent. No doubt he practiced the same mien with many factions: the South Vietnamese authorities and the Viet Cong who taxed him, the local forces that kept the roads safe for passage, and now, interrupting his aperitif, an American investigator.

The waiter delivered a glass of pastis, centered it upon a faded lace doily. "What are you having?" asked Gavet. I judged him to be in his mid-sixties.

"Too early for me, thanks."

Almost imperceptibly, his smile widened. I suspected that I fit his stereotype of the blasé American.

"And what about you, young lady?"

"No, thank you."

"You are here for what reason?"

"To translate."

"Ah. A service we shall not require. But I beg you to stay. You brighten this old room." He turned to me. "Major, you are a policeman, correct? How does it work with your jurisdiction? Does it encompass foreign businesses in South Vietnam?"

I told him no, which he'd already understood. He'd asked the question as a means of setting a tone: I had no power here. He'd afforded me this interview as a courtesy, and he drew its boundaries as he chose.

He said, "Tell me about this investigation of yours."

"The Gavet Rubber Plantation in Tay Ninh Province is close to the site where a man died early on Sunday morning. He was a Caucasian out on foot and alone. We haven't been able to identify him or explain his presence in the rain forest."

"Yes, I read of the incident in the newspaper. The article was unclear about where it occurred."

From my leather pouch I took the map. Hunching over it, Gavet's shoulders squeezed uncomfortably at his neck. He wore a white sports jacket, and the sleeves rode up his blimpy forearms as he followed the tip of my finger to Hill 71.

"The location is ten and a half kilometers from the nearest edge of your plantation."

He relaxed from his exertion over the map, tugged his sleeves to their proper length. "We call it our western zone. I'm familiar with the landscape. Outside the perimeter, the foliage is all but impenetrable. Ten kilometers is a long way."

"I know. I pointed that out to somebody yesterday, in fact."

"Then you will concede that the incident cannot be taken as relevant to my company."

"The connection is circumstantial, so far."

His thick lip curled around the glass for a sip of the pastis. "Perhaps you can explain something to me. The newspapers said the fellow was lightly armed and equipped. What did they mean?"

"He had a rifle and web gear. A canteen of water and a few rounds of ammunition. Not enough to get him far."

"The weapon and equipment, were they American?"

"Yes. Even the Viet Cong carry American equipment they come across."

"Certainly. My point is, because you wish explore what you label as a *circumstantial* connection, I can assure you that our personnel at the plantation use only European military gear, supplied through the French Embassy. This is not by happenstance. We have no wish to be mistaken for Americans. As you are aware, France ceased its participation in the war a decade and a half ago. That one of my employees would be ten kilometers deep in the jungle, carrying American kit, is inconceivable."

"I agree, Mssr. Gavet. It's also unlikely an American soldier would be so deep in the jungle by himself. I'm just eliminating possibilities."

His mouth flattened. "As you define them."

"Do aircraft come and go from the plantation?"

"No. The roads are kept open nowadays, thanks to the Vietnamese Army. And yours."

On an unencumbered doily, I laid the original morgue photo of the unknown. "Do you recognize him?"

The morgue shot triggered a grimace. "No."

Quickly I retrieved the disturbing photo.

He said, "You should be cognizant of another fact quite pertinent. Only a few Europeans work in the plantation's western zone. They maintain our radio tower, and their whereabouts are accounted for. Everyone else is Vietnamese. So I believe you can rule us out without further importuning your time, or mine."

"Mssr. Gavet, please bear with me. I have no wish to unfairly associate your company's name with the incident. Is there someone who might recognize *all* the European employees of the plantation, to confirm that the man in the photo is not one of them? For the sake of certainty?"

"Regardless of my arguments, you're going to insist on pursuing this line, aren't you?"

"I'm afraid so."

Gavet clapped his hands once and the waiter stepped in. "Bring me a telephone." He dug in his coat pocket for a memo booklet. The phone arrived and he made the call in French, penning as he spoke an address on the back of his business card. He extended it to me. "Mssr. Hipolite is our administrator for personnel. See him at his office today at sixteen hundred hours."

No surprise that the French colonialists used military time. "Thank you."

"After you speak with him, I want you to cease references to Gavet Rubber in connection with this incident. If I hear otherwise, I will present a complaint personally to your superiors."

*   *   *

Forty kilometers inland, on a river writhing to an estuary, Saigon was a port town, a military town, a place of extremes. This was the upper First District. If the fish had gold teeth, they would be here.

A block away, the trees of the Botanical Garden were citron brushes against the sky. The rain had just cleared, and cotton-candy heads of mist tarried over the puddles and fallen tamarind leaves. Amid them we weaved, holding hands and scanning the facades for the Gavet Rubber Company's personnel office that Leon's penned address put on this street. We stopped at a gate where metal spires fronted a garden, and I pushed aside the bougainvillea to reveal a polished brass placard with the house number. After the second buzz, a caretaker, sandals slapping, trotted out and led us through a vine tunnel between the garden and the adjoining brick maisonette.

Mssr. Michel Hipolite greeted us at the side door. Gray skinned, beset with a severe five o-clock shadow, he might have been a decade older than me. He didn't offer to shake my hand, rather he creased his face in what he may have intended as a smile. In his office upstairs, seated in cushioned wicker chairs, we faced screened windows open to a spirited breeze. Gusts tried to snatch papers that a few eclectic nick-nacks strained to hold down, and Tuy braced her hands on her knees to keep her dress hem from flapping. When I introduced her, Hipolite said, "Bravo on shattering my preconceptions. For an American officer, you have a wholly unconventional assistant."

"Tuy speaks excellent French. I thought I might need her to translate. Mssr. Gavet did not specify."

"He is tight with information. With money too, unfortunately."

I asked, "Did he tell you the reason for our visit?"

"I am to deny something. What is it again?"

I handed the Frenchman the morgue shot and explained my inquiry. The photo provoked no grimace, and I had the impression that he genuinely culled his memory. He said, "I don't recognize him. I am instructed to tell you that we are missing no employees from our sites. Which happens to be true."

One of the nick-nacks on Hipolite's desk was a coin inlaid in a square of lacquered teakwood. I couldn't discern the lettering, only the distinctive parachute in the center. I asked, "Were you here in the First Indochina War?"

"Too young. Mine was Algeria."

The breeze puffed hard, and Hipolite's curios fought to preserve their papers. He might have closed the windows, but he was the type who needed the outdoors. How had this para settled to earth in the unlikely role of a personnel officer for a rubber company? Seeming to read my thoughts, he commented, "We draw many of our new employees from the French Army and the Legion. They come to Indochina for work that is hard to find in France these days. I meet all these ex-soldiers—my résumé lends me an advantageous rapport when the contracts are drawn up—so I know them. None are the man in your photo. I would not be surprised if your incognito turns out to have had a similar background, but he was not with Gavet."

"Who might recognize him?"

"Perhaps the French Embassy, though I would not hold out much promise. I doubt he was the sort to frequent the diplomatic cocktail circuit. Also, this incident has been in the press, and anybody who wanted to claim him should have stepped forward by now."

For the first time, Tuy spoke up. "He was close to the Gavet Plantation's boundary when he died. Yet he was not an employee you recognize. Are there employee files you don't handle yourself, Mssr. Hipolite?"

It was a question I'd have expected Hipolite to shrug off. Instead the Frenchman shifted his attention to Tuy. She showed no discomfort in his long gaze, met it boldly in a way Vietnamese women rarely did. In the humidity, her hair was as dark as it got, and Hipolite could not have recognized his French ego reflected back at him. After a moment, he commented: "You should take good care of her, Major."

"I know."

"As for your insightful question, Mademoiselle, it implies that some of the Gavet Company's business is too delicate for the regular staff to manage. For instance, sections of Gavet's land abut territory where the communists operate. The Viet Cong easily might render our business untenable, yet we continue. Presumably certain understandings are reached, special people consulted. These matters are outside my purview. If there are, say, quasi-employees, I cannot help you. I've never encountered them myself. Something like that would be in the hands of Director Gavet."

I asked, "Who else might know?"

"Possibly Madame Simone Nogaret, a businesswoman with a fascinating history. You see, the Gavet Plantation was assembled from the tracts of former smallholders, and the western lands once belonged to Simone's father. He was killed in the First Indochina War, along with her mother, by a communist landmine on the plantation road. A few years afterward, she sold the land to Gavet. She still holds a seat, ex officio, on the board of advisors."

"Any chance I can talk to her?"

"Only by way of Mssr. Gavet. And I predict you would be wasting your time to ask. He is protective of Mme. Nogaret, extraordinarily so. I once tried to gain an appointment with her myself, to cross-check an employment reference. I was refused. For most people, she is—how would you say?—unapproachable."

Day 3

Midnight. Saigon slept like a turtle in a pond's sediment. Through the screened window seeped cricket chirps and a breeze the pre-monsoon humidity thickened. The eddies carried to the roll-out straw mattress where Tuy and I curled like the folds in a paper fan.

Show me a rich cop and I will show you a crook, Trong once had told me. Show me a comfortable soldier and I will show you a fraud, I thought. My life was too cozy for Vietnam. It didn't matter that this was a temporary condition, or that at times it had been difficult and dangerous. Bedded with Tuy, I existed in a place too sensual to be war, too pleasurable to be allowed to go on. And it would not. My time with her was slipping; already I could see past it to a certain road in Massachusetts framed in maple trees. Men counted the days toward such a picture of home. The same vision terrified me, because she wasn't in it.

The solution was to take her with me to the United States. As a plan, it relied on two assumptions whose validity quivered like the legs of an overworked coolie.

One was that Tuy and my family would accept each other.

I trusted the kindness of the Tanner family, particularly the women. Tolerant and empathetic, they would sense discomfort in a person and sooth it with genuine hospitality. They were nonetheless conventional. Tuy wouldn't fit their notions of the Vietnamese; they'd misread her politeness and self-diminishing demeanor. Sophisticated, educated, prideful, she expected people to take her seriously.

I recalled a night in the time of the late monsoons—the inverse of the current season—when the tiger stripes of orange clouds had cut crossways over the moon. It was soon after our courtship began, and in contrast to the black slacks and white blouse she wore in the day, she'd donned a silk ao dai. The wind streamed back the tails of her garment as we strolled Nguyen Hue Street after a movie at the USO. Around us Saigon hummed in petty events: the aria of sirens and their abrupt discontinuance, the artifice of young prostitutes trying to look like big-city women, the jeers of American GIs who construed something funny in the girls' solicitations. We passed merchant stalls whose venders tracked us with their stares, no telling what thoughts we stirred, this American and his pretty Saigonese girl, of longing, envy, resentment, remembrance. We passed through the interwoven pools of light from street lamps and cars that streaked her with the plumage of a rare parrot. Turning onto Pasteur, one of the busiest thoroughfares in town, felt like entering an American main street: a surfeit of Caucasians. Number 137 had been the site of MACV's headquarters before it moved to Tan Son Nhut in 1967. Set back from the picturesque lines of plane trees were BOQs for military personnel and other official Americans who worked downtown.

Among the annoyances of Pasteur Street were the street urchins pressed into the beggar's trade. Obeying their tutelage to harangue foreigners for piastres, kids began to circumambulate us, loping backwards or chasing alongside. We'd gone a block like this when she stopped and asked an urchin, "Where is your *padrone?*"

The kid huffed.

"Go tell him I want to talk to him."

Her tone impelled the urchin to race off, and soon afterward a man arrived. He looked to be in his thirties, a knife cut shorter than Tuy, his hair ruffled but clipped, his steel-green trousers and black t-shirt clean. He had a wrestler's stance and musculature, his sandals on blunt feet, the toes clutched as if every centimeter of him were sculpted for violence. His confidence showed in the disdainful cant of his mouth. "What is it?" he asked impatiently in Vietnamese (as was their full conversation, which Tuy translated for me later).

She said, "I wish to walk down this street in peace."

"These boys have to make a living."

"It is *you* who make a living from *them*. But not from me. What do I look like to you, a foreigner?"

He held her gaze for a minute, then glanced off to the side, as if deliberating. After a minute he barked something to the children. When we resumed our walk, two of them stayed with us, at a distance ahead; they were clearing a path.

The man flicked a glance to me, perhaps to gauge the American who had earned this woman.

"Let's go," she said.

The second tentative assumption was more of a weak hope—that Tuy would agree to leave her country. Never had she hinted at a willingness to separate herself from Saigon or from her mother. The Vietnamese cling to the lands of their ancestors, and in this she hadn't wandered far from the old ways.

She spent the first decade of her life on a bend of the Saigon River, a place of weltering fields, groping marsh streams, and the hazy umbra of trees. The reeds climbed tall, and the children could watch their tips sway against the tropical clouds. It was a place of changing mists and light, continuity in all else, especially the ubiquity of water and the sprawl of birds. Her family lived in a house that pillars lofted above the patina, and she came to think of water as the true foundation for everything.

Her father printed his newspaper on turquoise paper the shade of a lily pad. Lined in the diacritical-laced Vietnamese script, it was a typical daily with its essential horoscope and sensationalist headlines. Copies flooded the house. As she recalled, the floor contained not a square meter of space that papers, books, guests, or tables of food did not fill. The guests were her father's friends or employees who spoke French and Vietnamese in equal measure, and they'd pause from their cigarettes and drinks to ask if she wanted to run her father's newspaper when she grew up. If the press still existed by then, her father would quip, careful to express his anti-government sentiments as innuendo rather than as outright criticism. His business required him to spend most of his hours in the company of others, and he practiced his art well, many people claimed him for a friend and consumed his time as if it were cheap opium. When released from their hold, he receded into the comforts of his wife and daughter and spoke wistfully of a future in which his moments with them would multiply to fill his days. In these fond sojourns, they sat together in their little triumvirate, her mother and father at a table, she cross-legged on the floor, and they would read newspapers. Sometimes they chatted, but mostly they read silently in a state she remembered as sublime peace.

Her father had a younger brother, a protocol warrant who never visited their home, not even during the New Year's holiday. Not all men could tolerate the presence of other people, her father explained, to which her mother rejoined that not all men were polite or dutiful either. On special occasions, they traveled to the uncle's house in the Third District, and it was as if they'd gone from the natural world to the artificial. The house stood on a cement pad within cement ramparts, and the trees grew out of cement pots. Absent flowers, it exuded the smell of them, as if somebody went about tweaking a perfume atomizer in the rooms. Posed delicately on tables, frail-limbed statuettes begged a child to pick them up, and within her uncle's house, Tuy sensed that the adults wished she were one of the statues, motionless so she couldn't break anything or venture where she wasn't supposed to.

When her father died, her life became like a dun tableau set with the objects in her uncle's house she could not touch. She heard the word *debt* for the first time, and she intuited that her father's newspaper had draped it across their shoulders, a coolie-pole whose baskets bulged with stones. At first her mother said that their stay with the uncle would be temporary; soon they would save the money to return to their own house. *Temporary* and *soon* proved as insubstantial as the mists over the water. In the city beyond the uncle's ramparts, poverty ravaged families like a dreaded disease, and her mother dared not relinquish the shelter he extended to them.

His largesse came at a price. He insisted that the single language uttered in his earshot be French. One day he took Tuy aside and reminded her of something she'd known but hadn't weighted as more than a stray fact: her grandfather had been a Frenchman. Proof of this, her uncle said, manifested in the restless coloring of her hair. Her heritage made her *different*, and though he offered no explanation of why this should be so, he clearly deemed it praiseworthy. To Tuy's thinking it was irrelevant, and she told him so. For weeks afterward, he communicated with her only by way of her mother, who admonished her to show no further contrariness; it was a luxury they could not afford.

When Tuy was fourteen, her school introduced English, increasingly the language of power. It was the subject she tended most diligently, and it gave her a new voice to remake herself in a way other than what her uncle had in mind. Henceforth she spoke French solely with him, or at the French social gatherings he insisted she attend. For a time the will of heaven favored her, for President Diem, in power now for four years, eschewed the French and exalted the Americans. She observed how resentment over this situation registered on the faces of her uncle and the French nationals he toadied to. Eventually they rewarded his loyalty by sponsoring him for French citizenship.

She was eighteen when her uncle announced he would move to Paris. Before he left, he exhorted her mother to appeal to these same French benefactors. He told her this as he arranged to sell the house where they'd lived with him for seven years. Once again they would be left without a home. By now, however, her mother had been able to negotiate her way out of debt, earning an income working with old friends, virtuous people who had known Tuy's father and who seemed to exist in every quarter of Saigon. She was able to rent a one-room apartment below Tran Quoc Toan Boulevard, near the Buddhist Institute in northern Cholon. Among the Chinese merchants, in a district where a single room often housed whole families, they were but two women.

So began their journey back from poverty, toward the station meant for them, had Tuy's father not died so young. Through their struggles, he watched over them from the principality of the ancestors—this she never doubted. When they sat together on the floor of the apartment, as her mother studied the real-estate ads for properties she might purchase for less than they were worth, Tuy could feel the presence of his benevolent spirit.

Through the influence of her father's old friends, and from the favorable impressions she made on those who met her, Tuy gained admission to the university, where she honed her English and digested the history of the Vietnamese people. Politics infused these latter studies, and inevitably she became acquainted with activists among the students and the faculty. Their views spanned from snobbish disapproval of the regime to fanatical resistance. To speak against the government of South Vietnam—a country facing an existential threat—demanded a mentality resigned to punishment. People were arrested. The pressure did not suffocate the political discourse. The Americans wanted to believe that President Diem upheld democratic ideals, and so as not to alienate his champion, he grudgingly tolerated some criticism from the students. When he chose to crack down, he claimed to be purging communists, but if a distinction existed between communists and other political opponents, those he arrested failed to perceive it. Just once did the authorities arrest her, during the student protests following the regime's infamous pagoda raids in August 1963. They accused her of association with a tainted professor, a frail man who accommodated his captors by wilting like a flower and dying soon after they threw him in jail. A day later, they released her.

Tuy's mention of the professor recalled my uncle, Vaughn Tanner. When I described him, she replied that she would like to meet this fascinating man.

The only relative of mine she ever expressed a desire to meet, a family exile, was dead.

* * *

In the dense air I strained to hear her breath. When I couldn't detect the sound, a panic invaded, and I had to lean close to her for reassurance. She was my ligature to a certain way of thinking, an enthusiasm for life like a narcotic to me now. If she stopped breathing, surely I would too.

Too late to reinvent myself. Reckless, this state of mind, to love a person from a land I must leave, to need her in a way that was almost incapacitating. I might not even be able to say goodbye. Like a miner in a tunnel under the earth, there were masses above me poised to fall, to seal me off from her without warning. Death was not the only one. I could be sent home to the United States, my extended Vietnam service deemed fulfilled. Or a rattle of the telex could see me transferred to the military police detachment in Da Nang, six hundred kilometers away. If she traveled across town to see her mother, as she regularly did, I might be gone before she returned home.

Maybe it was the trickle of rain on the roof, the sluggishness of the breeze, but the urgency began to drift. Crowley was not about to send me to Da Nang, not with the investigation running. I still had time to resolve things with Tuy. In a week, this strange inquiry would be finished, and we'd decide what to do.

* * *

I caught a scooter to the police headquarters, a gray-stuccoed edifice, another souvenir of the French colonial administration. Erected at the turn of the century, its ornamented colonnades and plinths evoked a pompous officialdom; off-color cement patched the bullet scars from the First Indochina War. I entered through a side door into a vestibule of desks, fans, and typewriters, passing policemen of the *Canh Sat* in their pressed white uniforms and detectives in civilian clothes. Everyone was smoking cigarettes. The office furniture, the uniforms, and the ashtrays came courtesy of American foreign aid. Above them, on the whitewashed wall, an immense framed photo of South Vietnamese President Nguyen Van Thieu.

In situation briefings, I'd heard more about President Thieu. He was an army general, and he'd grown up in a French colonial system that spooned out favors, lines of influence and control that traced between the loyalist and the patron. To those it benefited, the system was addictive. Yet he listened to the advice the Americans gave him. When we exhorted him to implement land reform, he did so. When we insisted that the villages be empowered and the village chiefs democratically elected, he made it happen. Too many refugees? He resettled hundreds of thousands. He understood how statistics stoked the success stories that Americans loved to hear, and he supplied them. The briefers said all this, and I could regurgitate it.

Was it true?

No idea.

A detective noticed me and shouted for someone to summon Trong. A minute later my friend appeared, took my hand, and led me toward the building's deeper recesses. We skirted a side office—the detectives' bullpen—where two men slouched as languidly as tree sloths. Like every branch of the Saigon bureaucracy, the police employed sinecures whose relatives were governors or ministers or military commanders. The patrons demanded services, and the detectives might apply themselves exclusively to these, ignoring their police duties. I had to think that Trong wished he could boot these bastards out the door, but in Saigon's way, neither he nor his bosses could do anything about them.

Along the corridor we crossed a boundary where the American aid money had run out and the walls reverted to the original moldy paint. We reached an office whose furnishings were a desk, fan, and chair, not much different from my office at the French Fort, yet I had the impression I'd been lured into the den of an exotic animal.

Trong said, "This is Giang, an expert on vice."

Giang had a young-old visage, and it took me a minute to recognize one who'd given himself over to addiction, probably to heroin. An authority on vice, he had become its practitioner. Heroin had emerged from the ancient opium trade as the cash drug to peddle to American GIs, and some of the white poison had found its way into the veins of Vietnam's own population. Giang's delicate hand with almost translucent skin and rosy nails held the dancer's marquee photo, while his eyes, the only parts of him not withering in cachexia, studied it with seeming hyper alertness. Standing politely to the side, Trong adopted a respectful silence, quite unlike how he related to the other cops. In the West, custom requires a man to resist death, whereas in the East he might have other options. Giang had chosen to accept his terminal declination without fear, and it rendered him the object of deference, even from his superior officer.

"I have made inquiries about your dancer," Giang said. From the timber of the few words not cracking hollow, his voice might once have been forceful. "A street peddler recognized her. He said her name is Kim Thi and she works in a club downtown."

"Downtown," Trong echoed, shaking his head slightly. "It is meaningless. There are too many girls from the villages. They come to Saigon by the thousands. Nobody keeps track of them."

An edge to his tone. Working in a club on Tu Do Street, dropping into the cash-padded laps of American GIs, a bar girl could make in one day what he earned in a month from his policeman's salary. How was he to protect his daughters from the currents wrecking the traditional society? Since 1962, in its counterinsurgency strategy to safeguard isolated populations and deprive the Viet Cong of potential manpower, the South Vietnamese government with American funding had mounted massive campaigns to resettle villagers into rural fortresses called strategic hamlets. Separated from their ancestral lands, the peasants tended to drift like scythed reeds tossed in a meandering river, and despite recent rural security improvements, most of them were never going back. People gravitated toward money, and here it meant close to the Americans.

In his sandpaper voice, Giang said, "I am concentrating on the good clubs. The better ones are in the First District. They have dancers worthy to take a picture of."

"Which clubs?"

He named several of Saigon's choicest establishments. "Their sponsors are powerful. They have top police contacts. If we show ourselves, much trouble. Tonight, I will send a young boy with the photograph. He will say he is searching for his sister, that the family is asking all over for her."

Trong added, "The clubs might be more helpful with a boy than with police who are not on their sponsor's payroll."

He and Giang segued into rapid Vietnamese. The only parts I understood were the inflections of approval or disapproval I'd heard so often from Tuy, and the patrons and the names of the various clubs. The patrons were well-known Saigon generals or bigshots—no mystery why my friends wanted to keep the inquiry discreet. Then I caught a name, which I was slow to recognize because Trong with his northern accent pronounced it differently than Tuy would have. I interrupted to ask him to repeat it.

"*Quartier Latin*," he said. "It's a nightclub."

"There was another name."

"Nogaret."

"Simone Nogaret?"

"Not Simone. André. He runs *Quartier Latin*. He is a *parachutiste* who stayed in Vietnam after the French war."

"I know of Simone," Giang cut in. "She is—how you say?—a socialite. She lives in the First District. André is her husband."

"Do me a favor," I said. "Concentrate on *Quartier Latin* above the others."

"You have a special reason?"

"I heard Simone's name yesterday. Maybe just a coincidence."

No second guesses. A universal truth: Cops hated coincidences.

* * *

Circling above Tan Son Nhut, a formation of jets showered the base with AVGAS fumes. The day hung sultry, the air barely breathable around an intersection where the MPs halted my jeep to let pass a convoy of troop buses whose diesel smoke further clotted the atmosphere. The 1st Infantry Division was sending soldiers home. Not all its soldiers—some were being distributed to separate units as fillers. Behind the grenade screens, the lucky ones whooped and waved.

The premise that the South Vietnamese would take over the war had lurched along for nearly two decades. The French had attempted to create an anti-communist Vietnamese army, and French-trained Vietnamese soldiers had fought alongside their colonial masters at Dien Bien Phu. Since the mid-1950s, American advisors had trained the South Vietnamese military, building forces that despite advantages in firepower had proven inadequate to preserve a government that had lost the support of its rural population. The solution—more training, equipment, and experience. On MACV's time-to-victory clock, the hands always had pointed to years.

Then the hands fell off. Last May, we'd mounted an assault on a North Vietnamese Army stronghold named Ap Bia Mountain near the Laotian border. Seventy U.S. and allied soldiers had been killed and ten times as many wounded in the battle dubbed Hamburger Hill. A few days later, the Americans withdrew and the NVA immediately reoccupied the mountain. It was a common scenario—remote terrain possessed no intrinsic value. Throughout the Vietnam War, MACV had emphasized an attrition strategy—the favorable kill ratio—that our prodigious ammunition capacity rarely failed to achieve. Hamburger Hill was a military success. Yet to the increasingly critical American public, it showcased a profligate squander of lives and the futility of the whole enterprise. Anti-war fever flared, public patience evaporated. President Richard Nixon thereupon dusted off the Vietnamization concept and announced the imminent withdrawals of sizeable U.S. forces. The pullouts to date represented a modest prelude for what was to come. Two weeks ago, the President unveiled a timetable under which more than ten thousand soldiers a month would be going home.

Ready or not, the turnover was happening.

At my desk, a message to phone Crowley. Facing the framed photo of President Nixon, the same glossy of the Commander in Chief every unit had to tack up, I dialed MACV headquarters and waited for the operator to put me through. Nixon and the humming pedestal fan kept me faint company, and I could no more feel the fan's breeze than I could the reassurance in his enameled smile.

Crowley's voice came on the line. "You on post, Tanner?"

"Yes sir."

"General Cobris wants to see you, ASAP."

"Why?"

"His staff assistant, Major Vangleman, called to ask what you've been doing, on a minute-by-minute basis. "He said the general disapproves of your procedures."

"Meaning?"

"I don't know. What *have* you been up to?"

"Standard actions. I sent you my report from the morgue."

The clickety-click of a cigarette lighter over the phone line. A minute passed, and he said, "The dancer's photo in the rifle stock. Weird."

"I'm trying to find her through my main contact on the Saigon police. And I spoke to a couple of Gavet Rubber Company officials."

"Sounds straightforward. Just explain to the general and answer his questions. Find out what's digging at him. Be at the MACV landing pad at eighteen hundred. A chopper will pick you up. I have no idea where it's going."

"Fine."

"Oh—I got you a ride to Tay Ninh Province Tuesday to meet Colonel Larsen. It'll do you good to spend a few hours with the real Army. Too much Saigon is bad for the soul."

Unsettled, I put down the phone. Two things were obvious: One, General Cobris was kicking around in my investigation; two, Crowley, my commander, a fellow military police officer, wasn't insulating me.

* * *

On the landing pad, I watched the sun plunge behind the sharp corners of MACV headquarters and the sky segregate itself into layers of amethyst, plum, lavender. Distracted, brooding over Crowley's feebleness, at first I didn't notice the dot on the lilac stripe above the horizon. It enlarged into the familiar dragonfly shape of a UH-1 Huey, its rotor thudding deep in my chest. When the chopper touched down behind the hurled wall of dust, the crew chief waved me forward. Troop choppers usually sat their passengers on the floor; removing the benches saved on weight and made the aircraft more versatile. This ship was different. It came fitted with padded vinyl seats, a bolted-down map board, and a headset the crew chief clapped on my ears. "Hey there, Major," said the pilot. "Push the intercom button to talk."

"Nice rig," I said.

"General Cobris's ship." The pilot extended his hand across the map board. "I'm Jason Stobe, Commander of the 29th Aviation Company.

Also, the general's personal flyboy. Beats haulin' ammo crates to the infantry."

"Where are we going?"

"Vung Tau on the coast. It's a twenty-minute ride, so sit yourself back and enjoy the scenery."

We swung over the plains of Tan Son Nhut until, from the right-side cargo door, I gazed out on the Saigon River reflecting the melon-tinted sky. The river flowed past the city's lower boundaries, writhing briefly eastward to merge with the mud-gray current of another river—the Dong Nai—that gradually widened into an estuary and blended with the cerulean haze of the South China Sea. When we ascended above the range of small-arms fire, the air grew deliciously cold, and I was disappointed when the crew chief tugged the sliding doors shut. He receded into a corner, folding into a sleeper's pose, leaving me to my thoughts and the opaque traverse of clouds through the Plexiglas. Soon we were over the estuary, where trawlers and tiny sampans tipped triangular wakes. We crossed the Rung Sat Special Zone, an intricate mangrove swamp, once a stronghold of the Viet Cong, now desolate. Tons of chemical defoliants had poisoned land that from above resembled an infected rash, the raw mud clumps and clotted streams oozing an oily film. Closer to the seacoast, the vegetation brightened, and into view panned the narrow cape of Vung Tau, its red-tiled roofs like a postcard scene from the Mediterranean coast.

The old French resort had metamorphosed into a haven for GIs bent on raucous times. The American MPs who patrolled the commercial zone generated mountains of incident reports, hence my familiarity with a place I'd never visited. At maintaining public order, the MPs were about as effective as they would have been at Mardi Gras, wading streets clogged with hundreds of nineteen-year-olds with fistfuls of cash to spend in bars, whorehouses, tattoo joints, and hash dens. The GIs were on short furloughs between stints in the jungle and fire bases, and into their hours at Vung Tau they compressed the wildest excesses. Heroin in particular flowed rich, destroying as many young men as did the NVA. There were lighter drugs too, pills and hash, the latter so pervasive that U.S.

commanders in Vietnam often declined to press charges for its possession. Weed was as inexorable as the smell of fish sauce.

We banked over the downtown district and along the outer peninsula shore. To the east, the South China Sea merged with the sky, and the freighters turning on their running lights became indistinguishable from the evening stars. The chopper approached a promontory thirty feet above the rushing surf, and easing power it hovered toward a private villa. On the landward side opened a lawn whose tables, chairs, and bar on wheels had been pushed aside, clearing space for the chopper to touch down. The only person visible was a Vietnamese guard who shrank from the rotor blast.

"Head for that stairway," Stobe said on the intercom. "It winds up the hill to the villa. Don't mind the gook guard, he's just for show."

I duck-dashed beyond the fan, and the chopper lifted off. From the now-serene lawn, the stairs curved languidly between manicured flower patches and swishing, coifed palms. Vistas opened to the ocean, but not until the stairway hooked around to the top did I notice anybody. The breeze tossed the edges of a yellow-striped umbrella spiked through a glass-topped garden table. Here sat an Army major, his collar brass marking him as an artillery officer, crabbed over paperwork he held down with one forearm. Unseen, a phonograph seeped a female voice, maybe Edith Piaf's, too indistinct to tell. The surf rushed over the chord of a woman's laughter.

The major leered up from the papers and mechanically extended his hand. "I'm Derek Vangleman. Remove your hat and have a seat. It will be a minute or two before the general arrives." In the chair he posed incongruously straight backed, the way a praying mantis would. His hair was black and thinning; a five-o'clock shadow darkened his jowls.

I said, "Impressive quarters."

"MACV owns the villa. The general comes down here to relax." Apparently the relaxing did not extend to Vangleman. He evaluated me through bloodshot eyes

"Mind if I ask you a question?"

"Not at all." He fluttered his pencil.

"Isn't a police investigation a bit down in the grass for the general to worry about?"

"It's up to him what he worries about." He forced the kind of smile you might give the neighbor's cat. "He feels you might have gotten yourself a little lost. This meeting tonight is to set you straight."

"Set me straight?"

"You heard me. The general will elaborate." He resumed his paperwork, and I was left to wonder how Vangleman had amassed his arrogance. A mere major, the lowest of the field grades, he'd bullied my boss, a full colonel. Unimpeded access to the general lent Vangleman throw weight out of proportion to his rank. Some officers gravitated toward a general's staff because it gave them a form of power without commanding troops—a role that demanded icy calmness of the soul. Soldiers glean steadiness in a leader, just as they sense the jitters, and Vangleman was the jittery type—tension wrapped him like a strangler vine. Efficient, he was going through the papers quickly, intensely focused on the details. It was a trait that generals liked.

The sliding door opened and Cobris strode onto the patio. As military protocol demanded, I sprang to attention, while Vangleman, apparently exempt from prosaic custom, stayed seated.

Lanky but not as emaciated as some senior officers whom stress had whittled to chopsticks, Cobris moved with the sang-froid of a Hollywood leading man. He was young for a brigadier general, in his early forties; the mottles of gray merely seasoned his brown hair. Since the panel of inquiry four months ago, his responsibilities had chiseled parentheses around his eyes and mouth. He wore a Hawaiian-print shirt and ivory slacks whose contrast to a military uniform did nothing to dispel the marshal impression surrounding him. He set a newspaper on the patio table from which Vangleman's work had vanished by some sleight of hand. The newspaper was the New York Times, and I caught Gribley's byline under the headline 'TAY NINH KIA STILL UNIDENTIFIED.' The story filled a column on the first page—the equivalent of a home run on the scorecard of print journalism.

Cobris gave me a few seconds to gawk at the paper before he spoke. "Tanner, I want to know why you interviewed Leon Gavet yesterday."

As I'd observed at the board of inquiry, the general rarely used the interrogative; his style was to make a declaration and pause, inviting you to disagree or elaborate. His eyes, the shade of blue baked into fine ceramics, settled coldly.

"It was a routine part of the investigation, sir."

"Answer precisely."

"I questioned him about the proximity of the incident to his plantation. I was trying to eliminate possibilities."

"To eliminate possibilities," he echoed. "My God, with that objective in mind, I could do anything I wanted."

Emerging with drinks he handed to the two officers, a Vietnamese servant in a white jacket turned to me to await my order. The drinks looked like Scotches, which would have tasted good about now, but I needed my mental acuity wholly intact, so I asked for ice water. The general gestured for me to sit.

I wondered how Cobris had heard about my meeting with Gavet. I'd written the report late this afternoon, in one original and one carbon, and posted the original to Crowley in a courier envelope as I was leaving the French Fort. It couldn't have found its way to Cobris ahead of me. He must have other sources.

"I read your personnel record, Tanner. It says you've spent thirty-two months in country. That's abnormal. You've heard of 'Nam haunts, men whose brains are so fried, their perceptions so distorted, that they can't function in the normal world. Maybe you fit the description."

His sneering commentary baited me to explain why I'd stayed so long. I was tempted to tell him that, to me, Vietnam *was* the normal world. But my reasons would have sounded self serving. Also, I didn't like him. "Sir, I'm just trying to do my job."

"You're not using this investigation to make a name for yourself, the investigator who's got the balls to pester one of the most important foreign businessmen in the country."

"No sir."

"Tell me how you arranged the interview."

"G-5 set it up for me."

Cobris glanced to Vangleman, who made a note. G-5 was going to get a call.

"Your procedures don't fit the situation," he declared, and now his demeanor metamorphosed from belligerent to relaxed. He leaned back, sipped his drink, and stared out at the estuary that in the last minutes of daylight looked like the vast blank page of a newspaper. "It may not be altogether possible for you to share my perspective, but I want you to try. In this matter of the unidentified dead man, my intent is front-end damage control. I do it all the time, in various ways, notwithstanding that the danger might seem a bit obscure to you. The general's art is to see beyond the horizon."

It did seem obscure, particularly when laced with euphemisms, but I wasn't about to interrupt. Across the table, Vangleman had a notebook open, the pencil poised.

"Among my responsibilities is our current policy of Vietnamization, turning the war over to its rightful owners. We face real challenges. As a fighting force, the Army of the Republic of Vietnam is still developing. At the higher ranks, it resembles more a chamber of commerce than a military organization. To mold the ARVN into a self-sufficient entity, we need time, and we are starved for it. The reason is this." He poked the newspaper. Filling the upper right quadrant was a story about an anti-war rally in Washington attended by thirty thousand protesters. The photo showed them overwhelming the police barricades. "Take a look. If all you see is a bunch of tie-dyed losers, then you're not a member of Congress. This is what Washington calls *raw pressure*, and facing it, the military can serve up the best arguments in the world, to no effect. Whatever public approval the war once enjoyed back home, the footage of body bags on the evening news has erased. The politicians are running for cover. Part of the fault is ours—we pissed away our credibility a few years ago by declaring victory too soon instead of gaining an unadulterated vision. Fortunately, a few national leaders like President Nixon know the truth, and they ask us to keep the lid on the cauldron, to do our job so the pressure doesn't cause them to break their promises. In return, we gain time to teach the South Vietnamese how to run a war and preserve our large investment from going down the toilet the minute we're gone. We have an element of moral justice to uphold.

"As it stands, we are beginning to withdraw our forces according to an ambitious timetable that will leave only aviation personnel, advisors, and logisticians behind. That pleases the politicians—American casualties are the lowest since our combat troops arrived in '65. When confronted with a big protest, President Nixon just points to the numbers—budgets, manpower, and casualties reduced—to show he's got it under control. On this side of the puddle, our advisors are doing what they can to shore up the dike of the South Vietnamese military. There are days when I'm hopeful we'll succeed. Then, along comes a vacuous piece like this." He flailed his arm dismissively at Gribley's story. "To perpetuate their theme of U.S. failure in Vietnam, the press doesn't need two hundred casualties a week, all they need is *one*, if they can sensationalize it enough, and the politicians will forget we're just a quarter-way down the Vietnamization timetable. The pressure will intensify to speed it up, withdraw everybody. Meanwhile, the NVA is stockpiling massive supplies in their border sanctuaries in Cambodia, indicating they're cooking up another offensive."

Cobris's face had re-forged itself into a rigid mask. One had to assume he believed what he was saying, yet—and perhaps it was my fault, for not having been around the higher echelons to witness his mode of thinking—in Vietnam, you had to use terms like *truth* and *moral justice* with caution. To mention moral justice and Vietnam in the same breath was a propagandist's line. To assert that Gribley's story might arrest the course of Vietnamization sounded like a conjurer who decried that a sneeze during a séance had kept the spirits from appearing.

Ice tinkled as the waiter delivered my water. Sipping it, grateful for the cold flow in my throat, I wondered what had motivated Cobris's pontifications.

"Now, as to how this concerns your investigation. Deke, pull out the telex from the Pentagon Security Division." I blinked and the general already had the sheet of paper in hand. "After a theater-wide accountability call—meaning every unit and service and civilian agency in country affirmed every swinging dick—I requested a comprehensive review in Washington. I know people there, and they hotfooted for me on this. They compared the dead man's fingerprints to those on file with the Department of Defense, FBI, and other organizations. They found *nothing*. So I'm certain of the results—he was not an American soldier or other government sponsoree. Whoever the unlucky bastard was, he damned sure wasn't one of ours. No basis exists for a formal investigation."

He reclined in his chair and took another sip of his Scotch. So he'd close the investigation now, I thought. He must have staged this excessive show to explain his logic.

Fine with me.

He was still talking. "People on the outside describe the U.S. military as if it were a dictatorship. In fact, it's an organization that embodies many democratic ideals. People can talk back, and they do. I mention this because not everyone agrees with my reasoning. Colonel Larsen, the Second Brigade Commander in Tay Ninh Province, is the kind who talks back. He's a bigger thorn in my side than you are. He's standing his ground with the chain of command. Larsen is hard headed. I have to live with guys like him. But you do see what I'm getting at, Tanner. We already *know* the outcome."

"Yes sir."

"Important for you to understand, because it drives how you proceed. Without context, even a smart fellow like you can go astray. Try to step up to the level of strategic thinkers for a minute and comprehend that you can't apply the same template to every problem. You involved the Saigon police in your investigation."

In Cobris's style, it was a question. "Yes sir. They're trying to find a person who I believe can identify the casualty."

The creases in Cobris's face multiplied. "Here's what I *believe*. What had been under my control has been relinquished to grafters who now are in a position to issue alternative statements on the incident to sideliners like this reporter Gribley. We tell the press we're certain the unidentified KIA was not an American. Gribley then goes to the Saigon police and obtains a quote saying, on the basis of *their* investigation, he *was* an American. Christ, they might say anything. Look what you've set me up for."

"It won't happen. Your scenario."

"Never guarantee what you have no power over."

"It's not a guarantee, sir. I just know the people I deal with. They won't talk to the press. I trust them."

A snort from Vangleman. It was a rude sound, and Cobris snapped him a glance like a whip cracked at an unruly circus cat. The effect on Vangleman was mild, no remorse evident—the Vanglemans of the world hold themselves to be irreplaceable.

Cobris said, "We're not going to have a shit storm over a dead son of a bitch who isn't an American to begin with. I don't give an old whore's fuck whether your *procedures* call for a tidy checklist wherein you *eliminate possibilities* with your Saigon cop buddies. What I want from you is one thing—a finding that the casualty was not an American. It's a statement, to which you will sign your name, attesting that your investigation was thorough and complete and officially resolved. I want that very soon, without a lot of extraneous nonsense. Tell me this is clear."

"Yes, sir. It's clear. But before I sign anything, I need to collect more facts."

Cobris stared at me. Vangleman sat motionless.

I must be the kind who talked back.

In the distance, the faint whop-whop of a helicopter rotor.

"Your ride," said the general.

He must have signaled to Vangleman, who was on his feet. I'd been dismissed, and I had the impression I wasn't moving fast enough collecting my hat. Vangleman was actually tugging at my sleeve to escort me down the stairs to the lawn, where, by the stacked tables, he went off like a grenade. "Jesus Christ! You're lucky you're still around. The Saigon cops? The interview with Gavet? What the hell were you trying to do?"

"Did somebody complain about my interview with Gavet?"

"Word reached the general, I don't know from where, saying you were wildly flogging around. Which appears to have been accurate."

When Vangleman had phoned Colonel Crowley this afternoon about my actions, Crowley apparently hadn't let on that asking for help from the Saigon cops had been *his* idea—he'd ordered me to do it. What kind of officer lets his subordinate take the heat for following orders? Yet I wasn't about to serve up an excuse, especially to a creature like Vangleman.

I said, "I'm not flogging around. Investigations are my job."

"Get it through your head, Tanner—your *job* is what General Cobris says it is."

The chopper materialized over the trees and descended deafeningly toward the pad. Vangleman leaned close to my ear and screamed to make himself heard. "You deliver the signed affirmation that your Caucasian KIA wasn't an American, so the general can shut down this controversy, and you're guaranteed any follow-on assignment you want. Maybe a promotion." He stared me straight in the eye, validating with everything short of a wink where the offer had originated.

When the skids touched, the crew chief hunched in the door and waved me forward. I scooted under the pressuring rotor, clambered into my seat, and by the time I'd buckled myself in, the g-force was tugging me into a crazy lean. We climbed past the treetops and over the villa. I scanned for Cobris and Vangleman. They were gone.

They were gone but somebody else stood on the patio. A woman in a wind-blown dress stared up at the chopper. It was too dark, and the ship too high, to see her face, but I could tell she had a trim figure and light brown hair, which meant she probably wasn't oriental. Her uplifted gaze followed as we swept over. The rotor wash shivered her hair and her dress and the yellow-striped table umbrella.

Day 4

In Saigon's alleyways, you'd be wise to remember that the slap of a droplet on tile makes the same sound as a gun hammer cocked back.

The logistical streams that had fed the hostilities these past twenty-five years still flowed. The place was like a sewer clot of sandbags and weaponry wrapped in barbed wire. Yet to those who'd been around a while, it was obvious that a certain quiet had settled on the town, palpable in contrast to Tet 1968, over two years ago, when any cop who stepped out to direct traffic in a Cholon intersection stood a fair chance of being riddled with bullets.

My role in the Tet counteroffensive had been to take the Vietnamese MP company I advised across the no-man's land between central Cholon and the VC-infested lower 6th District, a ramshackle neighborhood in the tail of the fish where you might traverse a square kilometer levitated six feet up on the shack roofs, vaulting the squeezed alleys each as wide as the reach of a man's arms. A fanciful notion, but you wouldn't have tried it, not during Tet. Below ran a maze, intricate because the streets and houses had been hit by artillery, splaying the walls and spilling the roofs like cards in a game of 52-pickup. The destruction compounded the chance you'd get lost, and you'd hear the nearby gunfire and the screams of your men and not be able to find them.

Tet happened before I met Tuy or Trong. The only Vietnamese I knew were the soldiers being shot to pieces in the narrow streets. The Cholon residents who crowded the control line formed a presence on the margins of my comprehension, like an animal noise in the dark. The soldiers had ordered them to stay low, and they squatted—supple, they could stay hunched a long time—and extended their arms pitifully while I guided the tanks forward and identified the targets. The people cried out; I didn't ask for a translation of what they were saying. Barking their concussive barks, the tank guns tore into the neighborhood from which we were taking fire. The impact of a tank round on one of those shanties was to blow it into scraps, like a puffed-up paper bag clapped hard. Then the tanks rolled over what was left, and in an hour I'd squashed flat a square block.

Afterward the inhabitants returned. The corrugated roofs purled steam like charcoal grills. When the people found the ruins of their houses, they squatted on the surfaces in their tire-tread sandals, picking through the shards, their tears sizzling on the metal.

Clumped together in the ruins we found the bodies of three Viet Cong and a young woman. The soldiers said she must have been fighting alongside the enemy, though her ao dai of patterned white silk wasn't the garment VC women typically wore. I stared at her blood-speckled figure on the ground. Gunfire continued to crack from the other neighborhoods. There wasn't much left to fight over in this one.

That week, an American officer, having just summoned artillery and air strikes upon a village named Ben Tre, told a reporter that it had been necessary to destroy the village in order to save it. Mesmerized by the line's apparent irony, the press reprinted it endlessly. Yet to me it made sense; I'd done the same to a district of shacks.

The horrors of war might permanently sear a man's consciousness. Or they might not. In the aftermath of mental shock, an officer gropes not for peace and innocence, but for lucidity and the ability to command. For me, the Tet Offensive imposed less a nightmare than a sense of place. And a question: How had I come to kill the girl in the white ao dai?

The books hadn't done much to answer it. So when I returned to South Vietnam for my second tour, I sought out Tuy, the window girl with the clear eyes that had regarded the upended jeep as if it were the history of her country. I remembered the house. Before I went, I inquired with Trong, who confirmed that the woman who lived at the address was not married.

I told her about the girl in the white ao dai, how the image had stayed with me, the speckled bloodstains among the patterns in the silk. She recognized no irony in my story. Her building was not many blocks from the neighborhood I described. Along her ceiling ran black streaks from the fires; the booms of the tank guns would have echoed here.

And now I spent my nights close to the neighborhood I'd destroyed. Afterward the residents had rebuilt their homes using what could be salvaged. The only traces left were the soot and scorch marks. And the war dreams.

* * *

In the morning, I phoned Hipolite and asked for Simone Nogaret's number.

"You're wasting your time," he said. "She won't talk to you."

He gave me the number anyway.

Soon afterward, Tuy and I crowded into a little grocery store on Dong Khanh. The store belonged to a friend of her mother—it was the place I gave as an address to Americans who might need to find me on short notice. I used its phone to call out when I had to. Phone lines were not all that common in residential Cholon. Tuy's building had none.

I dialed and handed the receiver to Tuy; whoever answered would be speaking French. I'd rehearsed with her what to say: She was to introduce herself as the secretary for an American officer conducting an investigation. I wanted her tone to ring officious, suggestive of authority, whereas in truth I had zero. Having disapproved of my meeting with Gavet, Cobris would take umbrage at an approach to a French socialite. I intended to leave it out of my report and hope the general wouldn't find out anyway, as he'd learned of my interview with Gavet.

Suddenly Tuy was speaking in mellifluous French, sounding anything but officious. The chatter went on for a minute. She paused and hugged the phone to her shoulder, whispering, "I've got Mademoiselle Dobier, Simone's *assistante de gestion*. She's gone to inquire."

Tuy dragged the phone cord behind her friend's counter, while he smiled, a pluggy, honest, good-natured man utterly lacking in Tuy's finesse. She'd known him since she was a girl, called him *bac*, for uncle, perhaps because he contrasted so starkly with her true uncle, the colonial functionary. I sat with him atop sacks of rice and spices, expecting her to reap a curt refusal over the phone.

She said a few more words and hung up. "Today at six," she said.

"You're kidding."

"I never kid, do I, uncle?"

Rising on his bandy legs, he squeezed his eyes in delight.

* * *

Tu Do Street, Saigon's Champs-Élysées, arrowed from the pink-hued Saigon Cathedral past the square where a bronze statue remembered the Vietnamese war dead, to the park at the riverside avenue Ben Bach Dang. In this district clustered fine hotels, foreign embassies, press bureaus, and the National Assembly building. Simone Nogaret's apartment tower climbed in yellow-brick and glass from a tree-shaded street tucked three blocks off Tu Do. Under the trees slumbered Citroën DS sedans, the latter-day cyclos for Saigon's wealthy set. As symbols of power, the cars were less telling than the plain-clothes French security men outside the building. Over their shoulders they slung submachine guns they fingered loosely with their right hands, while with their left they pumped Gauloises cigarettes up and down.

The security men made inquiries before they escorted us to the lobby, where an urbane Frenchwoman awaited us. I guessed her to be in her late thirties. Her bundled hair, indigo skirt, and pressed white blouse were imprimaturs of her narrow-ranging, non-negotiable dominion. In English, she said, "I'm Marie Dobier." She did not extend her hand. Flicking a sideglance at Tuy, she asked, "Your companion, Major?"

"Tuyet is my translator."

Dobier must have realized that Tuy was the one she'd spoken to on the phone this morning. I thought, how would the elite residents of this building regard a lovely, unmarried Vietnamese woman who accompanied an American military officer? Would this turn into another bout of stereotyping, as at *Le Cercle Sportif?* "Wait, please," Dobier said.

We lounged in the wicker chairs. Sultry air spilled through the requisite grenade screens. On the street, the guards scrutinized the cars and passers-by, almost in anticipation. Downtown Saigon was prowled by various denizens, yet this quarter was kept secure, the influential residents protected. What worried the guards today?

In ten minutes, Dobier was back. "Madame Nogaret will see you now. She has another appointment soon. Please be brief."

Rising to the uppermost floor, the elevator opened to an oval foyer with a single apartment door whose panels gleamed in spotless white enamel. A bolt clicked, and Simone Nogaret stood in the doorway.

In the angles of her face I looked for flaws and saw none, a rare absence, for nature invariably delivers faces in disproportion, either crooked or unbalanced. Hers formed a perfect teardrop tapering to a sharp chin. The only unevenness was in her color; her cheeks wore a streaky tan from a day of too much sun. Hair the shade of dried bamboo skimmed her shoulders, and a lock dangled like a pointer to her direct gaze. A hint of mascara blushed eyes neither green nor blue; they reminded me of the woods at dusk.

Off somewhere, maybe on the roof, hummed a potent air conditioner, which was why she could tolerate the long-sleeved sweater. Knit of white Merino, it featured a diamond-hatched pattern clenching to a finer weave at the neck. The long neck might be folded over; she wore it unfurled nearly to her chin. Her slacks were white too, snug on trim hips slightly in sway as she led us inside. Her walk might be described as purposeful, expectant of doors being pulled open in advance of her arrival. Ushering us to a sofa sheathed in a lustrous cream batik, she reclined into an absinthe-green leather chair, withdrew a cigarette from a gold case, and held it at arms length across the glass-topped coffee table. Tuy and I declined. I smelled Simone's perfume, a subtle scent that seemed to dwell between East and West.

On the sixth floor above the First District, the apartment must have featured a glorious view of downtown Saigon. No need for the tawdry grenade screens up here. Perhaps to block the impending sunset, she'd shut the drapes, leaving the room at the mercy of a set of table lamps that struggled to penetrate the smoke of her cigarette. She said, "You may be the first American I've hosted here, Major Tanner." She drew out her *s*'s, her voice like the brush of fingertips on a silk pillow.

"To what do I owe the honor?"

"A change in outlook. For years I found it impossible to see your countrymen as other than usurpers. You stood by as France lost Indochina. Then you stepped in, to fill the vacuum, so to speak. An old story, so old the resentment has faded. I've come to regard you with sympathy."

"Sympathy?"

"For your naïveté. Nothing your supremacy inspired has taken root. You've made Vietnam no more progressive, merely busy. Having failed, you undergo the inevitable reduction, as we did. Your exit may not be as dramatic as ours after Dien Bien Phu, but you are leaving with your tails tucked just as humbly between your legs."

I was tempted to point out that neither had she left after Dien Bien Phu, nor were the Americans leaving anytime soon, but I parried my irritation at being lectured by a French colonialist for the second time in three days.

She turned to Tuy. "I apologize for the politics. So boring, eh?"

Tuy smiled disarmingly.

"I won't take more of your time than necessary," I said.

"Are you in a hurry?"

"Miss Dobier said you had an appointment."

"I suppose I do," she said, her memory jogged either to the appointment or to its fabrication. "So you should go on with your business."

"Eight days ago, about ten kilometers south of the Gavet Rubber Company's Tay Ninh plantation, a man was killed. He was walking alone at night, and he roamed too close to an American infantry unit. The encounter's outcome was tragically knowable. His identity wasn't. I'm trying to find out who he was."

"Yes. I've heard of this incident. A reporter has been petitioning for an interview. Gribley is his name. Nettlesome, like all the press."

Recalling the bumpy sequence of inquiries I'd followed to Simone, I wondered how Gribley had done it. Maybe a few investigative skills lurked behind the reporter's pudgy mien.

I said, "Do you plan to talk to him?"

"My connection with the plantation is unofficial. What does it gain me, to speak to a reporter?" Her statement sounded rhetorical, still she peered at me as if she wanted my opinion.

"I don't see what it gains you either."

"Then I'll reject his request." From an imperialist, such a tone decided fates. I sensed Tuy go tense beside me.

Simone exhaled a cloud, tipped the ash into a jade ashtray on the glass-topped table. "So, you postulate that this poor man was a lost soul from the plantation. Mssr. Gavet must have made it clear this was implausible." She used Gavet's wording; she must have spoken with him. Not surprising. The surprising part was that she'd decided to see me anyway.

"There aren't many places the man might have come from," I elaborated. "One is the Gavet Plantation on foot. The other is the site of an air crash, which suggests the plantation as his point of origin, or his destination."

"The plantation has no airstrip. The closest is at An Loc."

"I'm sure that a helicopter could find a spot."

"Yes, if you wish to speculate. However, the plantation is not one of your free-fire zones where everyone shoots at everything and helicopters touch down as they please. The land is controlled, incidents reported. The management would have been informed of a helicopter landing."

"When were you there last?"

"You are interrogating me now, Major."

"I apologize. It's a habit of mine." From the leather pouch I fished out the photos. "I have two identifications to ask of you. One of them is unpleasant." I waited for her permission, which came with a resigned nod. First I handed her the morgue shot, the dead eyes of the unknown staring up.

She shook her head. "And the other?"

I passed her the original marquee photo of the dancer. From its ride in my folder, it had lost the curl. "Who is she?" Simone asked.

"I don't know. I found the photo among the dead man's effects, wedged in the rifle stock of his M16, an unusual and inconvenient place for him to keep it. Hiding it that way implies she was important to him. Good chance she would be able to identify him."

Abandoning her languid recline, Simone leaned forward. She aligned the photo on the glass tabletop to examine. Unlike the sedentary Mssr. Gavet, she sleeked effortlessly from one posture to the next, and I gathered that she could configure her body any way she liked. "This is too big to fit into an M16 stock well," she declared.

From this fashionable Frenchwoman, it came as a curious observation, but then she'd lived here through the two Indochina wars, had owned a plantation in the midst of an insurgency, so why shouldn't she be aware of the physical characteristics of the American assault rifle? The stock well was a small compartment to store cleaning equipment. Some M16s had one; the unknown's did not. "It wasn't in a stock well," I explained, "but between the buffer sleeve and the fitted hole in the stock it slips into, in which it was rolled up. To put it in there, he'd have needed a screwdriver and a few minutes."

Her perusal of the dancer's photo took a few minutes too; she studied it with care. When she lifted her face, a slight smile had settled, softening her persona from abrupt to friendly. I didn't know how to interpret the change.

"So you're trying to locate a club girl in Saigon. Surely you're up against the odds. How many like her? Thousands?"

"Yes. Luckily, I have contacts on the Saigon police with the acumen to find people."

"I'm impressed."

I retrieved the photos, tucked them away. "You've been most gracious, Madame Nogaret."

"Where are you from, Tanner?"

"Massachusetts. In our northeast."

"Ah. The people speak French there, no?"

"Some of them. Mostly farther north."

"Do you?"

"It would grate your ears," I said.

"After hearing Saigonese French all my life? I think not."

Tuy sat perfectly still.

"And your given name?"

"George."

"George," she repeated, her *g* resonating like cello strings under a bow. "Call me Simone. You shouldn't contact Mssr. Gavet again—you would upset him. If you have questions, please come to me directly. That way, no trouble, eh?"

"Thank you."

"Now I have my appointment to tend to. Time is for me, how would you say, a hellhound?"

An odd expression; I wondered where she'd heard it. As we left, Tuy in the lead, me next, the fabric of Simone's sweater suddenly pushed against my arm, the soft pressure of her breast. Had this graceful woman bumped into me? The slightest smile creased her face, and her lips pouted as if she were blowing me a kiss.

* * *

Simone's door fell shut, and Tuy and I stood in the alcove waiting for the elevator whose cables groaned beyond the sliding panels. I could still smell Simone's perfume, feel her breast against my arm. We entered the elevator, and Tuy stared straight ahead, as if we were strangers. I took her arm and she pulled away. "I just want to get out of here," she said.

She led us past the security guards, her heels clicking in the direction of Tu Do Street three blocks away. Her step was brisk. Two minutes along, at a small traffic circle, she stopped, scanning for the taxis that commonly lingered at such places. Nothing stirred, and the absence seemed to trouble her. The slender muscles on her jaw tightened into cat scratches.

I asked, "What is it?"

"Why is nobody around?"

The same spot that in its history might have witnessed grenades burst and men shot dead in their tracks slumbered peacefully. Save for the occasional bicyclist going by, it hosted a single human activity, a barber in coveralls who fussed over a man on a metal stool, the quiet so consummate I could hear the scissors snip the hair strands. In a stall that sold tropical fish, a black eel glided in an aquarium. I did not pretend to sense the city's undercurrents, but to my eye this circle posed no malice.

I said, "People are getting ready for the evening, that's all."

She breathed deeply. I held her arm, and this time she let me. Eventually a cyclo came along, and we squeezed into the space that normally accommodated two thin Vietnamese or one fat westerner. The cabby pushed off, his calves bulging with the strain on the pedals, and we left the circle and the barber and the eel behind. Minutes later, on the boulevard Tran Hung Dao, pedestrians and the city's familiar babble surrounded us.

I asked, "Are you all right?"

"That woman. I don't care for her."

"She's a spoiled colonialist who grew up here," I said.

"No, *I* grew up here; she is from the *outside*. Anyway, that wasn't what I meant. There is something false about her."

"False?"

"Deceit. It surrounds her like the smell of a dead animal."

"Why do you say that?"

"It's what I sense. I can't explain."

* * *

In the apartment, she hunched in the bathtub silently anticipating the steaming water I poured in. Most of the things I'd given her had been practical and small, like the Ivory soap and the portable radio. The bathtub was practical and big, an antique from an era that had judged its griffin feet as other than grotesque. It had adorned the bathroom of a downtown hotel, where a fourth-story balcony had proven handy for an American Army officer intent on ending his Vietnam tour early. The shaken hotel manager had told me he'd already begun remodeling the room to get rid of the accoutrements that American guests considered *passé*—as if the behind-the-times decor had provoked the suicide. I'd seized the opportunity to buy the tub. Fifty bucks and four sweaty laborers later, it crouched in the apartment's corner behind the door. Privacy came from a PX shower curtain I hung from a wire stretched between the adjacent walls, cold water from the hose I ran from the sink tap, hot water from a metal bucket on the electric hot plate. Because draining the tub proved tedious, I paid a plumber to fashion a pipe that ran along the floor's edge to a hole in the masonry through which the bathwater could dribble to the rain gutter. While I handled the logistics, Tuy decorated the space. On the walls she hung fabric strips in brilliant shades that overlapped in an arrangement I'd never seen before. The colors were like the three tones of her laugh, unique to her.

Hard to judge the mix of hot and cold, to keep the water temperature high without scalding. Tuy folded her reed arms around herself, and I thought I'd made it too tepid until I saw the vapor smooth against her cinnamon skin. She swooned under the sponge I ran over her shoulders, the water's ethereal trickle.

Since we'd come home, I'd pondered what she'd said about Simone, turned over the interview for the signs that Tuy had intuited as deceit. In the curls of steam, I found one. "Do you remember how Simone reacted when she saw the dancer's photo?"

"She was quite interested."

"At once she went from condescending to attentive. I thought at first she was simply curious about the dancer, but it was more than that. She examined it carefully. Why?"

Tuy rested her head on her knees, her eyes barely open. "After she saw the photo, she put on a different persona. She wanted to be friends. But she doesn't fit with friends like me."

"Or me."

She asked, "So you think it means something?"

"I don't know. Maybe deceit, as you said."

She dipped her head, touching her hair to the water. "Better to stay away from her. She portends bad things."

Day 5

Bad things.
Bad people.
Bad for the soul.
Crowley's definition of Saigon.
So he was sending me to a combat zone.

I boarded a resupply flight to Tay Ninh Province, part of the infamous War Zone C. Relatively close to Saigon, War Zone C always had merited a high priority. It featured aggressive NVA units, savage fighting, and easy access for reporters who wanted a quick taste of combat. Often they got their taste and more. The name had become synonymous with horror, enshrined in the soldier's ditty that played in my head as I buckled myself in:

War Zone C, War Zone C,
The place you don't wanna beeee...

The ride took thirty minutes in a Huey 'slick' hammering northward. The cargo doors were open and the wind billowed my fatigues and plowed back my hair. We crossed rain forests, elephant grass fields, and rice paddies. Rivers and streams and a paved road made shallow cracks in the vegetation. Occasionally we pierced round clouds that floated like cotton balls tossed in the air, and the fine droplets dashed my face.

The Second Brigade's tactical operations center occupied a jungle clearing. Like barber clippers gouging into a thick scalp of hair, soldiers had chain-sawed the trees to nubs ankle high. Tent ropes and the guy wires for sectional antennas made a spider's web; a pole bristled with arrows and signs reading LATRINE, LZ, MESS HALL, BUNKER; white engineer tape trailed to the sites that would be used at night, especially to the latrine that owed its privacy to stacked sandbags. The sandbags abounded. Around the TOC trailers, they climbed to chest height, reminding me how men always felt safer behind walls, even if the safety they afforded was make believe.

Awaiting my appointment with Colonel Larsen, I sat on an avocado-green food case called a Mermite container, the Tupperware of the U.S. Army in the field. The place hummed purposefully. Generators whined out current for the lights and the radios; doors banged on the trailers that connected to form an L, one wing for the staff and the other for the commander's briefings. When the doors opened, I noticed rubber pads like yoga mats lining the floor. A shotgun-cradling sentry guarded a smaller trailer—no doubt the commander's quarters—beyond the L's exterior angle. From it, an intestine of flexible plastic duct snaked to a chugging metal box—an air conditioner. Every piece airlifted in.

In the TOC's doorway appeared a reedy major who must have studied at the same school for manners as Vangleman. "Hurry up, the colonel's waiting."

He led me past staff officers in spotless fatigues and polished boots who peered intently at their map boards. Lounged in a nylon-webbed beach chair beside a console of radios, Colonel Andrew Larsen held his metal canteen cup like the flagon of a king. His eyes were the shade of an old tortoise shell and just as hard. Deeply tanned in the face and arms, his skin hung like a loose hide—the air-conditioner hadn't kept the jungle from sweating off his extra pounds.

"Welcome, Major Tanner. Thanks for makin' the trip. As you know, my brigade is attached to the 1st Cav Division to help secure War Zone C, a right nasty sector. I'm mostly stuck at my headquarters at Tay Ninh City, but I like to displace to the boonies every now and then. Keeps my folks on their toes."

"Yes sir. Thank you for hosting me."

His gaze roved over my jump wings and Combat Infantryman's Badge and up to the combat patch on my right shoulder. "I'm glad they gave the job to somebody who's been around the block a few times." Years in the Army had sanded his Southerner's twang to a homey inflection; I suspected he could dispense with it when he wanted to. He tipped the cup toward my chest and shoulder. "Where'd you come by those?"

"During my first tour, I was an advisor for a company of Viet MPs. We worked with the 101st Airborne busting VC ambush sites."

"Good on you. I was with the Screaming Eagles too, when they first got here." Along with a Marine expeditionary force and the 1st Cav Division, the 101st had been among the first major U.S. combat units to reach Vietnam in 1965. "What have you learned about our mystery boy?"

I related my findings from the morgue and described my plan to locate the dancer via the Saigon police. I laid out the Polaroid of the death face and the dancer's marquee pic I'd found in the buffer well. Sipping his coffee, he looked them over.

"As to how he ended up in Tay Ninh Province," I went on, "I'm betting on an air crash south of the Gavet Plantation. Based on what he was carrying and the unhardened condition of his feet, he couldn't have been walking in the jungle for more than two days, meaning that he set out from his point of origin at the earliest on Friday 17 April, at a radius of about ten klicks."

"That roughly matches the search grid we've been using," said Larsen. Stepping to the map board, he waved his cup as a blunt pointer. "Since the incident, I've ordered our choppers to keep an eye out for a downed aircraft, as a coda to their regular recons. Ground patrols are doing the same. So far, nobody has reported any signs of a crash. Over the years we've defoliated the hell out of War Zone C, especially the northern part, but this area where we operate west of the Saigon River features tracts of rain forest as dense and inhospitable as they come. A small aircraft falling unobserved into the triple canopy might as well be a needle dropped in a haystack. I'm considering shutting down the extra efforts—they bleed resources from other missions. And General Cobris doesn't condone the searches. He contends that we're chasing our tails for somebody who wasn't an American. He was pretty emphatic about it."

"With me, too."

"What did he say?"

"He wants a conclusion fast, to kill the bad press."

"And your reply?"

"I said I needed to collect more facts."

He grinned. "I'd like to have seen his face when you said that. Not many people stand up to him. And you're justified—the Army doesn't retreat from a valid inquiry because of the press. I don't understand his position. Why should he care about my search operations or your investigation?"

Static blasted on the radio. Startled, I jumped. Larsen calmly sipped his coffee while a staff officer ran over and reset the dials. The quiet restored, he continued. "Cobris is the smartest one-star in this theater. He's ambitious, surrounds himself with a staff so subservient to him they make you want to puke, plays angles nobody else seems to notice, and calls it seeing over the horizon. And he's vindictive. I insisted on an investigation; he probably has me down on his shit list for that. I intend to do my job as I see it. I have the stature to do that. You don't. As one old ambush-buster to another, watch your ass around Cobris. If you get in trouble, give me a shout, maybe I'll be able to help."

* * *

The helicopter hurtled eastward over scattered clouds. I could smell the rain forest's yeasty scents. The clouds spat rain, intermittent at first, then a downpour as we flared into Bravo Company's one-ship LZ. Ducked over, I ran across grass the rotor wash had flattened to the jungle's edge, where waited Captain John Ulrich.

A head shorter than me, packed with energy he constrained by force of will, in another profession Ulrich might have kept more bulk on his bones. Command and the jungle had sculpted him into a stringy greyhound. He ushered me along a machete-hacked tunnel in the bamboo to his company's position. Nothing here resembled the elaborate brigade TOC—there were no air conditioners, trailers, or floor pads, only soldiers in shallow foxholes camouflaged to blend in. Water dripped from the trees and the men; both were impervious. In the rear echelon at Tan Son Nhut, I didn't see many soldiers like these, the teeth of the U.S. Army in Vietnam. Within the perimeter, I was the only one not gritted and fatigued. They regarded me politely, a stranger among them. A tourist.

Ulrich led me to where Sergeant Henry Joshua waited. Two fallen jungle trees lay like parallel benches, and I sat facing Ulrich and Joshua. I'd studied their statements, but enlightenment rarely surfaces from the sterility of military prose, so I asked them to tell me what had happened at Hill 71.

* * *

Weaving and bending like a Chinese parade dragon over the undulating terrain, the eighty-man column of light infantry in mid-afternoon encountered a resistive thicket of giant, thorny bamboo trees, their quills as long as Bic pens. Nobody in the leading platoon had seen such trees before. The soldiers hacked into them with machetes and bore their stigmata—punctures and cuts in their hands, forearms, legs. They spent three hours cutting a meter-wide path. With dusk less than 30 minutes off, Ulrich knew he'd made a mistake to press through the thicket. He should have backed off and found a way around.

His planned night-perimeter location lay a kilometer away. Normally units set up their night defenses in the late afternoon, while daylight allowed them to see what they were doing. Night was when the agile enemy became truly fearsome. Emerging from beneath the jungle canopy near the apogee of a dome-shaped hillock, Ulrich faced a dilemma. He hadn't studied this terrain in detail, and to remain here meant to trust his unit to possibly flawed ground. To keep moving to the planned site risked walking into an ambush.

His soldiers were exhausted. He decided to stay put.

At an elevation of 71 meters, the crest was the highest point in a generally low zone. He observed old shell craters, which meant the enemy probably knew the place all too well. The open top offered an LZ, so he wouldn't have to cut a new one. On the eastern side, he evaluated what the map falsely depicted as an unbroken slope. The tree line dipped, indicating a gully below. From the hill's bottom, the crafty enemy could follow it like a tunnel to the heart of Ulrich's perimeter. There were mediations: He might elaborately booby-trap the gulch, or set up a listening post at the bottom. He disliked booby traps; animals could trigger them, and they had to be painstakingly deactivated in the morning. The LP was the solution. Whoever manned it had to stay vigilant—a high standard after the hours of hacking through the thorns.

For his LP team leader, he chose a soldier who'd often walked point for the company, Sergeant Henry Joshua.

Joshua's childhood on the outskirts of New Orleans had made him familiar with marshy woods. He'd lived at the edge of the coastal bayou whose intricate scents had taunted his nose. Forbidden to the children, the marsh had beckoned them, the trees and vines receding into a steam-shrouded maze. A kid who knew the paths could find places to smoke away from adults. If you didn't know the paths, better to stay out, the place harbored snakes, and gators deeper in.

Zero two hundred hours. In the listening post at the gully's mouth, Joshua crouched awake. He smeared more camouflage paint on the black skin of his nose and cheeks, to suppress the oil that glinted at night. He didn't mind the LP duty. This furrow between banyan roots was safer than the hilltop—an obvious target for enemy mortars. The LP site afforded him a rare visibility of his surroundings. In the monsoons, the nearby stream had overflowed its banks, scattering light-gray pebbles in a washout. When the rains subsided, the water had settled in its gentle course, and the pebbles spread like a tanning reflector over the darker jungle floor.

Soon fog began to intrude. If an enemy unit had been tracking the Americans, the mist was deadly. It occulted infiltrators. On nights like this, a stealthy crawler might slash a soldier's throat, and his friends a foxhole away wouldn't even hear the gurgle. The fog slinked up the gully like a white caterpillar, brushed wetly over Joshua's forearms. Alongside in the banyan root's embrace, Specialist Cagill's head poked out of his nylon poncho liner. Cagill was motionless but not asleep. He scanned the white curtain and loosed a sigh of recognition.

Joshua mentally rehearsed. In his lap he cradled a portable field telephone whose wire snaked to the platoon leader's foxhole atop the hill. If anything happened, he'd report over the field phone; if things went to hell, he'd detonate the claymore and charge one hundred meters toward Bravo Company, shouting the running password, "Margarine! Margarine!" It was a word the Vietnamese couldn't say, supposedly.

On fifty-percent alert, the troops on the hilltop manned their hasty positions, guns out in all directions. Automatic weapons and grenade launchers covered the gully, a lot of firepower to be sitting in front of, Joshua knew. He'd seen it happen—a rustle in the bushes spooks a GI, and he lets go a shot that avalanches the whole perimeter. In this ninth month of his tour, Joshua was acutely aware of the things that could kill him and of the steps he must take to stay alive. He didn't rely on other people to do his thinking. Clinging to his skills, he was hard to kill, and with three months left on the clock, he had a good chance of going home in one piece, as long as he didn't slacken. Diligence equaled life.

The trees blurred into vague creases in the white. He could taste the moisture on his lips. It slicked the plastic field telephone in his lap.

Clack-clack-clack-clack-clack. The instrument's ringer was set so low he couldn't hear it as much as feel the dance of the little pendulum within. He nestled the box to his ear and depressed the rubber push-to-talk.

"LP."

"What's your situation?" The new platoon leader.

"Quiet. Fog rolling up your way."

"Okay. Let me know if anything changes."

Joshua nested the telephone in his lap. *Let me know if anything changes.* Like telling a man to piss in a downwind direction. The platoon leader was starting out jumpy. He was the fourth lieutenant Joshua had served under in the same platoon. Of the others, one had been wounded severely, two reassigned. Each new officer brought weeks of angst while his jungle legs grew under him. An officer's education must be the most expensive in the world, Joshua mused, paid for in other men's blood.

From the mist, a splash.

He gripped Cagill on the arm. His partner didn't startle. Solid man, Cagill. Joshua was very selective about the soldier he took with him on LP duty. With hardly a whisper of nylon, Cagill slid from under his poncho liner, and his hand fell on the fist-size claymore detonator.

Hard to tell what was corporeal and what wasn't. On top of that, he was dead tired. Exhausted men hallucinated, saw purple dragons cavorting in the trees; he'd experienced such visions himself. Over the root he peered, keened his ears, breathed to Cagill as if to a lover, "Once you blow the claymore, wait for my word before hauling ass."

Aimed toward the washout, the convex mine pronged out of the soft soil only twenty meters away, technically too close, but what the book said didn't match the real world, conditions were never optimum. Twenty was as far out as their claymore could go and stay concealed. The ground-rise would protect the LP from the backblast—provided that the mine was oriented correctly. The claymore was directional; raised letters on its plastic face read 'Front Toward Enemy.' At night, you couldn't see the letters—you had to rely on the mine's shape and the protrusions. Like every soldier who'd ever set up a claymore in the dark, Joshua fretted over whether he'd done it right.

A twig snapped. Was somebody out there in the mist? As a boy, Joshua had learned to catch bayou snakes from an older kid who'd been doing it all his life. Some snakes you could grab with your hands, the kid had taught him. Others you had to use a stick. Didn't matter if the snake was poisonous, the difference was whether it would whip at your outstretched hand, or let you grab it as languid as rolled cookie dough. You just *knew*, said the kid. After a while, watching his friend handle the snakes, Joshua understood. Nine months in the jungle, and he knew in the same unexplainable way that somebody was out there.

Gripping the field phone, he thought of what he'd say to the jittery lieutenant. No small thing, to bug out of an LP. He cared about his rep among the old timers—they trusted him not to lose his nerve. He knew he could intuit bad shit. But what if he abandoned the LP and nothing happened?

Like frosted glass, the mist seeped ambiance. He beheld a shadow slowly separate from the cloud and coalesce into a human silhouette, rifle in hand. The figure treaded across the washout, barely paces from the claymore. Beside him, Cagill's breath halted.

Shit! Quickly Joshua scanned the forest. The man could be the tip of an attack, a unit converging on the gully. No, that didn't make sense. In the mist, the man's comrades would have lost sight of him. No unit movement was ever so fucked up as in the jungle at night. If men didn't stay close to each other, they'd lose contact and become widely separated. This one didn't act like he was part of an attack. He didn't walk stealthily, he just plodded forward.

No time. A few steps closer and they'd lose the advantage. Joshua set aside the telephone, leaned over his rifle, pulled the butt hard into his shoulder, soundlessly rotated the selector switch from safe to semi-automatic. Rough-sighting, he aimed for the dark breadth of the torso.

He couldn't hold even a fuzzy sight picture; the shot might go anywhere.

The figure was close enough to piss on the claymore.

"Bust it."

Cagill crushed the detonator, and in the flash Joshua saw a man suspended in air, legs and arms spread, an X on brilliant white. The backblast stormed debris over their heads; soil and pebbles pattered.

Clack-clack-clack-clack-clack.

Joshua felt blindly for the phone. Dun globs floated. The flash had erased his night vision.

"LP."

"What the fuck was that?"

"Blew the claymore on somebody who walked up on us."

"Withdraw immediately to my position."

"There was only one."

"You sure?"

"Yeah," Joshua said. As if he could see jack shit. A minute after the blast, his night vision was inadequate to notice an elephant on a bicycle. A rookie move, to watch the claymore go off at night. He should have covered one eye.

Silence on the line. Good, thought Joshua. The lieutenant was reconsidering the order. It would give Old Man Ulrich time to supply adult supervision.

Now Joshua could distinguish the lump on the washout. No movement behind the mist. If the man had been part of an attack, Joshua would have heard a reaction to the claymore burst, men going to ground, equipment clattering. No such thing as a noiseless infantry movement. Weird, a lone soldier roaming the jungle at night. Gradually he relaxed. Chemical smoke hovered pungently. A rivulet slalomed down his face. He counted time while his night vision mended.

Clack-clack-clack-clack-clack.

"LP."

"Change of plan." Restraint in the lieutenant's voice, no doubt following a lecture from Ulrich. Once an LP is withdrawn, it cannot be reinstated—security is compromised, not to mention the risk the LP team faces crossing into the night perimeter without getting shot. Another lesson toward the day the lieutenant found his brain in his head. "We're on one-hundred percent alert. Find out who it was you blew up."

"Roger."

Now Joshua was grateful for the enveloping mist. For a weapon he took the .45 pistol, better for stooping over a body, more controllable, less likely to snag on a vine. He knew he could pull the trigger three times in a second if he had to. Advancing, calculating his footfalls, he swung the .45 with each scan of his eyes. He hoped not to fire a shot. Up top, the men the claymore blast had awakened would have no idea what was happening. Their fingers hovered by their triggers. Tension and sudden noises, a bad combination.

His feet compressed spongy leaf layers stinking of decay. At the washout, the ground firmed. The expanse of gray pebbles left him exposed, as if on a stage. He peered into the mist along the streambed that furrowed beyond. Tuning out the incessant insect chatter, he strained for the telltale clang or click that only a human makes.

On its side, the face turned upwards, the body had the floppy posture of violent death. Joshua lightly pressed the gun muzzle against the man's temple; with his other hand he checked the neck for a pulse. Warm, gluey wetness. He fingered the other side. The man was definitely dead. Joshua found the rifle, an M16, and pushed it away, just to be sure.

What was he doing here, this lone walker? A Viet Cong deserter? Around the head, a bandanna damp with sweat. Hugging the torso, web gear. A canteen in its holder. An ammo pouch. A butt pack on the web belt.

The Mighty C contained some 700 miniature ball bearings. The exploding compound scattered them in a V pattern. But no explosion is perfect. The pellets snuggled in a thin plastic bed. When the claymore detonated, they fractured unevenly, single pellets and clusters cocooned in plastic. A cluster had caught the man below the belt and streamed his intestines out through the lower back, a gruesome sight in the shimmery mist.

The man's gear—the uniform, webbing, rifle—was American. Not unusual—the Viet Cong would fight with whatever they could get. Maybe this one had stripped it off a U.S. or South Vietnamese casualty.

He checked the legs. Cargo pockets on the thighs. He opened one, extracted a folded map. Adhesive acetate covered the sheet. In his mind, a warning rattled like the field-phone tumblers. The enemy used map coverings too, essential in the damp climate, but clear plastic bags were the common thing for them. Acetate was American stuff, too expensive for the thrifty VC.

What the fuck?

The rule: no lights at night; lights were a sure way to serve you up to somebody's rifle sights. He knew this as he unhooked his flashlight. Night vision impaired, what else could he do? He had to be sure. The mist should protect him, unless the enemy was close, out searching for this lost sheep. Making sure the red lens cover was screwed down securely, cupping it with his fingers to fashion a peephole of exposed lens, he bowed forward so that his body formed a cave above the dead man's head. In the red-filtered glow, a Caucasian face. Half-open eyes floated in an infinity stare. No expression. The burst had killed him instantly. Joshua cut the light.

A Caucasian face!

Crazy. How could an American solider be out alone in the jungle at night? Joshua patted for dog tags around the neck. Nothing. Some soldiers hated the chain's rub, kept their tags elsewhere. The morning light would help. He didn't want to touch the man again. "God bless you, buddy." The benediction came as a whisper inaudible but to himself and the vigilant dead. "Very sorry. But you fucked up. You were in a bad place at a bad time. You were stupid and wrong and you died."

Stop scolding! Enough to have killed him.

The body submerged into a shadowy mound at his feet. The company would have to evacuate the remains. There would be questions to answer and statements to write. No time to worry about that now. The LP was still in business. Against the banyan root, he rested two grenades that could substitute for the claymore, if needed.

After first light they came down: the company commander, the platoon leader, a medic, and a fire team for security. Joshua sat on the banyan root while the medic checked the casualty. Nobody spoke at first. He thought, it was so clear what had happened. On the washout twenty meters from the LP site, the splayed body. The nearby crater where the claymore had burst. Dark. Mist. Obvious.

He was smoking a cigarette when Captain Ulrich approached, took off his helmet, and sat on the root. "He doesn't have ID on him. Did you find any last night?"

"I checked, but no."

"You're not riding yourself for this, are you?"

"Never killed an American before."

"If he *was* an American. We don't know that for certain. Anyway, it was his fault, not yours. To be tracking alone at night through the jungle is incomprehensible. Suicidal, basically." Ulrich was silent for a minute. "As soon as a chopper becomes available, we'll evacuate the remains."

"Yes sir."

"Listen up, Joshua. I'd have done the same thing. An unidentified fucker approaching my night perimeter damn well *better* get dropped. That's what my report will say."

Then Ulrich was up and gone.

With his finger Joshua pushed the cigarette butt into the soft soil, leaving nothing for the enemy to find. He stared at the leaves. He didn't look at the body bag they carried past him toward the hilltop. Soon a chopper would bear it away. The company would resume its movement through the rain forest. The urgent business of staying alive would take away the face he'd seen in the red oval.

*　*　*

In the grove, defying the grubbiness from weeks in the jungle, Joshua evinced composure, even nobility, as he told his story. He'd performed his duty, and I sensed he trusted me to do mine with no less diligence. The sergeant was fortunate not to know of the politics playing in this case. He'd probably never heard of a general named Cobris who wished to settle for an open question.

I asked him whether he'd stripped ammunition or gear from the casualty. Joshua confirmed they'd sent him back with everything they'd found, the items I'd examined at the forensic mortuary. He recalled that one of the canteens had been missing—he'd noticed the empty pouch and scoured the ground all around. It was anyone's guess why the man had been carrying extra D-cells.

Ulrich related how, after they'd carried away the remains, he'd ventured beyond the ravine and located a set of footprints in the muddy ground. With the tip of a bamboo thorn, he pointed to the spot on the map, traced a line from the spot where the unknown had died through the site of the footprints; the line shot off toward the east, the evident direction of origin.

I asked, "Why might he have been heading toward Hill 71?"

"There's nothing there," said Ulrich.

Joshua said, "At night, he had to be goin' someplace he couldn't miss. The only place like that in this whole area is the highway." With the thorn he plucked from his commander's fingers, Joshua tapped a crimson line on the map four kilometers to the west. "He was trying to get his ass out of the jungle. Had a ways to go."

I noticed that Joshua's black-skinned hands and Ulrich's white hands were so equally gritted, cracked, and nail broken as to be indistinguishable.

"Why would he risk moving at night?"

"Just pure bad luck he ran into us," Joshua said. You had to have an ear to catch the grief. I understood now why Larsen had pushed for the investigation. "You gonna get us some answers, sir?"

"I'm going to try."

Day 6

Aching from the bumpy ground where I'd slept curled in a poncho liner, I sat up into soup. The same brand of jungle mist that had visited Joshua at the LP had slicked me overnight with a piquant hash: aromatic, musty, bitter. I shook my boots to make sure no snakes or centipedes had wriggled in, pulled them on, and rolled my gear. The guard with the shotgun handed me a cup of coffee so black and steaming that Sergeant Lopez would have blessed it.

At zero six hundred, summoned by Larsen, I joined him at the TOC's main map board. He peered through reading glasses at a complexion of green outlined in black grease-pencil lines. "We analyzed the sector we think the unknown passed through. This forest eastward is triple canopy. About eight klicks from Hill 71, beyond this tributary, the ground opens into a vast marsh. We call it Area Zulu. The place is too flooded and open for the NVA to hide, so we don't send ground patrols past the outer edges, just recon it from the air. I don't think your man crashed there; the water's not deep enough for an aircraft to sink whole, and we'd have spotted the wreckage. Area Zulu is tame—you can fly low without risking ground fire. Over other sectors, don't dip below fifteen hundred feet, or you'll be a target. The pilot will have binoculars on board for a closer look if you notice something. When will the chopper be ready, Sam?"

The reedy major said, "Zero six thirty, sir, at the LZ."

"Can you make that, Tanner?"

"Yes sir."

The briefing was over. The two staff officers who'd stood by walked away. I began to collect my gear

"Tanner?"

"Yes sir."

"Have a look at this."

Larsen extended a telex dated this morning, 29 April. It was an official order that in four terse lines directed his brigade headquarters to relocate to Cu Chi camp, northwest of Saigon. His subordinate battalions were being attached to other units, with separate orders pending. The airlifts would begin tomorrow.

"Did you know this was coming?" I asked.

"No. It's straight out of the blue." His eyes stayed on the mystifying telex.

"Do you think Cobris arranged it?" Guessing that our suspicions ran to the same end, I wanted to hear his affirmation.

"If he did, he'd have had to impose it on the 1st Cav, a Machiavellian feat since he's not in the tactical chain of command. In time, I'll find out how it came about. For now, I have no choice except to comply."

The mist was beginning to lift. In the doorway, Larsen pulled off his glasses and scanned the scene with his old soldier's eyes. "I wish you well, Tanner. The redeployment order means that your flight this morning will be the final search. Enjoy the view."

* * *

By the time the OH-58 observation chopper reached the eastern operating zone, the mist had burned off. We flew at fifteen hundred feet, above the range of small-arms fire. From here the ground lost its intimacy; the streams and the terrain mercatorized to a two-dimensional field. There were tracts of land bulldozed or chemically defoliated to deny the enemy places to hide. Across our northwest ran a reddish-brown streak. This was Highway 246, where gigantic bulldozers called *Rome Plows* had widened the road's margins to a hundred meters or more on each side to deter enemy infiltration. *Deter* was a briefer's word. What the measure accomplished was to *inconvenience* the enemy, but not enough so that, every night, North Vietnamese Army regulars didn't cross from their sanctuaries in nearby Cambodia. On this side of the border, we shot at them, napalmed them, and bombarded them, leaving their bodies half-in, half-out of shell craters. They kept coming, lithe figures who moved everywhere on foot, disciplined and ruthless, infesting War Zone C.

Our first leg vectored us to the unknown's terminus at Hill 71. The pilot banked so I could gaze down on where Ulrich and his company had set up their night perimeter amid the craters of an old bombardment. It had rained overnight, and the water-filled holes glimmered like a diamond necklace on a headless mannequin.

"Where to next, sir?"

"Head east."

We overflew grid after grid of rain forest. I hoped to spot a trail or other passage. None appeared. Kilometers to the north, a shading of lighter green. From it spiked a radio tower.

"That's the Gavet Plantation's antenna," the pilot remarked. "Best landmark around."

Too easy, to traverse the jungle by helicopter. I recalled the unknown's punished feet. Navigating through the dense vegetation, in two days he might have crossed a dozen klicks, a distance my pilot would cover in minutes.

The map was deceptively short on detail; my two fingers entirely covered the six grid squares representing Area Zulu. Lifting my eyes from the pattern of blue hash marks on the map, I peered through the Plexiglas at the real place, a tangle of half-submerged, bog-nourished roots yearning toward drooping vines. Fetid, hostile to the presence of man, it was literally a quagmire. Had the unknown crossed it, he'd have sunk to his waist in water and mud. Around its periphery ran a leaf portico whose main pillars were sixty-foot trees. Everywhere I looked, I could see through to the murky water. As Larsen had said, it wasn't deep enough to have swallowed an aircraft whole..

The marsh pooled below a slender tributary of the Saigon River. I measured the distance from the tributary to Hill 71, five klicks at its closest, within the radius of the unknown's calculated hike.

I asked, "Is that waterway fordable?"

"Maybe farther upstream. Too deep here. A patrol could build a rope bridge across, if they ever had to. Larsen's policy is to fly 'em over. Why expose soldiers out in the open when we've got lots of choppers?"

Larsen's patrols probably hadn't searched the tributary's banks. Even if they had, they would have been hunting for aircraft wreckage, not for the subtle traces the unknown might have left.

"Can you get lower?"

"If the enemy's around, he's apt to shoot at us."

"I can't make out details from this altitude."

"Hold on."

The pilot nosed down, flattening out at one hundred feet, shaving over the break in the trees. Choppers on patrol occasionally caught the enemy in the open. More than two years ago, on my first helicopter ride in a combat zone, I watched as the door gunner bored bullets into a file of men scrambling across a stream. The rounds kicked up founts as tall as the figures. One of them, maybe a Viet Cong, maybe an innocent, fell and managed to crawl into the greenery, leaving his fate and identity forever undisclosed. The people we blasted from the air were happy to return the favor, given the opportunity.

The pilot was right. No fords here. If the unknown had crossed the tributary, he must have swum across.

"Can you get down in the cut? I need a closer look."

"What are you trying to find?"

"The place a man crossed. What do you do when you get ready to immerse in a murky current like that? You take your gear off, waterproof what you can, and dump anything that's excess. In the process, you trample the underbrush."

"Have you ever crashed in a chopper?"

"No."

"If I guide her in there and we get hit, won't be time for me to take emergency action. We'll hear the rounds plink, the instruments will flash red, and we'll go down, either alive or dead. If we're alive, that's not so great either, 'cause chances are we'll be stuck in the wreckage when the fuckers who shot us down stop by to say howdy. You wanna roll the dice on that?"

"One pass, then we climb."

Maneuvering the ship directly over the trench, he descended between the trees. His face muscles tightened as he wiggled the stick to dodge the outreaching branches. Tricky business—a rotor strike and we'd crash in the classic careening flip, which, once witnessed, imprints its horror indelibly. We crawled along at ten knots. If the enemy appeared on the bank and shot at us, he couldn't miss. I scanned the edges for disturbances the unknown might have left when he'd crossed. How fast did the jungle restore itself? Over the ten days since his death, intermittent rains might have erased any marks he'd made.

The tributary widened to forty meters. From the banks poked fingers of sand and reeds extending a third of the way across. No tracks or disarrangement. The main stream alternated between rapids and deep pools.

The trees closed in again, and the pilot resumed his nervous squeeze under arching branches. "We're barely getting through," he said.

"Try a little farther."

"Sorry, this is as far as we go." His tone said he'd already breached the bounds of good judgment. He began a delicate pivot turn, and sweeping around I noticed a gap in the greenery, revealing a small clearing near the water's edge, and nested in grass and leaves, an olive-drab surface, unrecognizable save that it was a man-made object.

I pointed. "I want to get out and have a look at that."

"No way. I can't put you in here."

"Not here. At those sandbars we crossed before. I can work my way on foot along the water's edge. I'll need about fifteen minutes."

"Dumb idea, sir, to step out by yourself, especially after we just buzzed by. This bitch is *loud*, the noise carries a long way. Who knows what unwanted attention we've attracted already?"

"Fifteen minutes, that's all. Then come back and pick me up."

From the sand finger where I hopped down from the skid, the distance to the object I'd spotted downriver was roughly seventy meters. At once I realized that the trip would take longer than I'd predicted. With every step, vines and thorns grabbed at me like desperate beggars. I winced at the noise I was making. Two years had gone by since the last time I'd broken through the brush by a Vietnamese river. Back then I'd had legs for the jungle. Today, armed only with my .45, I was busting through here like a Saigon cowboy on Tu Do Street.

The NVA and Viet Cong didn't lurk everywhere, I reminded myself. There might not be a hostile force within kilometers. Yet the enemy was legendary at materializing whenever you showed vulnerability, like ants at a sweet spill. Overhead circled the chopper, and I could almost hear the pilot cursing himself for having agreed to drop me out alone. Maybe the return trek would be faster, since I'd already thrashed out a path.

At last I came upon the clearing, and I stepped into it with the feeling you get when you intrude into another person's private chamber. Spread on the ground, a plastic poncho on which lay two open C-ration cans. From one protruded a white spoon, which I eased sideways with my fingertip, amid swarming ants, so I could read the can's black lettering: Sliced Peaches.

The yellow remnants in the unknown's stomach.

Beyond the cans, a plastic canteen. Coated in the jungle's slimy secretions, none of the items would yield fingerprints, so I picked up the canteen, twisted the cap, and sniffed the faint odor of iodine. A few seconds later I found a tiny glass bottle of iodine tablets in the weeds. Soft wax sealed the lid, and when I shook it, the little pills rattled, dry and intact.

Closer to the water I uncovered the olive-drab object I'd sighted. Held it up like a trophy. A military radio, Model PRC25. A fold-up antenna called a 'long whip' dangled. Recalling the items on the morgue's storeroom table, I turned the radio over, flipped the lower latches, and wiggled loose the base cover.

A standard PRC25 radio operated on a single battery, an item-specific model that resembled a brick.

This one was different.

Five D-cells stared up from their cozy bed.

* * *

At the TOC, Colonel Larsen examined the radio. He fiddled with the knobs and pried a D-cell from the battery cover. "I've seen this conversion before," he said. "The Viet Cong don't have our special batteries, so when they capture our radios, they rewire them to run on flashlight cells. The bastards use the radios to listen in on our tactical transmissions."

I said, "Our man left the radio behind, sir. I'm certain of it. He stopped to rest at the tributary before he swam across. The canteen I found is the one missing from the pouch on his web belt. If you insert a patrol, they might be able to follow his trail through the jungle to a crash site."

"How far do you estimate the crash site might be from where you found this?"

"Probably not more than five klicks."

Larsen shook his head. "The battery conversion convinces me he was not an American. He was something else—a Caucasian Viet Cong, maybe an eastern European. Why else would he have had this piece of jerry-rigged equipment?"

"A Viet Cong wouldn't have been by himself."

"Why not? What if he was a courier coming back from delivering a message? Hell, maybe he just got *lost*. It's happened to our own soldiers. A man goes off to take a shit, nobody notices, and next thing you know, he's left by himself. I can't risk a patrol to backtrack five klicks through the rain forest just to figure out the whys and wherefores. If somebody stumbles onto a crash site at the last minute, fine, I'll send people to check. Other than that, we're out of the search business. The Brigade will be gone, bag and baggage, within thirty-six hours. We're done. And so are you."

* * *

I wasn't done.

In a row of sun-bleached trailers at Bien Hoa, the Army Property Book Office crouched like a construction project about to break ground.

Air conditioners churned noisily to suppress the temperature inside, while outside the sun blazed off the aluminum panels, the sandbag walls that separated the trailers, and the glossy mold ponds where the drip pans overflowed.

PBO kept track of equipment, or rather it catalogued items before units in Vietnam lost them, usually for Vietnamese civilians or the enemy to find. The officer in charge of the property records section, Chief Warrant Officer Hollis, might easily have delegated me to one of his staff of enlisted clerks. Maybe the prospect of tracking a salvaged radio through the system intrigued him. Whatever his reason, he listened as I related the sequence from the unknown's death to my discovery of the radio this morning on the bank of a tributary in Tay Ninh Province.

Straight haired, slightly balding, in a pressed uniform and jungle boots that never touched the jungle, his skin leathery though sweat rarely brined it, Hollis was the kind of soldier reporters didn't write about. Turning over the radio, he ran his fingertips to an engraving on the base, got up, and walked through the steel filing cabinets, his glasses reflecting the indices. He tugged open a drawer and plucked out a stack of cards.

"These show various radio acquisitions. This card covers the specific item, Transmitter-Receiver model PRC25. From the manufacturer's notation codes, we'll be able to tell whether your radio was issued to a U.S. or an ARVN unit, and approximately when. Determining anything else about it would be impossible."

I said, "I thought every piece had a life history."

"That's the kind of thing they say on TV. Somebody tore off the serial number plate. Without that, who knows where it's been?"

"So there's nothing more you can do to trace it?"

He stared at the radio for a minute. "You say somebody might have recovered this from the Viet Cong?"

"That somebody is who I'm trying to track down."

"When units find equipment, they're supposed to report it on a standard form. I can go through the files, but it's a long shot. Units are spotty about reporting recovered pieces, including our own stuff they pick up. Easier to keep it under the table. If an item is interesting, someone takes it home illegally as a souvenir. If it's functional, they use it until it breaks, then chuck it back into the jungle." He popped open his fist like a magician to expose—*presto*—a bare palm. "I'll check and get back to you within a week."

"Can you manage 48 hours? I'm on a tight timetable."

Hollis tapped his pencil against his teeth. The clink echoed among the file cabinets. "Tell you what. I'm short handed, but if you can you send me somebody who can go through a lot of paperwork without his attention wandering off, I can tell him what to look for."

"A sergeant named Lopez will be over to see you today."

"Deal." Hollis rested his hand on the radio. "And I'll keep this specimen for a while, if you don't mind."

* * *

When I told Lopez about the research project, I mentioned Colonel Larsen's comment about the soldier who got lost after taking a shit in the jungle.

He lit a cigarette. "That's happened to *me*. We were on long-range patrol. I stepped out of column to take a shit, and I spent so much time cleaning my ass that when I looked up, my buddies had moved way down the fucking way. I couldn't hear them, and it was dark as hell. So I chased after them, thinking they must have veered off in a different direction, and all of a sudden I heard 'uhhhhh.' I was *standing* on this motherfucker who'd sat down on the ground at the tail of the column. I tried to get off him, and 'uhhhhh, uhhhhh'—I was stomping all over his ass. He was mad that I stepped on him, but if you ask me, it served him right, for sitting down."

"He asked for it."

Lopez sucked on his cigarette, blew out a contemptuous cloud. "Fuckin' A."

* * *

Before I went out, I ate the dinner Tuy had cooked. We sat quietly, leaning over steaming shallots and rice, our chopsticks clicking on the plates. Finished, I looked up. "I have a favor to ask."

"Why not? It's been at least a day since the last one."

"I need to know more about Simone Nogaret."

"How would I learn such a thing?"

"Hipolite mentioned that she had a fascinating history. Maybe it's in the newspaper archives." I guessed that Tuy's father's friends in the local press could find old articles.

She said, "In the French-language papers? Or in others?"

"The French ones first, then try the English-language."

"And the Vietnamese last?"

"Last, or not at all."

A faint smile touched her lips. "I really am your contact, aren't I, Tanner?"

"My number one."

At the prefecture, I looked for Trong. He was away from his office. I found Giang sitting at a desk bereft of the usual files and reports— apparently he didn't deal in paperwork. The skin around his left eye had turned black, the eye was cloudy, and I guessed the sight in it was gone, the latest increment in his slow death. His yellowed nails lightly balanced a cigarette. He said, "You were right about *Quartier Latin*."

"Did you find the dancer?"

"I sent the boy in. He pretended to be a village kid seeking his big sister. The employees at the club chased him away before he could get inside. Very heartless, those people. So I sent him to another club. Not French, this one. Corsican. They listened to him and looked at the photo. They said it shows *Quartier Latin's* stage."

"The stage?"

"You can tell from this." He tapped on a blurred shape in the photo, in the molding below the dancer's kick. I hadn't noticed it before. "The carving of a rubber tree. Only *Quartier Latin's* stage has it."

"That's damn good work."

He tipped his cigarette, the equivalent of a shrug. "Now we wait. I put a policeman down the block in plain clothes. He has a copy of the picture. He will watch for her."

"How long?"

"A day. A week. Maybe longer. A cop has to be patient."

"Do you see the rabbit?" Supine on the straw mat, I pointed at the pattern the cigarette smoke made against the ceiling.

"That's a fish," Tuy said. She saw fish in everything.

The ceiling fan patted the smoke through the window screen. During the cooler dry season, the fan had hung dead. The humidity had resurged and become unbearable, and I found in the Cholon industrial market an electrician whose bulgy eyes suggested he'd been shocked enough times to know his trade. I'd stood at the bottom of his ladder while he repaired the fan, handing down clippings of fabric-sheathed wires as old as the building. When he'd finished, I asked, "Safe?"

He'd laughed. "Nothing safe."

He'd been around.

The fan, the tub, the electric griddle, and the woman who used them had shaped this space into my home. How could I leave? I thought, maybe I could return in the guise of an entrepreneur, the rep of some American outfit that peddled tractors, and Tuy and I could move to the safe First District, become the neighbors of Simone Nogaret.

An ungrounded wire. No such thing as safe. And we were not First District people.

I said, "It's all going to end, isn't it?"

"What?" She was still hunting shapes.

"Saigon."

"No. The Americans will end. Saigon will stay."

"How? We're part of it."

"Not really. You are like the ceiling animals, made of smoke."

"That's not nice."

"What do you want, nice or true?" She stubbed out the cigarette and rolled on top of me.

Day 7

I reached the French Fort just as Crowley phoned. He'd received another call from Major Vangleman. Since General Cobris's lecture on the verandah, three days had gone by, and I had yet to certify that the unknown wasn't an American. What was taking so long?

I explained about *Quartier Latin*.

"Let's see if I have this right," said Crowley. "A plain-clothes gook cop is hanging around by the door of a nightclub, waiting for the showgirl, on the assumption she might appear. Nobody has actually spotted her."

"He's not by the door. They put him across the street." That sounded better than down the block.

"Doesn't matter. I can't tell any of it to Vangleman."

"Sure you can. Tell him that if I find the girl, we'll know the unknown's identity. If he stops the investigation now, we won't know. If he wants to figure this out himself, he can go ahead."

"You've got one more day."

"Is that from Vangleman?"

The receiver clicked.

I thought of the Army like an old Roman road. Commanders were its stones fitted together to withstand heavy loads.

Crowley had crumbled like a clay clod under a boot.

* * *

At fifteen hundred I returned to the prefecture to find Trong in his office. Giang was with him. It was the first time I'd seen Giang out from behind his desk. Thinner even than Tuy, he stood with a slight stoop, like a dead tree on which people hung laundry.

Trong grinned. "Giang told you the news?"

"You've confirmed *Quartier Latin*."

"Yes."

"But you haven't found the girl."

"We will find her, in time."

I shook my head. "It can't wait. You have to go in and ask."

"Not possible. It is a protected club. Very powerful. General Huang." When Trong was upset, his English became choppy. I assumed his annoyance stemmed from General Huang's nexus to *Quartier Latin*. A luminary in the South Vietnamese Army, Huang controlled parts of the military district around Saigon. He was reputed to be one of its most pernicious profiteers. "Huang will not tolerate interference in his interests. He shelters Nogaret, who runs drugs out of Cambodia."

"You're sure about the drugs?"

My question about surety didn't resonate with Trong. He flipped his hand, which meant it was in the air, the bit about Nogaret and drugs and Cambodia, between fact and rumor, a tendril of smoke. For him, it was enough. "A dirty setup. Untouchable. Huang's involvement makes it so. I cannot send in a detective. A police commander foolish enough to do so would be ruined."

"Then I'll go."

Trong laughed. Then he saw I meant it. "I cannot help you in there."

"Just tell me how to find the place."

"*Quartier Latin* does not cater to Americans. It is very exclusive."

"I'll dress up."

"You could get killed."

Giang grinned, a death's head. The prospect of mortal danger evidently amused him.

Trong stared at the photo on the desk. He must have asked himself how finding a club dancer possibly could merit all this fuss. He was too polite, and his culture too restricting, for him to declare his thoughts directly. When his eyes flicked to me, they beamed a message: My insistence was reckless.

Giang said something in Vietnamese, and the two men exchanged clipped syllables that dissolved in silence. Stepping to the window, Trong seemed to weigh the consequences of my request the same way that Tuy had deliberated our jaunt to *Le Cercle Sportif.* He muttered, "You cannot say you're working with us."

"I won't. If they ask, I'm working on my own."

"No. You are not working at all. When you are inside, you are not a cop, simply a customer with money to spend. Throw a little to the bar girls. Not too much. Ask for a drink a fool would order, like a Singapore Sling. Pay for a drink for the girl who waits on you. She will come back. When she does, ask about the dancer. American sentimentality is well known; the club will weigh this when they find out you are asking the wrong questions. Maybe you will walk out in one piece."

* * *

Quartier Latin's doorway opened in a side street that hooked off Nguyen Cong Tru a block from the river. The facade was unremarkable except for a neon tube that squiggled above the glass showcase. In daylight, this was a buzzing commercial district where everyone competed—the rolling carts with the shops and the customers with the proprietors in spirited bargaining. At night the bargaining was of a different sort. The carts withdrew, the shop grates rattled down. Tepid illumination from the clubs splashed the sidewalks. Arriving by taxi, the customers scampered nervously to refuge inside. This wasn't a hangout for Americans. In the infamous bars along Tu Do, the GIs got a display that was loud, blatant, and artless. The few clubs off Nguyen Cong Tru offered something else. What was it? The swagger of the Saigonese nouveau riche? The sneers of the older elites? The pseudo worldliness of the Europeans? They all thought they were smarter than the Americans. Maybe they were.

In civilian clothes, I took a table in the shadows away from the stage. I made out the carved molding of a rubber tree—the feature the photo had revealed—in the center below the flailing spotlights. Two tables of Europeans occupied the foreground. They glanced at me to gauge if I was someone they should worry about or merely disdain. Apparently I was the latter, for they restored their attention to the dancer, Li Hoa. I knew her name from the showcase photos that depicted her in several saucy poses, the prints the same size as the one nesting in my pocket. The spotlight speared Li Hoa's abdomen in a brilliant circle, sculpting her muscles like ivory. Forward and back she banged her pelvis while the spotlight dot contracted and enlarged, the rhythm suggesting she was fucking the light beam. She mouthed a rock and roll refrain and the drums kept beat. Behind her, the mural of a Paris street scene—ochre edifices fronted by café tables topped with orange umbrellas—created a certain *je-ne-sais-quoi* effect.

When the tables were full, *Quartier Latin* might host tens of clients buying drinks in front of the stage show. The waitresses were village girls who'd flocked to the capital to take up their dual jobs as servers and that which is served; enough cash would buy them. Even Li Hoa, queen of the dancers, was surely available, though for more green than the casual bar dabbler would pay. And probably not tonight. With the pre-monsoons outside and a handful of placid European customers, I had the feeling the club wasn't going to get busy. Squirming in my seat to relieve the irritation of my .45 pressing into my back where I'd tucked it in the waistband, I ordered my Singapore Sling, paid along with a heavy tip, and tried to look worldly.

It didn't take long before I became the favorite of one of the waitresses. In a lace top frilled with sienna fabric that made her look like a moth, she watched me for a few minutes, surmised I was an American, and decided that her sexual subtlety should be on a par with Li Hoa's pelvic thrusts. She gave a few preliminary smiles and eyelash flutters, approached, and commenced plowing her long fingernails through my hair.

"Why don't you get yourself a drink?" I said.

She took my money, returned with a whisky glass, its sepia-tinted liquid probably cold tea, and slinked onto the second chair, a practiced act judging from the grace with which she pulled it off without jarring the drinks on the spindly table. On the stage, Li Hoa had reached the climax of her act; her hips gyrated like an electric mixer. When the music stopped, spinning the umbrella from my Sling, I asked the waitress, "You work here a long time?"

"Maybe three month."

"So you must know everyone."

"Sure."

"I'm looking for one of your dancers."

"Why?"

Over the tabletop I pushed a ten dollar bill—real currency, not the military-issued script. Halfway across, it brushed her fingertips and was gone.

"I saw her perform. I couldn't get her out of my head." I laughed my best fool's laugh, which emerged more naturally than I'd have thought. "I bought one of her pictures." I pushed across the marquee pic.

Her mirth fell away and she regarded me coldly. At once I regretted the line about the photo; probably they were not for the buying. She perused it without touching. Softly she emitted, "Kim Thi."

"Is she around?"

"Last time week ago. No come back."

"Too bad. I was hoping to find her. You wouldn't happen to know where she lives?"

Abruptly she got up and flitted off into the club's recesses. I caught sight of her in the shadows beyond the bar facing a man in a silver silk suit and a color-matched tie. Just once did she tilt her glance my way, enough to confirm that I was the subject of the conversation.

A minute later the silk suit came out from the shadows. Wending amid the tables, his hip movements a bit too flashy, he crossed the room to an alcove where a Caucasian with sandy hair and a striped chartreuse tropical shirt reposed at a table. Around forty, ruggedly tanned, he exuded gravitas, and I'd have put down money he was André Nogaret. The suited man leaned over and spoke to his ear. What I'd hoped would be a discreet inquiry about the dancer already had risen to the club's management. My choices were to stay or get out. Nobody stood between me and the door.

I could toss a few bills on the table and reach the street in twenty seconds, a safe exit, though it precluded coming back, at least in the guise of a customer. If I wanted to learn about Kim Thi, I had to play it through.

The suit swished to a doorway behind the bar and disappeared. He emerged a minute later leading a sinewy youth whose nose had been broken a few times. When he saw me, the youth twisted his mouth into a menacing snarl, lips curled back, so excessive he rendered himself farcical. Leaning against the wall, he playacted the muscle while the suited man, as graceful in his maneuvers as the waitress, pulled out the extra chair at my table and slid into it. Coiffed and ostentatious, he wore greased hair combed to bisect his scalp. His teeth were so straight and white they could not have been natural. At an earlier phase of his descent to this ledge of Saigon's underworld, someone had knocked out the real ones.

He flamed a gold-plated Zippo over the tip of a Gauloises. "You GI?"

"Yeah."

"What your name?"

"Bobby John. What's yours?"

"Danh."

"That's funny, rhymes with my name." I chuckled.

"You funny too, Bobby." Danh didn't laugh.

"I'm just a customer looking for something extra special."

"Extra special?" The query had the ring of tedium, as if his job was to solve minor problems. Confident on his own turf, he hardly needed the youth to back him up, and I guessed he'd brought the kid as a show, perhaps at the direction of the sandy-haired man. These were careful people at *Quartier Latin*. He asked, "What so extra special for you?"

"Kim Thi."

"I should know her?"

"She's one of your dancers. I saw her perform a couple of weeks ago."

I kept my face unreadable, while Danh sucked on his cigarette for so long I thought he might have asphyxiated himself. In a huff of smoke, he said, "No work here anymore."

"You know how men promise things to themselves? For me, the promise was Kim Thi."

"You cannot promise something not yours."

"If she says no, then okay. I just want to ask her."

"You go to lot of trouble. Plenty of other girl around."

"I'm very sentimental."

"California is for sentimental. Here, business." Gleaming teeth vice-gripped the cigarette. "Maybe I throw you out in the street."

I smiled at the sinewy kid whose repertoire was limited to grimaces, and who now flashed one resembling the paper dragons that writhed through Cholon's streets during the New Year's celebrations.

Danh didn't like my smile at his thug. "You officer, right? You look like officer. Bad idea you get in trouble downtown. Brass hear. Your career all fucked up."

When dealing with the Vietnamese, it was important not to contradict a man of authority in front of his subordinate, so I answered in a tone so low only Danh could hear. "I suppose it would be. The brass would find out. My career would go to shit. The brass would also hear about your club. Bad publicity."

If they got physical, I'd brandish my MP credentials. Roughing up a customer was bad for business; laying a hand on an American MP officer was an outrage even General Huang would frown upon. The creds were a last resort. They would proclaim that I'd come here on official business about Kim Thi, and I'd uncover nothing more about her, not until Giang could find her. Without information from the club, that might never happen.

He said, "Her address cost one hundred."

For the address of a Saigon bar dancer, one hundred dollars rated so steep that even a heart-achy American would balk at it. I paused as if to reflect. While Danh squinted impatiently, I reached in my pocket, folded three twenty dollar bills into the drink napkin, and nonchalantly slid it across. As practiced as the waitress, he swept his hand and the napkin disappeared.

"The rest?"

"Sixty now. The rest when I find her."

"How I know you pay?"

"Send somebody along."

Vietnamese sophisticates tended to think of Americans as an artless race, with the subtlety of a donkey. In enacting this negotiation, I figured that I'd progressed from a donkey to a clever monkey. "You stay here," he said.

He hipped to the alcove to consult with the sandy-haired man. As I watched, their discussion spanned two cigarettes smoked. Lead-in drums signaled a fresh dance act, and the spotlight snared the sequins of a dancer warming up at the stage side. I contemplated the dregs of my Singapore Sling, a bloody puddle that as the minutes ticked by resembled my melting enthusiasm for finding the dancer. What was I doing, enacting this pathetic pantomime, risking the ruin of my best police contact and friend, when all I had to do was sign Cobris's certification and be finished? In the stare of the club's employees, I felt like an act on stage, a donkey to be sure, and I was mulling over whether to leave when Danh slipped into the other chair. "Outside is a boy who will take you to her. Pay him."

"Thanks."

"Don't come back."

"No reason to."

*   *   *

Just before twenty-three hundred hours, a lightning storm dazzled the city. The rain scraped leaves from the trees and flooded the streets, momentarily restoring Saigon to its origins as a marsh on a river bend. In the district behind the docklands, through mist rising from the ankle-deep rainwater lakes, my guide weaved his two-seater Vespa scooter while I clung to its slippery rails. He was the kid who'd shown me the dragon face, and although his expression had reverted to normal, for the ride he'd donned an improbable Humphrey Bogart hat. I guessed his age to be 18, draft eligible. For males, military service was universal, though many tried to evade it. I'd seen would-be draft dodgers flee from the conscription squads, usually to be caught and hauled off by their skinny arms. He might be among the tens of thousands who'd deserted. Or maybe the kid's underworld patrons had bought him a pricey exemption. With his tough-guy hat, rolled-up black sleeves, and insouciant mien, he was doing their bidding tonight in the streets the rain had made our private sanctum.

We buzzed along a wire-mesh fence, beyond which, shrouded in wood smoke, squatted hundreds of cardboard huts, banged-up CONEX containers, and plastic tents. The refugee camp was a panorama of discarded U.S. military packaging. Fleeing their villages, hundreds of thousands of refugees had assembled in overcrowded, sordid ghettos that spattered the city. This camp cluttered over uneven ground, higher than the street in places, lower in others, and in the flooding it balanced its water level by puking out garbage and open sewage in pulpy washouts below the fence. Across these the kid maneuvered the scooter, until he banked toward a block of tenant houses opposite.

He pulled in at the mouth of an alley between buildings. We faced a lake deeper than the Vespa could power through. "We walk," he said. He ran a chain through the wheel spokes and around a vertical wall pipe and clamped on a padlock.

Following the kid, carrying my shoes, my trousers rolled to my knees like a sampan operator, I waded into the water. It deepened, and things slithered against my calves, threads of slime I hoped were not able to propel themselves toward my genitals. Uncomfortable to toddle through, the flooding nonetheless added a dab of security; nobody could follow us without making the same splashing racket.

My guide halted near an edifice of cinder blocks three stories tall. A rickety wooden stairway bridged a mound of garbage to the second-level entry. We stood at the joint of alleyways bent crookedly like the leg of an insect. Having just splashed through the upper limb, we faced the lower that receded into pitch black. Denizens, junkies, or fence-jumping refugees might lurk here unseen. The only light spilled weakly from a bulb by the stairs.

I said, "Where do I find Kim Thi?"

"Top floor." He held out his hand, no doubt as Danh had instructed.

I put twenty dollars into it. "The rest after I see her." I pointed to the lower steps. "You wait." The sight of him might deter anyone watching us from coming closer.

Halfway up the outer stairs, I heard shouts of anger or alarm from beyond. No telling if the disturbance had anything to do with me or was merely the normal ambiance so close to the refugee camp. For the first time tonight, I was tempted to draw my .45, but on the rain-slick staircase, I might drop it through a gap into the garbage beneath. Or somebody might see the gun, panic, and start screaming. I left it in the waistband under my shirt.

Through the maw of the doorway, waiting for my vision to adjust to the obscurity, I paused to tie on my shoes and roll down my trouser legs. I peered up the inner stairs to the single landing whose broken window pickpocketed the dim bulb. As I climbed, the smoke from the refugees' fires intensified and blended with urine, cigarettes, mildew. One of the doors canted open, and I glimpsed a black-stained porcelain sink sagging out of the plaster above sideways-turned floorboards, a former hiding place pillaged of its drugs or explosives; nobody was left to say. I swished away mosquitoes whose buzz blended with faint mandolin chords. At the stair top I stood in front of a door framed in orange light. I knocked and the music halted.

"*Ai do?*"

"Kim Thi. I want to see her."

"*My?*"

The door cracked open. In the slit, backlit in orange, a woman much older than the girl I was looking for. Incense wafted through. She studied me a moment, enough to determine that I was indeed *My*—an American. Rapid chatter in Vietnamese followed with someone behind her. Opening the door, she ushered me into a room where a lava lamp on a side table cast an unworldly glow upon four women, ages between fifteen and thirty, who sat on the floor staring at me, their expressions anticipatory. None resembled the woman in the marquee photo. I noticed on the ceiling a centimeter-wide crack bleeding water from the earlier rain. Wadded newspaper had failed to seal the fissure, and most of the drips missed the can set out to catch them. The wadding reminded me of a wounded Viet

Cong I'd once encountered who'd stuffed his bullet holes with paper to stop the bleeding. Then he'd died.

"What you want?" The question carried from an older man who sat cross-legged in a corner next to a mandolin on the floor. His balding scalp bore a long scar, as if in imitation of the ceiling. He held up his forearm to display muscles ablated above the wrists, a permanent disfigurement that a man obtains from having his hands bound over an extended period. "French," he cackled. He lit a cigarette and plucked a sad chord on the mandolin.

The older woman wore a maroon silk robe faded to the same blush of rouge as on her face, the makeup of an old whore. She barked to the man, who rose and slipped through a doorway of hanging beads to an adjoining room. Then she turned to me to determine if fate had delivered her—*tuyet vo'i!*—a fool on whom she could ply any number of inventive jigs to amplify her profit. "You pay me," she said.

"How much?"

"Ten dollar for girl. Five more for room."

I handed her fifteen in greenbacks. The man reappeared through the beads, his cigarette ash leading the way. A girl who wasn't Kim Thi trailed him. So far I'd counted seven Vietnamese in this room.

She tipped her head toward the beads. "Go."

Curtains sectioned the second room into cubbies. In the right corner, one draped slightly ajar, and I fingered it aside to find Kim Thi kneeling on a mat. She was the photo's likeness minus the costume and stage presence. Raven hair flowed to the satin pillow behind her, and her lean figure contoured the robe belted snugly at her waist. In the space that measured no larger than a double bed, she'd decorated the walls with yellow boas that might have been the scraps of a dancer's dress, looped in flower patterns that created the feel of a child's room. She'd tucked her various possessions into two side-turned, tinsel-wrapped cardboard boxes in the corner. More pillows lay about, and I guessed that the girl I'd seen pass through the beads slept here too. The others must sleep in the other cubbies or the dreary room where I'd come in.

Stooping, I entered and knelt alongside her on the straw mattress. My eyes stung from the incense and lingering opium smoke. Accustomed, hers shone like paper lanterns. Her honey-brown face evinced neither lines of age nor protuberances of bone; she might be eighteen or twenty five, I couldn't tell. She didn't know why I'd come to see her, so she assumed the obvious. "I am not a prostitute," she declared.

The scents, the bright colors, the muffled mandolin—all conspired to suspend the tawdry reality. After the foulness outside, Kim Thi's eyes seemed like the peace at the end of the world. Perhaps the man in the Tay Ninh jungle had loved her for this, to be in the presence of tranquility. The robe flowed to reveal in shaded glimpses the cleavage of her small breasts and the mounds of her thighs pressed together.

I brought out the marquee photo. "You gave this to a man. Could you tell me his name?"

"Where you get this?" Apprehension squeaked in her voice.

In a gesture of kindness, I lowered my gaze. Grief normally touches a woman's face like a wrecking ball. Kim Thi's features altered not a twitch. With a tissue she dabbed at her eyes, though I'd seen no tears.

"How?"

"He was killed north of Saigon, deep in the woods. He walked up on American soldiers at night. They blew him up. It was an accident."

"Accident?"

"They thought he was a Viet Cong."

She shook her head as if this were incomprehensible.

I repeated, "What was his name?"

She might not have heard me. "He due back Saigon Monday. For three days I go to meet him, still he no show up. I cannot work. Too upset. Today, I stay inside."

A rattle of beads, footsteps, a hip's indentation in the fabric, and the madame's crowed authority: "*Anh ay dang lam gi the?*" She must have heard our exchange and disliked the tone.

"*Cut di!*" nipped Kim Thi. My meager grasp of Vietnamese sufficed to understand that she'd just told the madame to go fuck herself.

I leaned closer, whispered, "I need to talk to you. I'll take you anywhere you want to go. Not for sex. Just to talk."

"I have no place else."

"I do. It is safe."

She studied my face. Who was I? Why was I doing this? Why should she trust me? What did I mean by *safe?*

No such thing. She'd been around.

She said, "This place belong to you?"

"It belongs to a woman," I replied. "My friend."

"She there, or just you?"

"She will be there."

More contemplation. Through the fabric, beads rattled, water dripped. The piccolo of voices. Her eyes darted side to side. What was she seeing, that I couldn't?

"Wait outside. I put on clothes."

While she dressed, I stood in the leaky outer room. The madame had posted herself like a checkpoint by the door. "You finish?"

"I'm leaving. Kim Thi is going with me."

"Cost more!"

I threw a fiver on the side table, and the madame's claw landed on my sleeve. "Twenty!"

I don't like to be grabbed, and when she seized my shirt, I flinched. With a clasp around her wrist, I twisted and she flopped amid the girls, bumping the table and tipping the lava lamp into a crazy jiggle. Like the audience in a wrestling match, the rope-scarred mandolin player watched her tumble. He wasn't about to get himself hurt—he'd learned that much from his sessions with the French. The curtain opened and Kim Thi came out, surveyed the scene, and trilled harshly to the woman. I guessed that most of the girls were meek mice the madame lorded over. Not Kim Thi.

I tossed a folded ten bill that landed on the mandolin.

In the dark stairwell, I held her hand. It was an improper gesture with a Vietnamese woman of brief acquaintance, but I did it for my own safety. She'd descended these steps many times. I hadn't.

She asked, "Where your friend live?"

"In Cholon."

"How you come here?"

"A scooter. Don't worry, I'll get us a cab."

At the second-floor landing, I peered down the outer stairway. The scooter kid waited at the base. Light from the single bulb glazed his shoulders; the flooded street winked. I went first, holding onto the spindly railing, trying not to trip. Then the kid took off his hat, and for an instant I thought his gesture showed politeness to Kim Thi. But he hadn't graduated from a school for manners. His dragon's grimace was gone; his eyes flickered oddly.

The kid was terrified.

A droplet slapping tile makes the same sound as a gun hammer cocked.

The slap came.

Two of them, pistols blazing. A bullet went under my chin. I spun, heard wood cracking, and it was me going through the railing. As I plummeted, I remembered the grin that had crossed Giang's face when I'd insisted on going to *Quartier Latin*—maybe that cloudy eye of his had foreseen my death. Pitching sideways, I landed in the pile of trash, and immediately I was thumped down with bruising force—Kim Thi must have leapt or fallen through the broken rail after me. The impact crushed me into the trash, face in the mush, and probably saved my life.

One of my bruises later would take the angled shape of the .45 that the fall slammed against my lower back. Now I clawed for it, pried it out, snapped down the safety, ascended like a fiery Phoenix from the pile, leveling the gun in the style of night shooting, not looking for the sights, I couldn't have seen them. Muzzle flashes illuminated the walls, mine and theirs. I carried seven rounds in the magazine and one in the chamber, and I put eight shots in the air in less than three seconds. The first shooter, exposed by the stairs, made a silhouette at point-blank range. He crumpled. The second squared in the space beyond, and in the flurry he had the advantage, but he scattered his shots and mine went slightly high and blew off the top of his skull. He hit the water and blood haloed his mauled crown.

Vomit surged in my throat. Legs trembling, I leaned against the wall. Reloaded the .45. My face was a collage of hot and cold spots. Adrenaline shock. I didn't see Kim Thi. Was she buried in the trash and not coming out? The shock drained the strength out of my legs, and if not for the wall, I wouldn't have been able to stand. I hadn't frozen, I told myself, I'd performed as I'd been trained, but no training could prepare me for that much go-juice in my system. Forcing myself to breathe, concentrating on the cathartic air in my mouth, I clawed for equilibrium. Move and breathe. I balanced in the water and studied the bodies. In the ambience from the light pole, I distinguished the dark skin and round eyes of Montagnards.

Until recently, Montagnards hadn't been part of Saigon's refugee scene. They were a tribal people who dwelled in the Central Highlands in their thatch villages, their culture so primitive that it approximated the stone age. Isolated geographically, eschewed by the South Vietnamese, they'd been courted by the Viet Cong, French, and Americans. A number of the tribes had found their way to the anti-communist struggle thanks to the intrepid efforts of U.S. Special Forces teams. The Montagnards had become loyal allies to the Americans. But taking sides had proved costly; local dwellings had to be abandoned, the populations conglomerated for security. Farmers were able to reach their tracts only in daylight and after trudging kilometers alongside armed escorts. Inevitably, some had fled the mountains and moved to the cities, where they found themselves adrift in economic and social currents beyond their comprehension. These two had become gunmen, probably on someone's payroll.

The scooter kid lay face down. His hair spread like a black water lily alongside the bobbing fedora. Maybe one of my rounds had got him, or one of theirs. It didn't matter. A parvenu of the gangster world, he'd earned his Bogart hat.

From the refugee camp, the crackle of fireworks, string after string going off. I glanced at my watch. Midnight. Maybe it was a holiday. Or the refugees were celebrating having survived through another day.

I found no trace of Kim Thi in the trash pile. She'd made it out alive. The women in the apartment upstairs might know where she'd gone. Trong could ask them, later.

Now was for other business.

Day 8

When I picked up the kid, silty water and blood poured off him in a cataract. I hoped the Saigon police would take their typical time reacting to the gunfire—they were unpredictable, and I couldn't count on my MP credentials to mollify them, not until Trong could be summoned. At the scooter, I dug the key from the kid's pocket, opened the padlock, straddled the seat, and draped him across my knees. I hadn't driven one of these, and saw-horsing a dead person wasn't the ideal way to start. Slowly I wobbled, buttressing the unbalanced bike with my feet. Twice I fell, and I had to remount the bike and rework the kid back on.

Curfew time. The clubs off Nguyen Cong Tru were emptying when I walked into *Quartier Latin* with the kid cradled in my arms. Blood and slime made me an apparition. Two nicely dressed Europeans in the doorway leapt aside, their faces shocked—the grim reaper hadn't been featured here tonight, n'est-ce pas? On the stage, the dancer was grinding out her last gyrations. I kept expecting somebody to confront me, but the help was busy cleaning the tables or counting their profits. A handful of customers lingered, late-stayers unaware of me as I threaded past, until I laid the kid's body on the hardboards by the dancer's feet. Glancing down, she tapped a few steps backward and screeched.

The music broke; the phonograph arm skittered. The spotlight beams jumped around, and in their chaotic effulgence I had about a second's warning of somebody stepping toward me. A head cut the beam. I recognized Danh, who cawed, "Bobby John, what you do?" Striding within range, he threw his left foot in an arc meant to crash into my head. I ducked and the foot swished over. In the instant it took him to regain his balance, I chopped my hand against his collarbone. It snapped like a rice cracker, and he staggered, bouncing off one table, then another.

Heads swam in the beam. Opening my billfold, I thrust my military-police credentials in the air, the plastic cover glinting. It stopped them, at least for a minute. The light caught the chartreuse stripes of a shirt. Everybody froze, their faces white in the glare. My arm was getting tired from holding up the creds, it smacked of absurdity, still I guessed the Statue-of-Liberty pose was the only thing keeping them from rushing me. Then the sandy-haired man waved his hand, and the tension subsided. I let my arm fall.

"What do you have to say?" he asked.

"I thought I'd bring back your boy. He didn't make it through the ambush outside Kim Thi's building. Two more are still in the water. Or maybe they're in the bed of a police pickup by now."

He edged over to the stage, placed his hand lightly on the boy's hair. No display of grief, just the resignation of experience. "Who are you, exactly?"

"Major George Tanner, U.S. Army military police."

"I'm André Nogaret." He motioned to Danh, who, cradling his arm, eclipsed into the shadows with the other employees. "I had nothing to do with your unfortunate incident, Tanner. Follow me, before you embarrass yourself further."

Aware of how easily they might have clobbered me if they'd wanted to, I stepped out of the radiance. In French, André ordered them to right the overturned tables. He said his apologies to the customers, the few who'd not already fled. Then he ushered me to a chair. His gaze was disdainful. "The boy has a family. What shall I tell them?"

"He was an apprentice in the wrong business."

"You seem to think he had choices."

I recalled the last look on the kid's face. André was right. The kid hadn't been offered a choice, by me or anyone else.

I said, "I saw your wife the other day."

His eyes flared. "You are a virtuoso of surprises."

"I spoke to her on business, the reason I'm here now." I told him about the investigation, showed him the soggy marquee photo of Kim Thi, explained how it had been hidden in the unknown's M16. Then I handed him the morgue photo. He leaned back, the photo on his chest, and studied it briefly before he tossed it on the table.

He said, "So you believe Kim Thi will recognize him?"

"That's why I went to see her."

Danh appeared. Still cradling his arm, looking a bit piqued, he leaned over and whispered to André, who scanned the club through the lingering cigarette smoke. He said, "Someone is here for you, Tanner."

Across the club I spotted Giang. He stood among the tables like a scarecrow. The employees stayed well away from him—they must have interpreted his desolation and wanted none of it. André seemed intrigued. He pushed back his chair to observe, and when he spoke, his tone was civil. "We can talk again tomorrow. For now, you and your spectral friend should leave."

* * *

Giang led me to an intersection along Nguyen Cong Tru. A Sony billboard streaked the wet pavement red and white, and the neon bled to a dented Fiat parked carelessly away from the curb. Against the door leaned Trong. "A bulletin said that an American had kidnapped a woman and killed two men. When I saw it, I thought I should come looking for you."

"They tried to shoot me."

"You were supposed to be discreet."

"The shooters didn't know that."

He folded his arms and regarded the reflections on the damp pavement. "What a mess you have made. There will be consequences. Enemies." New tones were slipping into my friend's voice, new tones for new enemies. Yet André Nogaret was not among them. I couldn't have explained to Trong, or even to myself, how I knew that.

I said, "Kim Thi ran off. I need to find her."

The detective frowned. My chits with him were not so many.

"What a mess you have made," he repeated.

He dropped me off near the Kinh Ben Nghe canal two blocks from Tuy's place. The pall of cooking smoke had dissipated, and the canal mirrored the city lights. A gunfight replays itself in jolts to the nervous system, and I treaded unsteadily over the paving stones I'd walked many times. Facing her building, I noticed that her apartment's single window was unlit. I took the two switchbacks of stairs, slid in the key. The door was pulled open before I could turn it. Air scented with jasmine puffed against my face.

More than a year and a half ago, when I returned to Saigon and found Tuy, she'd been standing in front of the airline office where she gave language lessons. In the sun, her hair had shimmered, the ends had twirled as she whipped her head. Rapid movements were her nature, no matter in which act she was engaged. She'd stared at me openly. She was like a magic picture card whose image changed in the angle of view. One angle was profoundly native, from a Buddhist family that traced back a thousand years, a woman in whom the Vietnamese culture was alive. The other flashed the descendent of a French Catholic from two generations ago, far enough so that the manifestations should have washed thin in her blood, yet the directness of her gaze and the variegated shading of her hair portrayed no woman of pure Vietnamese heritage. She spoke French and English flawlessly. Was drawn to western ideas. Had chosen me as a lover.

Tonight in the doorway she wore one of my t-shirts. Its hem reached her upper thighs. She must have awakened from a slumber; temporary lines and swellings surrounded her eyes that embraced me calmly, though I was covered with blood and dirt and the stink of the garbage I'd rolled in.

"Come in," she said. "Take a bath."

Sleep had tangled her hair, and she brushed it while I squatted in the bathtub. The first filling had purged the night's tangible and mental filth. In the second, I soaked restfully. She brought me a Scotch, hooked her thigh on the tub's edge, and tapped her cigarette into an ashtray on the pile of newspapers. The brushing and the drink were bridges to intimacy; her cigarette smoke blended into the steam. Yet hauteur traced in the way she moved, and I knew that it angered her to see me return home in this condition.

The jolts came less frequently now. Between them I succumbed to exhaustion. I tried to think, and it was like trying to focus candlelight through a magnifying glass. Then the adrenalin bit and I was talking. "I met André, Simone's husband, tonight."

"Is he like her?"

She meant elitist. I shook my head. "He's a former soldier. Owns a club downtown. Seems to be in his element there."

"So you have a new contact."

"I don't think so. I walked into his club carrying a dead body and dumped it on the stage. Then I broke the collar bone of one of his employees and pulled out my police ID."

"The French are not fond of Americanisms."

"There may be repercussions. I could be sent away."

She nodded at what must have seemed a reasonable sequence of events.

"We need to speak," I said.

She stubbed out her cigarette. "We can talk later." She was finished with her hair; it smoothed darkly along the sides of her neck. In the steam she pulled off the shirt, slipped into the tub, and settled on me.

* * *

In the morning, it surprised me to find Trong waiting outside. He leaned against the Fiat sedan, the same pose as last night. "Let us walk," he said. He adopted a slow gait toward the Kinh Ben Nghe. The French had called it the Arroyo Chinois, and in their time it had been a busy conduit for rice from the Mekong Delta. A small European cemetery came into view ahead of us. He held my hand in the customary way, and I was reminded of the conversation with my father after Vaughn Tanner's funeral.

"Your gunmen last night were Montagnards. No way to trace such people. We may never know their identities." He said it offhandedly. People died, nobody knew who they were, just more victims, an aspect of the city and the times. But he'd not stopped by this morning to tell me about the Montagnards. He was my friend, no less correct in his ways, and we walked quietly for a minute until he had formulated his words. "There is trouble, as I feared. It arrived even sooner than I expected. You should have come to me after the shooting, not gone back to the club."

"What happened?"

"General Huang contacted my superiors. He phoned personally, so nobody could mistake his seriousness. They do not like Huang, but he is too powerful to ignore. He demanded to know why an American officer was shooting people in Saigon last night. And he has your name. Who did you give it to? Nogaret?"

"Yes."

"Unwise. Nogaret must have communicated with Huang, his ally. And my friendship with you is known. So they have turned on me."

No point reminding him that the shooting had been in self defense, or that I'd come within a centimeter of taking a bullet in the face. Or that bringing the dead kid to the club had been an act of courtesy. None of it mattered to the corrupt interests that backed the nightclubs.

"The people in the building told the police that you kidnapped Kim Thi. Nonsense, of course. Huang repeats it only to justify his involvement. An American officer kidnaps a girl, it becomes the business of the Army. Huang has put out orders to find her."

"Why does he care about the girl?"

"I don't know."

I remembered how the two shooters had materialized when Kim Thi and I had reached the outer stairs. If they'd wanted to kill me, they'd had opportunities to do so before I entered the building. Was it possible *she* was the target? Why would anyone want to kill a club dancer?

A block from the Kinh Ben Nghe, we reached the European cemetery that occupied a discreet mound behind a wrought iron fence. Set in crumbling cement, the bars spiked to tips in the shape of teardrops, while on the other side, the gravestones lined the low promontory like crooked teeth. Names embossed the surfaces alongside bullet scars from a forgotten gun battle. Trong noticed the bullet pocks too, and he stopped as if to survey the scene of a crime. It was a warm, sticky morning, but from the sight of him, hands tucked in the side pockets of his work shirt, he might have been on the chilly streets of a northern city. "I was ordered to halt my involvement in this affair. I must obey."

"I can't find Kim Thi without you."

"Giang will continue to seek her in his discreet way, among people who do not otherwise talk to the police. But he must not approach the club or question the employees. He will not be able to learn who sponsored the two Montagnards, or search openly for the dancer."

"I'm grateful anyway."

He shook his head. "His chances to find her are poor. Now that Huang is interested, his people probably will get to her first. When they do, they will deliver her to him."

"And then?"

"What he wants from her, he will take."

* * *

On my desk I found two messages. The first was from Hollis at the Bien Hoa PBO—*please call.* The other was to phone Colonel Crowley immediately. I did. "Stay put at your office," he said. "I'll be there soon."

After a few hours at the French Fort, you no longer noticed the rice-paddy smell outside. The same held in reverse; an absence restored the odor viscerally, and when I sat down to type my report, I might as well have climbed into a dung barrel. Whether it was the unpleasantness or the latent tremors at being shot at last night, I had trouble rendering my impressions on paper—of Kim Thi, the shooting, André Nogaret. They seemed borne in murky runoff.

I left out mention of Simone Nogaret.

Crowley arrived at ten. His face wrinkled when he smelled the paddy fumes, reminders of the country he despised. No doubt he wanted to turn around and flee. I didn't wish to think about his submissiveness to Vangleman. It shouldn't have surprised me—most men buckled when confronted with a power greater than they could handle. But I'd expected better from him.

I pushed the typed report across the desk. Dropping into one of the metal chairs, he read it slowly, making me think that my prose must run as syrupy as my thinking. When he looked up, he said, "Vangleman phoned this morning. He said that General Huang of the Capital Military District has made a complaint about you. They say you killed two men in a gun battle. They also say you kidnapped the woman Kim Thi."

"What about the third victim, the scooter driver? What about the commotion at the *Quartier Latin*?" I'd mentioned both in my report.

His dipped brows could have plowed up the dung garden. "No, nothing about that."

"But the complaint contained my name?"

"In full. Major George Tanner."

If, as Trong suspected, André had given up my name, why hadn't he mentioned the dead scooter kid? Or the bedlam I'd caused at his club? Why throw around a false accusation and leave out true ones?

Crowley tucked my report into the manila folder he carried. "Vangleman said that General Cobris is irritated as hell. He wanted this to be fast-tracked, but thanks to you, the South Vietnamese Army is involved."

"How else was I to learn the identity, but to have a go at the club?"

Crowley didn't answer.

I said, "So Cobris will close the case?"

"Not yet. He doesn't want to look like he's backing down in the face of a complaint from General Huang, a notoriously corrupt figure. And Cobris knows you didn't kidnap anyone."

"That's reassuring."

He didn't pick up the sarcasm. "You still haven't done what he asked—to certify that the unknown wasn't an American."

"I still don't have the facts."

I must have sounded irrational; he stared at me in apparent disbelief.

I said, "My PBO contact may have traced the origins of the radio. I'll drive to Bien Hoa to see him. Unless Kim Thi shows up, that's all I can do."

*   *   *

In the clammy PBO trailer, the air conditioner huffed, a fluorescent bulb flickered, Hollis's balding pate glistened. Hollis and Lopez had organized stacks of paper-clipped records. Rising above them like an exhibit at a science fair, the PRC25 radio. "With the serial number eradicated, it's impossible to be certain. Our starting lead was the manufacturer's code stamped inside the casing. We got lucky—the series arrived in country in one shipment in May of 1968, with sequential serial numbers. The radios were distributed between two American units: the 1st Cav and the 9th Infantry Division. If the PRCs had gone to the South Vietnamese, we'd have been dealing with an insurmountable problem." He'd attached the antenna to the radio; he must have replaced the batteries too, for when he clicked the *on* dial, it crackled immediately. Absently he spun the frequency knob, as if he expected his favorite country crooner's voice to emerge.

"Here's where Sergeant Lopez earned the fresh coffee I brewed for him. He went through two years of property records. Patient fellow, Lopez, he keeps his attention. Of the May '68 shipment, he found twenty-three crossed off the books, all missing in action or damaged beyond repair." Enthusiasm lit Hollis's expression, and I guessed it was the rare occasion for the warrant officer to flip back the shroud of anonymity and show off his competence. "Next we turned to two sets of documents, the Found Property Register and the repair slips. As I mentioned, units are notoriously spotty about reporting stuff they find, no surprise that none of the twenty-three serial numbers surfaced in the register. So we went through the repair slips." He tapped a pile of pink carbon copies. "A radio handed in for repair can go to a number of facilities, including to the States for depot-level work. Here in 'Nam, we keep radio repair records for a year. So we're talking long shots. We examined over two thousand pink maintenance copies. Sergeant Lopez culled through them until he hated the color pink. All for this. A single hit."

He held out the top sheet as if it were a high-denomination bill rather than a ruffled square of onion skin overprinted with numbered spaces. "The 151st Maintenance Battalion at Long Binh prepared this form in

March of this year for the repair of a PRC25. Read the entry in block seven."

"Serial number 117134."

"Turns out it's one of our twenty-three expunged radios from '68."

"The radio I found didn't have a serial number."

"Correct. So how do we know it's the same one? Read the entry in block ten."

"Repair certification 03/30/70. A.J.."

"The repair techs initial their work." Hollis plucked the radio off the table by its corner handle, turned it sideways, pulled off the battery cover, and pointed to a slender paper sticker on the radio's inside lip. "The rubber seal keeps this surface from the weather, otherwise the sticker would have worn off while it sat next to your tributary."

The sticker read 'Inspected 03/30/70. A.J..'

Hollis smiled like a geometry teacher who'd explained a theorem to a puzzled student. "There were two unusual things about this repair. One, it was a high-priority request. This is a common tactical radio—there are lots of them around. Why the urgency? Of course, some people want everything in a hurry." He stared at me.

"What was the other thing?"

"Look at the remarks section."

"'Turned in without a battery cover,'" I read.

"*Without* a battery cover. When you consider that this one's had been converted for D-cells, the reason becomes obvious. The modified cover would have signaled that it was found property, and the repair facility would have notified PBO—they do so at our standing request. Nobody ever reported the recovery of this radio. As far as the property records go, it's still missing."

"So when they repaired it in March, it had a serial number?"

"Yes. Somebody chipped it off afterward. Incomprehensible, unless you're trying to disguise where it came from."

"Who sent the radio in for repair?"

"The 29th Aviation Company at Tan Son Nhut. I thought of phoning them to ask about it, then I figured you'd want to do that, maybe pay a visit. The unit is located at Building 2451 at the airfield. The company commander is Major Jason Stobe."

The name chimed in my memory. I recalled the jolly helicopter pilot who'd chauffeured me to Vung Tau.

Major Stobe. General Cobris's personal flyboy.

* * *

A knife's edge of somber clouds slashed overhead. I thought I might beat the rain—the jeep I'd drawn this morning ran well—but motoring toward the gate, I nosed up behind a stopped convoy of U.S. Air Force flatbeds. The road was too narrow to pass, and I idled in the diesel-laced air while the MPs directed traffic and big raindrops began to avalanche.

The truck beds sagged under loads of wooden crates in two sizes. The wind whipped the tarps, and I could read the stenciling. The larger crates were MK-82 500-pound aerial bombs, the smaller were kits that fitted the bombs with flip-out fins to slow their descent, so the low-flying planes that dropped them could get away.

I recalled recent news reports, denied by Washington, that the United States had been bombing NVA bases inside Cambodia. Two daggers of Cambodian territory—nicknamed the *Fishhook* and the *Parrot's Beak*—stabbed into South Vietnam north and northwest of Saigon. From these and other Cambodian sanctuaries, the NVA fed men and war materials to their units in the highlands, War Zone C, and the Mekong Delta. International law forbade breaching the border of a so-called neutral state, so U.S. and ARVN forces stood by while the NVA thumbed their noses at us from across the frontier. Cobris had told me that MACV suspected that the enemy was stockpiling supplies for a new offensive, another Tet. A disturbing prediction. I pictured the people picking through the embers of their homes, the dead woman in the white ao dai.

Then I remembered that the news reports had said *B-52s* had been bombing the Cambodia sanctuaries. They flew so high you couldn't hear them from the ground. Their bombs didn't need drag fins. Plus, they weren't based in Vietnam—they came from Guam, hours away by air.

The ordnance on the trucks was for a different kind of warplane—those that flew low in support of infantry.

The MPs signaled for me to pass the bomb trucks. The convoy stretched longer than I'd thought, half a kilometer of identical loads of MK-82s and drag-fin kits.

When the Vietnamese wanted to discern the future, they looked for signs.

The trucks were a sign.

* * *

If the 29th Aviation Company kept paperwork on the radio, one swipe of a hand could make it disappear. I figured the less warning I gave them, the better. I parked a street over from the headquarters. A jeep makes its own stage entrance, a man on foot is hardly noticed.

Supply rooms usually roosted in the rear of a unit's headquarters, and I strolled around the cinder-block building next to an aircraft hangar and entered through an open set of double doors. Signs conveniently labeled the tall wire cages: WEAPONS, SPARE PARTS; LAUNDRY TURN IN. I found the supply office in a corner festooned with nylon airlift slings and gas masks in their canvas holders. Over a file box hunched a gangly sergeant, his arms entirely scrimshawed in tattoos. He must have heard the cage door creak when I walked in, for his head swiveled and he slowly regained his height over the box, his mouth forming a buck-toothed grin. Spivey, his name tag read.

"Looking for something, sir?"

"I'm Major Tanner, Military Police. I need to ask you a few questions." I hadn't thought about how I'd present myself, friendly or officious. A look at Spivey decided it. The lavishness of military supplies had made South Vietnam a candy store for profiteers, and nothing rattled them more than somebody like me pitching up on their doorstep. Not long ago, I'd investigated a supply sergeant who, claiming to be the victim of theft by a local-hire Vietnamese mechanic, had asked his commander for permission to mount a 'recovery operation' at the mechanic's house downtown. As if raiding Vietnamese homes fell within his authority, the officer had approved. The sergeant and a truckload of armed soldiers had stormed the residence and retrieved fifty vehicle tires. The incident might have been forgotten, just another episode at the convergence of power and stupidity, but it had played out in the full view of the Vietnamese neighbors. Enraged, they blocked the street, threw rocks, and broke the truck's windows. A riot ensued, and the Vietnamese police became involved. With Trong's help, I gathered evidence that the sergeant had been black-marketing tires through the mechanic. When the scheme had failed to net the anticipated cash, the sergeant had hatched the raid to recoup his merchandise. The Army ultimately court-martialed him and relieved his commander, who wasn't corrupt, merely an idiot.

"I want to see this item," I said.

Spivey peered at the pink repair slip I'd borrowed from Hollis, and which I held up, not letting him touch. He flashed coffee-stained incisors, making me think that if I grabbed his arm to keep him from escaping, he'd promptly chew it off. His first worry would have been that I'd traced government property he'd traded or sold, and he seemed to relax when he saw that it was a radio. Apparently he didn't traffic in those. If he'd had any presence of mind, he would have summoned an officer from his chain of command. Instead he was in motion, checking the serial numbers of the radios on the metal racks. "We don't have many of these, sir, they're not a helicopter mount, more for admin use. Hmm. It's not on the shelf. Let's see where it went to."

He moved nervously through the dangling nylon slings that licked his bald pate like the tongues of snakes, returned to the wooden box, and flipped to a layer of yellow slips. "Let me check my hand receipts." At the end of the intricate tattoos, his fingers diddled through the copies, stopped on one, read it, then flashed past it quickly. Too quickly. I was leaning close to afford him no chance to palm a document. When his eyes darted up, I caught their panic. "Well, sir, maybe you should talk to the XO or the First Sergeant." He pointed at a soldier passing by outside the cage. "Hey, Janowicz, go ask Top to come back here."

I reached over and lifted out the slip he'd scrolled past.

"Sir, wait a minute..."

But I already had the paper, a temporary hand receipt whose upper right corner, in hand-printed text, read radio, PRC25, serial number 117134. Across the bottom ran a signature, Jason Stobe, and a date, 27 March 1970. Three weeks before the unknown died.

I asked, "What did Major Stobe do with this radio?"

He stared glassy eyed, and without looking he closed the wooded box. Maybe it harbored a hand receipt that would trace to M16 rifle serial number 537629. I considered whether I should seize the whole box as evidence. But then the cage door creaked, and I knew my brief rampage at the 29th Aviation Company had run its course.

In the doorway posed the First Sergeant. Tall, black, present and distant at the same time, intrinsically menacing, he sported a massive forehead that cragged like a portable Mount Rushmore. He took in Spivey's stricken face, then mine, and immediately comprehended what had happened. "That's a company record, sir. Why don't you hand it back to Sergeant Spivey, and we'll go to my office and straighten out whatever problem you have."

I folded the hand receipt into a neat square and tucked it into my shirt pocket.

"You can't be taking our paperwork, sir."

"Can't I?"

The First Sergeant watched as I buttoned the pocket below the embroidered jump wings and the Combat Infantryman's Badge. His stare narrowed, and I sensed the cyclone of his fury whirling at this intruder who dared to confiscate his unit's records. Then his eyes roved to the MP insignia and major's rank on my collar, and the cyclone blunted itself against the impenetrable edifice of the military structure.

"Sir, I believe you should have a word with the company commander."

"Lead the way."

I'd only seen Stobe in his pilot's seat. Absent the cocooning aircraft, he was as tall as the first sergeant, with a linebacker's torso. A millimeter of hair coated the cube of his scalp on which the discoloration of birthmarks seeped through like the grease stains on a bag of fried egg rolls. His lips had trouble wrapping the big teeth he exposed in a genuine smile. "Nice to see ya again, Major. Come on in." His powerful voice was the kind meant to whoop at cheerleaders from the football team's bench. He loped over from his desk and closed his office door. "I take it you've done scared our supply sergeant half to death. Those supply boys don't take well to the military police."

"He can rest easy. He's not who I'm after."

Stobe settled his elbows on the desk and regarded me calmly. Many people I could intimidate; he wasn't one of them. He said, "My First Sergeant tells me you pocketed one of our hand receipts. Mind if I have a look?"

"I'm taking custody of it. Potential evidence."

"Kinda serious about this, aren't you?"

"On 27 March, you signed out a radio, a PRC25, from your supply room. You then turned it in for repair, which was completed on 30 March. Could you tell me what you did with the radio after that?"

Stobe folded his hands on his lap and tweaked up the edges of his mouth. I might have just asked him about his miniature golf score.

I fished the photograph of the dead walker out of my folder and handed it across. "Know him?"

"Can't say I do."

"He was killed twelve days ago in Tay Ninh Province. He's still unidentified. But he left something behind—a PRC25 radio on a river bank. The same radio that had been in your possession. You must know how it got from your hands into his."

"Plainly you're a smart fellow, Tanner, but you can in no way prove that statement."

"Before you gave it to him, you chipped off the serial number plate. You intended to render it untraceable. Why was that?"

"Why don't you slow down for a minute and think through what you're sayin' and who you're sayin' it to. Reflect on the implications, like whose purpose your actions serve. Didn't I drop you off with General Cobris the other night? Aren't you working for him, same as I do?"

"You're telling me Cobris is behind this?"

"I didn't say any such thing. Just asked who you were working for."

"I work for the Army."

Stobe laughed. "Seems to me you're too seasoned a fellow to be playing the zealot. But maybe I misread you." He stood up, as imperturbable as ever. "I hate to be impolite, but I have flight operations to attend." He ushered me to the orderly room, where stood Spivey, his face ashen, evidently in anticipation of a session with his commanding officer.

"This way, sir." The First Sergeant didn't like me afoot in his company area, and he led me to the rain-doused parking lot. On him, everything was oversized, from the Rushmore head to the baseball-mitt hands he planted on his hips, to the barge-scale jump boots on whose mirror-polished tips the rain beaded. He leaned uncomfortably close. "Major, I wish you a fine day. If you ever come back here, which I sincerely hope you don't, please make an appointment and do your business through the chain of command. That's how the Army is supposed to work." Waving a disparaging salute, he went inside, thumping the door shut behind him.

The rain had pooled on the jeep seat, and I squeegeed it off with the edge of my hand, tugged the poncho over my head. Turning the ignition felt satisfying, the jeep's choppy energy balancing my own. I recalled a story Tuy had told me, about how rats had gnawed a hole in a farmer's rice bin, and nobody noticed because the hole was low in the shadows, and the rice disappeared in such tiny increments that the surface barely sagged. One day the farmer's wife went to fetch rice, and it collapsed under her scoop to the bottom. A metaphor about corruption, so endemic in South Vietnam that it was both a root cause and an effect of the war.

Nothing quite tests the character of a man as when he gets what he wants. After the general's pressuring lecture the other night, I'd wanted so much to defy the bastard. Now I knew that Cobris was disingenuous in a way I could neither prove nor define, but the certainty chugged like the jeep's engine.

I was halfway to the French Fort before I realized that it didn't matter.

* * *

Two hours after my tête-à-tête with Stobe, Crowley summoned me to his office at MACV Headquarters. When I entered, I sensed that my relationship with him had changed; I read it like the red shift in celestial light that indicates a body receding at great velocity.

He said, "I received another complaint about you. Perhaps you heard."

"I can guess."

He leaned into the corner of his chair, away from me. I might have tracked in the dung from the French Fort. "Vangleman says that you accused the Commander of 29th Aviation, Major Stobe, of giving a radio to the Tay Ninh unknown. Please tell me you're not that big a fool."

"The radio had a document trail that led to Stobe's supply room." I started to describe how the PBO had traced the radio.

He swished his hand as if to shoo away a fly. "Some things just aren't *done*. You don't confront the general's pilot. Didn't I tell you that Cobris was backing you up against accusations of kidnapping? And you did *this?*"

"Sir, you've got to go around Cobris."

Crowley again adopted his stare of disbelief. Normally he reported to the MACV Provost Marshal, but in that officer's temporary absence, Crowley himself occupied the role. Above him were the deputy MACV commander and Commanding General Creighton Abrams. A case this volatile, involving one of MACV's senior officers, should go directly to Abrams.

I said so to Crowley.

"Not without substantiation," he replied.

"Sir, whoever the unknown was, whatever he was doing, Cobris was aware. Stobe as much as admitted it. Cobris has intruded on the investigation from the beginning, to keep anyone from finding out what's going on. He moved Second Brigade out of Tay Ninh Province to get Larsen out of the way."

"That's absurd. An accusation like that could get you relieved."

"Only if it's not true."

"Wrong. What counts is whether you can prove it. Can you?"

"No."

"Can you tell me Cobris's presumptive motives for any of this?"

"I don't know."

Crowley's laugh was full of pathos, for me and for himself. "You want me to approach General Abrams with a case you've pulled out of your ass?"

"If I can see the connections, Abrams will see them."

"Your job was to learn a man's identity. Instead you caused *incidents.*"

"Sir, if you won't go see Abrams, I'd like to."

"Out of the question." Crowley swiveled his chair toward the window and steepled his fingers. I'd lost him. More accurately, he hadn't been there from the beginning. "You were supposed to conduct a professional investigation. You were given latitude. What you did was to act irresponsibly and beyond the scope of your authority."

I wondered how much of his lecture replayed what he must have heard from Vangleman. I said, "Please think about it, sir. I have no reason to invent any of this."

"Stop talking. I'm very close to relieving you myself, and I may have to." Past the chair, all I could see of him were the steepled fingers. "Just get out."

* * *

I had to talk to Tuy. My time was almost eclipsed; orders might be waiting as early as tonight giving me 24 hours to be on an outbound plane. There were no more days I could squeeze, nobody I could appeal to. Crowley would be as eager as Cobris to be rid of me. I was an embarrassment, an officer in whom they'd lost confidence, one they had to make excuses for.

They were right. A soldier does not have the luxury of cutting his own way. Even authentic leaders like Larsen and Ulrich did what they were told. Though they might recognize the folly of some of their orders, they never lost sight of their place in the military hierarchy. My looseness meant that I'd lingered too long in Saigon, adrift in its post-colonial artifice, the swimmer whose feet never touched the firmament, only water.

Gripping the rails of the scooter cornering the darkening streets, I rehearsed what I'd say to Tuy, and the words fell into place easier than I'd expected. I had to engage her in a way so as not to catalyze her stubbornness. The thought quickened my footsteps across the broken pavement, past the crooked tree and the garbage bin, and I'd reached the base of the enclosed stairs before I saw the man in the hat coming at me. I reached clumsily for the pistol in my leather pouch, wondering why he hadn't yet opened fire.

"Don't shoot, it's only me," said Giang.

"Christ, you scared the shit out of me."

"Come. We go see Trong." Taking my hand, he led me toward a car at the end of the street. "We must hurry. There is danger."

"What danger?"

"We found Kim Thi."

* * *

The prefecture loomed behind floodlights that blinded a crowd of protesters. They blocked the entranceway, and signs pumped up and down from the lake of black hair. Unintimidated, Giang pushed through. Once inside, straightening my uniform, I asked, "What was that all about?"

"No pay."

"You mean those are *cops*?"

"More than normal this time."

"Isn't it a bad idea, to let cops go unpaid?"

"We have plenty bad idea."

We descended a flight of steps into the clammy spaces beneath the building, veered at the bottom into a dank passageway whose floor must stay perpetually wet from the poor drainage. Following masonry walls, their mold sketching camouflage patterns, we approached a trapezoid of light from the open door of a decrepit detention cell, an artifact of the French era, now serving as a storeroom. Within, Trong leaned against a crate. He said, "Today Kim Thi went to a police station. Luckily, the commander is a friend of mine. He called me, and I brought her here."

"Where is she?"

He flicked his head toward the corridor. She must be in one of the other cells.

I assumed we were meeting in this dungeon because it was the least likely place for him to be seen with me. Then I thought of another reason. "You think Huang will try to grab her?"

"Worse. A contract is out on her."

"A contract?"

"To kill her. It is known on the street." He said it as if everyone but me were already aware.

"Who?"

"Maybe André Nogaret. Or General Huang."

I said, "If it's Andre, maybe I can get him to call it off."

The facial muscles he made a habit of keeping placid twitched too fast to read. They steadied to his rare just-fucking-listen look. He said, "A contract is a powerful thing. Expensive. Complicated. It takes 48 hours to set up. Once started, it is almost impossible to stop."

"She's a club dancer. Why would someone pay to kill her?"

"Why is not important. She has been here too long already. You must take her to an American base. Nowhere else will she be safe." He'd never asked for anything in return for all the favors he'd done for me. Now he wanted Kim Thi off his hands. He wasn't a farmer who could quit the police and go back to his land. A man of integrity, he survived at the whim of a corrupt bureaucracy he couldn't afford to ignore.

"All right. I need time to arrange it." I thought of the bridges I'd set ablaze this very day. Could I rebuild them? "While I'm doing that, she'll have to stay at Tuy's."

His eyebrows peaked. He opened his mouth as if to warn that this was unwise, then stopped, realizing it was the only choice either of us had.

He left to get Kim Thi.

* * *

She stood behind the prefecture, in an alley below sooty buildings fettered in clotheslines. The twenty-four hours since I'd seen her had blemished her formerly serene face. Swellings rimmed her eyes, her lips bulged where she'd bitten them, and a bruise smirched her forehead. Her wrinkled and stained ao dai made her look like a pauper. From far enough away that they wouldn't provoke the police, real paupers watched.

Trong spoke to her in the voice he reserved for his children, soft but insistent. I caught fragments and gathered he was trying to convince her she'd be safer with me than on her own in the city. Considering that the last time she'd been in my escort, she'd been shot at and forced to leap through a broken rail into a garbage mound, it must have been a hard sell. Somehow it worked, for she let herself be ushered into the dented Fiat's back seat. I climbed in alongside, and Giang started the engine, his fingers like bird talons around the steering wheel. Trong remained at the prefecture. On his controlled mien, he forced a smile.

The way Giang leaned forward and squinted, I doubted he could see far past the hood. By hazard or design, he took an indirect route, swerving near the nocturnal canal whose surface glinted picturesquely, the window reflections shimmering on the water. The rain had stopped and the roofs glistened. The clarity was rare. Most of the time, the traffic fumes and smoke from the cooking grills melded the cityscape into a fuscous smear.

The tiny back seat jammed me against Kim Thi. Leg to leg, arm to arm, I could feel her body tense each time the Fiat creaked. She regarded our driver, an escapee from a tomb. When the car rattled around a corner, the bumpers scraped the pavement, and her eyes widened in terror. They reflected me darkly, and I wondered what I looked like to her, if not an ominous figure with a foreign voice. When I spoke, I tried to modulate it, which was like trying to keep a phonograph needle steady on a bronco ride.

"It's all right," I said. "I know where he's going."

"Okay." She sounded anything but comforted.

"Can you tell me who he was, your friend?"

"Who he was," she echoed, as if I'd reminded her of the tragedy she'd managed to put out of her mind. She accepted the cigarette I offered, and I cupped my hands around the Zippo flame as best I could in the jerky ride. "Gerard Penelon," she said, and in doing so she pronounced him dead and released the coiled tension. She leaned into me, and her breath came like the puff of a sleeper. She lifted her ao dai's hem to blot her tears, revealing the pantaloons and her sleek dancer's legs pressed together.

"Gerard was French?" A guess.

"Yes. My fiancé."

"You said you were waiting for him. Where was that?"

"We always meet at the cathedral square."

She meant the square at Saigon's Notre Dame Cathedral. In 1964, the South Vietnamese government had renamed the plaza in honor of the late President Kennedy. Americans called it JFK Square.

"When?"

"For three days I go there to wait. Thursday I stay home, until you come. I afraid he crash his helicopter." She said it offhandedly, as if I already knew about the helicopter. I thought about the woods east of Hill 71. Colonel Larsen's men had searched the area. Not thoroughly enough.

"Where did he fly his helicopter?"

"Across the border."

"Cambodia?"

She nodded.

"You both worked for André Nogaret. Is that right?"

She glared at me in a way I couldn't interpret.

"Do you know who sent the gunmen last night?"

No answer. Having leaned against me, she now sat upright, her guardedness returned, triggered by the utterance of a name.

Nogaret.

Giang rounded a familiar corner, and we squeaked to a halt outside Tuy's apartment. Over the canal, fresh rain clouds migrated toward Saigon, darkening the street and leaving the dancer almost invisible scurrying from the car to the enclosed stairwell. When I left to follow, Giang caught my arm.

"They have threatened Trong! Huang's people."

"How?"

"A phone call. For his safety, he must stay out of this."

I tried to step toward the stairwell. Giang still clung. "The girl is *yours* now, understand?"

"Yes."

In her typical way, while I was fumbling with my key, Tuy opened the door and immediately turned back inside. She dropped to sit on the straw mattress, her back against the wall. On the floor around her spread newspapers in the familiar fan pattern.

"We have a guest," I said.

She looked up, from me to Kim Thi. First she noticed her attractiveness, which must have disconcerted her, this woman arriving in my presence. Then she saw her dishevelment, weariness, and fear. Tuy stood, approached, and gently laid her hand on Kim Thi's shoulder.

And so began a night of twitter in Vietnamese, woman to woman, excluding me, forcing me outside to the landing while Kim Thi soaked in the bathtub. Their laughter penetrated the door and rang in the stair shaft where I smoked.

*   *   *

"Are you awake?" I asked softly, so as not to disturb Kim Thi sleeping across the room. Tuy glanced protectively to the blanketed form.

I pushed up and folded into my Buddha. A comfortable silence wrapped us for a minute, until I said, "They'll send me home soon."

"A month ago, you said the same. And the month before that. You are still here."

"This time it's different."

I lit a cigarette and she beckoned for it at once. It flared as she dragged on the filter, her eyes torched red, locked on mine. She'd detected in my tone an urgency I hadn't consciously introduced, telling her to listen closely.

I said, "I want you to go with me to the States."

"And leave my mother?" Her voice was barely audible, and I had the feeling she was thinking too of her father, though long dead, as if the realm of the ancestors were another of Saigon's districts.

"Maybe just for a time."

"A long time," she said.

"Yes."

The light through the window split her face, one side sulfurous, the other amber in the cigarette's glow. The twin hues seemed to project the rift she felt. I thought she might be waiting for me to make a hopeful declaration. Nothing felt certain enough.

"I need time to think," she said.

"There's not much."

She handed back the cigarette and settled on the mat.

Day 9

In the morning, the questioning resumed. Tuy's sisterly kindness had soothed Kim Thi like a balm, and I tried to preserve her mellow state of mind with a compatible tone. To build rapport, I asked about things that mattered to the average Vietnamese: her family and village. Next I gently raised her engagement and wedding plans. Her tears summoned Tuy's comforting arm over her shoulder.

I said, "You mentioned that Gerard flew to Cambodia. Why?"

"I only know what he tell me. I do not know the reason for anything."

"When he went, how long did he stay away?"

"He go two time. First time for a week. Second time same, but he no come back."

"Where did he live?"

"A boarding house by the central market."

"What's the name of the boarding house? Or the street?"

"He no tell me."

I pictured the mishmash of side streets around the high-roofed, crowd-frenzied central market. I'd never find the boarding house without an address.

"Is that where you went, when you were together?"

"We go to..." She said something in Vietnamese.

"The kind of place where they don't ask for names," Tuy translated.

Gerard had hid his relationship with the girl he loved. Why?

"Where did he get the helicopter?"

"I don't know."

"Where did he keep it? Did he mention an airfield? A hangar?"

She said something to Tuy.

"By the seacoast," Tuy translated.

"The seacoast. Was it Cape St. Jacques?" The French name for Vung Tau.

"Yes. The cape. He tell me that."

"The cape is a big area. Did he describe the place where he landed?"

"No."

"Did he mention a villa that faced the ocean?"

A shrug. "He only say the cape."

"Where did he land in Cambodia?"

"He no say."

"Who was he working for?"

Kim Thi cast an imploring glance to Tuy, who said, "She doesn't *know* these things."

"Please relax. The questions are normal, just part of the process. Don't be upset."

Tuy spoke, and Kim Thi gave the slightest bat of her head.

"Did he fly alone, or did others go with him?"

Another exchange between the women. "She doesn't know," Tuy repeated.

"Who was he working for?" She *did* know, I was convinced.

She folded her arms and turned her head away.

"Kim Thi?"

"No more," she said.

*　*　*

I found Tuy's hand and turned it over in mine, studying it like a tropical flower. "Have you thought about what I asked you last night?"

"Yes."

"Will you come with me?"

"I haven't decided." As if preoccupied, she stared toward Kim Thi, who lay across the room, face to the wall.

"Will you decide soon?"

"Yes. What about her?"

"I'm going to try to get her onto a U.S. military base. In the meantime, she has to stay inside. She mustn't go out, the streets are too dangerous for her."

Digesting this, Tuy's face shaded over as I'd not seen before, her eyes flecked with doubts.

I said, "Don't worry. She's safe here as long as nobody knows where she is."

"Who *does* know?"

"Us. Trong. And one of his detectives."

"Too many by my count," she said, softly, so Kim Thi wouldn't hear.

*   *   *

Sited in the same block as its American counterpart, the French Embassy was as much an icon of central Saigon and almost as busy. A notable difference was the absence of military uniforms at the French legation, and mine may have explained why the receptionist responded helpfully to my inquiry. She summoned a young consular officer, Mademoiselle Juliet Devereaux, who led me to a vaulted anteroom off the lobby, to a tired chair whose back might once have been straight, in front of a low table whose many coats of varnish failed to smooth the nicks, and I wondered if, on the undersides of these pieces, property tags showed 1887, the year France had annexed Indochina.

Taller than me, Juliet sported washed-out fawn hair and sunless arms lilting from a short-sleeved linen dress. Her bloodshot, bulgy eyes had seen too much since she'd left the Paris school for diplomats. Across the table corner under the whirling ceiling fan, she seemed to ponder whether to insist that I take my questions through official channels.

"Why are you interested in Mssr. Penelon?" She opened her notebook on her bare knee. In a different dress and style of hair, she would have been striking.

I said, "MACV is seeking civilian pilots to fly helicopters. A local contract. His name came up. I'd like to confirm his status and sponsorship."

"For a military police officer to inquire about a French pilot for hire is a bit unusual, wouldn't you say?"

"Perhaps you can explain to me, Mademoiselle Devereaux, how you decide what is unusual, and what is not."

A smile tweaked the edges of her cracked lips. A lover of irony, this one.

"Wait here," she said.

* * *

The scooter buzzed across the cobblestones, cutting through the narrow mercantile side streets and the wider boulevards. With one hand I clutched my leather pouch so Saigon cowboys wouldn't snatch it away, with the other I gripped the bumper rail. The driver craned for maneuver space, found an opening, darted through. The crowd released energy in a chase of boys, the march of a clique of women whose straw hats meshed like pagoda roofs, a crippled war veteran who waved his tin beggar's cup in an agitated arc. The rain evaporated and the people drifted in a white steamscape.

I told the driver to head for the nightclub *Quartier Latin.*

"No open yet," he said.

"Go anyway."

Knitting his brows, apparently concluding that my stupidity was my own problem, he skirted JFK Square, zipping around pedestrians like racing pylons. Two blocks down he skidded to a halt behind a jam of cars. Ahead, the intersection of Tu Do and Le Loi was closed—a crew was felling a row of plane trees for some reason—so I dismounted, slapped piastre bills into his palm, and set off on foot.

Scents filled the air: tea and orange, dust and diesel, incense and fabric. I turned to find a sidewalk vendor hawking bolts of silk. He held one for me to view, striped coral and white—electric colors that might complement Tuy's decorations. But I couldn't afford the time, and I continued along the decorative yellow sidewalk tiles, past a hissing grill whose cook flipped fish. An urchin in a burlap dress dashed up and tugged on my trouser leg. I tossed her a 50-su coin, and at once three other urchins joined her. I told them to go away. They followed me along the four blocks to Nguyen Cong Tru and its side street. When I reached the door of *Quartier Latin*, they halted and backed off, as if they sensed something dreadful.

In the doorway leaned Danh. Arm slung below his broken collar bone, silvery suit jacket draped over his shoulders, he sulked. "Go tell André I'm waiting," I said. He was better at obeying orders than at fighting, and he left and was back in barely a minute. I followed him through the tables and upturned chairs to the alcove where André Nogaret sat in the cigarette smoke that erected a fourth wall around him.

"A drink, Major?" He gestured to the second chair.

"No, thank you."

He waved a match against a Gauloises, drew on it fiercely, puckering his lips. His face was redder than I recollected, his sandy hair unkempt. He must have been plowing his fingers through it distractedly, like a man balancing his troublesome account books.

I took out the morgue photo. "Remember him?"

"Your wanderer."

"His name was Gerard Penelon. A Frenchman and helicopter pilot. Former French military. Also, former resident of Bui Thi Xuan Street west of the central market."

"Congratulations." He lifted his glass. "The name and the residence too."

"The place is a cheap boarding house. I stopped by this morning. His room was cleaned out, the bill settled. The manager didn't remember much else. Seems like somebody slipped him some piastres, the usual way things are done in Saigon."

"Unfortunately so."

On the table posed his pack of Gauloises cigarettes and two bottles with labels in French. One enclosed a clear liquid, maybe Vermouth, the other an opaque amber spirit. In his glass, they blended to the color of a French officer's kepi. He squeezed in the juice from a sliced lemon.

Served to a customer, the cocktail might wear a little umbrella, though I doubted that anyone else drank this concoction.

I said, "The French Embassy has papers saying that Gerard Penelon worked for you."

"I was going to tell you. But you have ruined my surprise."

"He was a friend of yours?"

"I merely sponsored him so he could get his local license."

"Why would you do that?"

"A common arrangement. Why do you care? You told me you were trying to discover whether or not your dead drifter was an American. Now you have your answer."

"There's a contract out on Kim Thi. Was she really your employee, or was that an arrangement too?"

"She was one of my dancers." His eyes clung to the table. "I heard about the contract. Very bad."

"It needs to get turned off."

"Can't be done. She should leave Saigon until the situation settles down."

"What situation? Why would anybody want to kill a showgirl?"

"I don't know." He said it as if he'd pondered the question himself. "I suspect it has to do with you, an American, poking into affairs that are none of your business. Saigon is suspended in an equilibrium, which you and your power-drunk country unsettle. Whoever is after Kim Thi might relax if you left matters alone."

"Can't be done," I mimicked. "Turns out that Gerard was involved with some U.S. military officers."

"Your problem."

"He crashed near the Gavet Plantation, for which your wife serves on the board of advisors. His lover was one of your dancers. His papers say he worked for you. It's not only my problem."

This may have resonated with André, who asked, "So what was his business with the American officers?"

"Ever since my investigation started, an American general has been trying to smother it. I traced a radio that had been in Gerard's possession to an officer who works for the general. Whatever the reason that Gerard ended up in Tay Ninh Province that night, they were helping him in some way."

André nodded slightly, as if he finally comprehended why I'd come to see him. "The general complicates your job, doesn't he?"

"Yes," I replied.

"And why would he be involved with Gerard?"

"I don't know."

"Surely you can imagine a reason."

"I can't prove anything."

"Let's hear what you can't prove."

"Gerard flew between Vung Tau and Cambodia. The antenna at the Gavet plantation is visible at night; he may have used it as a landmark. My guess is that it's a drug runner's route. Heroin entering Vietnam originates from the so-called Golden Triangle in Burma and Thailand and passes through Cambodia."

"And how was your general involved? Was Gerard sharing the profits with him?"

"I don't know."

"Those are your three favorite words."

"I believe it's all linked."

He scoffed. "All linked. It's what an amateur says."

André's eyes showed a yellow tint, perhaps from an old fever. Having drained the glass, bottoming-up his kepi drink in a move that might have snapped a neck less thick than his, he began mixing another. He regarded me as if he pivoted on a decision, to speak or hold his tongue, a judgment that goes poorly when soaked in booze.

I said, "General Huang issued a complaint about me yesterday. It carried my correct name and alleged that I'd killed two Montagnards and kidnapped Kim Thi."

"You seem to have provoked his ire."

"The complaint didn't mention the dead kid or the commotion at your club."

"Why should Huang know what happens here?"

"The police say he's your partner. That you're a smuggler of narcotics."

"The police are easily confused." I thought he might elaborate, but he seemed to have undergone another transformation. A minute ago he'd been attentive. Now he looked bored.

I said, "Nobody else had my name."

"Nobody? The way you bandy it about?"

Remembering how the Frenchman had perked up when I'd mentioned his wife the other night, an instinct shot in front of me like a chameleon across a dinner plate. "What happened between you and Simone?"

"What happened? Marriage. Life." He said it dismissively, yet the fancy drink coursing in his blood spurred him to talk. "Nogaret is her maiden name; I took it when we married. One of my many concessions. My Marseille origins had served me well in the rough-and-tumble world, but she considered them coarse, not the lineage she wanted appended to her. For myself, I was happy to climb society's ladder. Her lofty status captivated me, though I suppose it was not my milieu."

"But it was hers."

"Oh yes. Hers is a natural sophistication, the sublimity of the elite, with herself at the pinnacle. She represents a race that is becoming rare these days, that of the born colonialist. I don't think you have people like them in your country."

"We have them, maybe in a different form." I was thinking of the American brands of elitists, the arrogant bankers on Wall Street, or the residents of the Panama Canal Zone, nicknamed Zonians. I'd spent a few months training in Panama and had run across this privileged breed, the rulers of their American enclave who looked down their noses at everyone else, including the soldiers who protected them.

He lit another cigarette. "They are not the same as her, you can be sure. When she enters a crowded room, everyone rests their eyes on her. They might not know who she is, yet they will act deferentially, to the point of absurdity. It is the expectation she creates, a quality she wears like an aristocrat." He watched the smoke drift upward like an embodied memory. "Remarkably, she selected *me* out of such a room. It was 1954, around Christmas, and I was at a party I might not have been invited to. I was not of her class, but the world was disordered then. The defeat at

Dien Bien Phu had shaken the rigidity out of the social structure, and I was a former officer of paratroops, self-confident in a way that set people's minds at rest. Not that I lacked charm, I could fill a white gabardine suit as well as a set of fatigues, chat at dinner parties in the same hour I inspected the perimeter of guards. For a while I protected her. But I was never a colonialist." He said it with conviction, as if the title unsettled him.

"Later, the circumstances changed. She sold the plantation and became the consultant to people who accommodated themselves to the communists. They obtained peace in exchange for certain payments and freedoms of passage. When that transpired, my soldier's skills suffered a decline in their premium. I became the one who ran errands. Ennui and my old malaria supplanted each other in turn, like two skeletons on a see-saw."

"You wax poetic," I said.

"The truth is, I grew tired of it."

"So you moved to Saigon and took over the nightclub?"

"By way of other things. I didn't acquire the club until 1963. Simone had her own interests too, by then." I hoped he would expound on those interests. He didn't. Purposefully, as if sighting on a moving target, the Frenchman positioned the empty glass between the two bottles. "This is how life plays out. I can't say I wasn't to blame."

"That was a long time ago. Yet you're still married to her."

He grimaced. I'd breached a forbidden topic. Then he shrugged. "Why should she bother with a divorce?" Across the club, somebody swept the floor, the phone jingled and went unanswered, all passing André by. I wondered if he made a daily rendezvous with his drinks, caught in a reverie that roiled over him like a storm. If he'd started with a full bottle of the clear stuff, he had downed a third of it already.

I asked, "Was she connected to Gerard?"

He squinted like a man staring into the sun. "You are in *your* milieu, aren't you, Tanner? You would interrogate me forever, if left to yourself." He shook his head. "Go now. Don't make me summon Danh. It was hard enough to keep him from bashing you the first time."

On the street, hailing a scooter cab, I tried to make sense out of what André had said. If his booze-sopped tale conveyed a message, it was as jumbled as the traffic on Nguyen Cong Tru.

Trong had warned me about André. But Trong breathed the city air where truth and rumor tumbled amok—André conspired with his partner General Huang to murder the showgirl Kim Thi; he might try to kill me too; he was a drug smuggler, and nothing he said could be genuine.

I couldn't fit my mind around Trong's reality. He would scoff at me for trusting André, but I did, at least insofar as I believed the Frenchman wasn't out to assassinate me or Kim Thi.

Better than nothing.

* * *

Toward Tan Son Nhut on Cong Tuy street, my scooter joined the queue of vehicles at a drop gate blotched with a red and white bulls-eye sign: 'HALT!' Nearby, like two repulsive toads, ARVN and U.S. armored personnel carriers baked under the sun. An American sergeant in a track-commander's helmet occupied a pathetic wafer of shade. I dismounted the bike, walked over to him, and asked, "What's going on?"

"Checkpoint for extra security, sir. You should keep up with the news. We invaded Cambodia yesterday." From the tread, he picked up a copy of the Pacific Stars and Stripes and handed it to me. Units of the 1st Cavalry Division and the 11th Armored Cavalry Regiment had punched across the Cambodian border at locations in the Fishhook to the north, and the ARVN in the Parrot's Beak northwest of Saigon. I pictured the swarm of forces: tanks and APCs crashing through the bamboo groves, helicopters darkening the skies—Hueys to ferry troops, the big twin-rotor Chinooks slung with artillery for the forward fire bases, the even bigger CH-54s to lift trucks and bulldozers. On TV, President Nixon had explained the operation's purpose—to destroy the sanctuaries where the enemy assembled supplies and staged infiltrations into South Vietnam in violation of Cambodia's neutrality. Nixon's rationale had done nothing to mollify the political left, which decried the invasion as an outrageous expansion of the war.

I asked, "Trouble around town?"

"No sir. Situation under control." He said it with certitude, not having witnessed the war come calling on Saigon as it had in Tet 1968. I was sorely tempted to turn around and head home to Tuy, just to reassure myself she was safe.

The traffic line started moving, and my driver frantically waved for me to get back aboard the scooter. We glided through the checkpoint toward Tan Son Nhut.

*　*　*

At the French Fort, an envelope lay on my desk.

HEADQUARTERS, MILITARY ASSISTANCE COMMAND, VIETNAM
OFFICE OF THE PROVOST MARSHAL
1 MAY 1970
OFFICIAL ORDERS
INVESTIGATION NUMBER H-7406 IS HEREBY CLOSED. PERSONNEL ASSIGNED SHALL ASSUME THEIR REGULAR DUTIES. ALL MEMORANDA, FILES, AND RECORDS SHALL BE REMANDED TO THE CUSTODY OF THE PMO, MACV.

FOR THE PROVOST MARSHAL
CROWLEY(ACTING)

I punched two holes in the onion-skin copy and fitted it onto the flexible metal prongs in the folder. When I looked up, Sergeant Lopez was standing in the doorway. He must have guessed what the orders said. "A courier delivered it last night. Then Colonel Crowley phoned. He said he wants you to sit tight and wait. He didn't say for what."

"They're preparing my transfer."

"To where?"

"Someplace I'll be helpless to follow up." If they wanted to keep me in country for a while, they might send me to a unit near the DMZ, or to the Mekong Delta—they had plenty of woebegone spots to choose from. I thought of an installation I'd visited during an investigation, Can Tho Base Camp on the Mekong, utterly flat, an infinity of puddles. It was only 80 miles from Saigon, but it might as well be five hundred.

Or they might book me on the next Freedom Bird to the United States.

I'd left Kim Thi at Tuy's apartment, the two women sitting on the floor staring up at me. What would become of them if I didn't return tonight?

The thought burned like napalm.

Maybe I could get to General Abrams. Like all commanders, he upheld a so-called *open-door* policy, meaning that any soldier who wanted to see him could gain an audience, one time, to state his complaint. In practice, at Abrams's level, the sessions happened only rarely. Subordinate leaders almost invariably resolved problems before they reached the commanding general. If a petitioner insisted on pressing forward, he must explain how his leaders had failed to treat him according to the regulations. This was the policy's true purpose— to install a warning bell in case the chain of command malfunctioned.

What would I say to Abrams if I insisted on seeing him under his open-door policy? That Cobris had amorphous ties to a dead Frenchman? That he'd interfered in an official investigation? I pictured myself in front of the commanding general's desk dispensing the fragments of evidence I'd collected. At some point, Abrams would phone Cobris, who in a few well-chosen words would discredit everything I'd said. Crowley would agree, and when he abandoned me, whatever credibility that attached to my investigator's mantle would vanish. Unless I delivered proof so compelling that it convinced Abrams on the spot, I'd never be taken seriously again.

Without intending to, I'd settled into my seat at the desk.

"You okay, sir?"

"Yeah. I'm just thinking."

Thinking was insufficient. I couldn't piece together the scraps I'd gathered. Gerard had been carrying a radio that belonged to Major Stobe, Commander of the 29th Aviation Company. An isolated fact—

what did it mean? That Stobe, and by extension Cobris, had prior knowledge of Gerard's activities? But who was Gerard, what was he doing, and why did Cobris care? Why had Stobe given him a tactical radio? Kim Thi said Gerard had been flying a helicopter between Cambodia and the Cape, yet this was another uncorroborated assertion—nobody had found a helicopter. What role had Andre Nogaret played? Why would anyone put out a contract to kill Kim Thi? I evaluated what I knew, straining for a single, tangible thread.

To present this to General Abrams would be like Thich Quang Duc dousing himself in gasoline and striking a match.

The roar of a C-141 momentarily drowned my ruminations. I could smell the aviation gas suffusing the air over the base. The fumes spread from the continual logistics flights that fed the war. More bombs. Ammunition. Radios.

Stobe had given Gerard a radio. Maybe a rifle too. Gear to be used on the ground.

Stobe was an aviator.

Might he have given the Frenchman a helicopter?

The notion was preposterous. A helicopter was an expensive piece of machinery, with its own air crew, a team of mechanics on the ground, other teams to gas it up, calibrate its instruments, fuss over it in every conceivable way. Even with thousands of military helicopters in country, they were all accounted for. Surely.

"Sergeant Lopez?"

He still leaned in the doorway. "Yes sir?"

"How long would it take to put together map sheets of the area from Vung Tau to the Cambodian border above Tay Ninh? Full coverage."

"The Special Forces S-2 shop has every map series in country. I can ask a buddy of mine over there."

I tossed him the padlock keys to my jeep.

* * *

We pushed my desk aside, and the tile floor became a placard for twelve map sheets. We trimmed their margins, aligned them, taped them together, weighted down their outer ends with chairs. Crawling backward over the maps, I extended the string Lopez held steady at Vung Tau on the coast, where the blue matte of the South China sea washed the palm-tree-shaded shoreline at MACV's villa, northward to Tay Ninh Province and the symbol for the radio tower at the Gavet Plantation.

If my instincts were right, the string marked Gerard Penelon's flight route.

Lopez applied a piece of tape to hold it steady. "You said his destination was the Fishhook in Cambodia. That's farther north. Why should he go to the antenna?"

"Air navigation is tricky at night, even for a trained military pilot. Gerard needed a reference point. With its red lights, the antenna is a perfect marker. American pilots use it, why shouldn't he?"

"What makes you think he flew at night?"

"Most of what I've come upon in this investigation I've had to pry loose from some attempt to conceal. This is a well-traveled air corridor, full of troop ships and recon and logistics flights. If Gerard had flown this route during daylight, every aircraft in the sky would have spotted him."

I stretched a second string from Hill 71 to the spot on the tributary's eastern edge where I'd found the radio, extended it in a straight line to intersect the flight route. The strings crossed over printed blue sprigs.

Marshland. Area Zulu.

"Cover for me as best you can," I told Lopez.

"Where are you going?"

"To see Larsen."

* * *

Toward Cu Chi I drove northwest. In the distance, water buffalos made black dabs next to the pointy ticks of their straw-hatted tenders, an alphabet of two characters that said everything. No boundary existed between Saigon and rural Vietnam. Agricultural lands and rain forests rimmed the city, and to go a few kilometers was to be among peasants and in the realm of the Viet Cong. Not long ago, the woods north of Cu Chi had harbored an enemy stronghold called the Iron Triangle, infamous for its intricate tunnels into which whole VC battalions could disappear. The U.S. Army never had found a way to destroy the tunnel network, and so the VC might have survived had they not swarmed out to fight above ground in the Tet Offensive. Juiced by their own propaganda, the VC had expected the people to rise up and fight alongside them against the Saigon government. The people didn't rise up, they ran for cover. Battling in the open with U.S. and South Vietnamese regular forces, the VC died by the thousands. According to MACV, the enemy in the Iron Triangle had been decimated, the area pacified, as if Larsen and his soldiers might have done fine without their sandbags and barbed wire and machine-gun bunkers.

At the Cu Chi camp, I passed rows of decrepit Quonset huts. Saddled with age, the seams seeping rust, the huts resembled a ghetto. Between the buildings loitered soldiers, probably from Larsen's headquarters element. Some shot hoops or lazed on sandbags, smoking cigarettes and drinking from soda bottles. The scent of marijuana drifted across my jeep. Among these young men, the tedium of camps spawned almost as much destruction as the pungi stakes, snipers, and mines. Drugs and indiscipline weren't new to the U.S. Army in Vietnam, but it seemed strange to run across them today, with the Cambodia incursion afire just to the north.

I had phoned ahead and exhorted the staff officer who'd answered to schedule a meeting with Larsen right away. I found the colonel in his headquarters sipping coffee out of his eternal metal canteen cup. We were alone in the building, and I guessed that he'd cleared out everybody else in case our meeting aired topics he didn't want them to hear.

"When I called, sir, I half-expected them to say you were in Cambodia."

"Somebody has to keep the roads open." The bitterness diminished him, and he seemed to know it. His voice now rose an octave. "I'm surprised to see you too, Tanner. Seems like they'd have pulled the plug on you by now."

"They did. The investigation officially was closed last night."

I unfolded Gerard's map, laid it on the table, and related what I'd learned, knowing that Larsen the tactician would see the mosaic emerge from the fragments. I tapped the intersecting lines I'd grease-penciled. "He crashed here."

The leathery skin squeezed. "We searched Area Zulu."

"From the air. You missed something. I need a ride and some soldiers to help me search it from the ground."

"I don't own that turf anymore. It belongs to the units mounting the Cambodia operation. To insert you, I'd have to coordinate with them."

"There's no time to coordinate, sir. You'd never get permission anyway."

In Larsen's eyes, tiny specks floated like steel filings, the filter through which he viewed the world. Since the last time I'd seen him, his face seemed to have slackened, no doubt from the tranquility of occupying a pacified area. Now he modulated his voice so it wouldn't escape the corrugated walls.

"Tanner, you asked me to hear you out, and I've done so. To my thinking, your premise strains credibility. You say that this Frenchman kept a bootlegged helicopter at the MACV villa in Vung Tau. I've been to that villa. The lawn extends barely far enough to land a single chopper. Hiding one there would be impossible."

"So maybe he didn't keep it at the villa proper. There must be another facility nearby."

"There *must be*? You're speculating. And you say that from Vung Tau, the pilot flew all the way to the Fishhook in Cambodia? That's damned far."

"One hundred ten miles. Double that for the round trip. With a light load, it's within the operating range of a UH-1, just over an hour in the air each way."

"According to you, the pilot was a civilian. No civilian with any sense would fly a route like that at night."

"He was French ex-military. Maybe they trained him in night flying."

"More speculation."

"Yes sir. But not unreasonable."

"What you're asking me to do is to send young soldiers on an uncoordinated mission, to a place I can't give them fire support. How do I explain if they run into trouble?"

"Cobris pulled you out of Tay Ninh Province so you wouldn't find the chopper."

"Keep your goddamn voice down!"

"Look where he dumped you." I gestured at the seedy metal hut.

"There's no proof he had anything to do with it."

"Not evidence that would stand up in court. But the pieces fit together to form a picture. It's a scheme of some kind, with Cobris behind it."

"What does finding the chopper accomplish?"

"The only guarantee is, if I don't try, Cobris wins."

"Seems like you're itching to bag yourself a general."

"That's not the reason. I have friends who are at risk because they helped me. A corrupt warlord has threatened my Saigon police contact. And somebody put a contract out on the showgirl Kim Thi. Two nights ago, I shot it out with two thugs who tried to ambush her in an alley."

He stared into his coffee cup, and I was reminded of André searching the depths of his drink as if wisdom might bubble up. "A warlord, a showgirl, a shootout in an alley. Do you have any idea how fucking crazy it sounds?"

"Yes sir."

"After twenty-six years in uniform, there's a chance I'll get my stars, if I don't fuck up. Then I might be able to do something to save the Army from sons of bitches like Cobris. From everything you've said, to back you would be a fool's gamble."

"The cop and showgirl are my people, sir. Backing them isn't optional for me."

"Your people? They're Vietnamese."

I didn't comment. Larsen didn't strike me as a bigot; he was merely puzzled by a brand of loyalty he hadn't encountered before. Outside, a flight of helicopters roared over heading northward toward Cambodia, and in the whop of rotors I could almost hear his thoughts. He was thinking about backing his people up. It was the reason he'd insisted on the investigation in the first place.

He placed his cup gently on the table. Perhaps he resisted the urge to slam it down. "You got a weapon?"

"I brought my .45."

"We'll scrounge up a set of web gear and a rifle. If you run into the enemy, firing a handgun will only let them know how weak you are." He leaned over the map. "I don't see a landing zone near your crossed lines, but Area Zulu is low risk, so you can go to treetop level to scout for one. A squad from the brigade's recon platoon will assemble in twenty minutes and lead you to the helipad. There's a chopper there on standby." He checked his watch. "It's afternoon already. I can give you about two hours on the ground, one time only."

* * *

The rotors churned nervous energy into Lieutenant Zuniga and the six men from the brigade recon platoon. They sat fidgety on the chopper's floor, their eyes watchful. Zuniga belonged to the category of officer who was competent and who didn't like to be around those who were not. His face had gone taut when I'd explained our mission. Nothing incenses a soldier so much as to think that his superiors have handed him off to a crackpot.

The pilot's voice in the headphones: "Coming up on Area Zulu."

"Cut across the center," I said over the mike. "Then loop around to the south."

Zuniga leaned over water ribbed with half-submerged trees and toothed with broken trunks. "Looks like shit down there," he shouted.

The pilot said, "I don't know if I can put you down in that." He swung over a patina the shade of chocolate milk. Like an exploding can of green paint, a flight of parrots scattered from our intrusion. I judged that we were near my crossed lines, but there was no obvious place to insert us.

"Circle around again," I said.

He did so twice more. On the third circuit, I noticed a meadow of marshy grass jutting from submerged copses, pressed the push-to-talk button. "There!"

"That surface won't hold the skids. You'll have to jump."

"What if there's no bottom under that grass?" yelled Zuniga.

The sunlight blinded off the water, obscuring the depth. "Take us closer," I said, and the chopper hovered down to a few feet. Past the skid, I made out mottled earth below the surface. Good enough. I pulled off the headphones. "Let's go!"

The plunge immersed me to my waist. Pain shot up from my ankles. Zuniga and the recon team dropped in after me, their curses drowned in the rotor blast. They were traveling light: weapons, water, ammo, and commo gear only. Still it took ten minutes to get everybody out and to a mound of spongy ground.

Leaning against a spindly trunk, oozing water from the chest down, Zuniga pulled off his floppy cap and wagged his smooth-shaven head. "They told me you were an MP from Saigon. I never expected you to leap out of that chopper."

Our insertion point was more than five hundred meters from the intersecting lines. On the azimuth I plotted, we marched northwest through the bog, sloshing through the groin-deep water, zigzagging around marled roots and deeper pools. The wetness seethed; to breathe gave the sensation of drawing on a hookah pipe. The mosquitoes found us and bit through our wet fatigues.

Zuniga advanced a security team and staked everybody else in pairs. We formed a human comb that glided through the roots and reeds. Soon he splashed over to me. "Let's stop here for a few minutes," he said. "I'm going to take one man to recon a clearing we just skirted. We might be able to use it as an extraction LZ—the water there looks only ankle deep. The chopper can hover low enough so we can climb on board. Those pilots hate to power their skids out of the muck."

"All right."

"How long do we have to stay out here?"

"Until we reach the objective," I said. "Then we search across a half-klick radius."

"The *objective*? It's nothing but swamp. Colonel Larsen ordered me *not* to get stuck here after dark."

"We won't."

He peered at me, no doubt to discern if he could trust my judgment. He was right to be worried; we were isolated and vulnerable. Luckily he hadn't asked me how I'd determined the site, by crossing strings that Lopez and I had stretched over maps taped together. A string's width equaled thirty meters on the ground. Incomparable, to walk those meters in this bleak wetland. If Gerard's flight route had been different from what I'd guessed, or he'd veered widely in an emergency descent, he'd have landed far off where the strings indicated.

Ten minutes later, Zuniga returned, and we resumed. In four teams of two, we made a dashed line, a formation that seemed orderly in the morass, imposing the illusion that I knew what I was doing. My partner was a private named Wells, a skinny kid with straight hair that drooped over his forehead. He wore his floppy cap rodeo-rider style behind his neck on a cord. No older than nineteen, still trusting the wisdom of his leaders, he was accumulating cynicism like pounds on his frame, the process sped by today's experience.

"This is a wild fucking goose chase, right sir?"

"Maybe."

"At least we ain't dodging bullets."

Indeed, the only reaction we stirred was to scare up water fowl, singly or in flocks. The birds weren't used to people in their soggy habitat. As Larsen had appraised, no soldier would have much use for this place, even as a hideout.

We came upon a turret of dry ground bulging out of the water. A soldier spotted two empty C-ration cans, which Zuniga prodded with the muzzle of his M16. "No rust. Somebody left these here recently. Could be the enemy."

I said, "I know who left them. He junked other cans by a tributary a few kilometers from here."

"Whaddya wanna do, sir?"

I examined my map. To assume that Gerard had jettisoned the cans meant we should pivot along an adjusted line. It was a calculated risk, cutting off nearly half the original search area. Meanwhile, the clock was running.

I said, "We need to turn southwest."

"You sure?"

"Yes. Reorient your men." The assurance in my tone clawed at me. Wells had branded it correctly—this was a wild fucking goose chase. What had impelled me to bring these young soldiers out here today, gambling their lives on my guesswork?

Like a swinging gate, the line shifted until we faced our lengthening shadows. The water glimmered emerald. It grew shallower, only shin deep, and I no longer had to squint to see the root knobs. After twenty minutes we came upon another small mound. The sun picked out tree roots protruding from a clay bluff in the distance.

Zuniga said, "Looks like dry land ahead. Dry terrain means the NVA or Viet Cong. We don't want to bump into either one."

"Then we'll shift southward."

Zuniga edged close, spoke in a hoarse whisper. "Sir, there is *nothing* here. The chopper will be on station in fifty-five minutes, and we need to set up the LZ."

"Keep going," I said. "If we don't find anything in thirty minutes, we'll call it."

*   *   *

Twenty minutes later, sloshing along, I wedged my foot under a root and twisted my ankle. I thought, wouldn't these infantrymen just *love* carrying me through the bog? Somehow, Gerard had endured ten klicks, his journey ending in a white flash he probably never saw, at the hands of men he wouldn't have encountered save for their delay in a thorn thicket. Enter the jungle and you played by its rules.

While the ankle pain subsided, I paused to drink water, and a wide leaf broke off overhead. Weighty on the stem end, it caromed awkwardly. The trees were taller in this part, the canopy forming black weaves where the branches and vines laced together, and through these the leaf jolted until it plopped in the water. Waves pulsed at my shins.

On the surface, a vague luster.

Oil?

I looked up.

In one of the weaves, I saw an olive-tinted surface. A succession of rivets chased around the edge.

An outline materialized.

Wells asked, "Whatcha lookin' at, sir?"

"Go get the lieutenant."

Nose down, the helicopter traced a disturbing form, like a human skull gleaned amid the clutter of an attic. Hard to discern which parts had sheared off in the crash and which the tree occulted. The rotors were missing; they must have fallen into the water or become snagged in the high canopy when the chopper impacted. Gone too was the upper tail fin. I imagined the grinding descent, the groans as the chassis bent, the nesting into vines. Jagged branches had breached the fuselage. Ensnared, the chopper might dangle for years before it settled to earth.

I'd brought a 35mm camera and was snapping pictures when Zuniga walked up. "Shit," he said, probably feeling the same shudder as I had when I'd spotted the wreck. "That is a creepy sight. You say there were survivors?"

"One that I know of."

His voice dropped. "Somebody might still be inside?"

"The only way to find out is to climb."

"Daylight is slipping on us, sir."

"I'll go as fast as I can."

I deposited my gear with him, minus the .45 that I buttoned in my right thigh cargo pocket, and the camera, secured in the left. Boosted by Zuniga and Wells into the lower branches, I scaled upward. The fuselage hung like a slumbering bat that slipped in and out of my vision. They talked me along at places where I couldn't see past the leaves, and I nosed through a resistive thicket headfirst into a jungle spider's gluey web. The spider waved its hairy legs centimeters from my face. I blew hard and it receded. Gripping to a vine, I swung in an uneasy rhythm with the trapped ship.

"Watch it, sir. You don't wanna pull that bitch down on top of you."

For the first time I had the fuselage in clear view. This close it lost its eerie vibe and gave off the same mundane aura as the husks of ruined cars along Highway One. The coat of unreflective olive was ordinary too, until you hunted for markings. Army helicopters normally manifested subdued black lettering on the tail, and units typically emblazoned their insignia on the nose. This one had no markings at all. I took out the camera and snapped more shots, for what they were worth, capturing a ghost ship from nowhere.

In its airy repose, the chopper over time would have traded its characteristic fuel scent for the odors of the deep marsh. The tang of aviation fuel lingered, proving it had crashed recently. No other flights had gone missing over War Zone C. I had no doubt I was looking at Gerard Penelon's ride.

Standing on a branch, I kicked the frame a few times to make sure there wasn't a snake or a bee's nest lurking inside. The sole reaction was the blur of an ochre lizard across the riveting.

"You sure that's advisable?" Zuniga challenged.

"The vines arrested her descent. I think they'll hold. If not, you probably should stand back." I heard my lookouts sloshing rearward, while I stretched half in, half out of the wreck. It gave no detectable slippage. I looked for something to hang onto. The nylon hand loops slumped against the ceiling, now a vertical wall to my left. In what had been the rear bulkhead I found one of the hinged metal cargo links, folded it out to grip, and balanced on the doorway lip. The fuselage shuddered.

I scanned the cabin. Thank God, no poor soul had been left here.

Jammed open in the crash, the near-side cargo door hovered above me like a guillotine. The opposite door had popped off its tracks and braced against the frame. No seats in the cargo compartment. Standard gray quilted insulation covered the interior walls and ceiling; the vertical floor showed bare aluminum with raised nubs for traction. Everything looked clean except for a honey-brown oil jib over the nubs. Side-stepping along the doorframe to get a better view of the cockpit, I stretched for another grip. My foot slipped, and my fingers clawed across the oil.

I pitched headlong into the catcher's mitt of vines.

"What the fuck are you doing up there, sir?"

"It's okay," I rasped. Nested in the vines, pulse drumming wildly at the side of my neck, I panted. My mouth, the only dry thing in this whole goddamn Area Zulu, tasted like I'd poured a can of talcum powder into it.

If the chopper had held through that, it would withstand any stress my puny one hundred sixty pounds might add. I gripped the skid brace and hauled myself back up and inside, not trusting my footing until I'd locked my fingers around clamps. From my perch, I gazed into the pilot's compartment. The seats seemed undamaged; so did the instrument panel except for a burst seam sprouting plastic-coated wires. The left windshield had popped out, opening a gaping socket. Past the dangling shoulder belts, I spotted the buckled Plexiglas in vines at the chopper's nose. Below opened a tunnel in the vegetation, through which I could see Zuniga and Wells. Maybe the tunnel was how Gerard had climbed down.

The pilot had been extremely lucky—the central cabin had stayed intact. In a chopper crash, the rotor blades striking an immovable object could torque out the drive train, usually frontward, half a ton of hot steel mashing everything in its path.

I needed the aircraft number. I poked around for a data plate, not expecting to find one. If Stobe had repainted the fuselage to obliterate the outside markings, meticulously chipped the serial-number plate off the PRC25 radio, he wouldn't have overlooked an obvious plate inside the cockpit. He'd have had more trouble hiding the origins of the engine that bore multiple numbers inscribed in the metal. But the engine compartment rested *above* the cabin. To check it required climbing through the vines and removing the cowl. There wasn't time.

Gingerly I dangled into the cockpit until my feet rested on the avionics array. There were hollow wells where instruments commonly fit. The radio rack was empty. Finding an intact gauge, with my belt knife I turned the plate screws, tossed aside the faceplate, and extracted the instrument that was about the size of a small loaf of bread. Severed the tethering wires and rotated it until I found the data plate: Attitude Indicator, Model 2061C-12, Serial 16028.

I leaned over the windshield socket. "Don't try to catch this."

"What?"

"Just get it out of the water fast." The instrument shot through the vine tunnel and splashed.

"Jesus!" exclaimed Zuniga.

"You got it?"

"It nearly got me!"

Bracing on the seats and doorframe, I laddered toward the cargo compartment, and it was pure chance that I caught the glint of color from a crevice where the aluminum skin had popped loose from the rib. Whatever the item was, gravity had tugged it beyond my outstretched arm. Eventually I contorted far enough to scissor my fingertips on the edge and ease it out.

You don't expect to find a silk purse in the jungle. Orange, delicately embroidered, it had stayed pristine in the crevice. A closed zipper protected objects I could feel through the fabric, but to unzip it here risked spilling them into the unforgiving trees and marsh. I tucked the purse into my button-down shirt pocket.

The discovery inspired an idea. Instead of reversing my path, I climbed down by way of the window socket and vine tunnel, as I guessed that Gerard had done, not the fastest route, but he hadn't had the advantage of daylight. The descent took six minutes. I'd have gone quicker, but I paused along the way, searching the vines and the protruding thorns, until I found what I was looking for.

Day 10

Midnight at the French Fort. A glow through the closed louvers—Lopez had left the lights on for me. The desk surface was bare. No messages.

I phoned Hollis at his unit, waited minutes while the duty NCO went to get him. Examined my legs for swamp leeches I might have missed when I'd checked before, until his groggy voice came on the line: "Whaddya got, sir?"

"I need to trace an aircraft instrument." I read him the plate numbers on the attitude indicator.

"Where did it come from?"

I told him.

His yawn filled seconds. "An engine number would have been better."

"I know. It was the best I could do."

"How soon?"

"Tonight, if possible."

"It's not. I can't access the file stacks before morning. The soonest I can get back to you will be tomorrow afternoon. The *absolute* soonest."

"This is important, Chief. My investigation fails without it."

A pause. Hollis must have heard my disquietude over the crackly phone line between Tan Son Nhut and Bien Hoa. He said, "If the stakes are so high, you'd be smart to put your money elsewhere. You were lucky on the radio. Snake-eyes lucky."

"Guys like you make for all the luck in the world, Chief."

"That's bullshit, sir."

"First thing tomorrow, Sergeant Lopez will bring you the instrument."

* * *

Motoring into town at zero one hundred hours, I had to pay the scooter driver an enormous tip, for curfew had fallen an hour before, and I made it through the checkpoints only by flashing my MP identification. The streets of Cholon lay deserted; a puce vapor lingered on the tile and corrugated roofs. Half a block from Tuy's building, I waited by a tree until I spotted the glow from the police sentinel's cigarette. So Trong was still helping me, despite the risks. A few steps farther and I saw the yellow rectangle of Tuy's apartment window. A light burned inside. No doubt she would have been asleep this late but for her chats with Kim Thi.

On the smooth-worn floor, in a close coven under the lamp, Tuy and Kim Thi knelt with me as I spilled out the orange purse's contents. The light glittered on a necklace, earrings, and bracelet all in brilliant gold and inlayed ornately with diamonds.

"They are beautiful," said Tuy, smiling at Kim Thi. "Gerard must have bought them as a gift for you."

Like a jeweler, Kim Thi held the bracelet to her eye. I guessed that the dancers at _Quartier Latin_ developed expertise in every form of currency. She said, "Fine gold. The diamonds half carat or bigger. This set cost many thousand dollar. Gerard not have so much money." She fingered the purse's embroidery, turned it inside out, felt the stitching, sniffed the fabric as if it were a used garment she might buy, and held it up for Tuy to smell. Tuy, who never wore perfume, pronounced, "Exquisite."

Silently Kim Thi restored the purse and jewelry to the floor.

From my pocket I laid out the item I'd found in the tunnel below the chopper, a tassel of black threads eight centimeters long, ordinary until you felt the texture. "The helicopter crashed into the vines," I explained. "The climb down was at night; there was no way to avoid the thorns."

Tuy rubbed the threads. "Wool and silk."

Kim Thi stared at the tassel.

I struggled to keep the insistence out of my voice. "André Nogaret wouldn't say what Gerard was up to. Can you tell me?"

"You know," said Kim Thi.

"I want to hear it anyway."

Perhaps Tuy's presence had kindled trust, or the dancer was just tired of resisting. "Gerard the pilot for one passenger. Important person."

"Who?" asked Tuy.

I filled in the silence. "The threads are from a woman's sweater. The purse and the jewelry belong to a woman. What woman would have been in that helicopter?"

Kim Thi didn't answer. She gazed straight ahead at nothing. It was how people lived with the ambiguity of a guerrilla war. She stood up, walked to her blankets, and folded herself into them.

A minute later, ever the proper hostess, Tuy turned off the lamp.

*   *   *

Tuy wanted to talk, though not about whether she'd go with me to America. For power failures, she kept candles. She lit one, and the flame illuminated the notes in her lap.

"On Friday, I reached a friend from my father's old circle, to ask him if he could find archived stories about Simone Nogaret." Her voice barely surmounted a whisper, while across the room, Kim Thi slumbered in the aria of the rain outside. "Yesterday, he called to invite me to visit him. He said I should come at once; he had found something. So I left Kim Thi alone for a while. She was okay with it."

In the fracas over Kim Thi, it had slipped my mind that I'd asked Tuy to find old press clippings about Simone.

"His name is Huynh, and he engraves wood blocks. It is an old art that the printers revived during the Second World War, when the paper quality became too poor for the modern ways. He has many acquaintances in the newspapers around town, and through them he located three articles, two from the Saigon papers and one from a Paris magazine."

I listened as Tuy related the details. In my early days in Saigon, it would have struck me as odd she'd have asked such a man to locate published articles. Her logic followed the city's warped paths. Only rarely did she glance at her notes, and I guessed she'd staged them as a prop whose purpose was to cloak the shine of her intellect, which if displayed might convey arrogance, a breach of etiquette for a Vietnamese woman. Even with me, her lover.

Huynh had taken her to his shop's back room, a place she'd never been, where stacks of wood blocks alternated with newspaper piles. Among the papers were some of her father's, their turquoise paper blanched to the shade of hemp. The stacks summoned to mind how he'd collected the back editions around his desk, where she'd played among them as if they'd been the parapets of a fort, and her delighted screeches had resounded with the parrots' squawks outside.

The three articles proved disappointing; they delivered none of the insights she'd hoped for. She said as much to Huynh, who replied that Madame Nogaret was quite discreet in her ways; the press had no access to her. Anyway, why did Tuy wish to collect information about this privileged Frenchwoman? She answered that she was simply curious, not a convincing reason, for Huynh knew she didn't care about exploring her French lineage the way some *métissés* did. She said her motives were private, no less important to her.

He said, "Private, not official?"

"You know I have no dealings with anything official."

"People say your lover is an American soldier."

"What is private to me *stays* private."

The reply seemed to satisfy him. They drank tea for a while, and Huynh's voice became whispery; she had trouble hearing him when he explained that he had a friend, a woman who had moved to Saigon from Tay Ninh Province, where, years ago, she had worked at the Nogaret rubber plantation. Might Tuy wish to speak to this woman? If so, he would bring her, she lived close by, and they could talk. Strange, the way he said this, and Tuy suspected that this woman, rather than the insubstantial articles, had been Huynh's true reason for summoning her. But why the subterfuge?

While she waited, she studied the pages of her father's newspapers from more than fifteen years ago, watched the cyclos glide past in the street beyond the shop panes. From the back room's doorway, she observed people stop at the locked front door, heard their taps. Huynh had given her instructions not to show herself; she was to linger in the shadows. She thought this odd, but of course she complied, she must respect the wishes of her friend who had closed his shop to venture out on her behalf.

When he returned, he had with him an older woman who introduced herself as Diu. A plain cotton ribbon cinched her brown-gray hair. Difficult to guess her age; she had the countenance of a grandmother, the tone and enthusiasm of a young woman. She claimed to be a seamstress, and for a while she went on about how she would like to open her own shop someday, and it would be as stylish and abundant with fine materials as the boutiques in the Eden Arcade downtown. Diu declared her ambition in earnest, as if her clothes were not harlequinesque patches sewn together. Was she crazy? Yet her voice sounded melodious and pleasing, and Tuy sensed that the older woman liked having one so attentive for an audience. Then Diu asked, did Tuy understand why she couldn't give her real name? Not sure she'd heard correctly, Tuy managed to reply that Diu must have relations in Tay Ninh to protect. The older woman seemed satisfied with this.

What a discerning eye Diu had, I thought, to perceive that Tuy wouldn't hand her over to the authorities. Coming face to face with a Viet Cong, a Saigonese might feel fear, hatred, ambivalence. If people harbored scant trust for the guerrillas, they had even less for South Vietnam's regime. In the run-up to the Tet Offensive, the Viet Cong had staged thousands of fighters on the outskirts of the city. Their presence must have been noted, many people might have informed. Yet the attacks had achieved overwhelming tactical surprise.

Diu's quaint talk went on seemingly aimlessly, leaving Tuy to wonder if Huynh had explained to this woman the reason they were here. To interrupt would have been impolite, so Tuy listened patiently to Diu's stories about her youth in Tay Ninh. Forty minutes passed before the older woman brought herself around to the subject of Simone Nogaret.

As she spoke, Tuy guessed that the long lead-up had been Diu's way of preparing a topic that had great significance for her, and that revealed her as capable of dealing with terrible things.

* * *

Simone's father, Diu explained, had been a successful French businessman. He moved to Indochina in the late 1920s and purchased a rubber plantation in Tay Ninh Province and a smaller tract twenty kilometers north in Cambodia. Where the Tay Ninh plantation bustled with activity, the northern sister drifted in the languorous mists, and it was to this serene site that Simone's mother traveled to give birth to her daughter in the year 1936. Just before the monsoons flooded the roads, the Nogarets brought their baby to Tay Ninh. The Vietnamese workers gathered to welcome the black Citroën with the luggage roped to its roof. Diu, then fifteen years old, caught her first glance of two-month-old Simone cradled in her mother's arms.

Six years passed. Diu labored in the rubber groves where she gathered the raw sap. She carried the buckets on a coolie pole to the drums that would be transported to process the contents for export. A slender, fine-boned girl, she struggled under the weighted pole. The pace and heat exhausted her, weakened her concentration. One afternoon, not watching her footsteps in the shady aisle between the closely spaced rubber trees, she tripped over a fallen branch and broke her ankle. She could barely walk, let alone haul the heavy sap buckets. Learning of her injury, the Nogarets brought her to the plantation house to help the maids and the seamstress.

In those days, the Nogarets employed ten house servants. They cooked, washed laundry, polished furniture, beat dust from the oriental rugs, chased snakes from around the house, sterilized the water, and served the European guests who flopped in the wicker chairs and fanned their sweat-beaded faces. Diu's house duties were minimal and intended only to keep her busy while her ankle mended, but to everyone's surprise, even her own, she discovered that her callused fingers could perform magic with a needle and thread. On her first morning, limping around the second-floor rooms swishing a feather duster, she noticed through the window little Simone playing amid the garden flowers. Diu pictured a dress whose sections took shape in her mind. The next day, out of scraps of vellum and gingham the seamstress had tossed aside, she fashioned the garment—which turned into a romper because the materials ran out. Assembled from mismatched leftovers, it was not elegant, save for one feature—the shoulder straps.

"Who taught you to sew these?" asked Mme. Nogaret.

"No one, Madame."

"Well, they are marvelously done, as slender and pristinely stitched as those on my dresses from Paris. Of course, the romper is too big for Simone (Diu had had no opportunity to measure the child). But perhaps you'll do better if I keep you here to make her clothes."

When Diu commenced work at the house, the Second World War had been underway for several years. The French colonialists had acceded to the Japanese, then dominant over all of Southeast Asia. To evade an oppressive occupation, the French had relinquished the ports and the production from the tea and rubber plantations. The Japanese in turn tolerated the *colons'* administration whose allegiance was to the collaborationist Vichy government in France. Simone's father oversaw his business as before, albeit without profit, and he pined for the day when the Japanese Empire would fall and the French be restored to their rightful power. Out of earshot of the Japanese, talk of this was open. One occasionally noticed Japanese soldiers in the big towns or on the roads, never at the plantation.

Simone lived amid the disquiet, yet she was by all appearances unaware of it. Diu mused that the little girl must be the war's most favored child. With no brothers or sisters, in a house full of servants who doted on her, she skipped as if the world had been created for her pleasure. Children emit the illusion that they embody the goodness that surrounds them, and Diu, having observed from a distance the pretty girl whose hair was the shade of dried bamboo, accepted the opportunity to be her seamstress with this caricature in mind.

The next day turned it on its head. Like a martinet, Simone ruled the wing that housed her *chambre d'enfant*. She shouted at the servants, even struck them from time to time. "Do not look her in the eyes," warned one of the maids. "It infuriates her." Simone refused to pose for the measurements. In hopes that she could catch the little girl in a sedentary minute, Diu clutched the measuring tape all day, her clumping step a muted beat to Simone's sallies around the house and grounds. Diu realized it was impossible. The child must be compelled to obey—in no other way could precise sizes be taken and the patterns created.

She asked the other servants for assistance. They demurred. Never had a servant confronted Simone; none was confident enough to discipline her beyond the dulcimer suggestions that she ignored. The servants clung to their stations, which meant light chores in the mansion's coolness. Unfamiliar with the heavy labor in the groves, they dreaded it and so avoided a provocation that might reap their shattering demotion. Diu didn't cherish the work in the groves, but she knew what it entailed, and in some ways she preferred its simplicity to the jittery life of a house servant. She harbored no terror at the prospect of being sent back.

After two frustrating days of limping after Simone, Diu admonished her. Gripping the child at the shoulders so she wouldn't dash off, in a steady tone she instructed her to stand still. Amazingly, the intervention produced obedience. From that day forward, alone among the servants, Diu wielded authority over Simone. For her part, the girl came to regard her new seamstress as an irreducible fact, like wet grass after the rain, or the snakes that always found their way under the house. No matter how ill tempered she might behave with the others, she heeded Diu. Decisiveness was a special quality of the girl's character. Diu understood that, to Simone, obedience was simply expedient; it did not imply fondness for her seamstress. Even so, Diu began to feel love for the child whose clothes she painstakingly created. Her love followed no logic, required no reciprocity. It simply existed.

If nature and circumstances had shaped Simone into a little empress, they'd also bestowed certain talents. Adeptly she categorized people and manipulated them to her will. She cast Diu as the beleaguering sort, which didn't mean her seamstress couldn't be used to advantage. The girl began to participate in the design of her clothes, and the two of them traveled to Tay Ninh City to select the fabrics. They became a recognized pair in the tailors' market, where Simone demonstrated an eye for finding quality that had become rare because of the war. Gasoline was rare too, yet Simone's father indulged his daughter and lent them the Citroën and a driver for these trips. Arriving in town, Diu always stared for a minute at Nui Ba Den—the solitary Black Virgin Mountain that loomed beyond.

By the age of eight, Simone was confident, clever, articulate. She used her voice with an imperious disdain that could intimidate even her parents, and they approached her warily when she stewed in one of her legendary moods. No less could she be gloriously spirited and engaging. Gifted at games, she invented matches that diverted the servants with whom she played. Her favorite game used picture cards of threaded human faces that Diu had sewn according to Simone's instructions. Some of the stitched faces were oriental, others French. The object was to collect the more valuable French cards and above all to avoid the worst card that one could be dealt, the Japanese face, which delivered instant loss.

One afternoon, field men happened to be working near the garden when Simone commenced her card game. The usual household staff clustered, the maids and kitchen helpers. Diu stood by the trellis and watched—she never participated, for one part because she knew the cards too well, and for the other because she knew Simone too well. Simone invited the field hands to join, and hesitantly they agreed. The game proceeded pleasantly until Simone grew annoyed at them. Worried that they might hurt her feelings, they engaged half-heartedly. Play earnestly or leave, she insisted. Still they carried on feebly, until one of them, pledging to use all his cleverness, stepped forward. His name was Khiêm.

The contest was balanced. Khiêm was an adult and a natural competitor, yet this was Simone's game, and she'd invented the rules. As the play progressed, it became obvious she was losing. Almost feverish with intensity, gritting her teeth, she whooped when she selected a favorable card, shrieked when she drew an Asian face. The maids whispered anxiously in Khiêm's ear, cautioning him of the child's notorious temper. Then Simone had a streak of luck, three French cards in a row. At once her deportment mellowed, and she played gracefully, pretty girl in her impeccable dress surrounded by the garden flowers and the doting Vietnamese. She had gained the advantage, the game was all but finished. Only two cards remained. Khiêm reached, chose one. A Vietnamese face. No gain.

Simone smiled and put down her cards.

"You must take the last card," declared Khiêm.

Plantation hands did not instruct Simone in what she must or must not do. A hush fell over the gathered servants. None of them expected her to pay attention. Why should she? The game was hers, and Khiêm had no say over anything. Yet in her decisive way, she swept up the card and gazed at what she had drawn.

The charm vanished. The servants vainly tried to calm the girl who screeched like a bird caught in barbed wire. Wildly she pulled at her hair. Hearing her cries, her father rushed out, and thinking that someone had mistreated his daughter, he demanded an explanation. None of the servants understood what had happened until her hand yielded the crumpled Japanese face card.

Simone insisted that he fire Khiêm.

Her father was a reasonable man. Gently he explained that the field hand had meant no disrespect. He allowed a week to pass, hoping that his daughter would relent. Perhaps it was his way of preparing her for adulthood, to leave to her a decision of such magnitude. He was fond of saying that all that he owned—his land, his wealth, and his power soon to be restored, once the Japanese were gone—would one day pass to her. Within earshot of the servants, no doubt to remind them, he called her his beautiful heiress.

Silently Diu observed. She doubted that Simone would change her mind. With a servant's perception for things the parents often missed, Diu detected a profound coldness in the little empress.

One evening during the week, a maid informed Diu that a young woman was waiting for her by the gate that separated the garden from the groves. The woman was Khiêm's wife. Her name was Lien, and like her husband, she was a field worker. Diu remembered her as a person of encouragement, with a ready smile. The smile was not evident now. Fingers clenching the slats, Lien appeared stricken. She said she'd heard that Diu could influence Simone. Could Diu intervene to save her husband's job?

Diu replied, "I'm sorry, but what you heard is not true. I have no sway over her."

Lien clearly had gathered the courage to make her plea. She said, "What if I speak to her myself? We have a baby—a little girl. Surely Simone will understand—she is so beautiful, she must feel kindness in her heart." Lien's panic was justified: The Japanese Army had commandeered the rice, and there was none to spare for Vietnamese who lacked work. These days, thousands starved to death.

For the first and only time, Diu approached Simone on behalf of another worker. She waited in the upstairs hallway for an hour until the girl arrived. Now Diu confronted her: "Did you know that Khiêm has a wife and a baby daughter?"

Simone snapped, "Then he shouldn't have spoken."

"What did he do, except to tell you to observe the rules?"

Diu hoped that Simone would respond as she had years ago, when Diu had forced her to stand still for the measurements. But Simone simply glared, as if she could not believe that her seamstress was speaking to her in this way. Then she stepped into her room and closed the door. Diu knew that to remonstrate further was pointless, even dangerous.

Lien still waited by the garden gate. Diu delivered the bad news. "Simone has made up her mind. Once she has done so, her heart closes like a trap."

When the week passed, Simone's father bowed to his daughter's will. From the second-floor window, Diu watched Khiêm and Lien carrying their baby and their meager sacks of belongings. Their forms shrank until they submerged into the forest.

Tears flooded Diu's eyes. None of it made sense. How could Simone's father have permitted this injustice? Until now, she had not thought deeply about the world in which she lived, in which the masters' authority simply prevailed, imposed without her permission, and against which she dared not speak no matter how impetuously or arbitrarily the masters behaved. Now it dawned on her that such power brooked no effrontery, not even reminders to obey the rules, because any resistance whatsoever called its legitimacy into question. She saw that, to the Nogarets, the Vietnamese were like the stitched picture cards, things possessing no depth, whose role was to be played.

The Japanese met their defeat, but only after they'd brutally deposed the French colonial administration they suspected of conspiring with the British and the Americans. When the surviving French set about to reinstate *notre Indochine*, the long-anticipated event didn't go as they had hoped. Vietnamese rebels had seized the opportunity to declare independence for a nation whose history of self-governance traced back more than a thousand years. The rebels were strongest in the northern provinces around Hanoi, where Ho Chi Minh became the President of the new Democratic Republic of Vietnam. To restore the colonial paradigm, the French turned half-heartedly to negotiations and vigorously to force. French soldiers arrived on American ships. In December 1946, the French attacked Hanoi. It was then that the decades-old rural insurgency, long an irritant the French had branded as banditry, erupted into virulent guerrilla warfare. The plantations came under threat. Even benign employers like Nogaret experienced troubles with laborers who abandoned their jobs without explanation. The roads grew treacherous. Nobody traveled at night anymore.

The First Indochina War had begun.

(Listening to Tuy relate Diu's story, I was reminded how irony lay as thick as the jungle mists over our quarter-century embrace of the conflict. Throughout World War II, U.S. President Franklin Roosevelt had argued passionately to prevent France from reestablishing her dominion over Indochina. He'd wished to build pathways to independence for the Vietnamese and other subjugated peoples. With his increasing illness and fragility, and his death in early 1945, America's attention drifted, and France's wishes to remount her imperial grandeur prevailed. The ships were the first increment toward what eventually would become America's war.)

In the late 1940s, Mssr. Nogaret accepted an appointment to the council that advised the French Commissioner in Saigon. He moved his wife and daughter to the capital. Diu glimpsed Simone in the rear seat of the Citroën that brushed haughtily past on its way toward the An Loc highway. The young passenger did not wave to the servants who had gathered on the road only for the second time in thirteen years, this time to say good-bye. Tears streamed down Diu's cheeks. Quickly she wiped them so the others wouldn't notice. In Saigon, the Nogarets would employ servants. Diu they no longer needed. Exposed to the city's elegant emporiums, Simone immediately preferred the chic, imported fashions over the clothes her seamstress would have crafted for her.

The family's departure marked the end of a way of life. Mssr. Nogaret visited the plantation once a week. Occasionally his wife accompanied him; Simone, never. The drive through the countryside was too risky. Diu recouped her former job as a sap carrier in the groves. For a time, her life grew simple again, while, around her, everything else became more complicated. Representatives of the communist guerrillas—the Viet Minh—approached men and women seeking volunteers. Diu wanted nothing to do with them. Though she was poor, her life was without bitterness, and she had no desire to entwine it with a fanatical endeavor. She anticipated that a representative from the resistance would call on her, and she knew what she must say. She practiced her reply in a tone that conveyed refusal without arrogance or disrespect.

One morning, cloth cap in hand, a man waited where the trails merged. Edging to the far side so she could pass, she glanced up and noticed that he looked familiar. She stopped. In the cleft angles of his face she recognized Khiêm, who had played Simone's card game and copped his own severance. He smiled. "Hello, Diu. It is good to see you again."

"What do you want?"

"I represent the movement. I came to ask for your help."

At once she told him to go away. She wanted no part of the resistance. Her answer leapt from her tongue more abruptly than she'd rehearsed, and afterwards she fretted that she'd given offense. Still, wasn't it preferable that Khiêm hear her true feelings? He retreated so readily she dared to hope she would be left alone. But to abandon an objective was neither the practice of the Viet Minh nor in the character of Khiêm. A few days later, he stood again at the trail crossing. This time his wife Lien accompanied him. In a shaded spot off the path, he explained that he was the leader of the cadres in the area. He spent a few minutes asseverating political truths, as he called them, about the struggle's justness and how the people yearned to rise against their foreign oppressors. He seemed to think in terms of slogans. As she came to learn, they prefaced almost everything he said.

Then Lien spoke. Her gentle manner contrasted with her husband's intensity. Not everyone wished to fight, she acknowledged, and she had no wish to impose a heavy burden on Diu, a respected worker. Yet the resistance needed her—everyone knew of her skills. Ripped field harnesses cried for repair, one of the intricate and essential tasks at which women excelled and men fumbled.

Diu asked, "How can you be part of a movement that puts your daughter in danger?"

Lien's eyes fell. "When we were sent away, there wasn't enough food. Our daughter starved to death."

Diu was too shocked for words. Finally she managed to say, "Please forgive me."

"Why? It was not your fault."

In the end, Lien's simple humanity rather than Khiêm's political exhortations convinced Diu to join the movement. She became an auxiliary, called upon only occasionally, and she never carried a weapon; they were too scarce to be given to those who lacked the temperament to use them.

Usually she interacted with the lower-ranking Viet Minh, but occasionally she saw Khiêm. When he greeted her, his features softened, as if the sun had passed behind a cloud. Sometimes they found themselves alone together, and they chatted about simple things. Always he promised to pass along her fond wishes to Lien. She enjoyed these conversations, for his smile was affectionate and his interest genuine, not simply the technique of a good commander. The conversations never lasted long; invariably one of his men would arrive to deliver an urgent message, and his responsibilities would fetch him away.

In Tay Ninh Province, the guerrilla war swayed between tumult and slumber. Some days, hundreds of French soldiers marched through the groves. Then, for weeks afterward, she would see only her fellow laborers.

Explosions split the night, and in the morning it was as if nothing had happened. She glimpsed vehicles damaged by landmines and abandoned on the roadside. The smoke she smelled always seemed to come from a place unseen.

Stories reached her of the situation in the north. There the war was different, and terrible. The French used artillery, aerial bombardments, tanks. Hundreds died in the fierce clashes. The only reassuring aspect was that the north was far away.

Late in 1953, the plantation's field hands were summoned together and notified that Mssr. and Mme. Nogaret had been killed. Their Citroën had run over a landmine on the road between Saigon and Tay Ninh. Their deaths must have been fated, for the French military vehicles escorting the car from the front and behind hadn't suffered a scratch. The news saddened Diu, but she felt relief to be working in the rubber groves and not on the household staff. Her livelihood, the harvesting of sap, would go on. Nonetheless she found herself thinking of Simone, who had not reappeared at the plantation since her family had moved to Saigon four years ago. What would become of her? Surely she must sell the plantation and leave for France, the country where she belonged, where she would be safe.

But Diu was the one who ended up leaving.

She was carrying her empty sap buckets when a Viet Minh messenger stepped out from the trees. He instructed her to follow him to a truck that awaited them at the plantation's edge.

"Now? What about my work?"

"Leave your buckets on the ground."

"Will I ever come back?"

"Yes. It is temporary."

"What does that mean?"

"Six months. Or until we win."

Half a year sounded like an epoch to her. She rode northward in the bed of an old truck. They were headed for the real war, said the messenger, and they would traverse the Central Highlands, the lofty plateau in the Annamite Mountains. The roads soon vanished, and Diu and the other passengers disembarked onto the muddy jungle paths.

When the shoes she'd worn at the plantation fell apart, she donned sandals with soles fashioned from tire treads. Her feet blistered and cracked. Among the things she carried was a wooden bowl, and twice a day she held it out to be filled with rice. At times she was so weak she doubted she could walk another step, yet when she gazed down, she saw her sandaled feet slapping on the trail.

She joined a larger column of men and women who struggled as she did. No one complained. These were mere discomforts, not war. To whine brought dishonor. She sensed no danger until they reached the hills above a French fortress named Dien Bien Phu near the Laotian border. The siege already had started, and she was astounded at the number of Viet Minh assembled, thousands of them. Without disturbing the sheltering trees, they roped artillery pieces up the steep slopes to caves they had dug out of the hillsides. Rice and ammunition arrived on bicycles heavily laden and pushed great distances along jungle trails. Her task was to lug 75mm shells, one at a time, two kilometers from the offload point to the cannon she supported. She worked with a frail teenage girl named Mai. Often they chatted while they clambered up the rocky streamed toward the gun. Diu came to regard Mai as her daughter, and she protected her as much as she could. She let Mai rest along the way and shielded her from the other shell carriers who might rebuke her.

Weeks into the siege, hauling empty shell canisters down the hillside, they heard something buzz overhead. Abruptly the men dropped their loads and scattered. Through the leaves she glimpsed a plane tilted nose down, as if the pilot intended to crash. Suddenly it arced up from its dive, and a bomb lanced into the trees. It happened so fast she didn't seek cover. The shock wave from the explosion staggered her. Shards of bark pattered in the white smoke. Coughing, the Viet Minh searched for casualties. The blast had sheared off branches, and they pulled away the debris to see if anyone lay underneath. Nobody said anything.

She found Mai below a clutch of men. Squeezing past them, Diu sat cross-legged on the ground, resting the girl's head on her lap. One of her shoulders had been blown away, exposing the jagged bone edges and the pink lung tissue. She was unconscious. Please don't wake up, Diu begged under her breath. Mai never did.

The Viet Minh had said Diu's service would be temporary. After the French fortress fell, she learned that temporary was a word the leaders used at their convenience. Not six months but three years passed before she received permission to return south. She joined a column that retraced her long journey through the highlands to Tay Ninh Province.

The country had changed; the war had split Vietnam. Below the 17th parallel, the new nation of South Vietnam was ruled by Ngo Dinh Diem, whose devout Catholic faith and hatred for the communists endeared him to the Americans. He plotted merciless campaigns against his enemies. When his security officials learned that Diu had gone off with the resistance, they arrested her cousins merely for being her blood relatives. The southern communist cadres mounted a struggle to unite the south and the north. Not until this campaign was well under way did northern leader Ho Chi Minh acknowledge the fervor with which the southerners fought and begin sending supplies and people to help.

At a camp in the secluded forest not far from the Tay Ninh plantation, Diu's column linked up with the local guerrilla force. Its commander was Khiêm. Leaner than she remembered, formal and correct in front of the others, once alone with Diu he greeted her as an old friend. He related what had happened in the period she'd been away. The saddest news was that Lien had been killed by a South Vietnamese military patrol. Diu wept.

He had more stunning revelations. Simone Nogaret had returned to the Tay Ninh plantation. A beautiful young woman, she'd astonished everyone with her acumen. She'd married a French ex-paratrooper who used his skills to organize the plantation's defenses. Diu still pictured Simone as a child, and the revelation that her former charge had wed such a man made her feel old.

Khiêm's overdrawn language had not changed. He explained how he wanted to get rid of the French plantations and restore the land to the people. "I want you to stay with me and help," he said.

"Stay with you?"

"I apologize for my abruptness, but if I don't speak now..." For the first time her old commander appeared unsure of himself. "I want you to stay with me as my wife. All these years I have thought of you, hoping to see you again. In my enthusiasm for the resistance, I have risked much, and I regret what I have sacrificed, for Lien to be killed, and you to be sent away. It is my wish that you should not be lost to me anymore."

She found her answer as if she had prepared it, as when she'd encountered him years ago on the trail. "What I want is to live a normal life. Whoever marries you can only be wed to the resistance."

She expected to hear another of his patriotic speeches. He merely said, "I will arrange for you to be transferred to my command. Once this is done, you will be a civilian again."

He kept his word. Deactivated from the cadres, she moved into a village close to the place where she had lived as a child, in an area he controlled. Few of her relatives remained; the rest had fled or were in prison, arrested during President Diem's anti-communist campaigns. Diu and Khiêm were married in a small ceremony in the shade of mahogany trees. In the distance, like wedding fireworks, artillery thumped from cannons the Americans had supplied to the South Vietnamese.

She tried at first to keep herself away from the work of the resistance. As was perhaps inevitable, she began to help them in modest ways, mending their torn packs or caring for wounded or sick soldiers. More importantly, she assumed the role of trusted advisor to her husband. Marriage with Khiêm meant abiding with his bravura, repeating his slogans in the presence of others, and, in private, critiquing his ruthless schemes. She felt like an idolater before a deity that oozed blood. Having internalized discipline in the cause, admiring the resolve of those who struggled year after year for a united Vietnam, she found herself under the coolie pole of its relentless stress, which she thought was the reason she never was able to conceive a child.

Savagely Khiêm fought the war of national liberation. Among his enemies was Simone, whose plantation he attacked with the same earnestness he had shown during their card match in the garden. When he came home, he described his actions, which were calculated to make the plantation untenable. He scared away the workers, mined the road, burned the outlying facilities. He availed himself of the weapon of terror. If he heard that a Vietnamese outpost guard had fired his rifle at the guerrillas, his men would cut off the guard's hands. If he learned of a village chief who spoke favorably of the plantation's masters or Diem's government, he had the chief murdered. Within a year, he had achieved progress. News arrived that Simone was selling her property to other Frenchmen, no doubt fools who had more money than sense.

One steamy evening, Khiêm returned home, and she saw that the creases in his face had deepened to canyons of frustration. He announced, "The French wish to pay us to stop attacking them."

"So? What does their money mean to us?"

"The Command thinks we should compromise."

They sat quietly for a time. The failing light played off the rough teakwood beams that held up their roof. The sky was purple, bisected by palm trees that outlined rectangles like huge windows. She said, "We spilled our blood at Dien Bien Phu. How can the French be allowed to keep their lands? Do idiots command the resistance these days?"

His eyes beamed rebuke. "The Americans are the problem now. The French are harmless. Resources devoted to them are wasted. The plantation's new owners claim they have no interest in politics. They wish simply to tend their business. They agree to pay us taxes in secret. It is the best way."

"You believe this?"

"It is not important what I believe. They wish to meet with us to negotiate the amount of the taxes. I have been ordered to send an emissary who speaks good French." He pressed his fists against his eyes. Schooled in the wisdom of the movement, Khiêm lacked a way to adapt when it went awry. She felt pity and anger spinning together like the threads from two spools. She never thought she knew the resistance well, but in this minute she understood how it worked, the exchange of a greater evil for a lesser one, a fine bargain as long as the calculations were exact.

"I will go," she said.

He nodded. It seemed this had been his wish all along.

They discussed what she should say.

* * *

The meeting was timed for the hour of dusk, at the easternmost grove where the plantation's road blended into a jungle trail. She was familiar with this corner; she had broken her ankle here many years ago. To one side lay a peasant's graveyard where the stone markers sketched rows on a gentle slope, as if the dead were in attendance at an amphitheater. The beams from the perimeter lights spread like the arms of ghosts.

Khiêm had briefed her thoroughly. The plantation's new owner was Leon Gavet, a pragmatic Frenchmen who cared only for his profits. He was willing to pay the cadres in exchange for peace, the exact sum to be negotiated. Gavet or his deputy might show up. Gavet was tall and fat, the deputy, Cecil Cocteau, short and fat. Cecil had an easygoing manner, therefore he was the more formidable in negotiations. Both were clever. She had no idea how the resistance had obtained its information about Leon and Cecil.

It did not matter, for neither one appeared.

From the white car that halted at the edge of the grove stepped Simone Nogaret.

Diu marveled at the tall woman who approached her. Twenty-two years old, Simone strode gracefully despite the uneven ground; her bamboo-shaded hair shone like the lacquered tables that had adorned the Nogaret house. The pressed creases of her twill slacks scissored the air as she moved, and in a leather shoulder holster, a pistol's handle nudged her left breast. Recalling the little girl who had played cards in the garden, Diu had to squeeze her jaws to keep her discipline from shattering. How odd, when she regarded Simone, the predominant emotion she felt was affection.

Simone gave neither a greeting nor a smile. She stopped, glanced around, and smacked her lips. "I came here to meet the enemy, and I find my old dressmaker instead. Somebody is having a joke at my expense."

"You found who you expected. I am the one who must doubt *your* credentials." Diu's words leapt without forethought. *Be careful what you say to her!*

"What exquisite irony, for me to prove my bona fides to you." Simone lit a cigarette. Her face was a yellow moon in the match light.

"The Gavet Company asked me to negotiate with the locals I knew growing up. How literal it proved, they never could have imagined."

Simone stepped very close. So tall and bold, her presence was incredibly intimidating, and the urge rushed Diu to step backwards, the way a servant would. All her life seemed to flow together in this moment—the march to Dien Bien Phu, the months in the jungle, the girl Mai dying in her lap—and she beseeched her ancestors for the strength to keep her feet motionless.

"So what are your demands, dear old seamstress of mine?"

"We shall have free passage of the land." She fought to suppress the tremor in her voice. "You will pay us a percentage of your income. You will not cooperate with the government or give them information about us. If you do, we will find out, and we will hold you to account."

"Next, you'll have me planting mines in the road for you." Simone's voice was mocking and accusatory at the same time. Diu wanted to say that she had had nothing to do with the deaths of Simone's parents, yet she knew she must not show sympathy.

"What's the percentage?"

"Twenty."

Simone laughed. "Don't be absurd."

"Thirty," said Diu. Khiêm had instructed her to negotiate this way, for shock value. She was not sure she had it in her.

"My little dressmaker, you have no concept of money. You are bluffing. Tell your friends twenty is too high. If they wish to negotiate, they should send a cleverer bargainer. Go now."

"*You* go," said Diu. Tears and rage choked her, to be dismissed so coldly by this girl she had tended with love. She felt the wind on her face and hoped the dark would hide her tears.

Abruptly Simone stalked off.

For the next meeting, Khiêm sent one of his lieutenants who spoke passable French. Simone did not reappear this time. Her husband André represented the plantation owners.

They agreed on twenty percent.

* * *

Folding her notes, Tuy said, "I do not think I will see her again."

From her vivid account, I pictured Diu, the remarkable woman who had delivered such insights about Simone Nogaret. Tuy was right. Diu would disappear into the folds of the Viet Cong infrastructure; she wouldn't risk a second meeting.

"Did Diu say anything more about André?"

"No. She never met him."

"What happened to the land Simone's father owned in Cambodia?"

"Diu didn't say. I doubt she knew."

On the western edge of the protrusion known as the Fishhook, the Nogarets' Cambodian plantation had been an oasis of seclusion. I imagined it now, helicopters swarming over, tanks and armored personnel carriers roaring through the groves, artillery shells shearing off the fronds. If Simone still owned the land, her net worth had declined.

Easing out of her clothes, Tuy pinched out the candle and rustled under the sheets, waiting for me. But I wasn't ready for sleep. Cross-legged on the mat, I sat thinking, listening to the rhythm of her breathing.

"Tuy?"

"What?" Her voice was groggy.

"What happened to Khiêm?"

"He died during Tet."

"Where?"

"Somewhere in Saigon."

In the distance, a river barge gonged in the fog.

* * *

Half a block from Simone Nogaret's apartment building, I waited at a café table. The morning was peaceful. Birds sang in the tamarind trees. People walked hand in hand. Balconies gracefully laddered the yellow-brick facade to her sixth-floor penthouse windows where the sun-braised clouds reflected like bubbles in champagne.

Nicknamed the Pearl of the Far East, Saigon owned a few pearls of its own, and this street was one of them. A person who lived here would view the world differently than would the residents of Cholon or Tan Son Nhut. To be sure, it was the choicest cut of the colonial city, styled to remind people of Paris, and the French expatriates could blush with pride when they walked under its umbrella trees. A purely rational man does not make a good colonialist; it takes a romantic able to reconcile facts intrinsically at odds, for instance how France's foot on Vietnam's throat might be an enlightened gesture, and how the Vietnamese who resisted were striking at the heart of France. For the French Army to have fought to preserve the colony did not take much convincing. The military officers were the most romantic of all, they required only a hint that Saigon was an extension of their nation. Wasn't Paris too a city on a river, a grown-up village on a marsh bend? On these streets, you needn't stress your imagination, you could see France in the facades, smell her in the perfumeries, taste her in the patisseries and restaurants, hear her language. Even the street signs in Vietnamese bore her imprint in the Roman-alphabet transliteration a French monk had invented more than a hundred years ago.

On this street lived Simone, a woman who'd spent her life in Vietnam. This was her Saigon.

At ten hundred hours, I spotted the reporter Alton Gribley shuffling in his rubber-soled Hush Puppies and yellow linen pants. The morning heat had flushed his cheeks. When I'd phoned this morning and asked him to meet me here, he'd needed a minute to put aside his bafflement.

The waiter brought a bowl of fruit and two cold Pepsis to the table. Gribley took a grateful gulp.

"Recognize the neighborhood?" I asked.

"No. Should I?"

"You tried to get an interview with Simone Nogaret. She lives in the building behind you."

Gribley craned over his shoulder for a glimpse, a quick one, he was discreet enough not to stare. His question came low toned, matter of fact. "So you went after the Gavet Plantation angle?"

"Yes. It turned out to be a good lead."

From his shirt pocket, Gribley slid a pen and small notebook to his lap, below the tablecloth, where the waiter couldn't observe.

"The dead man's name was Gerard Penelon. He was French, a helicopter pilot." I explained Gerard's flight route from Vung Tau, how the chopper had gone down in the marshland known as Area Zulu.

"Penelon. Spell that." Gribley wrote down what I told him. He said, "A Frenchman. So there's no unknown soldier after all. The investigation must be over."

"Closed officially, two nights ago."

"Is MACV going to issue a statement?"

"Eventually. They'll probably phrase it in a way to discredit your story."

Disharmony clouded Gribley's features. "Is that why you called me, to wring out a retraction, so you could show off how well you did for General Cobris?"

I popped a grape in my mouth. "I called because I need your help."

"With what?"

"My investigation."

There was no flashy display of comprehension; Gribley knew how to keep a straight face. The momentary absence of a question meant he was listening.

"Everything led here, before it was turned off." I tipped an orange slice toward the yellow bricks. "Whatever Gerard Penelon was doing, Simone was involved. So were Cobris and his boys. Beyond that, I can't make much sense of it, and frankly I wouldn't give a fuck except that they've threatened my people. They know I'm on to them, and they're going to transfer me out. There's not much time."

"Your people? Who are we talking about?"

"A Saigon cop. And a showgirl. There's a murder contract out on the girl."

Gribley made a notation. He was the first American I'd met who seemed to accept my loyalties to my Vietnamese friends at face value. He looked up from his pad. "What do you want from me?"

"To confirm another lead."

His pencil scratched furiously as I explained.

* * *

In the yellow-brick building's lobby, the concierge connected me to Marie Dobier, who asked, "Why do you wish to speak to Mademoiselle, Major?"

"I have an item that belongs to her."

"And what would that be?"

"Just tell her what I said."

I heard the phone clunk noisily as Marie, protective of her mistress, went to inquire. I had the impression she was as diligent as she was doctrinaire, meaning I might not have to wait long. Two French security men edged so close I was in the drift of their perspiration odor.

Simone's silky voice came on the line. "George?"

"I'm in the lobby. If you can spare a few minutes, I'd like to come up."

"A new development?"

"Yes."

She cleared my passage with the guards, who escorted me in the mirror-plated elevator. She awaited me in the penthouse doorway. In tight peach slacks, an orchid short-sleeved blouse, and fashion sandals, she looked stunning. Her widely spaced, subtly shadowed green-blue eyes regarded me without expression. Gliding to the cream sofa, she motioned for me to sit, and she reclined into the absinthe-green chair. The corner of the glass-topped table separated us, and she picked up a lighter from the jade ashtray and flamed a cigarette. She must go through a lot of them, there were layers in the air, to drop onto the sofa was like an elevator ride through an Eiffel Tower made of smoke. Refracted sunlight dashed a spectrum across her blouse, and I wondered if she was the most beautiful woman in Saigon.

The curtains hung open to admit the surging sunlight. There were not many buildings around as tall as this one, none to obscure the view on three sides. On the south horizon, I could make out Cholon's rooftops. On Thong Nhat Boulevard a few blocks away, a corner of the U.S. Embassy, and at the far end of Tu Do, the spires of Saigon's Notre Dame Cathedral.

I asked, "Have you lived here long?"

"For years. I own the building."

"It must be the best real estate in town."

"It was. Now I think I shall sell." A puff frosted the air between us. "You told Marie you have something of mine."

A little push sent the orange purse across the table's surface. She scooped it up and checked inside, closed the zipper, and restored her gaze to me. No wariness there, only the shading of amusement, the way an owner regards a pet that has done something cute.

"Last week, you wore a white sweater with a long neck and sleeves." Unabashedly I scanned her bare arms and neckline. "Your bruises have healed."

She leveled a stare that had no meaning aside from the absence of other signals. An aristocrat becomes practiced at issuing dismissals, and by her repose she invited me to proceed.

"My job was to learn the identity of a man who died in the jungle. To do that, I've had to ask a lot of questions. The answers have taken me beyond the bounds of my imagination."

She tapped her cigarette against the jade ashtray.

"You were wearing a black sweater that night—a helicopter gets chilly at altitude. When the instrument panel blinked red, you would have been able to see the lights of the plantation antenna in the distance. It must have been strange, so close to where you grew up, to realize you were dropping into the rain forest. Then came the impact in the treetops, the engine gears ripping, glass and rivets popping out. Afterward, the only sounds were your breathing, both of you cased in the electric sensation of being alive."

Reverie in her eyes? Impossible to tell.

"Yesterday I stood in the wreck. I climbed down the same way you did, through the vine tunnel, past those grabby thorns into the water of that smelly marsh. It was an awful place to find yourself at night. Two things worked in your favor. One was luck. To ride a chopper into the trees and walk away uninjured, you needed plenty. The second, you were with a good man. Whatever you paid Gerard to work for you, he earned it that night. He would have tried to send a distress transmission from a dry mound you came upon in the swamp. It didn't help—nobody was answering. At dawn, soaked, the two of you began slogging westward toward the road, a long way off but the single course that made sense to you. He showed you the map location where he guessed you'd crashed. He carried the radio and the other gear. A compass too, which proved vital in finding your way. Tell me, did Gerard prepare the emergency kit, or did Major Stobe set it up for you?"

No answer. Tilting her head to show the unblemished curve of her neck, she blew smoke at the ceiling.

"All day you sloshed ahead. The adrenalin burned off and the fatigue set in. You emerged from the swamp into the thicker rain forest, only to find your way blocked by a deep tributary of the Saigon River. It inspired a decision, as such places do. Here was a clearing to rest. At the water's edge, you might be spotted from the air. You knew somebody would come searching for you, but you couldn't be sure how long it would take. So you decided that Gerard should continue on, swim across, and reach the road, far away though it was. To hedge your bets seemed wise. Leaving the radio with you, he set out, probably in the late afternoon. Before he entered the water, he took pains to protect something important to him. He sealed a photograph of his Vietnamese fiancée in the buffer well of his rifle. He never showed you the photo or told you about the girl. It seems you trusted him, but he didn't trust you."

I thought Simone might react to the last line. I was wrong. Through the smoke, she regarded me detachedly.

"That night you stayed on the riverbank, until, in the morning, you finally heard a response on the radio. Again you got lucky, because your batteries were running out. Gerard had forgotten to leave you the spare D-cells he'd rolled up in his poncho. When Major Stobe found you, his crew lowered a rescue harness from the helicopter to pull you up, and it was all you could do to hang on, so you abandoned the radio. You also left behind the second poncho and canteen, the C-ration cans, and a bottle of iodine tablets. You kept a few items. A flashlight. The weapon Gerard handed you—a nine-millimeter pistol. You probably had other maps, to cover the remote areas the helicopter flew over. I'm betting you tossed the maps in the water, but maybe you took them with you."

At my revelations, her eyes crinkled—all the affirmation I was going to get. I knew about the pistol from the solitary 9mm bullet; he wouldn't have left her unarmed. The flashlight was obvious—it was the only way he'd have found the vine tunnel at night. He wouldn't have taken the sole flashlight, leaving her without. The maps were a guess; I'd found no trace of additional maps either in the helicopter or by the river. I didn't mention the screwdriver, I hadn't found it, but somewhere nearby, or maybe in the tributary, was the one he'd used to open his rifle stock to fit in Kim Thi's photo.

Animated now, pumping her crossed leg, she stared at me, her dusk-in-the-forest eyes lively. "You didn't come here to regale me with your cleverness."

"No."

She lit another cigarette. "What do you want?"

"To help me keep someone alive."

"Who?"

"Kim Thi. The dancer in the photo."

"You found her?"

"Yes. There's a contract for her assassination."

She tossed her head, and her hair flayed out and curled back precisely on itself. "You are a man driven, George. I sympathize. But how can I help you with that?"

"I need to find out why somebody is trying to kill her."

"Have you spoken to my husband?"

"Yes."

"You should speak to him again."

I thought of the moment, as André had described, when sixteen years ago she'd walked into that room, and he'd turned with everyone else to behold the teenage aristocrat, the beautiful heiress who refused to listen to the adults urging her to abandon Indochina and leave for France. The sinewy insurgents who planted mines in the road hadn't frightened her. With her ex-para mate, she'd fought to keep her colonial birthright. The years of war should have carved more lines in that perfect face. She'd handled everything, the war, her failed marriage, the helicopter crash, with the same aplomb she evinced now.

The dismissal came in a subtle shift of her posture. When I rose she followed me, smiling softly, a reward for picking up her signal—she knew how to train her men. "Thank you for returning my jewels, George. Perhaps we shall meet again."

The two French security men stood outside her door, where I suspected they'd waited since she'd let me in. They escorted me to the lobby and out.

* * *

Tuy had asked me to buy towels and a few other things for Kim Thi, and for half an hour I perused Cholon's market stalls where I haggled lightly with the vendors. When I got to Tuy's street, the wind had picked up. The hanging clothes leapt like puppets. I lingered in the tree shadows looking for Trong's sentinel. He wasn't there. A clatter like a dropped plastic saucer wobbled eerily. Against the stucco, her second-floor window made a dark rectangle.

Had the women gone out, despite my warning? If so, would Tuy have left a note for me?

The soggy canal air muffling my footsteps, I crossed to the stairwell door, prepared to use my key, found it unlocked, not unusual for the afternoon, but Tuy's awareness of the threat against Kim Thi made it inexplicable. I entered the stairwell and strained for the timbre of a woman's voice or the music from the portable radio. At the switchback landing halfway up, I paused. A shift in the air as subtle as a breath. The staircase led nowhere except to her apartment; no others used it but for the cleaning woman who swept out the dust. Stairways inevitably collected scents, of cooking, mildew, sweat, but now a metallic acridness welled, as if from a broken moped. The smell grew prominent when I breached the plane of the upper floor. At the landing outside her door, I caught the odor enough to identify it.

Burnt gunpowder.

Somebody had fired a gun here.

The safety on my .45 clicked. For a minute, I froze against the opposite wall, staring at the brown monolith of Tuy's door. My heart hammered. Beside me, the landing window—the one in which I'd first seen her below the Roman frieze—threw pale swatches of light against the panels. What awaited me inside? I pictured her face and the panic mounted. Then I noticed that the door was not entirely closed; the shot-out lock distended from the wood.

A shooter would have had a better chance at me from the top of the stairs. Nobody was inside, I concluded.

Nobody alive.

I almost pushed the door open.

Doors. May 1968. Mini-Tet, they'd called it. The severed torso of a South Vietnamese soldier had dangled upside down in the tree branches, his boots still upright where his feet last had filled them, in front of a door he'd opened to search a house the Viet Cong had taken over in a skirmish in western Cholon. Below the suspended torso, a crowd of spectators had gathered, and like me they must have wondered why the soldier hadn't used the window—surely he'd been trained to avoid the doors of houses the enemy recently had occupied. Exploding behind the rigged door, the bomb had ripped away the house the way a ravenous mouth bites a rice cake.

I ran my fingertips along the inside edge of the jamb, to the bolt recess and over a bullet gore in the wood, nearly to the floor where, moving as gently as water droplets, they brushed the wire. It was half slack. I might have pushed the door open a forearm's length before the wire tugged out the pin on the grenade taped to the lower wall. Gently fingering the wire to judge its tautness, I slid my hand between the door and the jamb and gripped the grenade, the shape and texture revealing an American M-33. It was a good choice for a booby trap, more reliable than Chinese or Russian grenades, probably with the fuse shortened to one or two seconds rather than the standard four-second delay. My thumb on the handle so it wouldn't detonate, I pried it free, unspun the wire, and bent down the pin's edges to fix it firmly. The grenade in my hand was secure. Was there another?

It was a risk, a jackhammer turned loose in a house of mirrors, but I had to know what was in there, so with my foot I gave the door a shove, straining in the silence for the telltale zing of a grenade handle that would have sent me vaulting over the stair rail. The door arced open and thumped unimpeded against the bathtub.

I stared at an empty room, quiet except for the drip of the tub's hose. Where were Tuy and Kim Thi?

It is one thing to command yourself to logic, another to obey, as the vortex of panic whirls around your head. My fingers clenching the grenade had gone white. Roving the room, I saw the trail of wood debris on the floor, no other signs there had been a disturbance here.

Whoever had shot off the lock had not found the women. They would have killed them on the spot and not bothered to booby trap the door. I told myself the grenade was proof Tuy and Kim Thi were alive.

What if the women had been taken and the booby trap set to keep me off their trail?

Stand still and think!

Trong must have learned of the danger in advance and pulled the women out. He might have ordered the police sentinel to move them somewhere.

My choices were to wait here or to go searching for them. Best to find Trong first, I thought. No telling if the attackers had posted a watcher. If so, they'd know I'd disarmed their welcome-home surprise, and I might expect visitors momentarily.

Where to stash the grenade? From the landing, I recovered the bag of purchases, brought it to the table, and took out the towels. Under them I nested the grenade like a steel egg.

* * *

The people on Dong Khanh ignored me craning over their heads. It was the hour when they crowded the curbs for a ride. A cyclo was too slow—I needed a taxi or a scooter. Too hyped to wait my turn, I tried to crab past them, but they were quick and slipped into the vehicles ahead of me. Jostling along the sidewalk, I passed a side street whose specialty was coffin-making, and the notion of choosing one for Tuy—a narrow, tapering box—frenzied me even more. A woman stepped toward a yellow and blue Renault, and I bumped her aside, climbed in, and barked the name of Trong's street. Heads swiveled, men spat on the ground and uttered verdicts. The smoke from the fish cookers could have made a banner: *The Ugly American.*

Twelve years ago, journalists Eugene Burdick and William Lederer had published their memorable novel about how American naiveté had made us saps for the communists in a make-believe Southeast Asian country suggestive of South Vietnam. The title had become synonymous with our arrogant image abroad. The Kennedy and Johnson administrations had spoken of the book and its lessons. I'd read it. All of us had read it. Yet here I was, making a jackass of myself and branding my fellow Americans. I was the man who, warned over and over not to walk into a wall, walked into it, as if the wisdom of the past amounted to nothing, and all that mattered was my trepidation of the moment.

At Trong's house, I paid the driver to wait for me while I ran to the door and banged. It opened a few inches. His wife's face hovered in the slit, her expression as unmoving as the chain. "No here!"

"*Xin loi...*" I struggled for my few words of Vietnamese. "*Bao lau?*"

"He go."

"Where?"

The door shut and I knocked again. It cracked open. I said, "*Noi du'o'c Trong?*"

"Sureté," she trilled. The door thumped shut.

Sureté. She meant the police.

At the prefecture, the taxi driver refused my offer of extra money to wait, and I entered by the door where the demonstration had formed two days ago, now quiet under the rain-pending sky. The payless policemen were gone, having been paid or tear gassed. En route to Giang's office, I took a wrong turn into a corridor where dozens of men gawked at me from behind the bars of an overcrowded detention cell. The custodian yipped and shooed me away. Finally I reached Giang's door. It was closed. I knocked. No answer.

I headed toward Trong's office, hoping the door would be open. He could wink and lead me to a discreet place to talk. The door was shut; I had to stand there and knock. People in the adjacent hallway stared.

No response from inside. I didn't know the other detectives, and to ask them might invite trouble for my friend, so I said nothing. Cops froze in their steps. Perhaps they perceived panic in my ceaseless tapping on the wood. From a plainclothesman, in English, "He no work here anymore."

"Where does he work?"

Nobody knew.

* * *

Across the street, children chased each other along a concrete blast barrier. Every two meters or so, gray runoff lines segmented the wall, and the kids blurred from line to line like figures in an old film reel. It was comforting to see them indulge in the normal antics of children, not begging or peddling cigarettes. Rarely had the Vietnamese evoked my envy, but I envied these kids now for their heedless frolic.

I had to think clearly. Trong was neither at home nor at the prefecture. The plainclothesman had said he didn't work there anymore. A possibility clapped in my head. What if the two women hadn't been warned? What if they'd been out on their own? They might return to the apartment to find that whoever had set the booby trap had returned too, and was waiting inside.

A scooter cab snarled into view. Waving it down, I directed the driver to Tuy's apartment, tapped his shoulder, held out my fist, pumped it. The message connected—money for speed. We cut across a shopping street, threading between startled pedestrians, onto Dong Khanh where we shot through a popcorn popper of angry exclamations. Hooking a precarious right-leaning turn at Tuy's street, he kicked up the gravel in front of her building. Into his open palm I slapped piastre bills that he didn't count; he fishtailed away, the smoke and dust billowing.

Rain began to beat on the leaves. I was about to head up the stairs when I spotted a figure leaning against a tree. Perhaps Giang supported himself on the tree because he didn't have the strength to stand for long. The cigarette he brought to his mouth was as thin as the bones that held it. Folding his lips back from yellow teeth, he sidled closer, and his voice came low and raspy; it would have been low and raspy had he shouted. "You should not bring drivers so close."

"Where is Tuy?"

"A safe place. We go."

* * *

The rain cascaded; the sky orbed low over Giang's hood. He drove westward into Cholon, through alleys like flooded sewers. Twice the engine expired and he had to restart it.

"Trong too loyal to you," he said. "He get himself killed for you."

"He's my friend."

Giang looked like he might spit.

I asked, "When did he find out?"

"This morning."

"How?"

"He has other friends."

I related my visit to the apartment, the booby trap behind the door.

"They very bold," he warbled. "Even for Huang's men. Too much trouble for club dancer."

"She must know something that could hurt them."

"What could she know? Huang too powerful to care about her. She *nobody*."

Nobody. A shadow in a crowd. A presence unfelt. I'd fancied that I knew Saigon, but truly it eluded me. What could have lent Kim Thi the gravitas to merit a paid hit? My hip still ached from the fall through her banister when the shooters had opened fire. An hour ago, I'd nearly triggered a booby trap entering Tuy's apartment. All for a showgirl Saigon's underworld was striving to kill.

Giang u-turned and stopped briefly to watch for anyone following. From Pham Phu Thu he spun into Pham Van Chi. At last he swerved into a flooded alley between shanty walls of flattened tin cans nailed on like shingles. Splashing through puddles, he reached a wider space where I thought he'd do another u-turn. Instead he drove ahead, eased the car underneath a corrugated overhang, and got out. He led me along a walkway where our shoulders brushed the tin cans. I saw why Trong might have found advantages in this place, a nook within a labyrinth. Giang halted at a recessed door, tapped, and pushed inside.

On the straw mats sat Tuy and Kim Thi. They stared expectantly, and Tuy read the relief in my face. When she pressed into my arms, I squeezed her, and the sweet aroma of her hair almost buckled my knees. Across the room, Giang dropped weakly into the corner beside Kim Thi, offered her a cigarette that she lit with a candle. No longer wary of her skeletal protector, she smiled at him. The cigarette and candlesmoke blended into a thatch overhead.

Reluctantly I explained what had happened, the booby trapping of our home. The news hit Tuy like the death of a loved one. Never before had I seen her weep. She drew her breaths in short gasps, squeezed her eyes against the rushing tears. The rain plinked the tin cans. Rain and tears. I rested my cheek on her hair. How could I have delivered this misery to her life?

In the corner, Kim Thi and Giang, the dancer and the ghoul, regarded us with expressions between sympathy and indifference.

An hour later Trong arrived. He played father to everyone, arranging the containers of rice and chicken he'd brought, making Tuy and Kim Thi laugh at the mirth in his voice. He served the food, steaming hot and spicy, and the aromas and his presence calmed the mood in the little room. I couldn't help but be cheered too. Together we sat on the piled straw mats that kept the floor's dampness from seeping through.

While the others continued eating, he gestured me outside to the walkway and along to where he'd tucked his car. Spill from the sloped roof rutted the ground. Over the shacks I could make out a line of buildings pronging TV aerials, profligate even in Saigon's poor neighborhoods. He turned, and his happy facade fell away like a Chinese New Year's mask whose cord had snapped. "Huang has the whole city out searching for her. He has put big money on her head. You *must* get her to an American base."

"I'll try."

"To try is not enough!" From a man who would go far to avoid confrontation, it was quite an outburst.

"I will do it. But I must get permission. It won't happen before tomorrow."

"Huang has many watchers—soldiers, police, shopkeepers, children. In time he will find her. If you delay, she will be killed."

"I went to the police station to find you," I said. "I apologize, but I was worried for Tuy. They told me you don't work there anymore."

He had to force his eyes to meet mine. "Last night, they removed me from my position. Giang too."

"Jesus."

"I think they will transfer me outside the city."

"To where?"

"Maybe a provincial capital, or a backwater town. If I can, I will bring Giang. Otherwise, he has no place to go. Nobody wants him."

I thought of Trong's garden, his daughters and wife left alone. "I'm sorry."

He contemplated the rain spatters. "Now is wartime. Worse things happen to people."

What had I ever done to merit this man as my friend?

The rain pounded.

Day 11

Wriggling through traffic on the back of a Lambretta motorbike, I was half a block from the Caravelle Hotel when I spotted the woman in the miniskirt and low-cut sequined halter. I'd encountered so many weird things on Saigon's avenues that the woman would have been unremarkable, except that her stare had settled on me. Her head turned with the scooter rounding the corner. Any woman on Tu Do Street might be a prostitute, but her focus on me was too concentrated, especially for the first hour of daylight. As the scooter sputtered by, she traipsed a few steps in her stiletto heels, pointed at me, and screeched, "You Tanner!"

"Pull over," I told the driver. "Wait for me."

My uniform had a nametag which, standing so close to the street, she might have read, though it seemed unlikely. Something else was happening, impossible to interpret, and I'd have been smart to ride away rather than to approach her as I did now. "What do you want?"

"Come," she chirped. "This way."

"Why?"

She beckoned with a gathering motion of her wrist, the same gesture Tuy used, fingers turned down as if to stir bath water. In Saigon over the years, the communists had assassinated American and French soldiers—shot them from speeding mopeds, blown them up with grenades tossed under café tables. Why not use an aggressive prostitute who could read nametags? Warily I followed her to a plain, propped-open door, for the absurd reason that she'd told me to do so.

"Upstair," she said.

For the western elite, the rooftop bar of the nearby Caravelle had become a celebrated spot, its reputation handed down from the days when pioneer journalists had lounged in the sultry night air sipping their sloe-gin fizzes, while flares like fireworks blossomed over the swamps across the river. When I entered, I thought this might be a side entrance to the famous hotel, a discreet passage for the clientele to ascend to the rooftop bar. But no, the fastidious Caravelle would not have funneled its guests along this dim staircase. Venturing another step, I called, "Anybody there?"

"It's okay. Come on up." The American voice rang familiar. I squeezed past frayed electric wires and chipped bricks seeping moisture, a passage as derelict as the shack where Tuy and Kim Thi hid. In the accommodation-starved city center, westerners would rent any space they could find.

On the third floor landing waited Gribley in shorts and a white T-shirt. He swirled a red-labeled bottle of Vietnamese '33' beer that must have counted for his breakfast. Behind him opened a room that barely accommodated a sheet-crumpled bed and a side table where reposed a portable typewriter and a cairn of books: Bernard Fall's *Street Without Joy*, David Halberstam's *The Making of a Quagmire*, Jean Lacouture's biography of Ho Chi Minh, and a novel—Graham Greene's *The Quiet American*, all sprouting torn scraps as markers. The screened window overlooked Tu Do, and I could see my driver's leg braced against the curb.

I said, "I thought you stayed at the Caravelle."

"Too pricey for my nonexistent expense account. The desk takes messages for me."

"Who's the woman on the street?"

He grinned. "My friend Sally. I noticed you go by one morning last week, so I sent her downstairs to watch for you. She's not bad, eh?"

Was I so predictable that this reporter's doxy could fish me out of traffic? It meant I was absurdly easy to kill. Alarming, but I'd known it already, hadn't I?

He tapped his cigarette ashes into the '33' bottle. "It was tricky, confirming what you saw. Partly I wasn't asking the right people. And I admit, I really didn't believe it was true. People glimpse things and get the wrong idea. And you said it was dark and you were ninety feet in the air."

"More like sixty."

"What's the difference? It provoked skepticism. You can ask a question and get the stare of disbelief only so many times before you give up. I almost did." He tossed the ash-mouthed empty into a bucket of bottles in the corner. No wonder he was pudgy. "My hat's off to you, Tanner. You were right. Whatever it is you MP investigators do, you're good at it."

I thought of Tuy and Kim Thi sitting in a ghetto shack, of Trong and Giang removed from their jobs, of me about to be sent off to God-knows-where.

I was good all right. Like a Rome Plow.

* * *

At Tan Son Nhut, I drew a jeep and headed for Bien Hoa, driving too fast past the burned car skeletons. Edgy, my nerves frayed, I must have freaked out Hollis when I walked in on him. He jumped up from his desk, moved at once to the air conditioner, and adjusted its fan to high. The whirring machine masked our voices and sent his papers flapping. Hands pressed on stacks of carbon-copy forms, he said, "I thought you were coming over yesterday."

"I couldn't make it."

"Too bad." His voice was barely audible above the air conditioner, and I had to lean across the desk to hear him.

"What's wrong?"

"This morning, my commanding officer got a call from MACV. They told him that your investigation was closed. I was to lend no further assistance and to refer all inquiries to them. I never got instructions like that before. Is it because of what we found out about the radio?"

"Partly."

"Will I get burned for helping you?"

"Not for your help before the order was issued. After, you might."

He opened a drawer, extracted some paperwork, and held it tipped toward his chest, a poker hand in a tight game. "You got this from me *before* the order, right?"

"Couple of days ago, I recall."

On the table he spread three documents: a printout page and onion-skin carbon copies of a defective component record and an aircraft incident report. "This printout shows the serial number of the attitude indicator you retrieved. It arrived from CONUS in November '69. This form records that it was installed to replace a defective instrument in a UH-1 helicopter, tail number 87J-19. Your lucky streak continues—the defective predecessor was just a few months old, so the replacement was covered under the contract warranty. Otherwise, no record would have existed outside the chopper's working file, and I'd never have found it."

"What happened to the chopper with that tail number?"

He picked up the second carbon copy, the aircraft incident report. "It crashed in January. Nobody was hurt, but the airframe was a total loss. Or so the report declared."

The form revealed that the chopper had belonged to the 41st Air Recon Squadron. My eyes shot to the investigating officer's line. The carbon signature was illegible, and, contrary to practice, the name hadn't been typed in.

"Who was the investigating officer?"

"It took me a few phone calls to find out. Normally the squadrons appoint their own people. Sometimes, they get too busy—which seems to be what happened in this case. On 20 March, they handed off the investigation. Luckily, the 41st kept 87J-19's working file. It contains a memorandum of transfer to a new investigating officer—Major Jason Stobe. Same guy who had the radio." Hollis's tone bore no hint of triumph. "What's your bet, that he wrote up the chopper as beyond repair, took possession of the airframe, then had his mechanics restore it to serviceable condition?"

"Sounds about right."

He handed me the carbons. "This is beginning to look like evidence, huh?"

I opened my leather pouch, slid the copies inside, removed my .45, and tucked the gun in the belt at the small of my back. "I need a last favor from you. I'll try to keep your name clear. No guarantees."

He brushed a piece of lint off his starched fatigue sleeve. "I've been in the Army too long to believe in guarantees. But I've almost got my twenty in, and I can't afford to end my career in a court martial."

"No you can't, Chief."

He glared. "What's your favor?"

"Get the squadron's working file with the incident-investigation transfer memorandum. When you do, put them in here. Stash it in a safe place until I come back."

"What if you don't come back?"

"Then you'll be cozy with your orders."

Accepting the pouch, Hollis's expression resembled Giang's death-mask grin.

* * *

The two-story, pre-fab-metal headquarters of the Military Assistance Command Vietnam—MACV—was the centerpiece of a complex of buildings whose collective vibe was frustration. Created by President Kennedy in 1962, MACV had not yet accomplished its mission: to defeat communist aggression and make a secure country out of South Vietnam. Cobris had told me we were running out of time. Today's front page of the Pacific Stars and Stripes newspaper pictured MACV Commanding General Creighton Abrams shaking hands with South Vietnam's military chiefs. They were touting Vietnamization, the policy to prepare the South Vietnamese to take over the war. We'd leave behind a democracy capable of its own defense.

Or we'd just leave.

I passed through the security barriers and upstairs toward General Cobris's office suite. The waxed linoleum floors bore giant whorls from an electric buffer, and in them the floor and a glass display case mutually reflected each other, multiplying the shelves of war mementos and photos of the MACV edifice showing bullet scars and smoke plumes beyond.

During the Tet Offensive in late January 1968, in one of their bolder moves, the Viet Cong had attacked Tan Son Nhut airbase. Breaching the western perimeter, they'd charged across the meadows toward the parked aircraft and the cantonment area, where military and air police had fought to repel them. The VC hadn't gone much farther—only a handful reached the buildings. In the photos, among the whitewashed trunks and blown-off palm fronds, their bodies lay strewn. I wondered if Khiêm, Diu's husband, counted among them.

Somebody must have phoned to say I was on the way up, for sharp heel clicks emanated from the adjoining double doorway. The air conditioning kept Vangleman's starched khakis stiff as he tapped across the floor.

He said, "Where the hell have you been?"

"Is General Cobris around?"

Adopting an expression that could not have been more pained had he stood barefoot on a punji stake, he faced me from an arm's length away. "What is it with you, Tanner? Are you so fucking arrogant that you pay no attention to orders? The investigation was closed, yet you kept on? You flew up to Tay Ninh Province without authorization. Did you think we wouldn't find out?"

I was halfway through the door before he realized he wasn't intimidating me. "Wait!"

I waited.

"You're directed to remain here until otherwise notified."

I laughed.

"That order comes from General Cobris." Reflected in the waxed floor and the display case, Vangleman's figure became so many disarranged bits, not unlike someone who'd walked up on an exploding claymore. "You think this is funny? I'll call for the MPs to detain you."

"Go ahead."

He folded his arms. As I'd guessed, he made no move to summon anybody.

"I'll be in my office," I said calmly. "You have an hour to get me an appointment with the general." He was an intelligent fellow; there was no need to explain. It was only important that he see no hint of the bluff, because I still had no answers or evidence. If I'd had evidence, I wouldn't have been here anyway; I'd have been in General Abrams's office using it to burn down Cobris and Vangleman like spindly rice shacks.

Down the stairs, out through the open doors, I gratefully drank the breeze that swished the palm trees. The airfield, less than a kilometer away, must have been directly upwind, for I could smell the pungent AVGAS and hear the helicopter engines shift pitch lifting toward Cambodia.

* * *

"You've dug yourself into some shit, haven't you?" In his baggy fatigues, Lopez looked like the neighborhood gas pump guy with a rag hanging from his pocket, harmless until he pulls out a machinegun.

"Did somebody call?"

"Major Vangleman. He kept asking where you were. Three times I told him I didn't know. He said I was lying to him—the son of a bitch."

"That's him."

"He said a jeep will pick you up at nineteen hundred hours to take you to General Cobris. If you don't show, you'll be arrested. I asked him to repeat the last part, and he said, 'You heard me.'"

"Don't let him worry you."

"He should worry *you*, he's the general's shit dealer."

"You think you can hang with me a while longer?"

"Bad career move though it would be?"

"Yeah."

"Tell me you've got evidence, sir. Something that *weighs*."

The silence answered him.

"You're playing them. You're playing the goddamn general. I thought I'd seen everything." He kept the wick on his Zippo trimmed high, and now he blowtorched a cigarette. "Why not just walk away?"

"It's like your story about the bug in the crapper. I just can't relax, knowing the bug is down there."

For a minute he pondered this. Then he wagged his cigarette at me. "That ain't no good reason."

Darkness falls suddenly in Vietnam. Caught in the day's final lumens, the ground-hugging air meanders like a water buffalo, and the temperature might dip a few degrees before the suffocating night settles. By the time I climbed into the jeep Cobris had sent for me, the sun already had sunk over the horizon. The driver motored toward our destination, dodging past a running garrison unit that had timed its PT to catch the ephemeral coolness. The on-post traffic rules said vehicles could not exceed 10 miles per hour when passing formations in the road, but the driver, another of the general's empowered sycophants, gave not one shit about regulations and roared past the men. I caught the cadence caller's receding lyric that mocked death:

> *"Two old Harleys and a black Cadillac,*
> *My daddy keeps in his yard in back.*
> *Under the shade of the sycamore tree,*
> *Bury me beneath them three."*

The jeep deposited me outside the Officer's Club, in front of a parked VIP sedan whose air conditioner huffed condensate on the windows. The one on the driver's side rolled lazily down. Vangleman asked, "Are you armed?"

"A pistol."

"I'll take it until you come out."

I slipped the .45 out of my waistband and presented it grip-first. He tossed it on the passenger seat. "The general's a card player. You'd better hope you are too."

"We'll see."

"Look for this car when you're done," he said.

Tonight, in celebration or remembrance of something, the O-club featured a formal dinner by the poolside. I could hear the live music. A few officers tapped down the steps, nineteen-thirty their Cinderella hour, their dress uniforms drooping in the humidity. I stopped by the

Vietnamese concierge at the reception dais. A functionary of the American recreation machine, he forged his mouth into a crescent so stiff it might have been gouged with the point of a bayonet.

"General Cobris's table," I said.

He flicked a disapproving glance at my fatigue uniform. "Wait. I ask him first."

Waiting didn't suit me at the moment. "Never mind. I'll find him."

I walked through the doors to the pool patio. The underwater floodlights glowed up at me. At each corner hummed a pedestal fan, and the artificial breezes curled together to shudder the pool's surface into wavelets like so many colorful prisms. Silverware clinked on china and strings resonated from a trio of military musicians on a low stage. Laughter joined the swish of palm trees, their trunks spiraled in white Christmas-tree lights. Above each table, a striped umbrella, in case rain might spurt from the tropical clouds.

At the patio's far end sat Brigadier General Kyle Cobris.

Beside him, Simone Nogaret.

It was a long walk to their table. Or I thought so, as the lights winked up at me from the fan-ruffled water. I'd not expected Cobris to be so open about his affair with her—both of them were married to other people, at least on paper. He could have met me in his office, but he'd chosen the O-club, with Simone and these little extravagances around the pool. There was a message for me in this brazen picture, Cobris showing her off, Simone showing herself off, and the message was that my knowledge of their affair did not threaten them.

He must have guessed that I'd found out. Why else would I have been so bold as to demand a meeting? Gribley had confirmed what I'd suspected: The general and Simone had been meeting secretly for months. The reporter had located a Vietnamese civilian who catered at the Vung Tau villa, and this savvy fellow had recognized Simone as the woman who frequented the place when Cobris was staying there.

The general's dress whites gleamed under the rows of his decorations capped by silver aviator's wings. He lifted his eyes from his plate of veal cutlets in wine sauce. "Good evening, Tanner."

"Sir."

I nodded to Simone, whose lovely smile compounded my sense of the surreal. In her black silk dress, she was one of the few women present and far and away the most spectacular. For some reason, to be in her stare was not discomfiting. She created the impression that I knew her better than I did, the kind of illusion you pry yourself from with reluctance. She said, "What a pleasure to see you, I hope you'll join us for a drink." A conventional statement, but nothing from her sounded conventional. Her voice and accent harmonized like violins.

"Sit, please," said Cobris, stabbing his fork at the third place setting.

The waiter tucked the chair beneath me, and I felt myself falling into it as if from a great height. Simone and the general, the pool, the lit trees—all gyrated. The waiter hovered at my shoulder while I stared at the drinks menu. Too disoriented to focus on the print, I bobbed like the turd that lands in the punch bowl. Finally I just pointed at something. When he reappeared a minute later, I was relieved to see that I'd ordered a Scotch. Cobris and Simone seemed to be working on gin and tonics. No fool's drinks at this table, no dainty cocktail umbrellas.

She mewed, "Poor George. You've had a rough time these last few days."

Wasn't much I could say. *So, how did you two meet?* Finally I replied, "Some others have too."

Her lips pursed slightly, her rebuff to a droll statement. Cobris curled a thin sliver of veal expertly around his prongs. He said, "You're good at your game, Tanner. Now, Deke Vangleman is a fine staff officer, an intellectual to an extent, but he's young and rattles too easily. You, on the other hand, have an impressive instinct for mental poker."

Gazing around the club, Cobris seemed relaxed, his eyes slightly watery. I wondered how many gin and tonics he'd put down. Not enough to make him drunk.

As stunning in her dress as the moon over the Mekong, Simone patted the general's hand as if he needed comforting before he dealt with the likes of me. "Could you excuse me a minute?" she said. I didn't catch the cue. Maybe there hadn't been one; these two understood each other. Cobris and I stood as she left the table and went off to socialize, striding beside the pool whose shimmers caressed her, a jewel held up to the light.

"A woman like her comes along once in a lifetime," Cobris commented. "When she does, you cannot bargain, though the price may stagger you. In case you're curious, I have informed my wife I will be filing for a divorce."

From his tunic he slid a cigarillo, unwrapped it, lit its tip with a pewter lighter engraved with a brigadier's star. "You know, Tanner, anyone who aspires to be a general can look forward to solving about one hundred problems every day. Of these, about ninety are perfunctory solutions; to resolve them is a matter of giving an order or answering a question. Another nine are what I call *grapplers*, cases that involve research, deliberation of secondary effects, the apportionment of finite resources, taking from one to give to another—the nexus of calculation and seasoned judgment. Those nine problems eat my energy from before dawn until late into the night. You work long hours, Tanner, but mine are longer." He smiled indulgently. "Keeping track?"

"You're short one problem."

"Yes. The hundredth. A different sort of problem, not necessarily some intractable conundrum, it might even be simple, but unique for the reason it cannot be solved. What do you do with such a problem?"

"If it can't be solved, it's not really a problem."

He waved the cigarillo. "Precisely. So the best course of action is to get rid of it, pass it on, toss it to Washington for rework or further study—a number of deflections avail. If I can't jettison it bureaucratically, I try to reduce it—break it into component parts, or feign that it's under control and create the illusion of progress, the way we're doing with Vietnamization." He leaned back in his chair, and across the smoky air I saw myself reflected in his ceramic blue eyes. "You're thinking that my explanation refers to you."

"Doesn't it?"

"Don't take this too hard, but I've had plenty of experience with people who cannot recognize futility. I'm hoping you won't be one of them. If you are, the fact is, you won't take me more than a few minutes to sort out."

Which wasn't true. I could create a scandal that would cost him more than that. Perhaps a lot more. He knew it too, but he was playing his hand through, maybe to see who he was dealing with.

"You are transparent, Tanner. You think that I lied to you. That I allowed you to pursue a frivolous effort because I knew about this fellow Gerard all along. That I engineered a property scam so I could give a woman free rides over Vietnam."

Now it was my turn to be impressed, by how fast he shifted from banter to a cold challenge, which I would answer directly or fall apart, fumbling out a denial. Slowly, as slowly as I could without being blatantly insubordinate, I sipped my Scotch and replied, "You did lie to me. You also lied to Crowley and Larsen. You interfered in my investigation. You misappropriated government property for personal reasons. You let me walk blind into a situation that almost got me killed."

His normally piercing eyes had gone vacant, as if my commentary had bored him past his limit of concentration. "I have a story for you," he said. "It's a bit of a metaphor. You up for it?"

"Sure."

At an adjoining table, somebody shrieked raucously, and Cobris glanced over to reassure himself that the club's decorum wasn't at risk. When he spoke, his voice was uncharacteristically soft, and I had to lean forward to hear. "There once was a woman who lived in a country at war. She was not a participant in the war, and so she was able to travel, and the place she visited from time to time was a house on a fine piece of land her parents had left to her. They'd died many years ago; you might say that the place was the last vestige of their existence. Through the long conflict she tended it like a shrine, and to do so inspired her inner peace. Getting there was difficult—she had to pass through military checkpoints, navigate the warring forces, even cross an international border. But both sides came to recognize her and to leave her alone, for she portended them no harm.

"The woman was married, by law. In reality the couple had fallen apart long before. The marriage should have been over, yet for selfish reasons, her husband clung to her in a way that was closer to obsession than to affection. She asked him to grant her a divorce. He refused. He had no reason other than a cruel compulsion to intrude upon her life, and this he accomplished."

I lit a cigarette, and in the flame I saw André lost in his kepi drink, his indignation when I'd pointed out that he was still married.

"Though they'd been living apart for years, her husband approached her with a request. He said that when she visited her sanctuary, a stranger would arrive. The stranger would hand her a parcel, and she was to carry it to her husband. For this simple chore, she'd receive a generous sum. She needn't concern herself with what the parcel contained. At once she comprehended what she was being asked to do, and it filled her with revulsion. She refused, but her husband persisted. He threatened her: If she wouldn't help him, she wouldn't be allowed to cross the border.

"How could he do this? You see, in the country at war, the military ruled the checkpoints. One of the local generals was her husband's ally. This corrupt officer had an interest in the parcel—of which there were certain to be many more—and his soldiers could keep her from passing through. It was extortion, at which her husband and his ally were well practiced."

Now I understood why Cobris hadn't fired me after the complaint from General Huang.

"The woman would have been under her husband's thumb, but she too had an ally, likewise a general, though not the kind who sought to profit from his position. Her ally was powerful, and he gave her wings so that she no longer needed the road. It was a way to free her from the tyranny and manipulation of evil men." Cobris sipped his gin and tonic. "I served a tour in Special Forces. You know their motto."

"De oppresso liber. To liberate the oppressed."

"Correct. It's an expression of virtue, why we're here in this country. You, me, all of us, are called upon to act virtuously."

I tapped my cigarette ash into the dregs of my Scotch.

"I don't usually sketch things out for people, but I wanted you to understand why it happened this way. The helicopter, the other activities—sure they're against regulations. But what would I be if I didn't use my power to save this woman? To liberate her, if you will."

"The shrine you referred to, that would be her father's old estate in Cambodia?"

"You knew about that already. You *are* good, Tanner."

"I had only fragments. Like the radio and the helicopter. And Simone. When I flew over your patio at Vung Tau, I saw her."

"That was careless of her."

"Not as careless as I've been."

He blew out a mouthful of smoke. "State your point."

"This investigation has put some friends of mine in danger. I got them in trouble and I want to get them out of it."

"Friends."

"Two Saigon cops, my girlfriend Tuyet, and a club dancer. There's a murder contract out on the dancer. General Huang is behind it, I think. The other three are in the line of fire in one way or another."

"You're straining at the leash because of your girlfriend, two Viet cops, and a showgirl." Cobris laughed. Then his smile fell away, and he dabbed a napkin at the corners of his mouth. "Christ. Here I was thinking you were some kind of fanatic, and all you're trying to do is fix your own problem. You might have come to me earlier."

"It wasn't so easy."

"You're right, it wasn't." He sat quietly for a minute, drawing on his cigarillo, occasionally glancing to Simone a few tables over, as if balancing her against everything else on his mind. "You must have a proposal. Let's hear it."

"I want a safe haven for the dancer at a U.S. military facility until the danger to her is over. And I want you to use your connections to get Huang to call off the murder contract and the pressure he's putting on the cops. Once that gets resolved, the rest of it, your arrangement with Simone, can slide."

He wiped his hands on his napkin. "The safe haven is easy. Is tomorrow soon enough?"

"Yes, but it can't be later than that."

"As for the other part, dealing with General Huang, that's where you have to let me be the judge of how to proceed. I should tell you that we share the same problem."

"I don't understand."

"Mind you, I didn't know about the contract on the girl. But there are pieces *you* are unaware of. Surely you have asked yourself why a despot like General Huang would want to harm her." A master at systems analysis, he'd pinpointed the question that had clanged in my head for days. "You've met Simone's estranged husband, André."

"Why would André care about the showgirl?"

"He doesn't. His object is Simone. You remember my metaphor, about what he's trying to do."

"How he wants to coerce Simone into running drugs for him?"

"Correct. And he can't. I beat him. He is a bad loser. A blunted thug. He would kill me if he could, but that is beyond his scope. Even his friend General Huang can't do anything against me. So he has a single recourse—to inflict pain indirectly. He knows Simone was very fond of her pilot Gerard, but Gerard too is beyond his reach. So he strikes out at Gerard's fiancée, the wrath of a cruel and petty man. Petty, but not without venom through his corrupt ally."

I clenched my jaw to keep it from dropping. "I'm not sure he's capable of what you just described."

"Oh, he is capable of that and more. He is my hundredth problem, you see."

The tinkle of glasses was in my head, and for an instant I closed my eyes. When I opened them, the general was picking up a fresh drink. Classy, sophisticated, he licked his lips, tasting the gin, and when his eyes settled on me, they shone with a diamond's hardness. "You understand that this conversation never happened."

"Yes sir."

"A promotion might suit you."

"That's not necessary, sir. My tour is over. I just want to get my friends off the hook and to keep the dancer safe, then to leave and take my girl with me."

He acknowledged this with the slightest nod. When he spoke, empathy laced his tone. "Wise and reasonable." He glanced at his watch, and for an instant I felt the burden of his rank and those hundred decisions a day. He said, "I don't know why I bother to wear one of these.

I always know what time it is, to the minute. Time stalks me like a hellhound."

So she'd gotten it from him, the hellhound expression.

He asked, "Where is the dancer?"

"Tucked away in a shanty house, in a little ghetto of refugees."

"Where?"

"Off Pham Van Chi Street in lower Cholon."

"I'll need a few hours tomorrow to line up a place for her on post. Plan to bring her to the gate in the late morning or early afternoon. Vangleman will convey the details."

His expression changed, and I perceived I'd been dismissed. Cobris and Simone were alike in that way. I stood, but already he'd shifted his attention to Simone, who was working the tables expertly, holding the partygoers transfixed as they buzzed in the privilege of her presence.

Above, the flies made frenzied patterns around the lights.

Vangleman waited in the sedan. The air conditioner hadn't saved his starched khakis from crumpling in the mushy air. His face looked as withered as his uniform. He asked, "Did it go as you'd planned?"

"Just read from your script, Vangleman." Stretching across him through the window, I took my pistol from the seat. "The general has an errand for you tonight. Make sure you don't fuck it up."

"Such a hot shot, Tanner. You thought you were going to outplay him."

"I thought that, did I?"

"You figured you were going to pressure him because you'd found out about Simone and the helicopter. Here's a fact for you to *collect*—don't go out to Tay Ninh Province and expect to find a chopper hanging in the trees. Did you think we were going to leave it there?" Eyes squeezed nearly shut, he resembled a weasel with a duckling in its mouth. "A lot of guys want a place at the general's table, but they're only prepared to play one time. At his table, you've got to play the game day in, day out, and that is infinitely beyond your skill. You're a loser, and you don't have any cards. So heed your own advice. Don't fuck up."

Day 12

I woke up alone. Where was Tuy? The stiletto point of terror was at my throat. Then through the flimsy curtains I saw the aluminum-framed windows and the airfield lights beyond. After leaving the O-club, I'd gone to my BOQ room at Tan Son Nhut, the one I kept but rarely stayed in, and fallen asleep.

The air conditioner panted at my sweaty chest. In the distance, a C-130 revved its engines. The noise had wakened me. Looking over at my PX-bought bedside clock, I saw the digital figures flip from 4:43 to 4:44, triple pitchforks. How appropriate. Closing my eyes, I tried to hurry back to oblivion, to stay ahead of reality, but I was too slow. The forks skewered me.

I could have brought Cobris down. Instead, I'd cut a cheap deal.

He'd said I amounted to little more than a nuisance. His game had been to suppress my confidence, my willingness to push what I guessed on top of what I knew. I hadn't challenged him. What would have happened if I had played a better hand? Demanded that he resign within 48 hours? Instead I'd sat like a toady and given him a few conditions, which he would meet with perfunctory solutions: *To resolve them is a matter of giving an order or answering a question.*

Vangleman was right: I was a loser. Cobris had sorted me out in quick strokes. He'd intimidated me, appealed to my nobility—that was why Simone had been there, so I could behold her in her evening dress, a beautiful woman, what men live to protect. The general's unvoiced corollary—how could I bring myself to hurt her? And I'd bought it. To save my people, I'd swallowed the baited hook.

It wouldn't amuse Trong to learn that I'd joined the ranks of the corrupt. He'd assumed I was immune, untouchable, and yet I'd fallen. Naiveté was not the trait to show off in this city where to succumb was easy, all it took was to *want* something, or to have something you couldn't afford to lose, and Saigon owned you. The best you could do was to nurture the scraps of integrity that remained, the way Trong did. It was why he kept me as his friend. It helped him preserve his sanity.

How would I preserve mine?

Tuy and Kim Thi were safe, I reminded myself. Nothing else counted.

I thought of the music and the lights, Cobris across the table with his cigarillo playing like he had a few drinks under his belt, all an act—his mind had been as clear as the swimming pool water. He'd staged it perfectly.

How had he dismissed me, when he knew he'd won? A glance at his watch and one of his pompous lines, *I don't know why I bother to wear one of these. I always know what time it is, to the minute. Time stalks me like a hellhound.*

Time.

I sat up in bed.

They said I was good at my work. They were wrong. I'd learned the tricks and then forgotten to use them.

On the nightstand lay a memo pad. I picked it up and began to sketch out a chart.

* * *

By zero nine hundred, I was at the hideaway, delivering bottled water and freshly cooked rice and fish that I'd bought at Cholon's market stalls. Bent over the steaming tin containers, the four of us ate with relish, even Giang, who balled the rice in his bony fingers. I'd picked up newspapers for Tuy, one each in Vietnamese, French, and English. The papers featured front-page stories of a shooting at Kent State University. The Ohio National Guard had gunned down protesting students, killing four, the latest fallout from the Cambodian incursion.

I sat beside Tuy to catch up on the news I'd missed. I read about Cambodia, a country I'd paid little attention to until now. Cambodia had been part of French Indochina, and I wondered if it was as complicated as Vietnam. If so, it seemed that we should be wary of getting sucked into another quagmire.

Kim Thi and Giang ignored the newspapers. I asked him, where was Trong? He shrugged.

The climbing sun braised the walls. The heat today would soar. I reassured the women that they'd be out of here before evening. Tonight they'd sleep in soft beds in military quarters.

"For how long?" asked Kim Thi.

"A week or two. Until General Huang agrees to lay off."

Her expression stayed dubious. I didn't wish to explain how I'd arranged the deal. For once, I was glad not to see Trong. He would read everything too accurately.

* * *

The *Quartier Latin* club's showcase lay on the sidewalk, the pink neon tube sectioned like a snake run over by a harvester. Stepping over it toward the entrance, I was less curious that the marquee was down than why nobody had picked it up. Broken glass crunched under my boots. The lights inside were smashed, and the only illumination spilled feebly from the open doorway over what resembled a field of reeds: the legs of upended tables, strewn bottles, the backs of demolished chairs, and the crumpled stage curtains minus a torn strip that stretched like a sampan sail from the carved rubber tree to the ceiling. Three employees, including Danh, his arm slung, clinked through the ruins in search of things not broken. They were empty-handed. At first I thought I was viewing the aftermath of a bombing. Then I saw that the front door, walls, and pillars were unmarred, and I detected no charring or smoke odors.

Toward the far side I heard a moan whose volume peaked when I entered the kitchen that now served as an operating room. Sprawled on a carving table, his legs and arms dangling over, a Vietnamese man endured stitches to a gash on his forehead. An older gentleman pulled the bloody thread while two others struggled to hold the victim still. A step away, André watched. Blood dabbed his white shirt, and his face was so crimped that he might have bitten into the lemon from his kepi drink.

He saw me. "More questions, Tanner?"

"This time I have something to tell you."

He led me to the stage base, righted a table, found a surviving bottle of '33' beer, two chairs that retained their legs, and from somewhere came up with two unbroken glasses. "They burst in last night as we were closing, Huang's men, swinging wooden poles. They smashed everything and hurt two of my employees: one you just saw; the other is in the hospital. Is this sufficient to convince you I am not his partner?" He poured the beer, four fingers to each glass. He wasn't in much of a drinking mood.

I asked, "How often does Simone visit your club?"

"Your quips about my wife grow tiresome."

"It's just a question."

He studied the foam on the beer. "She stops by occasionally. Why not? She owns a stake in the business."

"Makes sense. It's familiar and safe. A place she discreetly could meet with Gerard."

"Please get to the point."

"They're going to kill you, André."

He laughed. I was indeed an infinite well of non-sequiturs. "Nonsense."

"I'm in a hurry, I'll spare you if you're not interested."

Lighting a cigarette, his hand shook slightly. "Please do explain. It was a long night."

"For me too. Last night a man told me that time stalked him like a hellhound, not germane to anything, except that it reminded me I hadn't been paying enough attention to time."

"You've only become more cryptic."

"I'm talking about a chronology, the examination of when events occurred, and in what order. It's a tool to determine causality. For example, a man dies in the jungle, an investigation follows, and a murder contract materializes on a showgirl. Last night, I thought about the contract on Kim Thi, and I asked myself, when did it start?"

He lit a Gauloises. "And this is pertinent how?"

"The shooters were waiting for her outside her place on Thursday night, so the contract was running then. It wasn't active before Wednesday, because she was out in public that day, at JFK Square, hoping Gerard would show up. She went there for three days, Monday through Wednesday, and nobody bothered her. It means that Gerard's death didn't trigger the contract. Not of itself. It was something that happened after."

"Something that happened after," he echoed sardonically.

"I have a friend on the Saigon police who says it takes forty-eight hours to set up a contract. To choose the killers, instruct them, orchestrate the conditions. The two Montagnards who attacked us Thursday night probably had waited for hours, maybe all day, for Kim Thi to come out. Subtract forty-eight hours from Thursday, and you get Tuesday. So the starting point was Tuesday, or possibly the night before—the night of Monday the 27th."

"So?"

"Come on, André, you told me yourself, in your little speech about Americans upsetting the balance, remember?" I took a sip of the beer that somehow had preserved its coolness.

"All right. Tell me what happened, the night of Monday the 27th."

"I showed Simone the dancer's photo. And her demeanor changed. It wasn't dramatic—she's nothing if not adept at keeping her composure—but I noticed, though I had no idea what it meant. I'll bet she recognized the club's stage in the photo. She may even have called you that night to ask about the dancer."

No comment. I hadn't expected one.

"Simone realized I'd find the girl and learn about the helicopter. But what of it? The revelation posed no risk to her. She had to be worried about something *else*. What might have menaced her so much that she'd set up a contract?"

"You have an answer for that too, I assume." His gaze didn't rise from the beer glass.

"She trusted Gerard completely. He flew for her, knew where the helicopter came from, understood everything. Nobody trusts another person that much without a reason. I'm betting they were old acquaintances. He'd proven himself to her before, maybe as one of your ex-soldier buddies who protected the plantation."

His eyes narrowed as if in remembrance. Tricky to read affirmation in a man's expression. I read it in his.

"Simone must have puzzled over why her pilot had bothered to conceal an affair with a Saigon showgirl. Then the implications hit her. If this girl had meant so much to him, what had he told her? Details of his business—which meant Simone's business? Even then, the showgirl wouldn't have been a problem by herself. It was when *I* entered the scene, searching for her with my Saigon police contacts, and the certainty I would question her, that she became significant. Without knowing it, I'd delivered a crisis to your wife."

He stared at me.

I said, "Simone didn't fly to Cambodia so she could rearrange the doilies on her antique furniture. Those were money-making excursions. They were especially rewarding because she didn't have to share the profits. I'm guessing that her slighted partner in the venture was General Huang. His involvement can't be a coincidence. With the helicopter, she could get back and forth without going through his checkpoints. What was she hauling, André? Heroin?"

"I don't deny that you are perceptive," he said softly. "But none of this concerns me."

"Kim Thi is not the only one who poses a threat to Simone. You know a lot more."

"She trusts my discretion."

"She knows you've talked to me. You're talking to me now."

"Are you *trying* to be a son of a bitch?"

"I'm trying to save your life."

"Why? As a gift for my cooperation? I'm afraid I cannot accept."

He knew there was no quid pro quo. Our conversation was a mutual hiatus made possible by the kindred spirits of soldiers. At his core, that's what André was, and I got along well with men like him. I probably would have gotten along nicely with Khiêm too, had he not been the enemy. And dead.

I said, "You locked her in a bad position. She can't risk a court case to divorce you, not when you know enough to destroy her. So what do you think she'll do instead?"

Maybe seeking the answer, André surveyed the wreckage of his club. The place was silent; the yelling from the kitchen had stopped.

Time to go. Wending through the powdery light, André trailing, we emerged onto the sidewalk where *Quartier Latin's* boys finally were dragging away the showcase. We reached the nearby intersection, and I began to scan the traffic for a scooter cab.

He said, "Why did you go to the trouble to deliver your grim warning?"

"Last night I cut a deal. It was my only way to protect Kim Thi and a few others. My part is to back off. You weren't part of the bargain, so I figured I could play it how I liked."

"Noble of you."

"No. The opposite of noble. What counts is to get my people clear."

"And after your friends are clear, as you put it, what will you do?"

"You mean, will I burn Simone?"

He nodded slightly.

"I don't think anyone would believe me."

A shadow passed over his expression. Perhaps it was gratitude. He asked, "So you think I should give her what she wants?"

"That would be smart."

"I'm seeing her today, at the Gavet plantation. She called me last night, soon after Huang's men wrecked my club."

"A coincidence?"

"I don't think so. You have your deal. I expect she will offer me mine."

"You're driving to Tay Ninh Province?"

"How else—do you think I have a helicopter too?"

A scooter cab reacted to my gesture, cruised to the curb. I climbed on. "Highway 13 is dangerous," I said. "Be careful."

Amusement lifted his tired face. He'd said all he was going to say, and my scooter already was swerving away from the curb. Glancing back,

I watched the Frenchman's figure recede in the saffron light. The driver banked suddenly—all scooter-cab moves are sudden—and I snapped my head instinctively as we dodged around a bicycle. When I looked again, André was lost to sight.

* * *

A lull in the wind. The trees in front of Tuy's apartment slouched. Passing them, I squinted up at the window. Three hours remained before I had to meet Vangleman. I'd phoned him to set the time—fifteen hundred hours. He'd been up most of the night and sounded groggy, and I might have gone light on him, but rudeness to the man had become requisite. No longer resistive, he answered my questions while I told him nothing. I didn't say I'd be bringing two women, not one, to the base. It was unwise to supply Vangleman with information that he'd use like a devaluating currency, to be spent while it still bought something.

I'd intended to leave Tuy in Saigon and to ask Trong to shelter her until I could take her with me. But the city was too treacherous now. Too risky for the women to return to the apartment to get their things, which was why I was here, to pick up as much as I could carry. Trong could recover the rest later.

Trong's sentinel no longer protected the side street, so I had the driver loop the block twice while I studied the rain-washed buildings. I scanned behind the fly-swarmed garbage bin and hanging clothes and chained scooters.

Nobody.

Off the bike, I crept forward, pausing every few steps to observe. At the stairwell door, I took out my .45 and snapped down the safety. The hours had dispelled the cordite; I smelled only the neighborhood's odors—fish sauce, wood smoke, wet leaves. Keeping to the stairs' edge where they creaked less, I reached the upper level and pivoted to cover Tuy's door. I touched it, felt it move, kicked it lightly to swing inward, spreading light across the scattered wood chips. The sole noise, the bathtub hose's torpid drip.

I stepped through.

A syringe needle jabbed into the side of my neck.

The pain seared. By impulse I flailed and knocked aside an extended arm, swung to shoot, saw the kick, too fast to stop. It smashed into my wrist and the pistol flew.

Glimpse of a bony face, long hair cut in imitation of a pop trend. A Saigon cowboy, ex-soldier gone to crime, a symptom of the war. He fancied himself a fighter, but he under-weighed me by thirty pounds. His fist brushed my cheekbone. With the butt of my hand I caught him aside the nose and felt the bone snap. His eyes rolled and he went down.

I plucked out the hypodermic. The plunger was extended—the cowboy hadn't gained the leverage to push it forward. In the glass tube opalesced a milky solution, maybe morphine.

The cowboy could have put a bullet through my head. Why the syringe?

A whiff behind. I spun and a wooden pole collided with my forehead. The pole broke, a sliver twirled. The room glazed over and my knees began to fold. In the blur stood another cowboy. He stared at the stump he gripped. He might have won by striking again, with the stump, his hand, anything. Instead he gawked, and my glands spurted the adrenaline to tilt me into a football block, shoulder to his chest, driving him to the wall and down. A head kick would have finished him, but it was my turn to gawk. He writhed up like a thrown cat, slashed a knife at my face. My left hand leapt to catch his wrist, and I tried to hit him. He twisted. This one had wrestler's moves. If we'd been in a ring, I'd have crushed him by weight alone, but this was Saigon and I had the wrong style. He squirmed until he was on my back, his left forearm monkey-gripping my throat while his right hand pressed the blade toward my eyes.

The cowboy wriggled his forearm tight. I tugged to break his grip. He was tenacious, to loosen him would have taken both my hands, and with the other I held off the knife. Riding my back, he dug his knees into my kidneys. I swirled and thudded him against the wall, accomplishing nothing, and the sinewy lever wrung my windpipe shut. A pall begin to descend. It occurred to me that an instant's blackout, the least relaxation of the pressure against his knife hand, and the blade would ram to the hilt through my eye socket. Panic has the feel of freezing water when it soaks through to the skin. My panting became a shrill cry, the cowboy heard it too, the whinny of my impending death, and it spurred him to flex his forearm all the harder while we pirouetted grotesquely in the window light in which the apartment's familiar sights—Tuy's hanging fabrics, the tub, the rolled-up straw mattress—whirled dizzily. No act was too desperate now, I would have hurled us both through the window if it hadn't been too high in the wall. The pall darkened, the knife waved like a snake's head two centimeters in front of my right eye, and I anticipated the screaming jolt when it went in.

Airless, turning a leaden dance step, the way you dance with your grandmother, I watched the room spin, and wandering into view, a stack of new towels...

My rider did nothing to stop me when I released his choking forearm and groped under the towels, wrapped my fingers around the grenade, brought it up like a starving man who finds an apple, molars on the metal pin, pulling, chipping teeth...

The cowboy knew what I had. He must have believed he was within seconds of killing me with the knife, so he clung. Consciousness folding, I staggered until the backs of my knees pressed against the familiar, rounded edge of the bathtub. I dropped the grenade behind me, heard it clatter in the basin, tipped my knees, still pushing the knife hand away, and the cowboy went over on top of the grenade.

He released his grip, the knife flew, his hands flailed. I slapped mine against my ears.

* * *

Time loses its consistency.

Like a stone catapulted straight up, I ascend toward the ceiling.

Aloft, I notice the window exploding outward, glass fragments and rusted screen rushing into gray sky. The hanging light fixture lies horizontal against the ceiling plaster, its bulb gone. The wire arcs in reverse, and I fall...

Face up on the floor, I am not yet aware of pain.

I detect movement.

The cowboy who damped the explosion with his body is not moving, of this I am certain, for I observe his head on the floor, a sculpted bust whose open eyes express surprise.

By the door, the first cowboy, the one who jabbed the needle into my neck, rises unsteadily. The tub's contours routed the blast upward, and he caught little of it save for the plaster dust. He shakes his head and a powdery cloud erupts. From his smashed nose, blood streaks along a white mime's mask.

He scans the floor. Steps, stumbles, rights himself. Abstractly, with no sense of alarm, it dawns on me that he is looking for the knife. He finds something. Not the knife. The syringe. Examining it, his face shows pique. The vial is cracked, some of the milky solution has leaked.

He finds me. I lift an arm, but I'm in shock. I cannot summon the strength to resist.

He is still on the hunt. For what? A neck vein. He rams in the needle. It hurts like hell.

This time he is able to depress the plunger.

Lurching, he vanishes out the door.

The dangling light cord oscillates. I count six swings before I no longer perceive anything.

*   *   *

A horn blares at the Tan Son Nhut airbase gate.

An American voice. "Easy, man."

Four hands tug me from the taxi and drag me to a cement bench by the guard house. Set upright upon it, I flop to the ground.

A military police sergeant grays over me, stooping to peer at my face. Alongside him, another MP says, "The cabby said an ARVN passer-by in Cholon noticed him crawling down the fucking sidewalk stoned out of his head. He stashed him in the taxi and sent him to the gate."

"Must have had a helluva night. Lucky bastard."

"Looks like somebody beat the shit out of him, there's blood all over his uniform."

"We get all the losers."

"Check out the insignia. He's an MP officer."

"What a fucking disgrace."

"If we report him like this, the motherfucker's career is over. Get a load of his pupils--they're so dilated they look like buckeyes."

"What should we do with him?"

"No broken bones. We'll take him to his BOQ to sleep it off." He checks my nametag and dials a phone. Minutes later, they curl me into the back of the jeep.

BOQs line the airfield's edge. Painted beige, the facades reflect the late-afternoon sunlight like sandstone cliffs. At Building 129, the jeep swerves into a driveway. The two MPs who unload me draw incurious glances from the Vietnamese gardeners who desultorily reposition the sprinklers to sustain the grass. The sprinklers spawn a swampy humidity through which the MPs lug me inside. In the hallway, they half-carry, half-drag me along the buffed linoleum floor. Like all military quarters, the place reeks of disinfectant and floor polish. A washing machine spins nearby. They find room 108 and drop me on the floor outside the locked door. I am patted for a key; none is found. A Vietnamese cleaning woman emerges from the laundry room, and they enlist her to open the door with her key ring. Inside, they dump me on the bed. I feel them unlace and tug off my boots.

"You hit the jackpot today, sir. If another sergeant had been at the gate when you showed up in this condition, he might not have been so sympathetic. But if I ever see you like this again, I'm going to write your ass up."

"For Christ sake, he can't hear you. Let's go."

But I can hear. The problem is not so much hearing but comprehending, for these men apparently choose their words out of a grab-bag and utter them like bingo numbers. I interpret no logic.

* * *

Night settles. I feel myself breathe. I'm aware of noises in the room. I sit up in bed.

Somebody is bashing out the window with a chair. I rise and drift alongside. The figure pays me no attention. He tosses aside the chair and clambers out through the newly broken glass.

I decide to follow.

The tilt-out window doesn't open very far, which is why he had to break the glass. The jagged edges slashed his thighs; blood drips from the cuts. Across the sopped grass he splashes. A gluey warmth dabs the backs of my legs. I reach down, feel the wetness, and lift a stained palm to the moonlight filtering through the swishing palms.

In my peripheral vision, I see a BOQ resident emerge. He must have heard the glass.

My clothes encumber me. I strip them off—pants, shirt, and underwear—and toss them on the wet grass. The oscillating sprinklers stitch my chest; the water dribbles to my thighs and turns red.

A shout from the reactive co-resident: "Hey, buddy, are you all right?"

I point to the chain-link fence wrapping the airfield perimeter. The man who broke my window is scaling over. Snagged in the barbed wire on top, he thrashes loose, drops to the other side, and resumes his run. Blood stripes his legs like peppermint sticks.

I follow. Dimly I apprehend that the runner knows where he is going. Various aircraft—fighter jets and helicopters—squat in the distance. I assume the helicopters are his destination.

A jeep engine roars; the wheels spray gravel. The vehicle swerves around a line of parked deuce-and-a-half trucks on the inner perimeter road. Behind the wheel, a black sergeant—he must be part of the logistical surge for the Cambodia incursion—shifts the clunky transmission. He switches the jeep radio to speaker mode, and I can hear his voice above the crackling static: "Hey, uh, Juliet niner, I'm by the east fence, and I'm driving up on some guy running naked..." crackle crackle "...bloody, cut thighs, beat up and bruised... running across the tarmac." He adds, "Motherfucker's headed toward the blue line."

I've never seen the blue line and don't think it's really blue. It denotes a boundary on the airfield a safe span from military aircraft. Ever since the Viet Cong attacked Tan Son Nhut airbase on the first night of the Tet Offensive in January '68, the security detail has stayed jumpy. The sentries have orders to shoot to kill anyone who breaches the blue line without permission.

Pounding to catch up with the runner, I squint at the blinding lights ahead. Under them, the sentries raise their rifles to take aim.

The airfield siren goes off.

The black sergeant guns his jeep. All military jeeps have something wrong with them, and I hear the gears grind. The engine fizzes, loses power. Then it catches. Military jeeps are not built for speed. Driven too fast, they may become unstable. I hope the sergeant doesn't push the machine too hard.

Ahead I make out the runner in the spotlights. He vectors toward millions of dollars of aircraft with their loads of 500-pound bombs and full fuel tanks. The shoot-to-kill orders are neither exaggerated nor discretionary, and I assume the sentries are about to shoot him when, behind me, the jeep engine changes pitch from a roar to a whine, coughs again. I hear a curse. A sentry traverses his rifle barrel, and I conclude he's picking up the runner in his sights.

For safety reasons, the jeep has no windshield. It sports an upright wire cutter jutting from the front fender like a defiant middle finger. The cutter nudges to within a body's length of me, and I muddle at why the sergeant follows so close. I puzzle too over why the sentries haven't shot the figure I'm running after. Certainly he's crossed the blue line by now—do they not comprehend their orders? As I ruminate, the jeep engine catches again, and I glance to see the sergeant aiming the wire cutter at my back. The jeep groans, the gears turn to mush, the speed droops. "Fuck you!" he curses. Suddenly the jeep leaps, and I stare at the wire cutter so much like an extended arm groping for me. I try to dart off to the side but it hooks me and the upright pole passes over.

Air Force security jeeps converge. Their downturned spotlights resemble the legs of an insect. Sirens wail, men shout, and in the bluish smoke of the burned rubber, the black sergeant dismounts. The sentries still aim their rifles. A bullhorn barks, "Put your hands in the air!"

The sergeant complies. Behind him, oblivious to this human welter, a jet with a full bomb load waddles toward the active runway for a night mission.

A lieutenant in a lacquered silver helmet liner, bullhorn in his white-gloved hand, struts up. "You're seventy-five meters past the blue line, Sergeant."

"I figured it was about that far, sir."

"You can put your hands down. Let's see what's under your wheels."

At the grill, two air policemen pluck me from underneath. The wheels didn't go over me; the wire cutter swatted me like a cockroach into a face-down slide on the tarmac. I note two bloody tracks—the skin from my forearms—receding under the jeep. Aware that they pertain to me, not otherwise concerned, I twist my head to gaze at the rolling jet. Where did the runner go?

The lieutenant asks, "Who the fuck is he?"

"No idea," replies the sergeant. "I figured I had to stop him before he got shot."

The officer shines his flashlight in my eyes. "He's on something, big time."

An ambulance, siren ululating pointlessly, joins the corral. The air policemen lift me by the arms, a raw, bloody hunt trophy.

"Better cuff him," the lieutenant says.

I oblige them by collapsing to the tarmac.

Day 13

At the U.S. Army hospital, I occupy a private room on the second floor. My behavior alarms the staff, so they shackle my ankle to the bed frame. When this proves inadequate, they buckle a canvas strap over my thighs and band me to the mattress. Rubbing against the strap, my leg cuts bleed, and the sheet soon resembles a butcher's apron.

I awake to a white-garbed doctor who jots notes on the clipboard at the foot of the bed. Short, balding, he wears standard black-framed glasses that magnify his eyes. I ignore him until he speaks. "Hello, Major Tanner. I'm pleased you're awake. My name is Dr. James Wilcott. You can call me Jim. How are you?"

"Get out, you little fuck."

"I just wanted to ask how you're feeling..."

"I said GET THE FUCK OUT!"

Frowning, he departs.

* * *

Later Wilcott reappears, unlit cigar in his mouth, ego resurgent. He examines the clipboard.

I ask, "Do you have another of those cigars?"

He seems to consider this. He sidles to the bed, reaches in his tunic pocket, and serves up a Havana. I hold it in fingers that poke from the gauze to jagged nails rimmed with dried blood. The gauze wraps my forearms to the elbows. Blood seeps through, polka-dotting the white.

"Right nice of you," I say. "Got a match?"

Flicking a glance at the ceiling fan that turns in a hypnotic stupor, he remarks, "The air doesn't circulate well in these rooms." He shows his own cold cigar.

I glare at him until he hands me a Zippo. I manage to sit up.

"How about a mirror?"

He fetches a stainless-steel bedpan. In the distorted reflection, a bandage bridges my nose, a cayenne scar smears my cheek, and the black of my puffy eyes melds with the pan's silver. As a kid in the little league, I saw a teammate errantly hit across the eyes with a baseball bat. I look like he did.

I set the bedpan aside.

He says, "I have some questions for you. About what you remember."

"Go ahead."

"You suffered a massive overdose from a narcotic, an opiate of some kind, injected crudely in your neck, some into the vein, more in the muscle tissue. It left quite a bruise. Nobody would inject themselves that way. Whoever did this probably intended to kill you."

"Yeah. You should see the cowboy."

"What cowboy?"

I don't answer. I light the cigar, holding the Zippo until the yellow flame imprints on my retinas.

"You're lucky to be alive," he says.

I study the smoke that wisps elegantly. "I feel lucky."

"Do you remember who did this to you?"

"Oh yes."

"Who? The cowboy?"

I suck on the Havana. "Do you know what I'm going to do to him?"

"Who are you talking about?"

"Cobris. You've heard of General Cobris?"

In the smoke nebula, his eyebrows notch downward. "I've heard of him."

"He's the one who did this to me. He's *mine*—you're not going to get ideas about that, are you?"

He ticks disdainfully.

Holding the cigar like a scalpel, I draw a flat oval in the air above the sheets. "I'm going to run the tip of my knife around his head, just above his eyes, lightly at first, round and round, to let him know what's coming. Then I'm going to turn the blade and cut. If a knife is sharp it cuts skin like paper, with the same crisp sound. I want him to hear it."

Wilcott fidgets with the collar of his tunic. "I've got to get that ceiling fan speeded up. Not enough air in here."

"After I cut him, I'm going to pull down the skin all around. Regular scalpings are up; they take the hair as a trophy. Not this time."

"Regular scalpings?"

"Right. This time I'm going *down*, from the eyebrows to the chin, leaving his face hanging around his neck like a foreskin. He'll scream, but I'll have him trussed up so he can't move." I wag the cigar like an instructor does with a pointer. "I might have to needle him with adrenaline to keep him from passing out. No problem, but it's worth considering." Cigar in my teeth, I concentrate on this important detail.

"Could I have my lighter back?"

"You know why it's done this way?"

"What?"

"Think about it. Why bother to scalp a man's face down? Why leave the hair on top?"

"Let's talk about something else."

"The sequence is critical. First I hold a mirror in front of him." I lift the bed pan to exemplify. "He's going to see his mug in it and freak, straight out of a horror show. That's not the best part. I'm behind him. In one hand I've got my .45, round in the chamber, the hammer cocked. In the other, I've got my hard dick. He looks past his face and sees the dick in the mirror, then the .45 aimed at the back of his head. Now he knows what's coming!"

Up and down I begin to bounce. The strapped legs propel me, chafe my ankle against the metal cuffs. The leg scabs break and bright red blood seeps through the sheet. I extend the cigar and this time it's the barrel of a gun. "Blam! A huge hole in his head. That's why you can't take the hair, see. You need it to grab!" With my other hand, I seize the imaginary dead head by the hair. The cigar has metamorphosed again. Now it's an erect penis, and I pump it furiously. "I'm going to SKULL FUCK the bastard! SKULL FUCK HIM TILL HIS EYES POP OUT!"

The ashes range to Wilcott and speckle his white hospital tunic.

He exits in a hurry. Has the presence of mind to snatch the Zippo on the way out.

Day 14

Immobile, I listened to Wilcott's voice. Fatigue pressed me like a weight-bent coolie pole that in my delirium had become a cross, and I hung upon it to atone for the arrogance of America's shooter-upper in Vietnam.

"You were given an opiate, possibly a cousin to morphine or heroin, and possibly doctored with an hallucinogen. We're not certain of the chemistry. We don't know how much of it got into your bloodstream. In this part of the world, people have been tinkering with opium derivatives for hundreds of years. Opium thrived because the colonial authorities exploited it—the drug helped subjugate the population. The Americans brought another boon—tens of thousands of cash-flush GIs willing to experiment. There have been so many addictions and overdoses, our soldiers are safer in the jungle. Your case is one of the strangest I've witnessed."

"I apologize for whatever I did."

"The narcotic put you in an agitated psychotic state for the past 36 hours. It's best that you don't remember. Means you're recovering. Until the substance completely dissipates, you may undergo episodes and experience drug cravings. That's why the ankle cuff and strap are still in place."

"I have no craving for that stuff."

"Let's wait and see. We should be able to remove the restraints by tomorrow. You won't mind them; your principal symptom will be exhaustion. You should sleep."

"Where is Tuy?"

He canted close. "Say that again."

"Tuy. Where is she?"

"I don't know who she is. Sorry."

"I need to find her."

He drew back. "You need to find yourself first."

* * *

The walls caught the light through the Venetian blinds. Half awake, I watched the sunlight doodle the shape of a wing, while in the distance jets roared off the runways. It occurred to me that God must be a graffiti artist. A door opened, the breeze rattled the Venetian blinds, and the wing shuddered as if it had been blown apart with flak.

Entering, Colonel Crowley. He sat on a chair situated to host spectators of the absurd.

"I'm glad you're still with us, Tanner."

With effort befitting America's grand enterprise in Vietnam, I twisted my head on the pillow to face him.

He said, "I've been in touch with Trong, your Saigon police friend. He had news for you. First, your girlfriend Tuy is safe. She's with his family."

With his family? Why not at the shanty house...

"Kim Thi has been taken. Trong said the kidnappers found the place she had been staying. Another policeman was guarding her. They killed him."

Giang.

"All this happened two nights ago, about the time you got run over at the airfield. Suspicions are that André Nogaret was behind everything. He's a drug runner—no doubt he was responsible for the attempt to overdose you. Kim Thi was his employee, connecting him to Gerard Penelon. It's all linked."

All linked. How had André turned the phrase? *It's what an amateur says.*

I'd told Cobris the location of the shanty house. He must have revealed it to Simone. The pain crunched my face. Crowley said, "Easy, Tanner. You're going to be all right."

I asked, "Where is André?"

"The Saigon police are looking for him. They haven't found him yet. Maybe one of his gangster friends is sheltering him. The police are searching for the kidnapped dancer too."

"She's dead."

"Dead? Hmm. I don't think we've heard that yet."

"It doesn't matter what you've heard. She's gone."

Digesting this, Crowley wrinkled his face. "One thing is certain: your Saigon is living up to its evil reputation. For years we've been trying to keep this place afloat, good money after bad as far as I'm concerned." He lit a cigarette. "I'm out, by the way. Next Freedom Bird."

Maybe I looked puzzled, for he smiled the kind of smile that precedes an embarrassing revelation. "Cobris summoned me to see him yesterday. In my life, I can't remember such a withering ass-chewing, and he didn't even raise his voice. He said I'd worked with you long enough, I should have known what I was dealing with. You're the kind of man…"

"Go ahead, you won't hurt my feelings."

"It's not your feelings that concern me, rather your discretion. But what difference does it make now? He said you're the kind of man who gets an idea in your head, and you won't let it go, heedless of the consequences might befall yourself and others, even your own death, and theirs. He said that some people might confuse you with a soldier, but in reality what drives you is a selfish impulse, the opposite of what a soldier does. A delinquent, the word he used. For a person of my experience to tolerate your behavior, and to facilitate it to an extent, meant I was a damn poor officer."

"What did you say?"

"I said I agreed with him."

I agreed too, but said nothing.

"He offered me an early end of tour in lieu of relieving me from my post. A graceful exit I was happy to accept."

"It's an exit, not graceful. You can still go to General Abrams."

"I would if I believed in your case. But I don't. Your evidence is mostly conjecture. Cobris left my career intact. I'll save my ammunition for a day when it really counts."

"Cobris left you intact because he's vulnerable. He concealed his own involvement and abused his authority."

He spiked on the cigarette. "Even if you're right, he must have had his reasons. The world is like a wrinkled blanket, Tanner. Every wrinkle is a doubt. You can pull the damn thing tight as a drum, but a taut blanket doesn't last for very long. So you live with things the way they are."

I didn't say anything. The chair clumped and he left.

At the airfield, jets whined toward the active runway. The Cambodian incursion must still be underway; the jet noises went on and on.

I felt it then. The craving. I pictured the white pus in the cracked hypodermic. Ugly stuff.

My veins licked their lips for the fix that would put me out.

*   *   *

Replacing the sun streaks through the Venetian blinds, wan smudges from the airfield lights. The wall clock read twenty-one hundred hours. I drifted in and out of sleep until I heard heels tapping on the linoleum and a figure descend onto the chair.

Across the bed rail, Vangleman's voice. "Hello, Tanner." A match whooshed and glowed red through my eyelids. Mentholated cigarette smoke blended into the ceiling fan's wash.

"The general is sorry it didn't work out for the dancer. Everything was arranged. If you'd have shown up, as we'd agreed, we would have had her safe. Too bad." He spoke as if he were talking about a golf ball he'd lost in the rough. "He understands that what happened wasn't your fault. He made a promise to you, and although the circumstances have changed, he still believes he can be of assistance. If you want, he can get your girlfriend Tuyet out, to some cozy stateside post like Fort Polk,

Louisiana. Some place with warm weather—I hear Viet women don't like the cold."

"Where is André Nogaret?"

"Missing. Or so we hear. Nobody has seen him for three days. Lucky for him." Lounging in the chair, he inhaled deeply, and the cigarette glow rouged his face. "You have to let go, Tanner. No more trips to Saigon to consult your contacts. No more climbing trees and digging through supply records. Bring your girlfriend onto Tan Son Nhut base until permission can be obtained for her to travel. In about a week, both of you can be gone and safe. Considering the events that have transpired since you met with the general, it's generous beyond any conceivable measure."

Vangleman was a pimp and deserved scorn. But the time for self indulgence was over. What he said was true. It was a sweet deal, an exit for Tuy and me.

Turning away, I stared at the Venetian blinds. "All right."

I heard him rise. "Don't contact General Cobris. I'll leave an envelope for you at the main gate about the accommodations."

He waited another minute, perhaps for me to reply, then his footsteps resounded. In the ashtray, the red cigarette ashes lived a few seconds before they became nothing.

Day 15

At my request, Lopez had fetched a clean uniform from my BOQ. Now I stood, smartly dressed, release form in hand, while Doctor Wilcott argued that I needed another forty-eight hours for observation. "Where do you think you are, Tanner? This is a fucking hospital. You're with us for a reason—you suffered severe physical and mental trauma. You almost died."

"Let me ask you, doctor, where do you think *you* are? This is fucking Vietnam. It's a barrel of shit begging to be burned."

Standing there, Lopez nodded.

"Jesus Christ," muttered Wilcott. He grabbed the form out of my hand, scrawled his name at the bottom.

Outside Lopez had a jeep, and he drove me into Saigon. His only stop was at a swarm of urchins where I bought two packs of black-market American cigarettes. By a roadside kiosk on Cong Tuy Street, I transferred to Trong's car, the same paint-chipped Fiat in which Giang had taken me to the shanty hideout.

"Any idea when you'll be back?" Lopez asked.

"No."

Trong spoke neither of Giang and Kim Thi, who were dead, nor of Tuy, who was alive. In his fingers over the steering wheel, he held a cigarette and weaved northward. With his cop's savvy for backstreets, he punched a shortcut across town, veering at the outskirts onto Highway 13. The landscape no longer resembled the French quarter downtown or the shabby refugee villes. Cinderblock or hewn-plank huts roofed with palm thatch crouched by fields in many shades of green. The stalks of men and women appeared in sunlight and vanished in cloud shadow. Trong needed gas, so he detoured into a roadside town. When we slowed, people gawked at the bizarre apparition I presented in the window. They recognized me as a white man, but the purple bruises and raccoon eyes threw them. Was I in costume for a foreign holiday?

On the highway he picked up speed. We skirted empty settlements, the relics of projects meant to win hearts and minds, lost instead to the expedient of evacuation. Fifteen kilometers later, sluicing through the dung-thick air, we passed a sign that read An Loc, 30 kilometers. Rice shoots swayed above the paddies, the water slurped at the base of earthen dikes and, closer in, reeds bearded the elevated road. Where the embankment thrust five meters above the surrounding wetlands, he pulled off. To the right, something had drawn a cluster of Vietnamese military police, their heads like seed pods among the swaying reeds.

"Go, have a look," Trong said.

Slowly, my legs none too steady, I descended the embankment. In the reeds I divined the contours of a Citroën DS, or the central part of it. The hood had peeled up, crumpled in waves; the roof was crushed on one side. Closer, I saw a body in the driver's seat, the toothy skull torched black. The ground squashed underfoot, miring my boots that made sucking sounds with each lifted heel. The Vietnamese military police eyed my much-punished face and stepped aside.

Burnt flesh smells worse than anything save an unearthed grave. I tried to keep upwind, but the fickle breeze kept shifting. Forearm over my mouth and nose, I stepped back to breathe, forward to view the roasted face, see-sawing from various angles. An image flashed of the self-immolated monk Thich Quang Duc. The sun poked around the edge of a cloud and illuminated the chin and teeth and the few surviving strands of sandy hair, and it was as if somebody had filled in a connect-the-dots sketch.

I recognized André Nogaret now.

For five minutes I examined the wreck. The soldiers grimaced when I thrust my head under the curled-back hood. The engine compartment resembled the inside of a fire pit, the rubber melted, the metal distended.

I tramped to the elevated road and breathed gratefully, letting the breeze take away the smell.

Trong said, "The car went undiscovered for three days. At first light today, a military patrol spied it in the reeds. They radioed the license number, and we traced it to him."

Walking the crest, we searched for the spot where the Citroën had left the pavement. The surface was concrete in good condition, an American project. We found nothing north of the crash and treaded back, traversing thirty meters before I eyed a ricebowl-sized pockmark and, beyond it, a gouge in the shoulder. In the grass off the road, a shaving of twisted metal amid so many windshield shards that the ground might have been seeded with diamonds. I toed a chrome chip on the opposite embankment. "Debris on both sides. An explosion right here."

"A bomb inside?"

"I found a penetration in the grill. Everything was blown inward."

"So a bomb hit the car?"

"A 2.75-inch rocket, shot from the north." I scanned for the place an ambusher might have set up. Attacks still occurred on these roads, though they were rare this close to Saigon, especially against a civilian vehicle. The nearest treeline painted a hazy stripe three hundred meters away, out of effective rocket range against a moving car. Around stretched fields of scruff and reeds.

On Tuesday, André had told me he'd be meeting Simone at the Tay Ninh plantation. When he'd set out on his drive north, somebody watching him had transmitted a message to a third party.

Fickle sunlight skimmed the fields. The haze flared silver, spanning from the reeds to the cobalt sky, too bright for my drug-dilated eyes to cope with. Squinting at the horizon, I understood what had happened.

The helicopter had hovered, rockets ready, the pilot watching for the car to enter a kill zone he'd have scouted in advance. Not until André crested the bridge would he have spotted the hovering demon. Whooshing at near supersonic speed, the rockets had spat their molten loads into his windshield and grill. He was probably dead before the Citroën tumbled and burned. If we searched the field to the southeast, we'd find the scars of rockets that had missed.

From here I could make out the torched death's head. I thought of André's wife Simone. Making the rounds at the poolside dinner, she'd known that her husband was to be killed the next day.

Cobris had known too. I recalled the pilot's wings on his dress-white uniform.

Some revelations overwhelm a man's belief mechanism.

The ARVN MPs pulled the corpse from the car. Trong watched. How many victims had he witnessed over the years? The MPs folded open a body bag, laid André inside, and stared up at Trong. He gave the slightest nod, and they zippered it up. He said, "The pressure from General Huang has stopped."

"You're off the hook?"

"Why should Huang trouble himself over a small fish like me? Those he wanted dead are dead."

*   *   *

Trong left us alone in the garden. Tuy wore perfume, a first for her in my experience. Having grown up in her uncle's house, obliged to abide by his rules, perhaps she considered the perfume a polite gesture with Trong and his family, the expected accoutrement for the proper Saigonese woman.

Or maybe she thought it would calm me down.

She poured Scotch in my glass. I didn't drink it. Instead I paced, while she sat on the step and watched me, her perfume mixing with the candle smoke. The garden's walls and the eucalyptus tree trapped the air. The leaves scattered the moonlight into triangles like scraps of paper clipped by a child, and the patterns and the scents and the sheen on her hair collaborated to summon peace.

It wouldn't settle.

A few hours ago, the ARVN military police had delivered André's remains to the old French mortuary, the same place where they dumped dead derelicts and addicts. Not to miss an opportunity, the cops had declared him guilty for the contract on Kim Thi, for the Montagnards in the alley, and for the booby trap and the cowboy attack in Tuy's apartment. No matter that the night before he died, thugs had wrecked his club. And who had murdered André? Naturally the Viet Cong. The authorities would mount neither a forensics examination of the car nor a tactical site study that would have ruled out a ground ambush. André was dead, his crimes were solved, and soon he'd be forgotten.

This was Saigon. He was forgotten already.

The candle smoke became a movie screen on which my mind projected Kim Thi. I saw her peaceful face in the cubby where I first met her; her terrified eyes in the taxi. She was dead because of me.

"No more thinking." Tuy touched my forearm to comfort me, and it was pure kindness, for she needed comforting herself. She'd been at the shanty hideout.

When I hadn't shown up, they'd waited. The hours had lapsed into the evening. The delay had brought no alarm—Tuy explained how I was often late. Giang had stayed to protect the women. It was long after nightfall when they'd decided to sleep. Tuy had curled up in her blanket when Giang rose, stepped to the door, pressed his ear against it. He'd heard a sound outside, a click discordant with the duck quacks, drips, and the rattle of the tin-can walls. He'd listened for a minute, then, brave skeleton, opened the door and got shot in the forehead, crumpling atop his own legs.

In the wrap of her blanket, Tuy had watched as they'd trussed up Kim Thi, whose last imploring look was through strands of hair before they slipped a burlap sack over her head.

Huang's men were pros. They didn't kill unnecessarily. They'd let Tuy live.

I should be grateful.

Weeping, she pressed her face into my hand.

Let it go, I told myself.

Not so easy. When a man reflects upon his life, its voices sing out, either an angelic choir or a thousand screaming protesters. Right now, the screamers had the street.

Within a few days, Vangleman would produce the paperwork for Tuy to accompany me to the States. U.S. entry permits for Vietnamese citizens had to work their way through the bureaucracy, and nothing happened on short notice unless you had connections. I had none, except through Cobris. If I strained at the leash, he'd cut them.

Let it go. And why not? I had what I wanted. Tuy could leave with me for the States. Pure rationality bade me to cooperate. If I didn't, I had no way of winning; I could only lengthen the roll call of the dead.

In my mind I saw smoke rising among the squatters, the bodies of the Viet Cong lined up alongside a young woman in a white ao dai.

I'd told myself I was helping my friends, but I'd only managed to get them killed. André had been right. Saigon had a rhythm. I was an errant note, a dissonance, no different from the whole American undertaking in Vietnam, trying to help insofar as we had any clue what we were doing in this country that made our heads spin. Fighting an elusive enemy, we'd resorted to massive firepower; counted bodies to measure our success; created free-fire zones; uprooted hundreds of thousands of peasants whose hearts and minds were one with the land they'd tilled for generations, the land we poisoned with defoliants. They grew to hate and fear us. We hated and feared them back. On the political side, we'd never insisted that South Vietnam's leaders uphold a real democracy that would have kept the people's loyalty. Instead it was the same corrupt burlesque as in Diem's Saigon.

Too tricky for us, this place. We should have stayed the fuck out.

Too late now.

My gifts to my friends had been a bathtub, bars of soap, propane stoves, a portable radio, fashion magazines, and my time, brief as it was. What else had I brought?

Destruction, displacement, death.

Now, like the American Army, I was leaving.

With her tear-drenched eyes, Tuy stared up at me. She didn't see my raccoon bruises, she peered beyond, to my roiling meditations. Standing up, she pulled me against her to smother them. "Stop," she said. "Stand still."

Day 16

We slept in one of Trong's rooms, a two-meter-square box with a screened window whose bamboo shade you opened with a rope through a ceiling pulley. The straw mat curled around us like a loose cigarette wrapper. Half asleep in the ambiance, I stared at a constellation of paint chips on the wall. The opiate still pulsed in my bloodstream, and I watched the chips reform into a dancer on a stage. She twirled to the music of the swishing trees and occasionally kicked a leg high.

Of all the ghosts of the marsh city, Kim Thi was the one who'd haunt me. Because I'd been stupid and slow, she was dead.

Deep in the night, watching the paint-chip dancer, I wasn't entirely sure she was a hallucination. Narcotized minds are not places where ideas assemble neatly. Ages lapsed before my projections in the shadowy room let me seize the question, longer still before its significance struck.

In the morning, I wedged myself into the corner. My desk was the flower pot's wooden base balanced on my knees. I wasn't sure how to create the tone. It had to be chatty and informal, absent venom or petty threats. Simone had to take me seriously, therefore I had to sound like her confident equal, no less relentlessly committed. I wrote carefully, crossing out errant words, re-styling the sentences.

By the time Tuy stirred, I had a first draft.

"What are you writing?"

"Letters."

Yawning, she sat up, stretched her arms, her torso a silhouette of sinewy curves. "Why?"

"This all started because two soldiers in a listening post saw a man walking toward them at night. They blew him up. It was what they had to do, because there was nobody else between them and their friends."

She blinked. What was I talking about?

I said, "Last night I remembered something that Diu told you about Simone. It stayed with me because it saw it myself. A rare quality she has."

"Her coldness?"

"Her decisiveness."

Perhaps Tuy understood; she asked no more questions. In the corner, the lines swam under my hand.

* * *

Our room became a steam bath from the boiling water Tuy poured into the tin washtub. Smaller than our porcelain tub, it was sized for diminutive people, and to fit I had to fold like a fetus—a posture my state of mind helped me attain. I squatted docilely, keeping the stitched cuts on my thighs from submerging. She mewed at my mélange of bruises, washed me with a sponge, rubbed lotion on my back, kneaded the muscles like stiff dough while I elevated my forearms so the gauze wraps would stay dry. Out of the tub, I did my sprinter's exercises. She inventoried my cuts and scrapes.

Reinstated to his job at the prefecture, Trong had resumed his old timings. He came home at midday and went to the garden where his wife served him soup and rice. Sometimes, after eating, like many Saigonese, he napped. Today, with guests in his house, he was politely awake when I approached him.

"You have an expectant look," he said.

"Another favor to ask." I held out one of the letters and explained what had to be done.

The detective took the envelope, which wasn't sealed, he might have opened it and read the letter. Instead he held it in fingertips and slightly away from him, as if it were a dead mouse. A minute elapsed before he said, "A wise man does not resist the will of heaven." A Catholic, he invoked a Confucian concept, his glare shivery as if he braced for rebuke. It was a breezy day, and the eddies within the garden walls swirled gently.

I retrieved the letter from his fingers. "Thank you for all you've done for me."

"My hope is for goodness for you and Tuy, and that you will choose wisely from now on."

*　*　*

Before I left the house, I gave the second letter to Tuy, with instructions.

I carried the first letter myself. I'd have preferred for Trong to have delivered it; I wasn't sure of the reception I'd get at the yellow-brick apartment building. The French security men appeared no warier of me than they'd been before, and they accepted the envelope addressed to Simone. Was she home, I asked? Yes, they thought so. Would Monsieur like to wait for a reply? No, that wouldn't be necessary.

At the office of the Randolph Press Syndicate, Tuy insisted on seeing Alton Gribley in person. She had to wait fifteen minutes until he appeared. She didn't introduce herself or say a word other than to ask him to confirm his identity. Then she handed him the envelope and left.

It was important that both letters be presented nearly simultaneously. Depending on how the recipients reacted, the delivery of one might interfere with the other. I was expecting problems at the gate at Tan Son Nhut, but everything seemed normal when Lopez picked me up and drove through.

Normally Lopez didn't carry a sidearm. At the French Compound, I wrote out and signed an order directing him to draw from the arms room a .45 pistol. He was smart enough to show the armorer the order, then to fold it into his pocket for safekeeping. Having lost my own .45 to the fight in Tuy's apartment, I signed out another. Then I reclined on the humidity-sodden cushion of the black vinyl couch Lopez dragged in. I had no trouble sleeping as the sun set and the breeze swept away the dung odor. Normally we locked the place after dark. Tonight it was open for business, Lopez at the desk sipping coffee, watching the moths cling to the screen, his right hand by the pistol in the open drawer.

Doctor Wilcott had been right; I hadn't recovered from the overdose. Amid syncopations of nausea and startling drug cravings, cataplexy quivered my lips. I gasped, thrashed, yelped. The substance must have burnished my retinas. Through them, the air wore a yellow tint, the shade of André's kepi drink.

Day 17

When dawn reddened the louvers, I took a whore's bath in the washroom sink. Peeled off the gauze, exposing a moonscape of scabs. I re-wrapped them in clean dressings and fell back to sleep. It was Sunday morning, and this corner of Tan Son Nhut drooped in the low-angle sunlight, even the new replacements compound slumbered. Occasionally I stirred to the tinny broadcast on Lopez's transistor radio, the Armed Forces Radio channel's censored news droning between songs by Melanie and Jimmy Hendrix and the Association. The hours milled on. By midmorning, the airfield had become screechy with jets—the Cambodia incursion still churned. After a while, I didn't register the noise.

Nothing seemed to be happening. What if, blunted and enfeebled, too pathetic to spark a reaction from my enemies, all I'd accomplished had been to cast myself beyond anyone's goodwill, past my chance to take Tuy out of Saigon?

Cobris was right. I was a delinquent.

In the dung-laced miasma, I sweated.

Eleven hundred hours. The phone jingled. Lopez handed me the receiver. "I asked who was calling. He wouldn't say, just insisted I put you on."

I said, "Tanner."

"Could you stop by?" Stobe had real self-control. I almost couldn't hear the stress.

"Sure, why not?"

I took my time getting ready.

At the door, Lopez waited for orders.

I said, "I don't think anybody will come after you, but if they do, or if it looks like I'm never coming back, get the file from Hollis and take it to General Abrams."

"You sure you don't want me along, to watch your six?"

"Not this time."

At the airfield's edge, the palm trees segmented an airliner leased to ferry home another increment in the Vietnamization exodus. The radar tower groped for things I couldn't see, while by the hangar doors, Stobe waited in his flight suit. He saw me, and I had the impression that he had to steady himself. He led me inside, past the mechanics who turned wrenches on choppers, to a ship budding its cowl panels for inspection. In the cabin, we sat on the facing nylon benches, and he slid the door shut.

"Something has gone wrong." He sucked a breath. To utter those four words must have winded him. The mechanics' tools clinked on the airframes, the sounds of dismantlement. I lit a cigarette, plainly in violation of the NO SMOKING signs posted everywhere. Enforcing regulations was the last thing on Stobe's checklist today.

"Simone came by last night," he said. "It was late, around twenty-three hundred hours, but she insisted that I fly her to her place immediately. She said the general had okay'd it. I shouldn't have taken her at her word."

I had to assume that being the general's mistress somehow afforded Simone, a Frenchwoman, the privilege to move around a military base. That was bad enough. The notion that she could show up and demand a ride on a military aircraft was too outrageous for comment. "Her place. Meaning Cambodia?"

He went on as if I'd stated a common fact. "I assigned a pilot I trusted. Certified and experienced in night flying. Then I called MACV, left a message for Cobris, and went to bed. My duty officer woke me a couple hours later to say that General Cobris himself had driven up, demanded his rig, and taken off, heading north. Alone."

"And neither of the choppers has come back?"

Stobe stared down. Simone had been gone for twelve hours, Cobris ten.

"So you've got three persons and two choppers missing, and you're asking me if the lights are flashing red?"

"I thought you might have an explanation for what's going on." His bloodshot eyes revealed a soul breached by doubts.

I said, "You have a bad habit of handing out choppers to people they don't belong to. Like the one Cobris flew on Tuesday loaded with rockets. What did you think he was going to do with those rockets, hunt tree monkeys?"

I might have slapped him. His face stiffened. Then he seemed to relax, a momentary flashback to the man who'd have laughed off the question. It didn't last. Casually I aligned the major's insignia on my fatigue cap; his eyes locked on as if it were a hypnotist's medallion.

"André was an evil man," he said softly.

"So I heard. How he tried to coerce Simone to run drugs for him and his partner, General Huang. Wasn't that the story?"

"The heroin went to American GIs. He deserved to die for that alone."

"As you head north on Highway 13, you encounter South Vietnamese military checkpoints where the soldiers search cars. How many checkpoints would you say? Three? Four?"

His bushy brows squeezed together.

I said, "Do you know who controls those checkpoints?"

"The ARVN?"

I didn't usually snicker when people were close to baring their souls, but this time I couldn't help it. "Come on, Stobe. You've been around long enough to know that the ARVN is not a homogenous organization. It's more like a collection of fiefdoms, each with its own warlord. So guess which warlord controls that sector?"

"I have no idea."

"Try General Huang."

"André's partner?"

"Not André's. Simone's."

He scowled. "That doesn't make sense. If she was Huang's partner, why would she need to fly when she could drive through the checkpoints?"

"Because she's not a very faithful partner."

Comprehension, or the beginning of it, darkened his face.

I went on. "As long as things were going smoothly, she could share the profits with Huang and still make plenty to pay for her lifestyle in Saigon and to prepare her nest egg for the future. But a couple of months ago, the situation in Cambodia changed. An ambitious general overthrew the ruler, and the place fell into turmoil. When that happened, our long tolerance for the communist border sanctuaries ran out. Simone realized that her time was running out too."

"There's no way she knew about the invasion ahead of time," declaimed Stobe. "Even Cobris didn't know about it more than a few days in advance. I was with him when the orders came."

"She didn't know. She *guessed*. She didn't need a soothsayer to tell her that the one piece of her father's legacy she still owned was about to be overrun, and her network in Cambodia disrupted, along with her profits. So she asked Cobris to help her close the old estate. She concocted a story that André was running drugs and coercing her so that she couldn't use the road. To liberate her from all that oppression, and with your assistance, Cobris gave her a helicopter. André helped her locate Gerard. The man who flew those night missions had to be solid."

Stobe winced when I mentioned Gerard. I suspected that this was the first he'd heard about André's connection to the pilot.

I said, "The helicopter allowed her to move more heroin than ever before. Had she driven the road, the product would have been noted at those alert checkpoints, and Huang would have taken his enormous cut. This way, she kept it all. So Huang wouldn't find out, she marketed it in Vung Tau, probably with Gerard's help."

Stobe tried to keep himself from spiraling like a rudderless aircraft. "Christ, Tanner, that's just nuts. A successful woman, why would she risk it?"

"There's no future for her in South Vietnam. Consider what she sees when she looks around: the Americans bailing out, the mandarins who run the place as corrupt as always. It's just a matter of time before the communists shut the place down. She doesn't want to be here when that happens. What she wants now is Paris, but not as some chased-home ragamuffin who only gets invitations to the lesser parties. Money fixes all that. She's been collecting her fortune for a while. The invasion of Cambodia just meant she had to accelerate things."

Stobe was staring at his buffed boots, the naiveté peeling off him like the skin from a charred corpse. He would have preferred that my soliloquy had reached its end, but I wasn't finished yet.

"By this time," I said, softly, trying to keep the edge off my voice, "André was a liability to her. He was doing his pathetic best to hang around. He let his own reputation take the hit for her drug smuggling—what did he care?—*she* was his reputation. What he wanted was for her to take him back. He was a dreamer, an outmoded vogue—too unsophisticated to hold her interest, too working-class to take to Paris, too shaky to jettison. Cut loose, he might divulge how she'd earned her money. The errand was too tricky to trust to Huang. So she found somebody else to kill him."

"Cobris went alone," he blurted.

"You got the ship ready, the rockets loaded."

It was no finger-pointing accusation, just a statement of fact: Stobe was an accessory to murder. The color drained out of his cheeks, his mouth twitched like a lab rat prodded with an electric probe. He muttered to himself, trying to cobble together an excuse, until he realized that I wasn't the best audience. I was the one who hunted down people like him.

I said, "If you want to know what happened to Cobris and Simone, we have to cross the border. Can you get another chopper ready?"

Perhaps wondering why I wasn't headed instead to MACV headquarters to deliver my evidence, he blinked.

"We'll need as many soldiers as you can suit up," I added. "There's no telling the situation on the ground."

Whether he agreed with me or was simply doing as he was told, grasping at whatever of his officer's qualities remained, he nodded. He stared at the door handle as if it demanded all his concentration to open. By habit he stepped briskly, made it only a few strides before he slowed to a shuffle, his back bowed as if one of his helicopters had landed on him.

*   *   *

Off the chopper's nose, the Saigon River wagged a brown dragon's tail over the landscape. We passed the Gavet radio tower at such altitude that I could see the Annamite Mountains bulging to the northeast. Ordinary scenery, until I looked toward the northern horizon. Ten days had passed since U.S. and ARVN units had invaded Cambodia. We'd captured tons of supplies and chased the enemy back from the border. For the most part, our forces had encountered only small NVA elements left behind to harass them. The firefights nonetheless continued, and supporting artillery raised a crop of smoke plumes ahead.

For years, the communists had sheltered in their border camps. Cambodia's ruler Norodom Sihanouk had disliked their presence but hadn't done anything about it. He hadn't done anything about the B-52 strikes either. The Cambodia incursion had rekindled press reports—denied by the U.S. administration—that we'd been bombing the sanctuaries for more than a year. A single B-52 unleashed 30 tons of explosives. When Stobe's helicopter crossed the frontier, I noticed square kilometers laid waste and pocked with hundreds of rain-flooded bomb craters, around which the broken trees lay like so many discarded cocktail umbrellas.

Could we deny *that*?

Whatever else they'd accomplished, the airstrikes apparently hadn't dislodged the elusive communists. In January of this year, when Sihanouk traveled abroad, his pro-American Prime Minister General Lon Nol had seized power and offered the United States an alliance. Here was an opportunity for us to expel the enemy from the border sanctuaries and buy time for Vietnamization to take root. Lon Nol wanted our help to buttress his new regime. For both parties, a deal too good to pass up. Too good. But if Lon Nol had been reading his tea leaves, he'd have noted that conflicts in this corner of the world spanned decades. The

United States already was withdrawing from South Vietnam. Who was going to step in to save Cambodia next time?

I sat in the copilot's seat. In the cabin behind hunched eight of Stobe's quickly mustered soldiers. They bore no resemblance to the seasoned recon squad I'd flown with to Area Zulu. Joining the incursion into Cambodia wasn't what they'd expected to happen to them today. Inadequately equipped, they had only their web gear, a mix of light weapons—M16s and shotguns—and minimal ammunition. A single item gave me reassurance—the PRC25 radio one of them carried.

I plugged my headset into the intercom lead to talk to Stobe. He had no crew for this flight, and no other headsets were active, so it was a private line between us. I said, "Can you talk while you fly?"

"Why not?"

"Tell me about the chopper you gave to Gerard."

"A friend of mine was the investigating officer for a non-combat crash in a rice paddy on the Plain of Reeds. Happens all the time, some hot dog bellies in. The unit sling-loaded the damaged airframe back and stored it outside their hangar. When I learned what the general wanted, I offered to take over the incident investigation. My friend agreed—nobody likes paperwork. I was able to get hold of the wreck, which I wrote up as a total loss. No questions were asked. I had my mechanics overhaul it nose to tail, replacing broken parts—essential components only. When the ship was ready, I flew it at night to a spot near Vung Tau. That's where I met Gerard."

"You repainted it and removed the data plates."

"Cobris specified that Gerard was to receive only untraceable equipment, and I did what I could to conceal where everything came from. I knew I'd have a problem effacing the engine inscriptions, but I figured that the chopper had an appointment with the South China Sea, once Simone was done with it."

"Where did you get the radio and the rifle?"

"Four months ago, I flew into an LZ after a firefight, and an infantryman loaded them aboard my ship. I gave them to my supply sergeant to stash away. The Viet Cong had refitted the radio for civilian batteries—just right for Gerard for emergency commo. But when I tested it, the damn thing didn't work. I had to get it fixed, and so doing created the paper trail you bird-dogged straight to me."

"Tell me about Gerard."

"I hardly knew him. Once he took possession of the chopper, he handled the functions himself: piloting, simple maintenance, even the fueling. A couple of times he asked for spare parts. Simone would pass the requests to me via the general and Vangleman, and I'd send back the parts. He couldn't have kept it up for long—maintaining a chopper is too complicated for one guy, but this was a short-time deal."

"And nobody in your unit thought it was strange, rebuilding a ghost ship and handing over those spare parts?"

"They assumed I was doing a favor for somebody. Units trade favors every day—parts, equipment, whatever they need. It's against regulations but greases an inflexible system. I used reliable men who kept their mouths shut."

I puzzled at his definition of *reliable*. The helicopter they'd refurbished had fallen out of the sky. With the general's mistress aboard.

Stobe went on. "Gerard was careful. He stored the ship under cover at Vung Tau and flew it only at night. A very professional character."

"He wasn't professional enough. He told his fiancée about Simone and the flights. When Simone found out, she tagged her for a threat and put out a hit contract."

"What happened?"

"They killed her." My words clanged over the intercom, reminding me that Kim Thi's death was my fault.

Capping a plateau whose sides plunged into dense jungle, the old rubber plantation's mint-green groves came into view. Stobe descended to skim above the treetops, a technique called 'nap of the earth' where he whipcracked overhead before anyone could take aim. The enemy reportedly had fled into the Cambodian hinterlands, but Stobe wasn't taking chances. Scanning for activity, he banked over the trees. Everything looked prosaic and unmolested.

Until the plantation house came into view.

The white-framed manor posed above a rectangular lawn. Artillery had gouged holes in the roof tiles. In front, resembling a dead weed, a fire-blackened tree. Behind were buildings I judged to be garages and servant's quarters, their roofs similarly marred. A truck lay on its side. Nobody was in sight. The invasion had passed through here like a bad dream, leaving the place to fall back into slumber.

On the front lawn squatted a helicopter, its rotors drooping. "That's the general's rig," Stobe said. "But where is he? And where's the other ship?"

"Put down and I'll have a look."

* * *

The skids bumped and I was out and running toward the general's chopper. Leading the squad was a young sergeant named McAdams, normally a door gunner. He surprised me by doing the right thing—he dashed to the overturned truck, the only worthy cover nearby, and spread out his men. As soon as we'd cleared the rotor radius, Stobe throttled his ship skyward—a chopper on the ground is vulnerable—and debris from the vertical takeoff peppered us and clacked against the truck.

Up close, the parked helicopter revealed bullet holes stitched across the engine compartment. Oil bled down the windshield and dribbled from the nose. Nobody was inside.

I radioed Stobe and described the damage.

"I haven't spotted the other ship," he came back. "I don't see anybody else. I'm going to do a wider circuit."

I shifted my attention to the house where Simone had been born. On meter-high posts that protected it from flooding in the heart of the monsoons, the timeworn edifice loomed, a creepy visage that reminded me of the helicopter I'd spotted in the tree. *Somebody might still be inside?* Shredded porch screens flapped. When I kicked open the door, a bird fluttered frantically out. The foyer smelled of mildew and explosive residue—an artillery shell had vented its energy here, erupting wood and plaster. Overhead, electric wires suspended a fallen ceiling fan at a crazy angle.

I entered rooms: a dining salon and a parlor whose overturned furniture evoked *Quartier Latin* on André's last day. Some things had stayed intact. On the flowered wallpaper hung oil portraits of women, their sharp chins hinting at their relation to Simone, their eyes gazing with detachment at the broken rear windows and swaying curtains. Through them I could make out the garage and a line of servants' quarters past a tin-roofed walkway. On a ledge by the stair banister rested a silver plate, meant for the calling cards the colonialists had dropped off when they'd attended the social gatherings. I imagined the men and women resplendent in their linen suits and silk dresses in which they socialized amid the comforting hum of their own language. Colonialism is a state of mind. To have commanded this splendid plateau must have evoked a peacock's pride, the Frenchmen raising their glasses to how they'd possess Indochina forever. Sixteen years after forever ended, I had to wonder why Simone had kept the place all tricked out. It was one thing to save her parents' Cambodian estate, another to preserve the past as she'd done. Some eras shouldn't be memorialized. They summon hate.

Peering up the stairwell to the second floor, I could see past the wood banister to the crashed-through ceiling where a shell had hit. I'd left the front door open, and the breeze swirled in and plucked at my hair, rousing the dangling ceiling fan into a drowsy pirouette. I was about to ascend when I heard footsteps pounding, and I turned to see McAdams leap over a tumbled divan as if it were a racing hurdle.

"Major Stobe just radioed," he panted. "He flew over a concentration of NVAs at the western woodline. He said they saw his chopper land, and now they're moving this way. We've got to clear out!"

I thought, the NVAs must have shot up the parked helicopter and waited, knowing that somebody would come looking for it. "How far?"

"Less than a klick away."

I had time.

"Sir?"

"Get ready. I'll be with you in a few minutes."

I was already on my way up the stairs. In disbelief, McAdams watched. He probably hadn't smelled the perfume in the air.

A hallway opened at the stair top. On the floor, footprints marred the plaster dust. The perfume lingered. I wasn't good at scents, but this one I recognized from the penthouse apartment in Saigon, a subtle fragrance mixing East and West. It seemed to emanate from close by. I eased toward the nearest door slightly ajar, and, remembering trip wires, quickly checked the edges. When I pushed it open, the tepid light through lace curtains revealed a seated figure enshrouded in a sheet, a bald mountain peak against a wispy sky.

As if the apparition might lunge at me, I crept forward, and with my thumb and forefinger pinched the fabric and tugged it up gently—there are superstitions about waking the dead—and exposed the oyster-white face of General Kyle Cobris. The thrown sheet had been an act of courtesy to keep the birds off. The bullet hole low in his forehead had hardly bled, a testament to how fast his heart had stopped beating. The killing shot had come from a small-caliber handgun at point-blank range—burnt gunpowder specked the surrounding skin.

On a table alongside, a jade ashtray, the sister of the one in Simone's Saigon apartment, a cigarillo butt, and the general's pewter lighter. He must have been reaching for the lighter when the shot came. The arm bridged to the face I conjured in its final illusions of potency. What a speech he must have made, pontificating about moral justice and virtue and seeing over the horizon, believing that his rhetorical theatrics would cow Simone into answering the questions he'd heard from the Randolph Press Syndicate preparatory to the release of a story. In the footsteps of his countrymen who'd resorted to force whose consequences they did not understand, he'd tried to intimidate her, managed instead to convince her that he'd get in her way, and he'd joined Kim Thi and André with a ticket to the land of the ancestors.

His horizon now was exactly zero.

How sad. I could hardly imagine a pair more made for each other. Elite, brilliant, confident, they'd regarded the world as an asset to be controlled, themselves as its masters, the one's image revealed in the other, a mutual narcissism. How far had their relationship progressed? Had she cared about him, or simply used him for what he could give her, freedom to fly like a wraith at night over a land at war?

In the end, she'd killed him as easily as she'd click out a light.

I pictured her tearing open the envelope marked *To Simone, From George.*

Dear Simone,

Having returned one set of jewels to you, I bring another, perhaps more valuable. A bit of advice: Leave Saigon. The press is about to become even more nettlesome, for I've given them your story, true and detailed. They are whetted for interesting news these days, as long as they can quote someone, and now they can. If you go today, you may beat the headlines. Sorry not to have informed you in person, but time is a hellhound for me too.

George

Like a grave robber, I slid the lighter into my hand.
A mortar shell clumped authoritatively in the orchard.

*   *   *

I intended to recover Cobris's body and carry it to the chopper. But first I had to check something.

Simone had come back here for a reason.

Returning to the first floor, I exited through the rear door and crossed the gravel turn-around to the garage, where I almost tripped over three cowering Cambodian plantation hands. Startled, they jumped up. I couldn't blame them for being terrified. An invasion, landing helicopters, shells going off, and up runs an American with a lemur's black eyes...

The garage doors hung open. I went in. Along the walls, farm tools rusted in the humidity—not much real plantation work had been going on here lately. In the center posed a couple as made for each other as Cobris and Simone: a red, three-wheeled Tri-Lambretta and a powder-blue Citroën *Deux Chevaux*. Behind the vehicles, a plain door on the back wall. I kicked and the flimsy hasp tore away.

An artillery shell had buckled the roof. Ceiling panels sagged. Glass fragments speckled a laminate table, the remains of odd-shaped beakers and metal tubing that dangled like the ivy my father used to rake off our siding in Massachusetts. Crunching over debris, I pulled open one of the lower cabinets and saw stacks of small, oblong boxes, U.S. military supplies pilfered and distributed on the black market. The lettering read: BAG, PLASTIC, CLEAR, 64 OZ, 100CT. There were at least a dozen boxes.

Heroin coming out of the Golden Triangle into Vietnam was reportedly the purest ever marketed, so potent that users could smoke rather than inject it. So why the lab? Had Simone's Cambodian property been a transshipment point, or something more? I guessed the latter. And that the men outside were not plantation hands; they were her henchmen who'd doctored the heroin to buck-up the effect.

No wonder I still craved the stuff.

The hiding place formed a cutout in the floorboards the size of a child's coffin. Probably it had havened the last hundred bags or so of the product Simone had come back to retrieve, no doubt to sell to her contacts in Vung Tau. Had her helicopter not crashed into Area Zulu, she already would have recovered the drugs and maybe a few keepsakes from her house. She'd have dismantled the lab. But last night she'd been in a hurry and left it for the Cambodians to clean up.

Maybe that was why they hadn't run away. They stood now at the garage doorway, their expressions confused and agitated. One of them wore a dent on the side of his head, an old war wound. More densely muscled than his companions, he was Cambodia's version of a Saigon cowboy—his army service probably dated to the First Indochina War, when, on behalf of the French, his thick hands and forearms had wrung the necks of rebellious peasants. He glowered menacingly.

I scanned the garage, found what I was looking for, a jerry can of gasoline, opened it, and sloshed the contents through the lab doorway and across the table and the broken beakers. Poured a trail to the driveway. Tossing the can aside, I pulled out Cobris's pewter lighter. This proved too much for the skull-dented Cambodian. Rushing to the Tri-Lambretta, he withdrew an M2 carbine, and he might have gotten the drop on me had he remembered his old army lessons, but he was still tugging on the charging handle, peering at the chamber, when I shot him in the top of the head. Down he crumpled into a seated pose against the vehicle's beak-like fender, his mud-covered boots kicked wide.

"Out!" I shouted. The other two backed away. I flicked the lighter and the gas trail came alive. Mango-colored flames licked the walls, smoke billowed through the lab roof and into the trees. For a few seconds, watching the flames engulf the vehicles, I mused that I'd vaulted the line of my authorities. But who else was going to stand for those who'd OD'd on the heroin this place had turned out?

I wondered if Giang, in the arms of his ancestors, was grinning that grin of his.

* * *

Running toward the squad, I still had it in mind to recover Cobris's body. The NVA mortar gunners must have traversed their tube to sight on the smoke; the shells started dropping close. One went through the roof, another into the trees, showering me with bark. I reached McAdams just as a round burst at the driveway's edge.

"They've got us bracketed," he remarked, rather calmly, making me wonder if his grace under pressure was real or vacuous unfamiliarity with what mortar shrapnel did to the human body.

I took the radio handset. "We could use a ride out of here."

Stobe's voice crackled, "Bad news. The NVA has set up two hundred meters to your west. All that's holding them is the hope that I'll land where I did before. If I do, I'll never get back into the air. You've got to hightail it to a better extraction site."

"Which way?"

"Move in the direction of my line of flight. I'm coming over you in about thirty seconds." A pause in the transmission. "What did you find inside?"

"Your boss. Dead."

"Are you sure?"

"He took a bullet in the forehead. You're welcome to have a look for yourself."

Another pause. "Negative. Out."

The wind shifted and the smoke from the garage and the now-ablaze house twined into an ebony column. Flames licked through the windows.

There was no possibility of recovering Cobris's body now. Rotor blades thudded and Stobe's ship arrowed due east through the smoke.

Toward the rubber trees we sprinted. We had to cross three hundred meters before the terrain swooped into rough jungle and cover. If we could get that far, Stobe could direct us to a place where he could land and lift us out.

The NVAs saw us. Their bullets sheared off the tree branches.

* * *

They chased us. Amid the rubber trees, their brown uniforms looked like dabs of mustard on celery stalks. Stobe dropped a parcel that crashed through the branches. While McAdams scooped it up, one of the soldiers stopped at a rubber tree to pump out rounds from his shotgun, making a fat target of himself. I barely managed to grab him by the collar and pull him back before bullets shredded the trunk.

It was all I could do to keep running. These soldiers were stronger than me—they were younger and hadn't just emerged from a hospital bed. Yet they didn't know what to do. Through the orchard they bunched together like teenage girls going to a movie. No time to train them to disperse, I could only hope they'd imitate me cutting diagonally across the orchard rows, to prevent the shooters from sighting a machine gun along a row and dropping us all in a single burst.

The grove ended and the land broke over a slope. No pause, I plummeted like a log down a mud chute. To slow my descent, I clutched to vines, but I was going too fast and they sluiced through my fingers. Alongside me, a soldier roller-coastered headfirst.

I crashed to the bottom. "Get up, keep moving!"

Through the marshy undergrowth, tripping over protruding roots, I reached the base of a banyan tree. The bark sported scars from some long-forgotten shootout. The jungle was a vast graveyard for Frenchmen, Japanese, Vietnamese, Cambodians. I thought of the wounded men who'd toppled into it, never to be found.

The scabs from my tarmac skid had opened. Blood soaked the gauze. Barely two days since I'd left the hospital, the overdose still coursed in my bloodstream, and my brain sputtered like a motor-pool jeep. I was patently unfit to be leading these soldiers. One by one, they stumbled up, pummeled from the chase but unhurt, each as blank faced as the next.

McAdams unzipped the package Stobe had dropped, dumped out a pair each of flares and colored smoke grenades for signaling, a map, and a compass. I unfolded the map and strained to focus on the squiggly lines.

Past the chorus of heavy breathing, I listened for the sounds of pursuit.

Noises are hard to isolate in the jungle. The harmonics span the chit-chit of insects, water dripping, wind fluting through the hanging vines, the screeches of parrots. The leaf canopy triplicates itself upward, each layer its own ecology that echoes in a different way. Below, moisture and insects dissolve prostrate things and secrete them into the soil with an incessant gurgle. Any sound might be close or far off.

Stobe had grease-penciled a loop around a hilltop a kilometer away, meaning it was the closest place he could land. To get there, I had to lead McAdams and seven first-tour mechanics or door gunners whose combat experience, if any, was from above the canopy. These kids were so jumpy they'd shoot each other by accident. "We have to move," I told them. "Make sure your weapons are on safe."

I tucked the map into my thigh cargo pocket and pushed up on wobbly legs. Taking point, I doubted I could hike a kilometer.

Deeper into the undergrowth we pushed. It felt like being wrapped in a gigantic spring roll bound with creepers. None of the soldiers had been in the jungle before, and they shuddered when we slipped into a rainwater-etched fissure. Weaving through the vine curtains, we startled lizards and excited the monkeys above. The upper limbs interlocked like the beams in a basilica, and the monkeys leapt in a ceiling mural gone amok, their figures breaking the frail sunbeams. We squashed through sediment full of leeches. No time to stop and pick them off.

Lightly equipped, we didn't make much racket, and I hoped we could stay concealed long enough to outdistance our pursuers, radio the chopper, and be lifted out before they got close. The danger was that the NVA knew this terrain, might guess where we were headed, and speed there on a parallel route. I paused only for compass sightings and to listen.

If the enemy was following, he was too far behind to detect. Tempting to think nobody was there. And suicidal. Stories from the First Indochina War still made the rounds, of the enemy stalking cut-off French columns for days, over many kilometers, just to get the kill. I had to assume the NVA soldiers were tracking us and would close the distance eventually. Stobe had to extract us or bring help—American or South Vietnamese units must be nearby. Yet the daylight under the canopy already had begun to dim. No rescue would come after dark, and we'd be left to face an enemy whose métier was the night.

* * *

At eighteen hundred hours, sweat sodden, we trudged onto the hilltop. Not much of an LZ—the clearing barely would accommodate a single helicopter—yet the area was too big to secure with the inexperienced group I had. I positioned them in a crescent facing downhill, the radio operator with me a few meters within the surrounding brush. My attempts to radio Stobe failed; I heard neither a break in the static nor thump from the ship's rotors. He must have flown back to refuel. Under my breath I cursed. Every minute narrowed our lead.

Half an hour passed before I picked out the whop-whop to the south. I grabbed the radio handset, reached him on the first try. "We're at your site."

"Pop smoke."

I pitched a smoke grenade at the clearing's downwind edge. A yellow cloud blossomed.

"Coming in on yellow," he miked, using the standard identify-color procedure that kept pilots from guiding on visual signals the NVA might use to confuse them or lure them into an ambush.

The shooting started as soon as he hovered overhead. From across the clearing, machine-gun tracers spat upward. I seized the handset. "You're under fire! Break off!"

A few seconds later, he radioed, "Keep moving on the same azimuth. I'll spot you a new LZ."

I took a step toward McAdams, and an RPG rocket whooshed. Expecting to see it trail after the ascending helicopter, I glimpsed it flash past level to the ground and explode. Something wet showered me. The radio man. His head and most of his torso were gone; chunks of the radio peppered the pinkish remains of his lungs. Attached was an arm whose hand held the handset, the severed accordion wire jangling up and down like an agitated monkey.

Having missed its aerial target, the NVA machine gun leveled to chop at us. Bark erupted. "Move!" I shouted. I tripped over a vine, and my outstretched left forearm slammed into a thorn. The ten-centimeter stiletto drilled through the scabbing. Never before had getting injured caused me to scream. I did now. I snapped off the spike. The wind had shifted. Yellow smoke floated from the LZ, and in its drift we were taking more hits. A soldier fell. I ran over, turned him in time to see blood and air bubble from a hole in his chest. He coughed once and his spittle settled on dead eyes.

I took his rifle.

Galloping, wheezing, my legs nearly bucking, I led them down the slope out of the yellow cloud. At the bottom, no longer under direct fire, I slipped along the line to count men. We'd left behind two dead; two more were injured, including McAdams. Blood spattered his shirt. "It's not bad," he said. "Pieces of the radio hit me."

The other living casualty had suffered a bullet wound in the upper arm. Fortunately it hadn't broken the bone. A spindly kid, eyes brown and watery, he resembled something the jungle would eat. "We're fucked, aren't we, sir?"

"No," I lied. "Our helicopters are nearby. They know where we are. We can't talk to them, but we have smoke and flares for signaling. If we can find a clearing, we can launch a flare. The choppers will pick us up. That's our game."

"It's almost dark."

"Better for us. The enemy won't be able to see us."

That calmed him. He didn't ask the obvious question—how would Stobe know we weren't already dead? I had no answer save for my odd trust in the blocky pilot. He wouldn't abandon his men; he'd stay aloft over this sector, until sooner or later we'd find a clearing where we could launch a flare. I had to believe it.

Pushing to the front, I resumed our frantic pace. The trick now was to gain distance. Through breaks in the trees, I could see the sky full of black serrations. Thunder rumbled; lightning torched the upper canopy. Rain whacked and the drops cascaded to successive layers. The rain would obscure our trail and buy us time. The downpour accelerated to an onslaught, and the last filaments of daylight vanished.

The enemy trackers no longer could guess our intended destination. There was none. We were moving blind.

* * *

Ahead, the outlines of a village. I guessed it was abandoned—no people or lights visible. It offered shelter from the rain and therefore was the last place we should stop. From the way we reacted, the NVA had to have concluded we were PX warriors, men who'd seek the illusion of safety behind bamboo walls.

I couldn't see the figures behind me. We hugged the descending slope, bracing against protrusions that kept us from skidding downward. The slope steepened, and it was impossible not to slide, heels dug into the loam, gripping roots that couldn't be trusted, slicking on our butts in the flow. In a few minutes we were muddied from head to foot. At the bottom, the rain and a glutted stream unified in a cacophonous rush, the forest a gray matte beyond.

We stumbled along for another hour, crossed the stream at a spillout through a cleft of rocks. With visibility barely beyond the reach of my arms, we progressed at a fraction of the pace we'd have made in daylight. I hunted for a place to stop until dawn, doglegged from our path until I reached a cavity between a fallen tree and the hillside. Ledging from the bark, the fungus made diving boards for insects; a rotten odor spilled from where things crawled to die. In a combat zone, concealment abides discomfort, and bunching inside here made more sense than crashing blindly through the vegetation. With two men awake for security, the others could rest in turns.

Mine came. I hovered, too depleted to sleep. On the screen of rain I saw Cobris. My machinations had killed him. Simone would agree, and if she chose to enact revenge, she'd go after Tuy in Saigon.

Day 18

I awoke in the pre-dawn. The mud coating had become a glutinous slime that made every twitch loathsome, and I wanted nothing more than to submerge in oblivion. Pain yields selfishness, and in war, selfishness equals cowardice. A leader thinks about others first.

Who was I kidding?

Birds made a hullabaloo in the canopy. One cawed the syllables "checkout, checkout, checkout" like an insistent command. As if obedient, I examined the two wounded men. Overnight their wounds had inflamed. I applied fresh first-aid wraps. We didn't have enough dressings for my forearms. The scabs had dissolved, exposing the raw abrasions. The left throbbed where the thorn had broken off, ballooning so I couldn't make a fist. The stitches in my legs had stayed intact, but left untreated in the wetness and filth, these and the other injuries would yield tissue necrosis.

We took an hour to ascend out of the valley. I hoped to come across a clearing big enough to land a chopper, but so far the trees and undergrowth were too thick. The map showed a washboard of minor ridges. Along these, the forest should thin out. The sun soared. So did the temperature. The jungle reverted to a steam bath. At a murky steam, I ordered the soldiers to fill their canteens and drink water. By the foresight of their unit's SOP, the pouches on their canteen holders stored little bottles of iodine tablets that they used for the first time.

Luck belonged to the seven us of who'd survived. Yet the adrenaline that had borne us this far had burned out. Nobody had rations, and we'd not eaten for at least eighteen hours. By the time we reached the midpoint of the first slope, we treaded listlessly, heads down, alertness fleeing.

I wondered where our pursuers had gone.

Surely they'd not given up the chase. Nothing shivered a soldier's spine more than to comprehend his enemy's fearsome determination. Throughout the French and the American wars, our foe had evinced tenacity, sublime understanding of the terrain, and the almost superhuman ability to operate at night. This was not from communism or culture. The enemy simply had competent leaders. Not far away, a determined young NVA officer was studying his map with as much intensity as I squinted at mine, both of us seeking a decisive course of action. He wouldn't relent any more than I would.

As if to echo my thoughts, shots kicked up the ground around us.

Everybody took cover behind trees. The blunt cracks of AK47s, distinct from the M16's sizzle, originated from the opposite slope. The fire was sporadic—I guessed there were only two shooters. The foliage obscured them. On the map, this ridge bumped laterally into a larger hill mass, a ladder leaned against a barn. To our sides ran other ridges; I guessed that the enemy was maneuvering along one of these. The shooting from behind was meant to buy time for the flanking unit to get above and block the ladder from the top.

I had to get us off the ridge. But which way? The maneuvering NVAs must be well along; the stay-behind gunners would have waited until the moving element had cleared the line of fire. Shifting laterally, we might slide beneath their tail. A gamble. If my narcotic-buzzed logic proved wrong, we'd get no second chances. We didn't have the combat power to survive a direct confrontation.

I gathered the squad and scaled higher. Our displacement might lead the shooters to conclude that I was following their game plan. Fifty meters up, under dense canopy, I swerved. The rifle fire plunged erratically. One of the men fell. McAdams was alongside him immediately. Blood trickled from a scrape on the side of his face.

McAdams said, "He needs a dressing on that cut."

"Later. Keep moving."

We bottomed out in a scree bed and scrambled up the opposite slope. The gunfire blunted itself against the now-vacant hillside behind. Nearing the crest, I slinked. If the maneuvering element was close by, our survival hinged on spotting them first and going to ground. Seeing no one, I arced over and dropped into a ravine.

Rumbling in the distance. Thunder? The noise was too cadenced; it had to be an artillery barrage. I aimed my compass at where it seemed to originate, plotted the azimuth on the map, and traced my finger across the green to concentric ovals more than a kilometer away.

Over my shoulder, McAdams stared at the whorl. "That sounds like a place we don't want to be."

"It's exactly where we want to be," I said. "The barrage is a signal from Stobe. He's telling us the way to our pickup site."

* * *

I hoped the sideways scoot over the ridges had scraped the NVAs off our tail. For a while it seemed that it had, and we advanced in quiet save for the occasional chopper above the canopy. Four hundred meters from the plotted hilltop, we came under fire again, and the only choice was to carom ahead, abandoning caution and hoping the enemy hadn't maneuvered an ambush in front of us. Bullets cracked through the branches. Our pursuers must have guessed where we were going. The fire missed widely, but accuracy didn't matter, they were simply trying to disrupt our progress so they could close within killing range. Coarse and effective, the tactics demonstrated a well-led and disciplined force pressing its advantages.

One of the soldiers fired back.

I'd been wrong to assume the NVAs were following our trail as a hunter tracks a deer. They were smarter than that. Understanding the terrain, they'd set up watchers to pinpoint our line of march. The NVA leader had organized his unit into teams that now would converge on us.

Another of the soldiers went down, shot in the lower leg. Without a word, the men slung him in a poncho they gripped along its slippery edges and occasionally dropped as we staggered ahead. I feared that the hilltop was going to turn out like the last extraction site, a hornets' nest of machine-gun bullets.

I'd managed to get us all killed.

A break in the trees. I could distinguish a wall of green, a grassy hillside. My hopes diminished further. We couldn't hide on that exposed slope. Visible for the first time since we'd dropped off the plateau at Simone's plantation, men in mustard uniforms shot at us from one hundred meters away. A bullet zinged past my ear. I took aim and fired. An NVA fell. Gunfire from our left flank; the bullets slapped the leaves overhead.

Picking up the wounded soldier from the poncho, I worked him over my shoulder. The slope loomed. "Run!"

An NVA raised a rifle-grenade launcher and fired. I followed the trajectory of the black projectile heading straight toward me. Leaning forward, I tried to sprint, but with a man on my back, it wasn't working.

* * *

MEMORANDUM FOR THE RECORD

TO: COMMANDER, 3RD BATTALION, 22ND INFANTRY

FROM: TASK FORCE FLYCASTER, 3/22 INFANTRY

SUBJECT: AFTER-ACTION REPORT OF CONTACT WITH ENEMY NEAR HILL 165, FISHHOOK AREA, CAMBODIA, 11 MAY 1970

1. At 1100 hours on 11 May, Task Force Flycaster conducted an air insertion at landing zone 'Tackle Box' (see sketch, attachment A). Upon assembly, I secured the LZ with one platoon and the mortar and recoilless rifle elements. In accord with my mission to attempt to locate and, if possible, rescue an isolated squad of

aviation soldiers, I ordered two platoons to
move westward toward the adjacent valley.
The lead platoon's point man was Sergeant
Haines Jefferson.

2. At 1157 hours, having traversed
approximately 400 meters, I heard gunfire to
the west. I moved to the head of the column,
where Sergeant Jefferson estimated that the
fire had originated from approximately three
hundred meters forward of us and downhill.

3. At approximately 1215, I again heard
rifle shots. This time, the fire was close
enough to identify as originating from AK47s
and a few M16s. I assumed that the M16s
belonged to the missing squad of aviation
soldiers. From the AK47s' heavier volume, I
judged that the squad was outnumbered and at
risk of being overrun and destroyed.

4. Immediately I increased our speed, hoping
to reach a vantage point from which I could
spot the isolated squad. Considering the
unknown size of the enemy force, I requested
helicopter-gunship support and received
notice that the gunships were en route with
an ETA of 1250.

5. At approximately 1230, an explosion
occurred to our southwest. Taking Sergeant
Jefferson, the RTO, and two soldiers for
security, I conducted a leader's
reconnaissance, moving until I was able to
see down the reverse slope. I spotted a
group of figures climbing the grassy
hillside in a direction that would have
crossed the ridge approximately one hundred

meters beyond my position. The lead figure bore a man across his back in a fireman's carry. The party was taking fire from several directions, and some of it was striking close to my recon position.

6. It was at this moment that Sergeant Jefferson, without orders, ran ten paces down the slope and removed his helmet. This entirely voluntary act on his part exposed him to enemy fire. To summon the aviation soldiers to our location, he could think of no better way than to show himself as a Negro, which he believed would erase any doubt in their minds that he was an American. Vindicating his risk, the soldiers, upon seeing him, immediately shifted toward him. The one carrying the soldier shouted, "We've got thirty NVAs on our ass." Immediately I ordered 1st platoon forward into a hasty ambush position at site B (see sketch, attachment B).

7. I wish to emphasize that TF Flycaster's rescue of the aviation squad developed as a consequence of the valorous actions of Sergeant Jefferson, subject of my recommendation (see attachment C) for award of the Bronze Star.

T.J. NELKEY
CAPTAIN, INFANTRY
COMMANDING

* * *

To the black soldier who'd appeared out of nowhere atop the slope, I managed to rasp something. I reached his outstretched hand, and he tugged me up into other soldiers who helped remove the wounded man from my back.

"Get down!" one of them said.

I found myself next to a captain who spoke urgently into a radio handset: "Quebec one-three, this is India one-niner. Close on me at full speed. Your entire element. Bring the medic. Over."

The handset crackled. "One-three, moving."

His soldiers were spreading in a hasty ambush position along the crest. Flanked by M60 machine guns, they formed a line of shooters fifty meters wide. Beside the captain, I gazed down the slope at the NVA force ascending toward us in the knee-high grass. An officer urged them on. He looked as young and determined as I'd imagined him to be, encouraging his men, leading from the front where they could see him. They climbed eagerly, bounding to their feet when they slipped, pulling their comrades up.

They'd have caught us in minutes.

The U.S. military in Vietnam held a single indisputable advantage— raw firepower. For each bullet the enemy expended, we fired thousands. A rifle in the ambush line barked, and beside the NVA officer, a man's head whiplashed in a cloud of blood. Then the American line erupted in full, and I saw the NVAs falling in the murderous barrage from the top. Launched grenades detonated among them. The NVA officer must have realized he'd run into a unit more formidable than the little group he was chasing. Signaling retreat, he waved his arm until a bullet clipped off his fingers. Still he extended the bloody stump, shouting so loud I heard his voice above the din. The NVAs ran, staggered, collapsed in the avalanche of bullets that sprayed blood over the grass. Defiantly the officer raised his rifle with one arm and shot at the top of the hill. A bullet whacked into his thigh, another struck his hip and spun him, a third hit between his shoulder blades. He sank into the grass and was lost to sight.

The gunfire ceased. I scanned the slope. The captain surveyed the scene for a minute through his binoculars, then he turned, took in the mudded insignia on my collar.

"You all right, Major?"

"Yeah," I wheezed. I read the nametag on his sweat-soaked uniform. Nelkey. I hoped I'd remember it.

In the dissipating smoke, nothing moved but the blades lightly swaying.

Day 19

General Abrams stared at me across his desk.

I'd had the chance to shower and rest in my BOQ room overnight. The pre-monsoons had billowed the plastic taped over my broken window. My scraped forearms kept bleeding through the new gauze the medics had applied. They'd pulled out the thorn tip, and the swelling had subsided enough so that, this morning, I'd managed to ease on the sleeves of a starched uniform, fumbling the buttons with my ballooned fingers. In the mirror, a scarecrow with blackened eyes had stared back. It was in this condition that I sat in front of the commanding general, flanked by two staff officers, to deliver my report.

I'd paid attention to stories about General Creighton Abrams because we were both western-Massachusetts men; his boyhood home in Springfield was less than twenty miles from mine at Tanner's Woods. A photograph showed him as a young lieutenant in his riding breeches and Sam Browne belt with the cross strap—the style of uniform vanished, the mentality of the cavalryman intact. In World War II, General Patton had called him the best tank commander in the Army. Across the desk he hulked, his cropped hair bristling over eyes steely and empathetic at the same time.

I told him the unadorned truth from beginning to end. Showed him the documents from my leather pouch I'd recovered from Hollis: the hand receipt, repair slip, the aircraft incident report; the photographs of the chopper hanging in the tree; the morgue shot; the dancer's marquee.

I penciled a sketch of the rocket attack that had killed André. Finally, I described the deal that I'd cut with Cobris and the letters I'd written to Simone and Gribley.

Abrams registered no emotion until I related the deaths of the two American soldiers at the hilltop LZ in Cambodia. Hearing how I'd left their bodies behind, he glowered, and in his expression I saw the bitterness of the long war.

When I finished, he said, "Be sure your report specifies the locations of the two KIAs. We'll bring them out."

"Thank you, sir."

He asked, "Where is the Frenchwoman, Simone Nogaret?"

"I don't know. Neither does my Saigon police contact. He guesses that she's left Vietnam."

"Do you believe that she had anything to do with the NVAs you ran into at her Cambodia mansion?"

"She probably had an arrangement of some kind with the NVA. Their proximity may just have been a coincidence."

Abrams grunted. Apparently he too hated coincidences.

He turned to one of the staff officers and instructed him to telex the Pentagon to request a formal investigation of the extraordinary circumstances of General Cobris's death. A minute later, the officer tapped me on the shoulder. The session was over.

I treaded across the Army-blue carpet.

* * *

Still reeling from accusations that the Army had covered up the 1968 My Lai massacre, the Pentagon immediately appointed a special investigator, a brigadier general. The new acting Provost Marshal phoned me at the French Fort with brusque instructions: I was to do nothing more on my own; my sole responsibility was to stand by to give a formal statement to the special investigator when he arrived.

When I hung up, I knew my career was over. I'd delivered an embarrassing tale to the press, an unpardonable offense in the Army's culture.

Other careers were ending too. Stobe offered to resign his commission. MACV turned him down, relieved him from command, and confined him to quarters pending an Article 32 hearing and likely court martial. Vangleman was loading files into his staff car in the VIP parking lot when the MPs surrounded him. They confiscated the files and led him to a room on the MACV compound for what amounted to house arrest. Colonel Crowley, having barely arrived in CONUS, received two phone calls. The first notified him of the cancellation of his assignment. The second summoned him to Washington. For the term of the special investigation, he would serve in a nominal capacity with no authority. It was the kind of purgatory where you became the subject of whispers and rumors, and you prayed they'd let you return to the real Army, knowing that it probably wouldn't happen.

An examination of airline manifests revealed that Marie Dobier, Simone's *assistante de gestion*, had left Saigon aboard a flight for Paris. No record was found of Simone's departure, but she must be gone too, perhaps under a false identity, or her own with the name left off the passenger list. Such omissions could be arranged.

I spent a few hours at the French Fort going through the paperwork to turn over to MACV. I worked alone—the Vietnamization reaper finally had bladed Sergeant Lopez. Duffel packed, he now waited to board a Freedom Bird at the departure-transfer station. He'd left a note for me under a coffee cup on my desk:

Sir,

They DEROS'ed my ass before I could say goodbye.
Nam is finally over for me.
You need to get out too, before the shit hits the fan.

Lopez

DEROS meant Date of Expected Return from Overseas. Mine wouldn't be far behind.

I received a last update. On the outskirts of Vung Tau, local farmers had been hearing helicopter noises emanating from a wooded compound.

The farmers informed a joint MP patrol, which located a landing pad, workshop, and tools. On the pad, a helicopter. It proved to be the chopper that had flown Simone on her final trip to Cambodia. Still strapped in his seat, the pilot had a bullet hole behind his right ear.

Forensics indicated a small-caliber handgun.

* * *

With the assistance of General Abrams's staff, I moved Tuy to Tan Son Nhut airbase, into a barracks under construction in a row of identical, plywood-sided structures. Meant to house forty persons, the barracks now sheltered two.

She glanced around, her expression empty. Somebody had swept up the sawdust and the discarded nails. The place nonetheless smelled like a lumberyard. I thought she must feel like the inhabitant of a strategic hamlet, plucked out of her old village and resettled behind barbed wire.

A quartermaster sergeant stopped by to ask if we needed anything.

"How about some drapes for the windows," I said.

He came back to report that the PX was out of curtains. He substituted white sheets that he tacked to the interior window frames.

Tuy said she liked the effect.

At a folding table, we ate dinner from cartons I'd picked up from the PX take-out. We sat away from the walls that radiated heat from the sun, now steeping into the paddies to the west. After, we carried our bottles of Michelob to the steps whose rails hadn't yet been installed. For a long time we sat without speaking, until she leaned her head against my shoulder and said, "You know, don't you?"

"Yes."

"How long?"

"Maybe always."

"Me too, I think. I couldn't admit it to myself."

She took a sip of her beer, and when she lowered the bottle I saw how the red sky picked out the lighter streaks in her hair. The sadness crushed me, and I couldn't speak for a while. Finally I asked, "Where will you go?"

"To my mother's, at first. She lives in a safe neighborhood."

Safe. No such thing.

But maybe there was.

"When?"

"Tomorrow, in the morning."

Thus a man finds his horizon. I'd once seen a helicopter whose tail rotor clipped a tree and sheared off. Spinning wildly, the chopper thumped atop a thatch hut, smashing it flat. South Vietnam was a new country overlaid on an old culture. America was a foreign power set on top, making for an unwieldy stack, the helicopter and the hut.

Had Tuy gone with me, it might have been a metaphor for us.

She didn't let it happen.

Day 20

In the morning I went to the PX snack bar to buy breakfast. When I returned, she was dressed to go, her meager bag packed and by her feet.

"I'm leaving now," she said.

"Can I give you a ride?"

She shook her head. No doubt it horrified her, the notion of riding in a U.S. jeep to her mother's neighborhood.

I drove her to the taxi stand by the gate, where I stayed with her waiting for a blue and yellow Renault to show up. She asked, "When will you leave?"

"A few days. A week."

Something in my tone must have stirred her perfect intuition. She peered at me, her eyes narrowing. "You're going downtown?"

"Later today."

"To see Trong?"

I nodded.

"I thought he stopped helping you."

"He's still my friend."

"But why go?"

"Last evening, you asked me if I knew. Now, I ask you."

Her eyes revealed the intensity of her concentration, and I was happy to see that look of hers, my brilliant Tuy. "She's still here?"

"Yes. Trong got a message to me."

"She's not your problem anymore. Why not leave it to others?"

"She *is* my problem. My hundredth problem."

"Hundredth?"

"It was Cobris's definition—the one you can't solve, so you pass it on."

She stared, not comprehending. A taxi engine growled, and her eyes drifted.

*   *   *

In violation of the order that I do nothing, I went downtown, to do something.

By late afternoon, I was where I wanted to be.

For all I knew, General Huang had posted his watchers along the quiet street only two over from Hipolite's, but I saw neither watchers nor guards as I walked along the bougainvillea-covered walls to the metal gate whose oiled hinges made no sound swinging open. Recessed from the street, occulted in leaves, the villa was a fugitive's paradise. I used the keys to the front door and entered a foyer of polished marble. Immediately I knew I'd come to the right house—against the walls leaned oil portraits like the ones I'd seen in Simone's Cambodia mansion.

I perused the fine villa. Its architectural twin probably could be found in the streets off the Champs-Élysées. In the muraled ceiling, the faces of pink cherubs. The floors gleamed. Whoever had built the house must have been thinking of the Pearl of the Far East, for what is a pearl other than a treasure in a hidden space?

The rear wall featured tall, glass-paneled doors, and through them I noticed a girl working in an enclosed garden. She squatted with her knees level with her shoulders, her black hair smoothing along her spine almost to her waist. Between the flowering oleanders she carved irrigation furrows, and somehow she managed to stay clean, even the fingers she occasionally raised to brush back her hair. Like the flowers, she lent tranquility to the space around her. I'd thought that Saigon had lost all charm for me. Now I felt it one last time.

A curving staircase led me to the second floor.

Simone stood in front of a copper-tinted mirror, in a room with an oriental carpet whose edges ran nearly to the walls. Natural light through glass-paneled balcony doors like the ones downstairs illuminated her back toward me, her ebony dress unzipped. In the mirror she noticed me leaning against the door frame, and the only sign she gave was a momentary halt in the movement of her hands as she fastened a clip in her hair the shade of dried bamboo.

She said, "Do you often enter a woman's bedroom uninvited?"

No questions of how I'd learned where she was or how I'd entered the house. She would have deduced very quickly that someone had given her up, and it was not important who, rather what to do in this moment. Her steadiness while she decided should not be mistaken for hesitation, I reminded myself. Across the room, finished with her hair, she proceeded with the ordinary movements of applying her makeup.

I found a chair, a gilded replica of a Louis XIV with a lozenge-green silk pad, and sat lightly so as not to break it. The .45 rested in my lap, cocked, the safety off. I said, "You think you'll charm your way out?"

"Of course."

"What happened to Kim Thi?"

Simone's mouth curved into a slight smile, revealing the edges of her teeth. "Is that why you came?"

"Among other reasons."

"Such as?"

"Nobody else was going to kill you."

"So you took it upon yourself?" Her laughter rang like the notes of a song. "Why should I be surprised? Isn't violence always the recourse of a weak man against a strong woman?"

"If you say so."

"You are extraordinary, Tanner, so persistent, like an overly attentive lover. I should have known what you were. Cobris thought so dismissively of you, it influenced me for a while. A mistake."

As she manipulated the lipstick tube, I watched her hands. Cobris, trusting her, never had a chance. I had a sense for how she'd move, but it is one thing to see it coming and another to get out of the way.

I repeated, "What happened to Kim Thi?"

"I am not inclined to know such details."

"She never revealed anything about you."

"She would have, eventually."

I thought of what they must have done to the dancer, her terror when they'd slipped the bag over her head. Whatever had happened, Simone had ordered it, yet my stereotypes of a lifetime refused to evolve, my mind could not reconcile the beautiful woman as she put on her makeup with what she really was, a murderer, a supreme imperialist who considered other people her property, subservient and disposable.

Simone, whose eyes never left me, knew her advantage. She was the snake that mesmerized its prey.

"Your place in Cambodia is infested with the NVA," I said. "They nearly chased me to death."

"Very pragmatic fellows, the NVA. Their liaison is necessary. One has to stay in business."

"You took it a step further. You adulterated heroin and smuggled it to sell to American soldiers. The NVA did well by you. Who wouldn't want his enemy hooked on drugs?"

She said nothing.

"You had a tidy alliance, you and the NVA. Not to mention you and General Huang; you and Cobris; before that, you and André. But all your liaisons are temporary, aren't they?"

The makeup radiated artfully around her eyes, the black within, a reddish garnet without. A mistake with those colors and she might have looked ghoulish, but she knew what she was doing. Her gaze stayed on me, and she saw the gun in my lap.

"The Montagnards who tried to shoot Kim Thi and me on the steps of her building, I thought Huang had sent them, but they were yours. It was only when you lost them that you turned to Huang. He was quite a partner—he did your bidding without asking a lot of questions. He didn't figure you were cheating him. But things change."

She straightened the straps on her dress. "You spoke with him?"

"Just today, actually." Trong had told me how to contact the general.

She viewed the completed picture of herself in the mirror. Turning around, in her audacious way she managed to infuse desire into her eyes, the kind of look that must have left Cobris's lean face hanging slack. Even the wisest man, offered such a visage, wants to believe it is real, done for him, not a woman's subterfuge.

I was a bit past that now.

"My lovely George. How I could use a man like you. What has your army given you, except an unpromising career?"

"More unpromising than you think."

She laughed. It is an odd sensation to know that your death cooks hot on another person's mind. The important thing is not to be easy to kill.

"What gets me, Simone, is that I was ready to walk away, if you'd have let things rest. But to rest isn't in your nature, is it?"

"You sell yourself short, George. You would not have walked away. Once you had your friends safe, you would have come after me. There is no rest in you either."

Her eyes were magnificent. They held me, they were born to hold me, and so I let myself be held. Turning slightly, she raised a slim cigarette to her mouth, dropped her hand to reach for a lighter, brought it up quickly. Too quickly. A magician's trick, mean to freeze my attention, for her other hand was moving, I knew it, but I was slow. She had the pistol leveled and the trigger pulled, and I was still staring at her eyes.

She'd done Cobris the same way. The difference was, she'd caught him from a few centimeters away, and I was three meters from the extension of her arm. Not far, but she wasn't an expert pistol shot, and the bullet hit me high in the torso rather than center, and I was diving off the chair at the same time I was shooting, once, twice, and the difference between Simone and me was that I was a very good pistol shot. On a silhouette target they call it the stopping zone, an oval in the center torso that surrounds the heart. 'Shoot here,' my range instructor had remarked, 'and the doctor can stay home.'

My two shots went there.

I lay on the floor, my cheek on the carpet, in the stickiness of the spreading blood, the only pain a dull pressure. An image flashed—the bubbly wound in the chest of the soldier at the hilltop LZ. Breathing out, I heard no bubbles. Pushed away the broken chair, tapped my shirt, saw the bloody palm come away. The coldness of shock mounted, the way a man in an open doorway feels the winter outside.

To stand upright, I braced against the table, staggered to her dresser, avoided looking at myself in her coppery mirror, no use feeding the shock. Saw the clump of ebony fabric on the floor. In her fingers, a chrome pistol. A fuzzy sense of caution dictated that I pry it loose and toss it. Her face was to the side, and I turned it skyward. Her neck was oddly compliant—you expect the person you have mortally shot to be resistive. Her eyes blinked once and focused on me, and I beheld her in her final beauty, her perfume floating up like a spirit. For a brief moment, my fingers brushing her cheek, there was intimacy between us.

On the way out, I picked up her gold cigarette case.

* * *

It was a long way down the curving staircase, long in state as well as distance, for by the time I'd reached the marble foyer, I could neither stand straight nor see well. Staggering along the pathway to the gate, through it to the sidewalk, I went as far as I could, until, back against the gatepost, I slid to the ground. The bougainvillea rustled. I could still smell the wisps of Simone's perfume, the scent between East and West.

Legs extended, I reposed.

In the villages, the people believed that the spirits of their ancestors watched over them. This wasn't a village, this was the callous city of Saigon, and the people were so removed from the old ways that if the ancestors appeared, the reaction would be to try to sell them something. Now I understood that the French colony and its American successor and all their trappings were thin layers of rice paper over the realm of the ancestors, for the spirits arrived. Some I recognized: Simone, Giang, Kim Thi, André, Cobris. Here were the Montagnards, the scooter kid in his Bogart hat, the two soldiers from the squad, the young NVA officer. Gerard, fit and handsome, smiled like an invitation. There were other ghosts too, strangers who regarded me distantly, as if my pending entrance to their principality was a mundane event.

Nobody among the living noticed me sitting by the gate until a cyclo glided along, the driver having glanced over and spotted Simone's gold cigarette case in my fingertips. The driver's act of kindness was to put a cigarette in my mouth and light it with his own match. Then he stashed the case in his pocket and pedaled into the gathering dusk.

The End

About the author:

Jeff Wallace is a former US Army officer. He lives with his family in southwest Virginia.

P 10 — White Cong

P 15. Bien Hoa — bowling alley etc.

P 23 draft dodgers & flower children

27 Gerald Hickey

P 25 — Pro worlds best army is a bunch of ragtags

P 27, My Lai

30. Ceramic elephants

P 55 People → money
94 Rome Alone?

Made in the USA
Charleston, SC
31 January 2017